Downsizing

Books by Lin Stepp

Novels:
The Foster Girls
Tell Me About Orchard Hollow
For Six Good Reasons
Delia's Place
Second Hand Rose
Down by the River
Makin' Miracles
Saving Laurel Springs
Welcome Back
Daddy's Girl
Lost Inheritance
The Interlude
Happy Valley
Downsizing

The Edisto Trilogy:
Claire at Edisto
Return to Edisto
Edisto Song

Christmas Novella:
A Smoky Mountain Gift
In *When the Snow Falls*

Regional Guidebooks
Co-Authored with J.L. Stepp:
The Afternoon Hiker
Discovering Tennessee State Parks
Exploring South Carolina State Parks

Downsizing

A MOUNTAIN HOME NOVEL

LIN STEPP

MOUNTAIN HILL PRESS

Downsizing
Copyright © 2021 by Lin Stepp
Published by Mountain Hill Press
Email contact: steppcom@aol.com

This is a work of fiction. Although numerous elements of historical and geographic accuracy are utilized in this and other novels in the Smoky Mountain series, many other specific environs, place names, characters, and incidents are the product of the author's imagination or used fictitiously.

Scripture used in this book, whether quoted or paraphrased by the characters, is taken from the King James Version of the Bible.

Cover design: Katherine E. Stepp
Interior design: J. L. Stepp, Mountain Hill Press
Editor: Elizabeth S. James
Cover photo and map design: Lin M. Stepp

Library of Congress Cataloging-in-Publication Data

Stepp, Lin
Downsizing: A Mountain Home novel / Lin Stepp
        p. cm – (The Smoky Mountain series)

ISBN: 978-1-7361643-4-1
First Mountain Hill Press Trade Paperback Printing: April 2021

eISBN: 978-1-7361643-5-8
First Mountain Hill Press Electronic Edition: April 2021

1. Women—Southern States—Fiction   2. Mountain life—Great Smoky Mountains Region (NC and TN)—Fiction. 3. Contemporary Romance—Inspirational—Fiction. I. Title

Library of Congress Control Number: 2020925282

DEDICATION

This book is dedicated to Mike Maples (1952-2019), a native
Tennessean and friend who loved the Great Smoky Mountains
and especially the Greenbrier area where this book is set. Mike
spent years hiking the Smokies, learning about the mountains
and their history and taking friends hiking on the trails and
pathways he knew so well. He was beloved by many and we were
happy to call him "friend." Mike often shared bits of history and
stories about his hikes and rambles with us—and we enjoyed his
company, his music, his many books about mountain history,
his blogs and videos, and his amiable warmth. Often called The
Smoky Mountain Jedi by those who knew and loved him, Mike's
memory—and stories—will always be treasured. Just living his
life and loving the mountains, he became a local legend.

Photo courtesy Susan Rudd

ACKNOWLEDGMENTS

"There is always, always something to be grateful for." – Anon

Acknowledgement and thanks go to all the wonderful people who helped to make this book the best it could be ...

To our photographer friend Jim Bennett who allowed us to use one of his wonderful Smoky Mountain black bear photos on the cover of my book.

To Matt Hills at M&D Hills Photography in the Glades in Gatlinburg and to our friends at the Appalachian Bear Rescue in Townsend who taught me a lot of needed facts about Smoky Mountain black bears.

To fans and friends in the Glades Arts and Crafts Community in Gatlinburg who shared stories with me, let me visit in their shops and watch them work, and answered a multitude of questions about the area.

To all the editorial and production staff at Mountain Hill Press who work so hard on every book published ... and especially to:
  - My daughter Katherine Stepp for her help with cover art and design and her ongoing creative assistance with our work.
  - My husband J.L. Stepp for always being the first, enthusiastic reader of my books and for his excellent production skills. He makes writing a joy and an adventure.

Thanks also to all my wonderful fans.
Keep reading and loving my books
and I'll keep writing them!

And deep gratitude to the Lord
for His help and wisdom with my work.

"Giving thanks always for all things unto God." – Eph 5:20

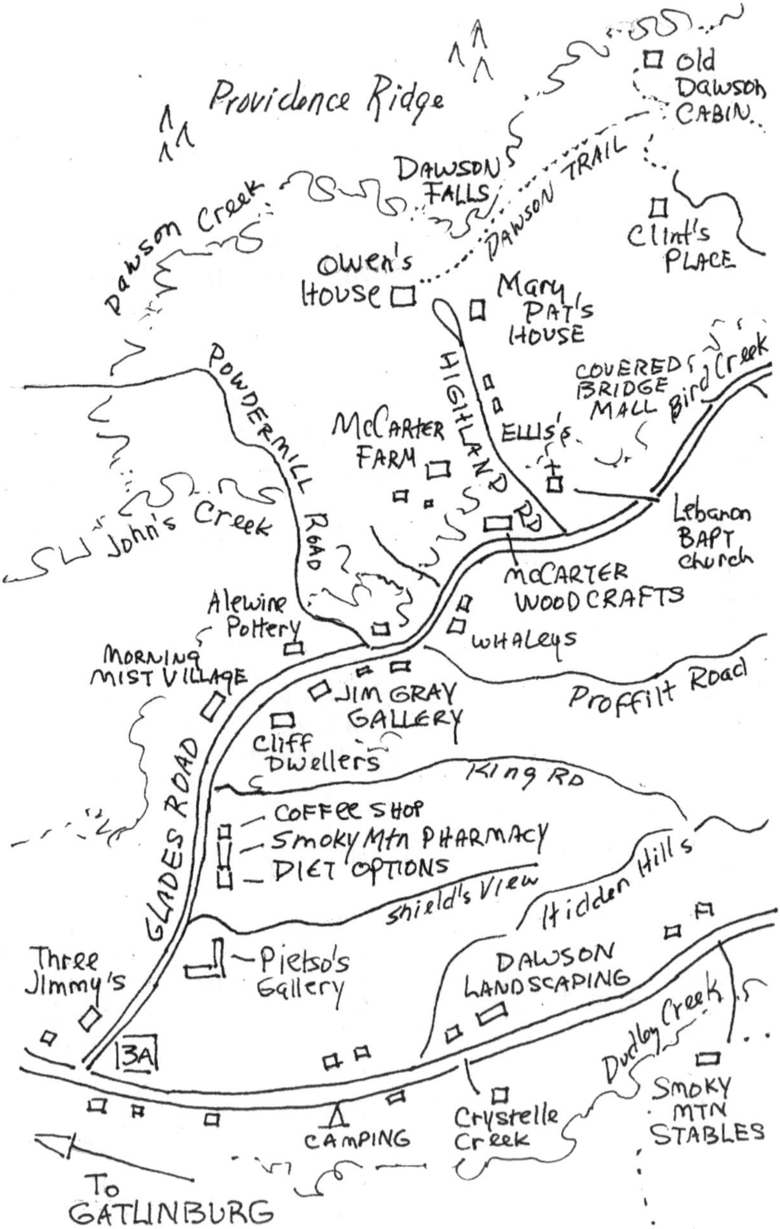
Providence Ridge
Old Dawson CABIN
DAWSON FALLS
DAWSON TRAIL
Dawson Creek
Clint's PLACE
Owen's House
Mary PAT's HOUSE
POWDERMILL ROAD
HIGHLAND RD
COVERED BRIDGE MALL
Bird Creek
McCARTER FARM
ELLIS's
John's Creek
Lebanon BAPT church
McCARTER WOODCRAFTS
Alewine Pottery
WHALEYS
MORNING MIST VILLAGE
Proffilt Road
JIM GRAY GALLERY
Cliff Dwellers
King RD
GLADES ROAD
COFFEE SHOP
Smoky Mtn PHARMACY
DIET OPTIONS
Shield's View
Hidden Hills
Pietso's Gallery
Three Jimmy's
DAWSON LANDSCAPING
Dudley Creek
3A
Crystelle Creek
SMOKY MTN STABLES
CAMPING
To GATLINBURG

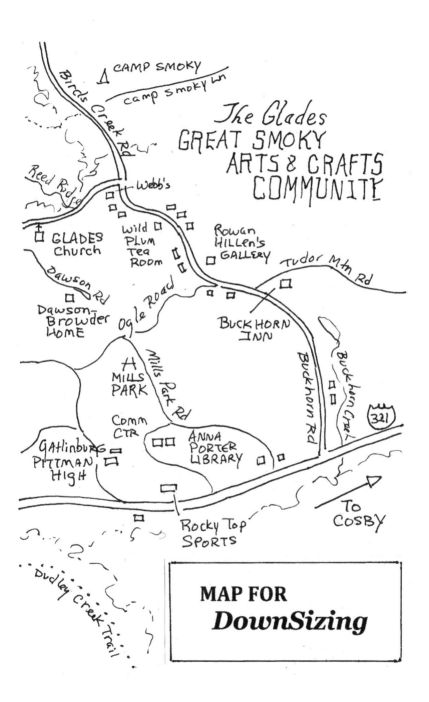

The Glades
GREAT SMOKY
ARTS & CRAFTS
COMMUNITY

MAP FOR
DownSizing

CHAPTER 1

Mary Pat glanced up from the kitchen counter where she stood frosting her latest cake masterpiece to see her husband Russell walking in the back door.

"Hi. What brings you home in the middle of the day?" She smiled at him, licking a dab of strawberry frosting off her finger. "Have you had lunch yet? I can make you something."

"No. I grabbed a bite at the hospital earlier between surgeries. I'm good." He moved over to a stool at the big kitchen island and sat down.

She lifted her eyes from the cake she was working on to study him. He still had on his lab coat, a staple of a doctor's wardrobe. His wavy hair was graying now at mid life, receding a little at the temples, and his face showed a few new wrinkles every year. He was still a handsome man, though, tall, distinguished, and confident, with an easy manner and a warm smile. He wasn't smiling now.

"Uh, oh," she said, adding the final layer of frosting to the top of her cake. "You look serious. Did I run up the credit card accounts too much during Christmas? I know I got a little carried away with all four of the children home for the holidays. The boys and Victoria are in apartments now and they need so many things. We don't see them nearly enough either. I know I spoil them."

She swirled the frosting on the top of the cake into peaks, looking at the iced cake with satisfaction. "Isn't this cake gorgeous? It's called a Pink Lady cake. It has a white cake base with strawberry gelatin and mashed berries added, and more fresh berries in the frosting. I'm making it for the Pink Luncheon we're having for the Ladies Auxiliary tomorrow. Janice Wright, Faye Hart, and I are decorating the meeting room at the country club in pink for the event, and everyone is dressing in pink to make the luncheon even more fun."

Mary Pat paused, remembering her shopping trip yesterday. Russell had already talked to her about curtailing spending this month with the holiday bills coming in. "I did buy a new pink hat and a dress I probably didn't really need for the luncheon. Are the bills totally out of line, Russell?"

"No, they're not a problem, Marian." He never called her Mary Pat as many of her friends and family did—always Marian. He disliked anyone calling him Russ either and insisted on Russell, not liking nicknames.

She finished the cake, arranging a few sliced berries across the top to make it prettier. Turning to the sink to rinse her hands, she looked back at Russell. "Are you sure you don't want a sandwich or a piece of the cream pie I made yesterday? It's no trouble. I can pour you a glass of tea, too."

"I'll take the tea," he said.

"Good." She beamed at him, still hoping to cheer him up over whatever seemed to be worrying him today. "I'll add some fresh mint to your tea. I'm so glad I bought that mint plant at the nursery to put in the kitchen window this winter. It gives us mint for our iced tea and for my recipes when I usually wouldn't be able to find mint." She got down two glasses from the shelf, pouring out tea from the pitcher in the refrigerator, adding a few sprigs of mint to each and sitting them on the counter.

Russell still hadn't smiled yet and Mary Pat felt uncomfortable with him popping in at midday like this. As a busy cardiologist, he seldom had time to get away from the office or the hospital during the day. Many nights he got called back into the hospital or simply worked late, too. His practice was demanding.

"We're celebrating Janet Harmon's announcement that she and Dave are expecting their first baby at our luncheon tomorrow."

She picked up the conversation again. "If I remember correctly, you work with Dave at the hospital. He's a gastroenterologist."

She put a glass top over the finished cake. "I'm sure you remember all the women in the Ladies Auxiliary are doctors' wives, too. Did you know that organization was established way back in the 1930s? A group of women started it to knit women together whose husbands were doctors in the Knoxville area. The organization will be seventy-five years old next year."

Mary Pat pushed Russell's tea across the island counter to him. "This whole week will be busy for me. The New Year has kicked in." She filled the too quiet room with words while she cleaned the kitchen. "I have my auxiliary luncheon tomorrow, a Junior League meeting later in the week, a church committee meeting, our big Friends of the Library fundraiser, and I promised to help Stella shop for the baby shower she's giving for Lesley's daughter. Lesley and Stella are in the Monday Girls with me. I'm sure you remember both of them, Russell, since all the girls in that group live right here in the neighborhood."

He patted the cushioned barstool beside him at the island. "Come sit down a minute, Marian."

"All right." She made her way around the counter and settled onto the barstool chair. "Aren't these new chairs comfortable? I was so proud to find them on sale this fall. They have nice memory foam seats and the color is so attractive with the new kitchen renovations we did."

Russell stirred his tea and sighed.

"Whatever is the matter, Russell?" she finally asked.

His eyes lifted to hers. "I want a divorce, Marian."

"What?" she said, trying to absorb the words.

"I want a divorce," he said again, saying each word more slowly.

"Russell, that doesn't make sense." Mary Pat put a hand to her heart. "We celebrated our thirty-fourth wedding anniversary while the children were home for Christmas. We've raised four children together. We seldom argue. We share a good happy life. Surely you can't mean that."

He frowned. "Marian, be realistic. We've been going our own ways for years. This shouldn't come as such a huge surprise."

"Well, it *does* come as a huge surprise." She felt tears well in her eyes. "In fact, it comes as a total shock. I can't even believe you're sitting her telling me this. Whyever do you want a divorce?"

"I want a change. I want some excitement back in life, more meaning outside of work. Someone to share things with."

"We share things."

'No, we don't. I go to work. I play racquetball and golf; I work out and run. I go hunting with some of my friends. You go to your clubs, meetings, and social events. You cook and shop. That's all you ever do or talk about. We do nothing together. We really have nothing in common anymore."

She felt the tears drip down her face. "I don't see how you can say that. And how can you say that's all that I ever do or talk about? I'm a busy, active person."

He crossed his arms. "You don't even see how you've failed to develop over the years, Marian. What happened to that young woman I married full of dreams and plans for her life? When we met, while you interned at the hospital, you were so excited about counseling patients, helping them to plan better nutritional habits and healthier lifestyles." His eyes drifted over her. "Now look at you. You're sixty pounds or more overweight, pushing obese now. Your doctor told me he was concerned that you weighed in at over two-hundred pounds your last visit."

"That's confidential information." She lashed out the words. "He had no right to tell you my weight."

"Well, you never mention it. How else was I to know, except by guessing?" Russell scowled. "How do you think it makes me feel as a heart specialist with my wife waddling around obese? I preach the importance of a healthy weight to all my patients every day. I'm sure it looks great when they run into me somewhere with you. I watch you struggle to get out of chairs now, and you can't even take a short walk with me in the neighborhood without getting winded. You all but waste your days, too. I can't find anything to respect or admire about you anymore."

She put a hand to her mouth, crying hard now.

Ignoring her tears, Russell pointed to the cake on the counter. "Honestly, the fact that you can make a pink lady cake just doesn't do it for me, Marian. Perhaps it does it for you, along with all those countless television shows you watch every day, the endless shopping trips you make, and the silly things you fill your time with. How can you find mundane, mindless things like that satisfying enough? How could you have let yourself go the way you have in every way? I simply don't understand it."

She hugged herself, every one of his words feeling like painful darts. "I had no idea you were growing unhappy with me."

He shook his head. "When younger we promised we'd stay fit and active. We always said we'd keep growing and learning, that we'd keep experiencing life. Savoring it. Sharing it. But we don't do that anymore. We haven't for a long time."

Mary Pat pushed her chair further away from him, beginning to grow angry now. "I had four children right out of college, if you'll remember. First Todd, then Craig two years later, and then Patrick two years after that. Four years later I had Victoria. It wasn't as though I sat home twiddling my thumbs all those years." Her voice rose. "I was raising our children. I seem to remember you encouraged me to stay home and not work. You always praised me and encouraged me for doing things with the children, helping them develop their talents and interests—scouts, soccer, football, clubs, all kinds of lessons."

Mary Pat scowled at him. "You certainly never had time for those things with them yourself, with the work schedule you kept. But I was always there. I kept their lives going and our home going, too. Was that so bad?"

He shook his head. "No, and I remember those early years as good years. I do. Then as the children grew older and went to school, you never returned to any interests of your own except for the little social groups and cliques you got involved in. Back then I did enjoy coming home and hearing about the children's lives.

But you had nothing to share about your own life even then. You sort of disappeared along the way, Marian. Then as the children grew older you began to get more and more overweight. It even embarrassed the kids. You sat around the house as your weight spiraled, not having the energy to do much. I kept changing, learning and growing, finding new interests, staying involved in life. The kids kept changing, learning and growing, but you just stagnated somehow."

He looked away. "I'm simply not happy with you anymore. I want a different life."

Mary Pat sat quietly for a few moments, hurt down into the marrow of her bones and trying to absorb all he'd said. How could this be happening?

"It might have been nice if you'd tried to talk with me about these things before now," she said finally.

His eyes met hers. "I *did* try."

She searched her memory. "I don't seem to remember any of those times."

"That's because you never paid any attention to me, shrugged off my words. I finally gave up."

"That's hardly fair, Russell, and not true either."

He made a face. "Well, look at you and look at your life. It says enough, doesn't it?"

Mary Pat wanted to throw something at him but instead she tried to stay calm, to think reasonably. What in the world was going on with Russell to make him act like this, so mean and hateful? It wasn't like him. Granted, he hadn't always been the most attentive, kind husband—frequently busy and distracted with his work—but never like this. What had suddenly changed him so much, made him think he wanted a divorce? Surely they could talk about this, work things out. If she got angry and screamed at him it would hardly help. What should she say to try to turn things around?

"How do you want me to change, Russell?" she asked at last. "We can work on this, make things better. As I said, I had no idea you were unhappy in our marriage or with me. We can talk, go to counseling if you like."

He shook his head. "No, I don't want to go to counseling or talk. I just want out. I've bought a condo over near the hospital. I've talked to a realtor about selling the house. She's found a buyer who wants to write contract."

Mary Pat felt her mouth drop open. "You want to sell our house?"

He shrugged. "It's too big for us now with the children grown and gone. I couldn't imagine you needing a place like this on your own either. Even with the children gone and so much time on your hands, I still pay for someone to clean the house for you and to take care of the yard every week. I don't want to do that anymore."

She felt her anger rise. "I see, and while you were so busy making new plans for yourself without even consulting me, where did you plan I should live since you apparently already bought a new place for yourself?"

Russell rubbed his neck. "With the sale of the house, you'll have enough to buy a smaller place or a condo. For a time if you like, you can move up to your parents' old place in the mountains above Gatlinburg. You talked me into buying their house when they moved to the Florida panhandle to start their café about twelve years ago. You insisted we'd all enjoy going to the Smoky Mountains for getaway vacations and holidays, but we seldom go up there." He sighed. "I told my attorney I'd sign the mountain house over to you since it had belonged to your parents; I paid out the mortgage a few years ago already. You can live there for a time and then sell it. You did grow up there. The street and area are familiar to you. Or you can move into a condo or apartment here in Knoxville and sell your parents' old house. Whatever you want. I don't care."

His words cut. How could he talk to her like this? So mean, as though she was a stranger or something? Granted, talking him into buying her parents' old place, the house where she grew up, hadn't been the wisest financial investment for them, but she'd hated to see the house, with all its memories, sold to strangers when her parents moved to Florida.

She stared at him, trying to figure out where the husband she knew had gone and who this new man was. *Whatever you want. I don't care*, he'd said.

"The fact that you don't care seems obvious from your words," she said when the quiet lengthened between them.

Russell didn't answer. He glanced at his watch instead, like he often did when he wanted to leave a boring party or escape someone cornering him as a doctor to talk about physical symptoms at a social gathering.

"You'll be all right, Marian," he said after a few moments. "I think this change will be good for both of us."

"No. A change will be good for you maybe. Or at least you seem to think so." She glared at him. "It won't be good for me. I laid aside my career goals to be a wife and mother for you all those years ago, kept your home, took care of your children, entertained your friends, joined the appropriate social organizations, supported you in every way I could to help advance your career and goals. I think it's cruel you're turning your back on me now after all these years, walking away without seeming to care how I feel or what will happen to me."

"That's unfair." He disagreed, a frown crossing his brow. "You won't be hurt financially. My attorney is working all that out. You can hire an attorney, too, if you wish, but you'll be well taken care of. The realtor is getting a good price for our house. She listed it at the top selling price and found a buyer without reducing the original price."

Shock and grief morphed into a slow anger now. "You make it sound so civil and nice, but it isn't. The last thing I ever expected was for you to simply cast me aside as we grew older, Russell Latham. Do you have a new wife picked out, too, to go along with this new life you're planning?"

She knew her words sounded hateful and sarcastic, but she watched Russell's gaze drop to his lap as she said them, watched him glance toward the door, as if wishing to escape.

Mary Pat thought back over his conversation. "Who's the realtor you've been working with?"

His eyes didn't meet hers. "Cherise Lavene. You know her. She lives in the neighborhood. She knows the value of the houses here."

"Yes I know her." Mary Pat watched him. "She's the woman you run with on the boulevard some mornings, isn't she? Widowed about five years ago? All the girls call her the barracuda—fearsome appearance, ferocious behavior—a beautiful predator on the hunt for a new man they say."

He looked up, annoyed. "That's hardly fair. Cherise works hard in the real estate business. She runs, goes to the gym, and takes care of herself. She doesn't deserve that kind of gossip."

"She's the one. Isn't she?" She pushed at Russell's chest, almost upsetting his stool.

"I admire her," he admitted. "I admit, too, she's exciting, interesting, and full of life."

Mary Pat knew he wouldn't admit more, but she also knew instinctively there was more. She'd heard the girls talk about the different men Cherise Lavene had targeted and pursued in the last years. She'd married an older, very wealthy man the first time. The girls all said she was looking for a new man along the same lines. Russell, at sixty-four, had been acting sensitive about his age for the last few years. He'd bought that sporty convertible last year he didn't need, and she'd noticed other signs. Obviously she should have paid more attention. She'd seen other wealthy men trade in their long time wives for a newer version but never imagined it could happen to her. Russell was ten years her senior after all, and she'd always felt that age difference a sort of protection. That and their long-term marriage, which she'd believed a happy one.

"I don't know what to say, Russell. You've decided our marriage is not enough for you anymore and that I am not enough. You've picked out a new place to live, a new partner, and you've already made plans to move on with your life, thinking little about how all these decisions will affect me or our children."

"Our children are adults now," he said with annoyance. "They've all finished college; they're working. They'll understand. It's not like they're little kids anymore."

She shook her head. "If you think this won't shock and hurt our children, you're deluding yourself greatly." She paused. "And I plan to let *you* be the one to tell each of them about this, too. You always made me be the one to deal out any disappointing news in past, but not this time."

He wrinkled his nose. "No problem. I'll talk to them."

"Good, and unless you plan to change your mind about filing for divorce, contact them soon. Since you've already talked with an attorney and started paperwork, and since Cherise has been marketing our home—I might add without my knowledge—word will soon get out. I'd rather our children hear about this from you before someone calls one of them and tells them about it behind our backs."

"I said I'd talk to them." He bit the words out.

She sat there, trying to think what else she could possibly say. Surely this wasn't really happening? She'd seen people she knew get a divorce, heard stories tittered on the wind, felt sorry for those she knew well. Never had she imagined it might be her. Not for a minute.

"What will I do, Russell? I haven't worked outside the home since we married. Any office skills I once had are sadly out of date. Any resume I might create would look ridiculous."

He shrugged. "You've apparently felt happy enough sitting around and doing nothing for the last twenty years since Victoria started school. I guess you can keep sitting around doing nothing if you want to, go to your little clubs and such. Your alimony will be pretty good. Divorce doesn't need to change your life very much if you don't want it to."

"That's a mean and stupid thing to say. Divorce changes everything." She snapped the words out. "And I never pursued anything else outside the home because I thought you were happy with the life I led. You never once encouraged me to get a job, to not be home whenever you showed up to eat dinner. You always seemed delighted to have me available to plan a dinner party for some of your associates and doctor friends, to run your errands, to handle everything with the children and with our home. You always told me you felt glad I was content to stay at home, that I made everyone else's lives so much easier that way."

"Maybe I said that when the children were smaller. But then things changed. You could easily have gotten back into some kind of meaningful work as the children grew older. Built a life of your own." He drank the last of his tea and stood. "I kept watching for you to wake up and want to change, but you never did."

She clenched her fists. "Are you saying I'm boring as well as fat now? Is that it, Russell?"

"What do you think, Marian? Go look in the mirror later. Go look at your life and you tell me what you think." He started toward the door. "I've got to get back to the office."

"I guess we can talk about this more tonight. We'll need to."

He stopped near the backdoor. "No. I don't think there's anything more to talk about right now. I have a late surgery scheduled today and I'm staying over at the condo tonight. I've taken some clothes and a few other things over as I could. I'll get the rest on the weekend. Don Pauley, my attorney, will be contacting you." He glanced around. "You take whatever you want from the house. The condo I bought came furnished."

She began to cry again.

Russell ran a hand through his hair. "Listen, Marian, I'm sorry if this has come as a big shock. But maybe fast and clean is best. I plan to sign the contract sale for the house this week. You need to sign it, too. You can't keep this place up alone financially. The house isn't paid for and the upkeep is high. Don will explain that to you. I've talked to him about all this. It's realistic to sell the house. We got a good offer, and we'll split the profits. The buyers want to take possession at the end of February. That's nearly two months from now. A lot of time."

Two months from now! Mary Pat wanted to scream the words out. Surely, he couldn't expect her to pack and leave their home in less than two months?

Fighting back a new sweep of tears and anger, she said, "Russell, surely you realize that only one short time to talk about this will not be enough for us. A lot of issues and decisions need to be considered. You don't walk away from a thirty-four year marriage after a short chat over iced tea one day."

He gave her a blank look, not seeming to follow her logic. "I really can't see what else there is to talk about. The attorneys will handle the rest. It's pretty straightforward. I think Don can answer any questions you might have. Cherise knows a good auction company that can handle the sales for anything you don't want to keep in the house. The company comes in, lists and itemizes everything, packs everything up, and takes it out in one day. It's less complicated than you might think."

Russell glanced at his watch again. "I've got to get back to the office. I have an appointment coming in. I'm sorry I was forced to be the one to recognize and point out that our marriage is over. But I hope when you think about it, Marian, you'll see this decision was the best for both of us." He offered her a smile and then left through the backdoor.

A smile. She wanted to scream and throw something at him. How could he just smile, wish her the best, and walk out? Like he would a patient he was dismissing after surgery and care.

She climbed off the stool at the counter and found her legs were shaky. In shock, she walked over to the big sofa across the room and sat down, pulling a soft afghan over her, feeling chilled. What in the world was she going to do? Her husband had just walked in and asked for a divorce in the middle of the day, as casually as if he'd asked her to drop off some clothes at the dry cleaners. Did he not have any idea how this had turned her life totally around? How unprepared she'd been to hear his words today?

Glancing around the familiar room, at the family photos lined up on the mantel, Mary Pat started to cry. She wasn't sure how long she cried. Barker, the dog she'd taken in a few years ago, padded into the room as she wept, climbing up on the sofa to lick her hand

and comfort her. It only made her cry harder.

Seeming frozen in time, Mary Pat sat curled up on the couch for hours after Russell's visit. She couldn't stand the idea of calling any of her friends or her family to talk. She felt so humiliated, so hurt. What would she tell them? What would she say?

Realizing the afternoon was fading, she suddenly felt afraid someone in her family would call her or that one of her friends would stop by. She wasn't ready to talk to anyone yet. She couldn't talk to or see anyone yet. Glancing around, she realized the idea of spending the night here alone terrified her. Everything around her made her think of her life with Russell. And she didn't think she could get through the night alone in this house filled with memories, sleeping in the bed where she'd always slept with her husband. In the morning she'd be expected to head to lunch with her auxiliary friends, all doctors' wives. They'd pick up on her feelings. Or maybe they would have heard something by then. Cherise Levene wasn't known to be a kind woman. Perhaps she's already spreading the word around that Russell is leaving me.

Getting up, Mary Pat headed into the kitchen to toss some snacks and food for herself and Barker into a bag. Then she ran upstairs, threw clothes, toiletries, and other items into a suitcase haphazardly. She had to go somewhere tonight. Anywhere but here.

CHAPTER 2

At the end of a long day Owen McCarter walked through McCarter Woodcrafts turning off lights, locking windows and doors. After high school he'd left the family business to go into the military, served over twenty years and then came home again. Funny how quickly he'd merged right back in to the old life he'd once been so eager to leave behind.

"Mr. Owen?" Wheeler Ellis grinned at him through the front window.

Owen opened the door for him, and Wheeler ambled in with that slightly swaying walk of his, offering Owen another happy grin that lit his face and crinkled his eyes. Wheeler was such a warm and loving boy, despite the birth defects that left his mind a little slow.

"I finished up all the mowing, and I raked and did the weed-eating. You wanna come look?"

Owen knew Wheeler liked praise for a job well done. "I'm sure you did a great job, Wheeler."

He pulled at his gloves. "I swept off all the porches and the steps, too."

Owen walked to open the front door, made a point of looking up and down the porch with interest. "I can't imagine anyone could have made the place look better."

The boy, actually a man now at forty-three, grinned with pleasure.

"I'm going to walk on home now." He looked at his watch. "Ma likes me home by supper."

Wheeler started out the front door and then stopped, turning back to frown at Owen. "There's a woman up there at the Jennings' place next to your house." He pointed up the road as though Owen didn't know where his own house sat at the end of Highland Drive. He'd built it on the upper end of the McCarter farm property after he came home.

"I think that woman might be sick or something."

This caught Owen's attention. "Why do you say that, Wheeler?"

"I'm supposed to look out for things up there," he answered, as if he needed to explain this to Owen. "You know I always mowed and worked for Mr. and Mrs. Jennings afore they moved to Florida. The man who bought their place asked me to keep looking after things. He sends mom a check for me to keep doing it."

Owen nodded. He knew the Jennings daughter and her husband bought the place about twelve years ago, before he retired and came home from the military. He hadn't seen any of them at the house for years though. His dad said they stopped by now and then but he'd never run into them.

"Why do you think the woman there might be sick?" Owen probed.

"She's acting sick. She don't look good or sound good." Wheeler glanced up the street again. "She was snifflin' and crying like you do when you're sick. I didn't think I should stop by but maybe you could. We don't want her to die up there or nothing."

Owen tried not to grin. "I'll stop by when I go home. When did you see the woman, Wheeler?"

"Just afore I came to do the yard here. I'd walked Mama's little dog Sadie up the street and back. I haven't seen no car come down the road since, so I think she's still there." He paused. "It's been worrying me."

Wheeler had a sweet heart. "I promise I'll check. You go on home."

Owen watched him amble down the steps and across the parking lot to head for the Ellis's small frame house on the hill behind the Lebanon Baptist Church. The church sat on one corner of

Highland and Glades Road, with McCarter Woodcrafts on the other.

Wheeler turned to wave before he started up the street and Owen lifted a hand in return.

A short time later Owen locked the front door of the store and headed up the hill in the Toyota 4Runner he'd bought to get around the mountain roads in. You needed a pretty tough car for some of the unforgiving terrain in the Smoky Mountains.

Highland Drive was a short side road off two-lane Glades Road that looped through the Arts and Crafts Community above Gatlinburg. The Glades area always seemed quiet and peaceful to Owen, next to the hustle and bustle of nearby Gatlinburg and Pigeon Forge.

He saw the bright red Audi Coupe in the driveway as he passed the old Jennings place. Sharp little car; pricey too. Some of the family must be up visiting. Owen hated to go snooping, but maybe he could walk over on some pretext or other to satisfy Wheeler's concerns.

His place on the left at the end of the road and the Jennings place on the right were the only two homes at the end of Highland Drive. The church and McCarter Woodcrafts sat the bottom of the hill, with a couple of homes on the right above the church, like the Ellis place. On the left behind the store and across the creek stood his grandparents' old farmhouse where his sister and her daughter now lived with his dad. For buildings, that was it—except for a barn and a few sheds—with only farmland and woods between.

After parking his car in the garage, Owen made his way into the house. He'd built a rustic home, stained a weathered barn red, on the hill at the end of the road when he'd retired. It sat on the foundations of an old cabin, once belonging to his great grandparents, that had burned down in a fire before he was born. He'd seen a grainy picture of it once. Owen had grown up with his parents and older sister Francine in the big white farmhouse on the lower end of the farm nearer the family business. The McCarter family owned all the property on the left side of Highland Drive from Glades Road to his place at the end of the road and up into the edges of Providence Ridge.

Owen dumped the rest of the beef and vegetable soup he'd cooked yesterday into the electric cooker to heat again for supper and then put his coat back on to head across to the Jennings' place. The Jennings, like the McCarters, were an old family in the Smokies area. Owen had known Paul and Regina Jennings well and remembered when they built their white cape cod house with its single gable when he was only a toddler. He and Francine had grown up with the Jennings' two children, too. He'd grieved when at West Point, learning about their son Brandon's death when he was killed in a wreck one winter. Brandon had only been twenty nine, working his first job, Mary Pat away in college. It must have been a tough time for them. Paul managed a restaurant on Highway 321 all the years Owen could remember, and Regina worked in a small sweet shop in the Glades. He'd felt sorry to see them move off to Florida.

As Owen climbed the porch to the front door now, he heard a dog barking. He knocked several times before he heard steps move toward the door. A woman peeked out, red-faced and distraught-looking, keeping the chain on the door. It took him a minute to recognize her.

"Mary Pat?" he asked, still not sure it was her after all these years.

"Owen?" she asked in return, then groaned and rolled her eyes. She pushed the door in, slipped the chain off, and opened it again a small space. "I'm sorry to seem inhospitable," she said then. "But this isn't a good time for me. Can I help you with something?"

He remembered his reason to come. "If that's your car in the driveway, you might want to put it in the garage and lock it— especially if you've left any food or drinks in it. We've had problems with bears around the Glades lately. One or two have gotten too socialized and, unfortunately, caused trouble."

"Ah." She seemed to consider his words. "I've forgotten all the things to be careful about living in the city for so long instead of the mountains."

He saw her dog poking his nose around her leg. "Be watchful about the dog, too. Remember bears and dogs are natural enemies. Your dog, being used to the city, might not know what a bad enemy—or playmate—a bear might be."

She actually offered him a small smile then. "Thanks." She opened the door wider. "Do you want to come in a minute? I could use help remembering how to lay a fire in the fireplace. I've turned the heat up in the house, but it's cold in here, and I know the temperature is dropping." She hesitated. "You'll have to put up with my looks, though. As you can see I've been crying. My life's just fallen apart."

"I can cope with that all right. And you look okay to me."

She started back into the house, holding on to the dog's collar. "Well, that's nice to hear after being told I've let myself become fat, boring, and completely expendable today."

Following Mary Pat into the house, he couldn't help noticing she'd put on quite a few pounds since high school when he'd known her as a cute little blond and Gatlinburg High's top twirler.

He saw she'd already brought in wood from the woodshed outside, put kindling in the fireplace and started to arrange the wood. He squatted to finish the job, stacking more wood and then lighting the kindling to get the fire started. After finishing he went out back to the shed to bring in more logs for her to put on the fire later.

Owen petted the dog before he went out and then when he came back in again. "Nice dog," he said, sitting in the chair across from her where she'd curled up on the sofa. "What's his name?"

"Barker." She smiled a little again.

He scratched the dog behind his ears. "What's the breed? A mix I think. Maybe some sheep dog?"

"A little sheep dog with bearded collie mixed in. A neighbor's dog dropped pups. My last child had just left home. You can guess the rest."

Owen remembered his soup then. "Have you eaten any dinner?"

"No." She leaned her head back.

"I put homemade vegetable beef soup in the electric cooker to heat before I came over. Walk back to the house and eat a bowl with me."

She sighed. "I'm not good company for anyone tonight, Owen. You go on back. And thanks for helping with the fire."

"Tell you what," he said, getting up. "I'll go get the soup and bring it back over here. An old bachelor like me doesn't get a chance to eat dinner with Gatlinburg High's Homecoming Queen every night."

She rolled her eyes. "I'm a long way from that girl."

He put on his jacket. "Dig us out a few bowls while I'm gone. I'll be back in a few minutes."

Owen came back carrying the electric cooker to find she'd set two place settings at the small dining table in view of the fireplace. Carrying the cooker into the kitchen to sit it on the counter and hook it up, he handed her a paper sack. "I brought homemade bread Mrs. Ellis made and a stick of butter, too. I didn't know if you'd had a chance to pick up anything."

She pulled items out of the sack. "What's this?" she asked, pulling out a folded over bag.

"A couple of fried pies Mrs. Ellis gave me, too. She seems to think a bachelor like me would starve to death if she didn't keep plying me with food every day or so."

Mary Pat leaned over and sniffed the bag. "I think I've died and gone to heaven just over the smell." She mustered up a small smile again for him. "I'm going to start a pot of coffee to go with these after the soup."

They sat down after a few minutes to eat.

Owen had only seen Mary Pat a few times through the years since high school but it felt surprisingly comfortable sitting here with her eating dinner. "Odd how comfortable old friends feel even after years go by," he said.

"I was just thinking the same thing," she said, cutting off another slice of the thick homemade bread to butter it. "Maybe it's because you ate dinner so many times with us here or because you and I spent so much time together growing up. My brother Brandon and your sister Francine were so much older than us. I think we were the only two kids close in age for miles. We either had to play together or play alone."

He looked across the table at her. "We got along well, too. Had a barrel of fun exploring these hills, playing, carrying on as kids. And we got along right well in other ways later."

Owen watched her blush.

"It's sweet of you to remind me of that tonight when I'm feeling old, fat, ugly, and broken-hearted."

"I still see the pretty girl in there that I knew," he said, being honest. "And you still have those beautiful blue eyes and your blond hair, touched up a bit perhaps."

"The hair color is mostly natural," she said. "When a little white started to show my hairdresser decided to help things along with a pretty white and ash blond look to even the color."

He studied her. "It makes me think of the white blond curls you had when you first moved here. I think you were three or four." He got up to get another bowl of soup. "We've been friends a long time, Mary Pat."

"God must have been looking after me to have you stop by tonight, Owen. Thank you."

He grinned as he sat back down. "You can thank Wheeler. It was his idea for me to stop over."

Her eyes brightened. "Mrs. Ellis's little boy? I remember him. I used to read my old storybooks to him. He loved them."

"Wheeler is forty-three now, hardly a little boy anymore."

She bit her lip. "How is he doing?"

"Pretty good. His mind's a little young, but he's as good as gold. He works doing yards and odd jobs for people around here and he helps my cousin Clint Dawson in his landscaping business. His mother Maydeen Ellis works for us at the store, runs the register, meets and greets the public. Warm-hearted and friendly. I know you remember her."

"Gosh, I do. You're bringing back a lot of memories." She looked across at him. "How are your parents and your sister? Catch me up on your family and your life."

"My mother died ten years ago. I came home on leave from the military to be here for a time before we lost her and I decided to retire and come home. I've been surprised at how easily I slipped back into this old life."

"I remember when your mother got sick. I know you must miss her." She smiled at him. "She was so proud for you when you got into West Point. She knew how much you wanted it. So did I."

He started to mention how hard it had been to follow that dream when he'd wanted her so much then, too. But he thought better of mentioning it. What would be the point? He'd gone on, into the military. She'd gone on to the university in Knoxville, then married. And now all these years had passed.

"Is Duggan, your dad, still living? I so loved him."

"Yeah, he's still fit as a fiddle, working in the store, whittling and woodworking, walking the trails, bossing everyone around." He grinned over the words. "He'll like hearing that you loved him. He was sure crazy for you."

"What about your sister Francine?"

"Francine, like me, took off to do bigger things. You probably remember she went off to Emory and Henry College in Virginia on scholarship. Majored in accounting. Took a job down in Charlotte, North Carolina, got married there, had a girl Larissa. Her husband was killed tragically in a car wreck a little over six years ago. Francine decided to come home then with Larissa. She moved into the farmhouse with Dad. After grieving a little she took over the books at the store, took over the books at Dawson Landscaping, and does some other jobs as she can work them in. We've all been blessed she came home."

"I remember she was always smart in math. I used to get her to help me with my homework." She paused. "But I'm sorry she lost her husband."

"It's hard and that's a fact."

She seemed to pick up on the changed tone in his voice. "I

thought I remembered that you married back in past."

"I did. The military life doesn't make for a happy life for a lot of women. The woman I married wasn't cut out for it." He changed the subject. "You can see others have marital griefs and sorrows they had to pass through. You going to tell me what's going on with you?"

She winced and hugged herself. "You probably don't want to get me started on it. I'm still in shock. Hurt, weepy. All that girl stuff. I don't have any idea what I'm going to do either."

"You'll find your way. Let's hear it. Maybe go back a ways first and catch me up on your family. You had kids along the way, too. Dad said he met some of them a few times when they came up here to see Regina and Paul."

She got up to take their soup bowls to the kitchen, rinsed them out, left them in the sink and poured them both a cup of coffee. "You want any sugar or milk in this? I don't have any creamer."

"I'll take a little of both," he answered. "But not much of either."

She brought their coffee back and then put the fried pies on two plates and carried them back to the table. She ate a few bites of the pie and drank a little coffee before she talked again.

"I met Russell Latham the summer before my senior year in college while doing an internship at the University of Tennessee Hospital. I was studying nutrition and dietetics at UT and I was really interested in being a clinical dietitian in a hospital after graduation." She sipped at her coffee, remembering back. "Russell was ten years older than me, starting practice as a young cardiologist. He really came after me. We dated, got engaged, and got married over Christmas break. I finished school a married lady, and soon pregnant, too. I had Todd in September, then Craig two years later, then Patrick another two years after that, and four years later Victoria. It was wild with four little kids so close together. Looking back, it seems like those years just flew by."

"I'll bet you were a great mom."

"I hope so. I tried, and I loved it." She smiled at him. "With Russell a cardiologist, we were blessed financially. I really didn't need to work, and my life was busy enough with the children and other activities I got involved in once they started school. Soon I was packing children off to college dormitories and before I knew it my youngest Victoria left and I had an empty nest."

"Where are the kids now?"

"Todd, always my bossy, responsible child, became a doctor like his dad, but an orthopedic doctor instead of a cardiologist. He's finishing his residency training and working at Vanderbilt Orthopedics in Franklin, Tennessee, south of Nashville. Craig, my somewhat geeky child, always fascinated with computers and technology, is a software development manager for Vistaprint's corporate office in Waltham, Massachusetts, not far from Boston. Patrick, who always reveled in the outdoors and especially loved the water and the ocean, became a coastal geologist. He works for NOAA Coastal Services in Charleston, South Carolina, and lives on James Island near Charleston."

She paused. "I got to keep my girl a little longer than the others, her being the youngest. She's a daddy's girl; this situation is going to hit her hard."

"What is Victoria doing now?"

"Like her father, she had a medical bent and just finished school at Belmont College of Pharmacy in Nashville. She's working her first pharmacy job at Green Hills Pharmacy nearby and loves it. I helped her move into a nice apartment with her best friend Carol this summer." She spread her hands. "So the kids are all over the place. Living their own lives now, calling home once in a while, and dropping in occasionally for holidays. It seems so strange sometimes that they're all grown and gone after the house was so full of noise and life for so many years."

"You're lucky to have that family. I know they love you, even if they're busy and far away now."

"I hope so." She got up to get a little more coffee and Owen walked over to stir the fire and add another log to it.

"You want to sit over here closer to the fire now?" he asked. "These January nights get cold in the mountains."

"That would be nice." She settled into the couch where she'd sat before and Owen dropped into the same chair near her.

"Here's the bad part of my life story." She sighed. "Today, Russell popped in unexpectedly at lunch time. He was acting odd and I kept chattering, like I do when I get nervous, thinking maybe I'd overspent at Christmas and he was upset as the bills started coming in. Finally I asked him if anything was wrong, and he said he wanted a divorce. Just like that. Out of the blue without any warning signs I can look back and see clearly. I was stunned."

"I'm sorry."

"Me, too. I'd hoped he might be open to counseling, to try to work things out, but he informed me he already had procedures started with his attorney. More shocking, I learned he'd already bought a condo for himself near the hospital and he'd had a realtor looking for prospects to buy our house. He let me know an offer had come in and he wanted to take it. If we do, I have to be out of the house by the end of February. Hardly two months from now. It's only January sixth."

She closed her eyes, obviously reliving the hurt, and he saw tears seep down her cheeks. "He talked to me like he might one of his clients about a needed but necessary surgery. Matter of fact, almost cold. I couldn't believe he was the same man I'd been married to these thirty-four years. When I lost it and asked him what in the world I should do, since he had his own new life so well planned out, he told me I could move up here until our house sold. 'I don't care what you do,' he said. Just like I was an old pair of shoes he was ready to throw out."

Owen watched her cry then and he fought the urge to go gather her up in his arms. But that wouldn't be right. "He's a real fool to let you go, Mary Pat."

She sniffed. "Well, that's nice of you to say, but he certainly doesn't think so. He told me he was ashamed of me because I'd gotten fat, when he's a cardiologist, and that he was disappointed in me because I hadn't done anything with my life. Apparently raising his children, keeping his home, entertaining his clients and friends, running his errands, and cooking his meals count for nothing. As do the various social groups I became involved in, many because he encouraged them, like the women's auxiliary of doctors' wives. I simply can't take it all in. It seemed like my husband morphed into another being right before my eyes." She paused. "Like one of the boys' transformer toys."

He chuckled a little. "I remember those."

She shook her head sadly. "Well, transformer Russell also let it slip that he also has a new wife or girlfriend picked out, a younger, sleeker model. She's a realtor who lives in our neighborhood and who started jogging in the morning at the same time as Russell did this fall. The same one who so conveniently found a buyer for the house." Mary Pat closed her eyes again. "I really should have figured that one out."

"I don't think you can stop someone who wants to cheat. And when you love well and hard, you are the last to know sometimes."

She looked across at him. "You sound like you're talking from experience."

"I told you my marriage didn't work out. You move on. You don't have any choice."

"I'm seeing that," she said.

"Who have you talked to?" he asked then.

"No one." She reached over to grab a tissue to blow her nose. "After weeping for a couple of hours and sitting in shock staring out the window after Russell left, I threw some things together and ran here. I was terrified to spend the night in that house, to face all my feelings in the dark where all the memories of my life would be all around me." She crossed her arms. "I kept imagining how awful it would be if one of my friends called me. Or one of the children. What would I say? This is so humiliating."

"Have you called your parents?" he asked. "Called your mother? You've always been close to her."

Mary Pat cried again. "What would I say, Owen? Everyone will think I'm such a failure. So pathetic."

"No, they won't. Russell is the one in the wrong here. The

villain, if you want to think of it that way. You need to call your parents. They'll be a support to you. Help you through this. Advise you when you're too upset to think as clearly as you should." He paused. "Have you contacted an attorney? Russell obviously has retained one. You'll need one, too."

"No. I haven't done anything. Or called anyone." She burst into tears again. "I told Russell that he had to call the children about this, too, that I wouldn't do it. What could I say to them?"

He got up and walked over to sit down beside her this time. "I know that you're upset and that this is hard, Mary Pat." He took her hands in his. "But I want you to call your mother. I remember your mother well, and I remember her hauling over to the school to chew out a few teachers and administrators when it was needed in relation to her kids. My guess is she'll head to Knoxville tomorrow to help you with this. And you need someone in your court right now."

She looked down at his hands holding hers, and he withdrew them and got up to go back to his chair again. "I'm going to go wash up our dishes, and I want you to sit here and call your parents while I do. Will you do that?"

"Okay," she said after a time of leaning her head back against the couch with her eyes closed, as if gathering her strength.

He watched her reach into her purse to get out her cell phone while he headed into the kitchen.

Owen could only hear snatches of the conversation Mary Pat had with her mother after that. He looked into the living room to see her pacing around the area a few times. When he finished cleaning up, he found Barker's leash, put on his jacket and took the dog out for a walk. He'd sure stepped into it, coming over to check on Mary Pat tonight. But Wheeler probably had one of those odd leadings he got that things were not good here. He was funny like that sometimes.

As Owen walked the dog, he prayed. He remembered all too well the pain of learning someone you loved and trusted was cheating on you and cared little for you when you'd built your whole world around them.

He let himself in the back door a little later, taking off the dog's leash and then walked into the living room. Mary Pat was standing in front of the fireplace, watching the blaze.

"You were right to tell me to call Mother," she told him, trying to offer him a small smile. "She's packing now, has already made a plane reservation, and I'm picking her up at the airport near Knoxville early in the morning. She's going back to the house in Sequoyah Hills with me, and Daddy has already called an old attorney friend of his in Knoxville to see Mother and I tomorrow afternoon. Mom said she'll stay until we can get everything figured out. She reminded me that we Jennings are strong people and that I'd be fine."

She reached down to pet Barker. "She and Daddy are also ready to shoot Russell. They can't believe he's doing an idiot thing like this."

Mary Pat walked over to wrap her arms around him. "Owen, I am so grateful you came over here tonight. Truly I am. I'd been looking at butcher knives, wondering if I could kill myself."

He pulled back in shock.

"Oh, I know I really wouldn't have killed myself, but I wanted to. I wanted to simply die. I felt so betrayed and alone. So awful and ugly." She hugged him tighter and kissed his cheek. "I really think God sent you here to save me tonight. I needed good counsel and someone to talk to more than I knew. I will always be grateful to you for coming and for staying around tonight. This hasn't been one of my better moments, I know."

"Will you be all right here tonight by yourself?" he asked. "I can call Francine and ask her to come stay over with you. I know she'd be glad to. She always thought of you as a younger sister. She'd love to see you, too."

"I'd like to see Francine again, too, but not tonight. I really think maybe I can sleep now. This was my home growing up. I'll be all right, and I have to get up early in the morning to drive down to pick up Mother. She said it was unwise for me to leave the house until things are resolved. There will be a lot to talk about and a lot to do." She walked over to warm her hands in front of the fire again. "I really don't know yet what I'll do or where I'll go."

"You'll figure something out. You're stronger than you realize."

"I hope so. I'll have to think about all of this and pray about it a lot." She turned to look at him. "Do you believe in prayer?"

"I do."

"I remember we used to pray and have funerals for little animals that died when we were kids, and we used to say prayers up at Dawson Falls and throw rocks in the water to represent our prayers about things. Do you remember that?"

"Yeah, I do. Dad always says 'all things work for good to those that love the Lord.' I've seen that happen, even after the worst of times."

"I hope he's right. I used to tell my children that there's always a rainbow after the storm when bad, unfair, and hurtful things happened to them."

Mary Pat glanced at the clock on the mantel. "You need to head home and get some sleep yourself, Owen McCarter. And thank you again for being a friend."

She paused. "I'm sorry we didn't keep in touch more over the years. I heard you'd come back home but I never seemed to run into you the times we came up here to the mountains. I usually had the kids with me—or at least one or two of them. They were teenagers or in college then. They had things they wanted to do while we were here and never wanted to stay long."

Mary Pat glanced down at herself. "Actually, I was ashamed to let you see me. I'd put on so much weight, and Duggan showed me a picture of you once. I knew you were still fit and handsome." She looked at him. "You still are. You've aged well, Owen. I feel dowdy next to you and I know we're the same age."

He wasn't sure what to say so he just nodded.

"Anyway, I know I'll come back up here to see you—and Francine and Duggan—again as soon as I get things straightened out a little."

"Will you stay here for a time?" he asked, realizing he wished more than he wanted to acknowledge that she would say yes.

"I can't say yet." She shook her head. "There's so much I have to deal with. But Russell said he signed this house over to me. Maybe I can come stay for a while if things work out. I don't know."

He pulled his wallet from his back pocket and pulled one of his business cards out of it. "The store phone is on here, and I'll write my home phone and my cell phone on the back. If you need anything you call me. You know Wheeler will keep watching out for the house, too." He glanced at the fireplace. "You'll need to stoke the fire during the night to keep it up. And be sure to put the fire out well before you leave. I wouldn't mention it ordinarily, but I know you have a lot on your mind."

"Thanks. I'll do that."

They said a few more niceties as Owen put on his jacket again and retrieved his soup pot from the kitchen. Odd how this time felt to him so much like the time he went away to West Point after high school, needing to say goodbye to Mary Pat but hating to say goodbye, too. Life sure had odd twists.

CHAPTER 3

A few weeks later, Mary Pat sat at the glass-topped table on the sun porch behind her Knoxville home with her mother. Papers and notes lay spread across the table and the last bits of lunch sat on two plates pushed to the side.

"Do you think you'll be okay if I fly back home in the morning?" her mother asked. "I can stay longer if you want."

Mary Pat reached over to put her hand over her mother's. "You've been here nearly a month now. You need to get home to help Dad at J.J.'s Café."

"January is our slow time at the beach. Dad's managing all right on his own for now. He wishes he could be here, too. We're both so sorry for what Russell is putting you and the children through." She reached over for her cup of hot chocolate on the table and sipped it. "At the attorney meetings and the house closing he seemed so unlike himself. So cold and detached."

"I don't think I'll ever understand it." Mary Pat picked up the inventory sheet of household furnishings to study them.

"Are you sure you want to let most all your furnishings go?" her mother asked.

"You did when you moved," Mary Pat reminded her. "You and dad moved to your new place at the beach and pretty much let all your things at the mountain house go. The boys hauled off most of your furniture, dishes, and household goods to their apartments."

Her mother waved a hand. "You know the beach house we bought came furnished, and our things at the mountain house didn't seem appropriate for our new place. Besides, those furnishings had seen us through all our years with you children. With everything a little old and shabby, we felt glad for the grandkids to come carry off what they wanted. We knew you'd want to redecorate the house to make it your own, too." She smiled. "You did really fix the old place up to be charming and welcoming. Dad and I love to go up there for vacations."

Mary Pat reached for the last cookie on her lunch plate. "Do you think I'm making a mistake to move up to the mountains for a while?"

Her mother lifted an eyebrow. "Do you?"

"No, especially not after some of the things that happened this week."

"You mean like those nasty Monday Girls telling you that you really didn't belong in their little group anymore now that you were selling your Sequoyah Hills home?" She shook her head in annoyance. "I still can't believe they had the nerve to call and eject you from their Monday get-togethers at a time like this, even if politely. You've been friends with those women for twenty years at least, ever since you and Russell bought this house. Some of those women are your closest friends, not just a neighborhood social group."

"I've certainly had some wake-up calls about my friendships since the word got out that Russell and I are divorcing and selling the house." She made a face. "I did consider two of the women in that group my very best friends. My other closest friends were in the Auxiliary. Judy Clifton called me yesterday to let me know that Cherise Levene applied for membership. Evidently she and Russell are planning to marry as soon as the divorce is final. Judy suggested the group could hardly deny her membership since she would, in fact, be a doctor's wife when she married Russell. She cleared her throat a few times before reminding me that I would soon no longer be a doctor's wife."

"You're not serious?" Her mother's eyes flew open.

Mary Pat sighed. "I am totally serious. Judy suggested I might feel awkward coming to the Auxiliary with Cherise at our meetings, and she also said some of the officers pointed out that I actually wouldn't be eligible to continue my membership as a divorced wife. The organization has a clause for widows to stay in the group in good standing after losing their spouses but nothing for divorcees."

"I simply can't believe what you're telling me." Her mother put both hands on her hips. "This is the same Judy you took care of through that lengthy recovery time after her hysterectomy, isn't it? The one you cleaned for, bought groceries for, cooked for, and drove to all her doctor appointments? I cannot believe she would talk to you like that! I'd like to scratch her eyes out, the little cat."

Mary Pat reached for her own cup of cocoa, stirring it before she took a few sips. "I've been really shocked, and hurt, at how many of my friends have pulled away from me in this time."

Her mother made a face. "I remember that ditsy little Faye called in a panic the morning we got home from the airport because you weren't coming to Auxiliary that day and bringing the Pink Lady cake you baked." She shook her head. "I could hear most of what she said to you. Even though you'd emailed and left her a message to explain why you weren't coming, all the woman was concerned about was that they might not have a cake for the lunch if you didn't come. She actually asked you to bring it over to the country club if you didn't feel like coming. I couldn't believe it."

"She came by and picked it up, though. Remember?" Mary Pat grimaced at the memory. "She was annoyed she had to drive out of her way to get it, too. Do you know what she said to me at the door, knowing Russell had just asked for a divorce the day before? She said, 'Does this mean you won't be rich anymore, Mary Pat?' Can you believe that? Not a hug, not a word of love, support, or encouragement."

Her mother shook her head. "I wanted to dump that cake upside down on her head after her nasty, uncaring phone call. I still can't believe those selfish women simply expected you to run right on over to the country club, decorate for a silly luncheon, and smile as if everything was just hunky-dory in your life."

"You sound like Russell now, Mom. He said all my social clubs and groups were silly, called them a waste of my time."

Her mother put a hand to her mouth. "Oh, honey, I didn't mean to imply that. I'm so sorry."

"No, it's okay." Mary Pat shrugged. "The way some of the women in my social groups have acted, I'm beginning to wonder myself about all the time I gave to them."

"Many of those groups do some fine things though, Mary Pat. Don't be too hard on yourself."

"I know." She tapped a pencil on the table thinking. "You've never been in many social groups, Mom."

"Oh, honey, I've always been working." She hesitated. "I never really had the option to stay home full-time, except for a short season when you and Brandon were small. I always needed to work, and clubs and groups asked for time, commitment, and money I didn't have to spare."

Mary Pat considered her mother's words. "You led my scout troop, took me to all my baton lessons and came to all my recitals. You worked in Bible School at the church when we were small. You and dad went to all Gatlinburg High's football games to see Brandon play and later to see me twirl with the band. Don't make it sound like you didn't do anything but work."

"Well, many of those things were for you children."

"Yes, and you were a good mom."

Her mother stood to gather up their plates and cups from lunch and gave her a kiss on the cheek as she did. "So were you, Mary Pat."

She studied her mother as she walked into the kitchen to take their dishes to put them in the sink. The resemblance was strong between them, her mother a blond with blue eyes, too, and about the same height at five foot four, but her mother was still slim and fit, and tanned, too, from her life at the beach.

Her mother Regina Jennings and her father Paul, that Mary Pat's kids called Gigi and Pops, both worked and ran J.J.'s Café, a cute shop that sold coffees, beverages, pastries, and sandwiches at

Grayton Beach in Florida where they now lived. When Mary Pat and her older brother Brandon were growing up, Grayton Beach on the Florida Panhandle had been their family's favorite spot to visit, and after she and Brandon left home, her parents continued to vacation there whenever they could get away from their work. Suddenly, about twelve years ago, her parents came home with the news that they'd bought a cute café in Grayton's colorful uptown area, a beach house not far away, and planned to move to Florida full time. Mary Pat knew they'd been happy since they moved and she often envied their warm camaraderie working together in their business, enjoying their work and life together.

"How are the children doing with the news about this divorce?" her mother asked coming back out on the porch. The afternoon sun made the glassed in porch a comfortable, cheerful place for work and a visit even in January.

Mary Pat hated to answer her mother's question. "The children are very angry about the divorce. To my shock, they're angry at me, too, as if I should have been able to do something to change their father's mind. Todd has just gotten engaged, and he says it's embarrassing to plan a wedding now with Allison, knowing his parents won't be there as a couple like they're supposed to be. Victoria will hardly speak to me. She was always a big daddy's girl and she keeps making subtle remarks to me that this situation is all my fault, that I let her father down in some way, that there are things I'm not telling her."

"Honestly. That girl. She always has been too outspoken, and your daddy thinks you and Russell spoiled her. Do you want me to call and talk to her?"

"No, and thanks for defending me. Victoria and I were always close as she grew up but then in her teen years she pulled away, became critical and surly, didn't want to spend time with me anymore."

"Oh, teenagers. They can be so selfish in those years."

"Was I?" Mary Pat asked.

"No." Her mother looked thoughtful. "You always had a sweet, nurturing personality and were loving to your family as well as your friends. You tended to put others' needs ahead of your own."

"Yeah, and look where that got me."

"Oh, sweetie. Don't blame yourself overly much in this. You wanted to go to counseling with Russell. You wanted to do whatever you could to change and to help save your marriage. But Russell Latham didn't. I am convinced that him falling into an affair with that woman, Cherise Levene, is the real key behind all this mess. The one time she stopped by the house, uninvited of course, to ask whether you wanted to offer any furnishings with the sale of the house gave me her number after only a short conversation."

"I told you all the girls call her the barracuda."

"Well, I can see why." Her mother shook her head. "I watched that woman look around at everything in the house with an accessing eye. I could tell she got annoyed, too, when you told her Russell said you could keep all the furnishings in the house or sell them. She nearly flipped over that, insisting they should be part of the estate. I certainly hope Russell knows what he's getting into with that woman."

Her mother hesitated, glancing around. "Are you sure you want to let go of all the things on these lists? You can put *everything* in storage, you know."

"No. I've talked to the children about things they want or things they want me to store for them. Some items I'm taking with me, of course, and others I've decided to keep until I'm sure where I want to live. And you know I bought all new furniture for the mountain house after you and Daddy moved. I do like all the furnishings there. I decorated that place myself, with no real input from Russell. I can live there comfortably until I decide what I want to do with the rest of my life."

"Have you thought any about what you want to do?"

"Yes, a little. I'm thinking of going back to school next fall, to upgrade my credentials in my field. The whole area of nutrition and dietetics has changed so much. I got my bachelors but never went on to finish the supervised internship or to take the comprehensive examination in order to practice. Most registered dietitians today have graduate degrees in the field now, too. The University of Tennessee still has a good program. I could commute from Gatlinburg and then move wherever a job opened when I finish."

Her mother smiled. "I'm thrilled you're already thinking ahead."

"I am. I'd like to be a clinical dietitian as I planned or perhaps go into one of the other field areas. It's scary to think about, but school would move me back into a disciplined work schedule. Despite what Russell says or thinks, I'm not stupid."

"No, you're not, and good for you for knowing that."

Mary Pat glanced over the sheets in front of them. "In the next two weeks, I'm going to pack up all the things I want to take to the mountain house, then begin to pack what the children and I have decided to store. I'll have the auction company come in to pack and take the rest later in the month. I have to be out of the house by the first of March, and I'll need time for a cleaning service to come in. I scheduled everything to be finished by that last weekend in February." She looked up with tears in her eyes then. "That's just over three weeks from now."

"I know this is hard, honey. What can I do to help you before I go?"

"Just you being here with me has meant everything. I'll always remember you dropped your life to come up here and help me. I'm so grateful."

"After you settle, come down to the beach and spend some time with your father and me. It will be a good break for you."

"I'll do that. I want you and Dad to come up to the mountain house, too, whenever you can get away for a break. Even with me living there, the house still has plenty of room for company. I know Duggan, Owen, and Francine would be thrilled to see you both, as would Mrs. Ellis and Wheeler."

Her mother looked thoughtful then. "It was kind of Owen to come over and be a support to you the night you went up to the mountain house. I got to see him several times over the years when he came home on leave from the military or for holidays.

He's known some heartache, too, you know. His mother Idaline told me, before she got sick and died later, that his divorce really hurt him. She said he hadn't wanted to risk any type of serious relationship since. So I guess he understood more than most how hurt you felt that night."

"Yes, and I'll always be grateful for that kindness." She saw her mother's eyes continue to watch her. "Don't get any ideas about me linking up with Owen, Mother. The last thing I want right now is someone else in my life. Even someone nice like Owen that I already have a sweet past with. It's simply *not* the right time for me to consider any type of relationship. I want to find myself again, learn more who I am on my own, not linked up with anyone else. These last weeks have shown me all too clearly that my current life and friends are not quite what I thought they were. I have a big transition ahead of me."

"You'll find your way."

Mary Pat started to say, "That's what Owen said, too," but caught herself. She didn't need to give her mother any more ideas. Mary Pat had already shown her mother too clearly how touched she'd been over Owen's kindness. He'd made her feel she wasn't ugly and worthless at a time when she most needed it. And Owen certainly didn't need her using him on the rebound, as if he'd even consider the idea with the way she looked now.

"Well, you call me if things get too hard here over the next few weeks, and I'll fly back up again."

The next day after driving her mother to the airport, Mary Pat pulled into the driveway in front of her home and had one of those moments. She stared at the house, the house that had been her home for over twenty years, and wept. She'd been so happy here, raised her children here, shared holidays with her family here. It was going to be very hard to walk away and say goodbye. The house, a beautiful large two-storied white colonial home had crisp black shutters, lush landscaping and a black ornate fountain in front, with a long, green lawn reaching down to the river behind to the boat dock where Russell kept his boat. Or where Russell had kept his boat. He'd moved it somewhere now.

Sequoyah Hills, where their house sat on the main boulevard along the Tennessee River, was a lovely old neighborhood full of moneyed families and gracious grand homes, meticulously maintained by the homeowners, with the help of a horde of garden services. When Russell's practice began to thrive, they'd been thrilled to be able to buy a home here, to raise their family in this neighborhood. Sequoyah was close to Russell's practice and the hospital, too. She'd walked the streets in the neighborhood many times in past, enjoying the flowers and the dogwoods in spring, the turning leaves in the fall. Granted, she'd taken fewer walks in the last years. She made excuses about how busy her life was but the truth was that walking wasn't the pleasure it once had been since she gained so much weight. She'd tried a lot of diets, lost, and then always gained the weight back again and more besides. Eventually, she'd just given up.

While her mother had been here this month, Mary Pat held back a lot of her grief, hating to seem overly emotional and immature. But she knew she had some bad days ahead of her now. Despite how everyone said 'things were only things' the things in her home had meaning to her and were filled with the memories of her married life and years raising her children. It would be hard watching all her possessions hauled out of the house. Sold or given away.

She possessed a sentimental bent about things, too. Silly, but true. She'd always been the sort to keep old school annuals, to press corsage flowers to save, to keep photos and mementos, to associate things with the significant moments of her life. Mary Pat expected a lot of crying sweeps over the days to come. And some lonely, lonely times.

None of the children had come home during this time to be a comfort either. They made excuses as to why, but she knew they were angry about the divorce. They didn't want to come home; they didn't want to see her or Russell or the house they'd grown up in that would soon be sold.

Patrick said, "Gosh, Mom, if yours and Dad's marriage couldn't make it, whose can? I don't think I ever want to get married now." She'd heard a lot of statements like that from the kids.

Mary Pat had told Russell the divorce would be hard on the children, but he hadn't believed her. He tended to avoid looking at or thinking about painful issues or feelings. She knew that a part of his way of viewing life had developed working as a doctor and surgeon for so many years.

"You have to keep a professional distance," he always told her. "You can't get overly involved." In his earlier years of practice, he'd wept sometimes when he lost a patient, but he seldom did now.

Taking a deep breath, Mary Pat got out of the car at last. She had a lot to do and precious little time in which to do it. In the kitchen she stopped to read the quote she'd put on the refrigerator door to encourage herself: *"Grief comes in two distinct stages. The first is filled with loss, denial, and heartache. But the second is filled with new beginnings and the making of a new life."* She needed to remember that and to look ahead instead of back.

CHAPTER 4

Owen sat around the big table in the little conference room upstairs with his father and sister on the last Saturday in January. They usually tried to schedule a time to talk before store hours every month or so.

"We had a really good holiday season," Francine was saying, giving financial figures and details to support her words.

Owen listened, around drinking coffee and nibbling on sausage biscuits Francine had brought with her from the farmhouse. But he found his mind drifting to Mary Pat, wondering how she was doing, or if she'd come back.

As if picking up on his thoughts, his dad asked, "Have you heard anything from the Jennings girl, whether she'll come back to the house for a time?"

"I haven't heard anything from her."

Francine got up to pour herself another cup of coffee. "If she comes back again, let me know. I'd really like to see Mary Pat. I don't think I've seen her since our college years when she used to come home for the holidays. Does she still look the same? I always remember she was such a beautiful girl—honey blond hair, pretty face, cute little figure, with a million dollar smile. I have to admit I sometimes envied her looks, with me so tall and angular looking and with the McCarter nose."

Duggan snorted. "There's nothing wrong with the McCarter's looks—strong, good, well-built people."

Francine made a face. "Oh, don't get sensitive, Dad. I grew into better looks with maturity. I know I look okay." She glanced across at Owen. "Owen got the best looks in the family though and he got mother's Dawson family nose."

"You've kept your figure and your looks well, Francine," Owen said, reaching for another sausage biscuit and smiling at her. "I see you as a beautiful woman and Larissa looks so much like you."

"You're sweet," Francine said. "Is Mary Pat still gorgeous?"

He hesitated. "In some ways, but she's packed on a lot of weight through the years."

"That's hard to imagine," Francine replied. "Did you ever meet her husband?"

"I think I saw him a time or two years ago on a holiday here. Never met him or spent time with him, though," he answered.

"You didn't miss much," his father said. "I talked with him a few times when he came up to the Jennings house to stay with Mary Pat and the kids. Wealthy, driven man, fond of himself, fond of money, and fond of folks with money. Big on appearances, the right clothes, the right cars, knowing the right people, always tossing out names to impress—you know the type. He always talked down to me like I was a poor old mountain man. Probably didn't know I owned enough land to buy and sell him even with his fancy doctor's degree."

"Dad, that's hardly kind," Francine chided. "Many people don't see the appeal of living a simple life in the mountains like we do. They don't understand why our way of life is satisfying."

"Maybe, but if Mary Pat has come to think like her husband, living the rich, city life for so long, I don't imagine she'll stay around here long even if she comes back for a space to lick her wounds."

"She did grow up here, Dad. I went away, lived in the city but I came back."

"Have you regretted that—moving in with your old, crusty dad in the old homeplace, working for the family again?"

She smiled. "I didn't *have* to come home after Davis died, Dad; I had a good job. I *chose* to come home; I wanted to raise Larissa here. If I hadn't been happy here, I wouldn't have stayed either."

Owen watched his father try not to show his pleasure at her words. When Owen had come home when his mother died, then decided to retire and fill the hole she'd be leaving behind in the business, he also decided he *couldn't* move in with his dad again and be comfortable. His father tended to be a little cantankerous and bossy, but it didn't seem to bother Francine. She stood up to him and Larissa adored him. His niece, now nine, had only been four when they came home five years ago and she'd quickly stolen Duggan's heart. She'd softened him up more since, too. He thought both he and Francine had created a good place for themselves now here in the mountains and in the family business.

"Your mama built up some weight in her last years," Duggan said, returning to their earlier conversation. "Maydeen has done the same. It happens to a lot to women in the middle years. Mary Pat had four kids close together. Childbirth has a way of adding a little weight to some women. You only had the one, Francine, but I remember you fussing some over your weight after. Imagine four babies close, staying home, entertaining and living that lush lifestyle Mary Pat did, and in the city where she probably didn't get out much. It ain't hard to see how it could happen."

"Well, don't worry," Francine said. "I won't say anything to her about it. I'm just sorry she's experienced so much sorrow lately, and I'll be glad to see her if she comes back to the Glades for a while."

A knock on the back door sent her down to let Wheeler and their cousin Clint Dawson in.

"Hey," Wheeler said to them all, grinning as he came into the room. His eyes moved to the pile of sausage biscuits still on the counter.

"Have a sausage biscuit, Wheeler," Francine said, sitting back down at the table. "You, too, Clint. You can reheat them a minute in the microwave if you wish. Wheeler, there's juice in the refrigerator, too, if you want some. Clint, I know you'll want coffee. Help yourself. You'll find creamer in the frig and sugar on the counter there." She gestured.

Clint nodded. The two men made themselves at home getting a snack before they sat down to join the others at the big table.

"You get that big wood shipment in at the business?" Duggan asked.

"We did and I can deliver a cord to each of you today if you want," Clint answered. "If you want to put some bundles on the side porch to sell to tourists, I can wire wrap about two dozen bundles for you and stack them on the porch, too."

"Definitely do that," Francine put in. "We made some good side money on bundles like that last winter. It helps offset our slow time financially in the store."

Duggan inclined his head in the positive, too.

"I can help wire all them bundles," Wheeler put in. "I'm helping Clint today and I know how to do that."

Clint usually picked up Wheeler for landscaping workdays since Wheeler didn't drive. He'd helped to teach him some good skills, too. They'd all pitched in to help Maydeen when she lost her husband as a young mother. Life hadn't been easy for her, but she was always cheerful and good-hearted, beloved by all in the Glades who knew her and by all who came into McCarter Woodcrafts.

"Guess what I saw afore Clint picked me up this morning?" Wheeler asked, leaning forward with his usual excitement over any happening around the Glades. "A moving van heading up our road. Not a real big un, but pretty big. I walked Sadie up the road to see where it went and saw it stopped at the Jennings' house. You reckon they're moving out and selling and that I won't get to care for their place no more?" His smile faded then.

"No, I think I'd of heard if they were selling or moving," Duggan replied. "It's probably Mary Pat bringing some stuff up to stay for a while."

"Is that the lady who was here before?" Wheeler asked Owen. "The one you said was the Jennings' daughter?" He paused. "I remember her. She used to read me stories a long time ago. She's nice."

"I remember Mary Pat Jennings, too," Clint put in with a grin.

"Owen sure was sweet on her in high school. Right moon-eyed about her if I remember right."

Owen glared at him. "That was a long time ago. We've all moved on a lot since then."

"Well, sometimes a little spark can get relit from an old fire." Clint teased. "You can fall for girls again that you knew back when, you know. Ain't no rule says you can't. If I could see how you look at her now, I'd know if there was some old spark kicking up again or not."

Wheeler's eyes widened following this conversation. "Do you mean how you look at Francine, Clint? Ma and I don't see how come you don't take her out and court her when you like her how you do. Why don't ya?"

Clint's face flamed and Francine's eyes shot open, her coffee sloshing across the table as she inadvertently knocked it over.

"You got a big mouth, Wheeler," Clint said, jerking out of his seat. "And we need to get to work." He started out the door, not saying goodbye. Wheeler followed after a minute, grabbing another biscuit on his way out and waving. Seemingly clueless of the big can of worms he just opened.

"Well, well. Who would have thought?" Duggan said with a grin after they left. "I guess we've all been about blind not to see Clint had a little interest. I guess I'm losing my old keen discernment about human nature not to have noticed." He laughed out loud. "Leave it to Wheeler to see it."

He looked at Francine then, a deep blush still staining her neck and cheeks. "All that blushing and spilling your coffee makes me think there might be a little interest on your side, too, girl."

"You're embarrassing me, Dad. And Clint Dawson has never suggested he has any interest aside from friendship in me." She paused. "Besides, he's my cousin."

"Third cousin," Duggan reminded her. "If you remember, your great grandfather Wiley Garrett McCarter was brother to Lavinia McCarter who married Isaiah Dawson, Clint's great-grandfather. That makes the two of you third cousins. Ain't no problem hooking up with third cousins, by legal or natural reasons. It's only first cousins that's a problem."

Francine stood, gathering up her papers as she did. "I don't want you two speculating about my personal life. I'm going over to the office at the house to work. It's Saturday and Larissa is there by herself. You two need to head downstairs to open the store. Maydeen had a doctor's appointment this morning and won't be in until later in the day."

She paused before heading out of the door, her blush fading now. "Owen, stop by the Jennings' place at lunch. Okay? If Mary Pat has come back, invite her to dinner. I planned to cook a pork roast in the oven tonight, bake some sweet potatoes, and stir up a jar or two of those green beans Maydeen and I canned this summer. I can easily feed one more and it will make Mary Pat feel welcome."

"That's thoughtful, Francine. I'll invite her if I see her."

She glared at her father again and then started down the stairs.

Duggan laughed again when she'd gone. "Lordy-dee, ain't life fun some days? I can't wait to geehaw with Clint's daddy about this one." He grinned at Owen. "I wonder if he knows?"

"If you tell Lamont, Clint will know where he heard it."

"Aw, it'll get out anyhow, and besides we need to start working on finding a way to get them two together." His dad got up to rinse his coffee mug at the sink and drop his paper plate in the trash. "It's a good match for both of them. Clint's always acted shy of women ever since that Lacey Harper broke his engagement back when he was younger. He hasn't wanted to take a chance on putting his heart out on a stick again. Like you, once burned, he's avoided relationships of any serious kind ever since that time. He needs to move on."

He started toward the stairs. "So do you," he muttered.

Saturdays were often one of the store's busiest days, except in the winter months like January and February. In the busier months, at least two of the family worked in the store with Maydeen Ellis— Duggan, Owen, or Francine, and usually Noble McCarter, Owen's cousin, in the demonstration shop. Noble's father, now deceased, a master furniture craftsman, had passed those skills on to his son Noble but without any of his social skills. It was a lucky day if you got more than three words out of Noble but folks loved watching him work, building chairs, tables, chests, and more, or caning chair seats in the wood-working area.

When Noble didn't work the shop, Duggan filled in whittling or making the skillfully-crafted wooden bowls from tree trunks he was known for. Owen could claim some skills of his own, too. He could build furniture as Noble did, but he preferred creating walking sticks or birdhouses or carving black bears or other wooden animals. The other woodcrafts in their store were supplied by various crafters who lived in the Glades or nearby, like Wade and Evalyn Dawson. Wade worked full-time with his father Lamont and his brother Clint at Dawson's Landscaping but he loved to build and work with his hands on the side. Evalyn had her own gifts, too, especially with home items for the kitchen area and children's toy shop.

Walking up to the front counter, he heard Maydeen telling some tourists now about the store. "Everything you see here in McCarter Woodcrafts has been handmade right here in the mountains. As you walk through the store you'll see signs denoting the different areas—the kitchen crafts area, outdoor woodcrafts area, children's crafts, and the hearth and home items in the middle of the store. To the back is the demonstration shop. It's glass fronted to keep the wood dust contained but you can watch our crafters working there. On our glassed side porch by the creek, that we call the birdhouse area, you'll find birdhouses, carved and painted birds, cute outdoor signs, and more. Just wander around and enjoy yourself and ask me if you need some help."

The group smiled and moved into the store with interest.

"You're so good with folks, Maydeen," Owen told her. "We're blessed to have you working here."

"I'm the one blessed. Your Mama and Daddy hired me after my man Merle got injured, laid up in the hospital, and died. We about lost all we had then. I don't know what I'd have done if Duggan and Idaline hadn't hired me and helped me pay out some of the bills that piled up. You've all been good to my boy Wheeler, too."

"That's what neighbors are for." He glanced back into the store to see his father talking to a couple of the visitors about a carved stool. "Speaking of neighbors, Wheeler said he saw a moving van head up to the Jennings' place this morning. Mary Pat Latham, the Jennings' daughter, might be moving to their place to stay for a time."

"Wheeler's been worried about her. You know how he is about hurt things. Said she's seen some problems. I was sorry to hear that."

He nodded. "Francine wants me to go up on my lunch time to check on her, invite her to dinner with us tonight if she's come to stay for a time. Since you're back, I'm going to run up to the house to grab a sandwich and stop in at her place."

"Your dad, Noble, and me will be fine here." She smiled. "When there's a need for it, I can get Noble McCarter to do his duty and talk to folks a little, too, even help me out when the store gets busy."

"Wheeler sure loves Noble. He can get Noble to talk like nobody else."

Maydeen frowned. "You know when Noble's mother died, his father Zebulon sent him out to stay with a woman that lived up Birds Creek while he worked. She abused him sorrowfully, repressed his spirit for a long season afore anybody realized what was going on. Noble pulled into himself then—he was only a little thing—and he's never really come out much since. When Noble's father learned about it, he got a contingent of folks and run the woman out of the area. Threatened to call the law on her if he ever saw her face again. I heard tell he threatened to burn her house down with her in it, too." She glanced back toward where Noble worked in the shop. "That's when Zebulon quit his job at the chair factory and brought his business home to the Glades. Others were doing that then in the area, too. He worked and sold his products right out of his old farmhouse down the road a space, and he taught Noble to work right alongside him."

"People know some sorrows, don't they?"

"They sure do." She reached under the counter. "You go on up to check on Mary Pat. She was a sweet girl. Used to read to Wheeler when he was younger. She's got a good, kind heart. You give her this banana bread I made. I always bring a little something down to work with me most days in case there's someone needs it. Food has a way of making a body feel better about life when it goes bad."

"I suppose it does. I'll tell Mary Pat you sent it, assuming I find her there. If not I'll bring it back."

As Owen drove his 4Runner into his driveway, he saw Mary Pat's red Audi again in the driveway next door. After he fixed himself a sandwich and ate it, he walked over to the house. The front door was open, with only the screen shut, and he could see Mary Pat bent over working in some boxes. The dog, spotting him, got up from where he napped on the hearthrug and barked—while waving his tail this time.

"I think Barker recognizes you," Mary Pat said, standing up to turn around with a smile. "And I forgot to shut the door when I brought that last box in."

Despite the smile, he could see she was red-faced and winded, just from moving boxes around and working at unpacking things. In some sort of stretch pants today and a loose overtop, he couldn't help noticing her weight again. It was a shame to see she'd let herself gain so much, hidden her natural beauty under so much excess weight. In the active military he'd seen little overweight and obesity, but he'd noticed more overweight among those discharged. He'd purposed to stay in shape since retiring and so far had seen little to no gain. Not that he didn't have to work at it with well-meaners like Maydeen plying him with food and sweets all the time. He looked down at the banana bread in his hands. Like this.

Owen reached down to pet the dog and then spoke to Mary Pat. "Looks like you've decided to move in for a while."

"For a time," she replied. "I'm not ready yet to make a decision about where I want to live, and I hardly had time to look for any other place, either, with all I had to do these last two months. It's been hectic."

He nodded and then held out the bread. "Maydeen sent you this banana bread, said she was looking forward to seeing you again. And Francine wanted me to invite you down to eat with all of us at the farmhouse tonight. She's making a pork roast, vegetables and such—says she has plenty. She's wanting to see you again, too. So is Duggan. We hope you'll say yes."

She looked around. "I have a lot to do, but it will wait, I guess. And that's a kind invitation. So I'll say yes. What time does she want me to come?"

"We all tend to eat late, about 6:30 most nights, since the store stays open until 6:00. Will that work for you?"

"It will." She glanced down at the bread in her hand. "Can you stay for a few minutes? If so I'll cut us both a piece of this banana bread and pour out two glasses of cola. I could use a break."

He nodded and followed her toward the kitchen.

"Set that box on the table on the floor and we'll sit there, " she said.

Owen did and settled into a chair. She soon brought them both a large slice of the sweet homemade bread and a frosty glass of cola.

He forked into his bread with pleasure, taking a bite. "Umm. Maydeen sure does make good breads." He started to add that he had to watch eating so much of her sweets, but then thought better of the words.

"Did you get most of the needed things settled out?" he asked instead.

"Yes. The divorce papers are signed, the house is sold, the woman Russell got involved with has announced to all that they're marrying as soon as the divorce is final. Most of my old friends have dumped me, my kids are all mad at me and hardly speaking to me. It's been a fun time."

Hearing the sarcasm in her tone, he smiled at her. "Sounds like your life has been interesting at the least."

She laughed a little. "Well, you could say that. I thought a few times I might die from all the grief, problems, and hurt, but I haven't. I keep waking up every morning, still here. My heart is still ticking, and my old self, I'd almost forgotten about, kicks up every once in a while. I guess I'll make it through like everyone else survives these things."

"You'll be all right," he said. "I remember you as a stubborn, determined little thing. When you set your mind to do something, you did it, and usually better than anyone else."

She looked across the table at him. "You have a way of saying the nicest things to me when I need to hear them the most."

"I imagine it's because I've known you longer than most people and know you better, too."

"Well, thanks." She finished off the banana bread and then said, "I didn't contest the divorce, Owen. I didn't make a point about Russell's indiscretions, either, although I could have. Both lawyers knew that, too. I signed a mutual-consent, no-fault divorce. Russell didn't try to withhold assets and he was fair, even generous, about finances, which helped. That means in two months, since we have no minor children, that the divorce will be final. Just like that after all these years. It seems unreal."

"Did your mother stay to help you through some of the worst?"

"She did. She and Dad have been terrific. I'm so grateful to them."

"I'm sorry your kids haven't been more of a support. They should have been on your team. I'm especially surprised your daughter didn't sympathize and come in to help, like your mother."

"I admit I hoped for that. Victoria and I aren't as close as we once were, but she certainly reaches out for my support, sympathy, and help when something goes wrong in her life. Vents, you might say. But she tends to fluff off my problems. A lot of times when I call her, I can still hear her texting or working at the computer while I'm talking to her, letting me know she's only partially attending."

"She's still young. Perhaps life will teach her to be kinder."

"I hope so." She stood up then. "Listen, thanks for stopping by. I know you need to get back to the store and I need to get back to work. Tell Francine I'll be down around six-thirty and that I really appreciate the kind invitation."

"I will. See you later." He got up to head for the door.

As he walked back toward his own house, Owen realized that he still carried some feelings for Mary Pat. He cared about her; he felt protective about her. There were certain moments in which he felt the old attraction he'd once known for her surface, too. But Mary Pat was different now, not only in looks but in all she'd experienced, and a lot of time had passed. When they'd been young and in love, they'd imagined being married, of course, sometimes talked about it. Made youthful plans and pledges. But he'd walked away for the life that called to him, the military life he wanted. Now she was here again, but she probably wouldn't stay. He imagined this was only a transition stage for her, as she suggested. After her divorce was final and she had a little time to make new plans, she'd move on.

They were just old friends now. That was what they should be and that was what they should continue to be. He had a good life, didn't he? But every time he was around Mary Pat he left conflicted. Wondering what might be if old sparks did light again? Or if they even could light again.

CHAPTER 5

As March began, offering a warmer day hinting of spring to come, Mary Pat decided to get out of the house for the day. She'd spent the last week settling in, enjoyed an evening at the McCarter's last weekend and an unexpected visit one afternoon from Maydeen Ellis and Wheeler. Now each day dragged. Despite Russell's harsh criticisms that her life was full of meaningless and silly social activities, her days and weeks had been full and busy ones. Her various clubs, organizations, and philanthropic activities kept her active and engaged with a calendar book full of meeting dates, luncheons, fundraisers, committees, and get-togethers with friends.

She'd called a few of her old friends since moving to the mountain house, feeling lonely and missing them. They'd talked rather gaily about this or that but not in the old comfortable way of the past. Most encouraged her to call if she came to Knoxville so they could catch lunch together, but when she mentioned a specific future date they found they were suddenly too busy at that time. The excuses they offered sounded good but somewhat contrived as well. Frankly, it hurt. It seemed obvious they felt uncomfortable with her changed life status. No one called her anymore either, when her phone once rung off the hook every day, her emails and texts sometimes too many to answer.

Talking to her mother early one Saturday morning, she said, "It's amazing how many of my old friends seemed to have liked me because I was Dr. Russell Latham's wife or because I lived on the Boulevard in Sequoyah Hills."

"What about your church friends?" her mother asked.

"When you stop going to church with them, they fade away, too. You realize they were friends only because you attended the same church with them every Sunday, the same committee meetings, the same women's circle." She paused, considering her words. "A few called to tell me they're sorry for all I'm going through. Some said they were praying for me, but none visited me before I moved. Not even the minister. It's been disappointing."

"Well, don't blame God for it." Her mother's voice softened. "He is always faithful, and He still loves you. Reach out to Him and He will be right there."

"I know, and I've been praying a lot and reading my Bible— looking for answers, wisdom, and comfort." She grew quiet a moment. "It's amazing how many scriptures I read about adultery this week, how ugly it is, and how God sees it. He talks about avoiding it, fleeing it, and about how it can hurt and destroy the soul. I can understand that better now when I've felt the hurt of it myself, seen how it's hurt my kids so much."

"Have any of them called you to be a comfort?"

"Craig called me the other night from Massachusetts, said they had ten inches of snow there. He just kind of talked to me about things, chatted about happenings in his life, like he used to. It was nice." She smiled, remembering. "Before he hung up he said, 'Are you all right, Mom? Is there anything I can do?'"

"That was sweet of Craig. See, they're getting past their shock and realizing how hard this is for you."

She sniffed, almost tearing up. "Craig asked me if I needed money, wanted to know if his dad had jerked me around financially or hid assets or anything. Evidently, that happened to the mother of one of his friends. Their father hid all his assets in the Caymans or something." She blew her nose. "I thought it was sweet he felt worried about me."

"It was, and Russell at least acted fairly in the financial settlements as far as we know," her mother said. "I've known many friends who fared very poorly in a divorce, got left in some difficult straits."

"I guess it could always be worse."

"Are you getting out any?" her mother asked. "Despite some of these hurtful situations and the friends who let you down, there are still good people in the world. Don't give up on people in general because of the selfishness you've seen lately."

"I won't. And, admittedly, I'm getting a little stir crazy sitting up here in the mountains by myself every day with no one but Barker for company. I'm not used to so much quiet or inactivity."

"You're an extrovert, dear. You need to get out more."

"I agree and I plan to do that today. I'm going to drive around the Arts and Crafts Community loop. It's a nice day for early March, almost spring-like. I think I'll poke around in some of the shops, see old places I remember and new ones, get familiar with the area again. I plan to treat myself to lunch somewhere, too."

"That sounds wonderful. You have a good day."

They hung up then. Mary Pat finished getting dressed to go out, walked Barker, and then headed out to explore.

She soon cheered herself up talking to clerks, storeowners, and crafters in the many cute, original, and interesting stores scattered around the Arts and Crafts Community loop.

"Do you know how this community of artisans and crafters started?" an older lady asked as Mary Pat stood watching her weave on a big wooden loom in one of the shops.

"I grew up here and used to hear people talk about the history of the area, but I've forgotten much of it."

"Well, back in the 1930s after the national park was formed and Gatlinburg began to grow into a tourist destination, many of the mountain people realized the crafts they knew how to make were salable. They needed money and began to go into Gatlinburg to work at different shops, making things and selling their work."

She moved the shuttle back and forth across the loom as she talked. "In the late thirties and early forties, some of the crafters decided to go home to work. Many already lived around the Glades area, so they chose to set up their shops here, many working right out of their homes."

"John Crowden was one," Mary Pat remembered. "I used to hike to his woodworking shop over on Birds Creek Road."

"Yes, and he's passed now, but he and many others like Dick Whaley, Charles and Claude Huskey, Lee Ogle, Elizabeth Reagan, Sally Compton, and others began working here, soon drawing more crafters to the area until the early years of the Arts and Crafts Community were born. With a little publicity over time its reputation grew."

"Elizabeth Reagan was a weaver like yourself," Mary Pat said, watching the woman work.

"Yes, she was. I never met her but I heard a lot about her. I learned my skills from my grandmother and through some classes at the Arrowmont School."

"It's a patient, beautiful work you do." Mary Pat held up the purse in her hand. "I'm buying this gorgeous woven purse you made. I love the color and the old English roses scattered over it."

The woman glanced at the bag. "It can serve well as a purse and it has a firm strap to drape over your shoulder."

"I know I'll love it, and I enjoyed talking with you and watching you work today."

After leaving the weaving shop, Mary Pat stopped to visit two art galleries she'd always loved, the Jim Gray Gallery and A. Jann Pietso's art gallery. She bought a small painting from each for the upstairs bedrooms at the house.

Walking back to her car, Mary Pat glanced at her watch, realizing it was after noon already. Hungry after her early breakfast, she decided to drive back up Glades Road to the Three Jimmy's Restaurant near the highway. It looked like a nice restaurant to try and she'd never eaten there before.

Studying the lunch menu, that claimed their hamburgers had been voted 'the best in town,' Mary Pat decided to order a cheeseburger with fries. For dessert, she added a piece of chocolate peanut butter pie, after seeing a customer nearby receive one.

"That pie looks so good," she said to the waitress.

"You won't be disappointed with any of our desserts at Three

Jimmy's," she replied. "Everyone around here loves them."

While Mary Pat waited for her meal she studied the map of shops in the Arts and Crafts Community that she'd picked up, deciding where to go next after lunch. The restaurant was a busy place with great food and a friendly staff and she knew she'd want to come back.

After lunch, she slipped into the restroom for a minute, feeling happy over her day. Outside her stall, she heard two young girls chattering about a cute boy they'd seen, making her think of Victoria and her girlfriends.

"Did you see that fat woman at the table near ours eating by herself?" one of the girls said. "She was huge, her butt hanging over the chair. I swear I'll never let myself get fat like that. Ever."

"She had a nice face, though," the second girl said. "If she wasn't so fat she'd probably be pretty."

They both giggled, and Mary Pat felt mortified. She pulled her feet up in the stall so they wouldn't recognize her shoes, staying quiet and hoping they wouldn't realize she was there.

"Did you see what she ate for lunch? That huge burger, a big pile of French fries, and that giant piece of pie. That explains a lot, doesn't it?"

The other girl snickered. "Yes, and it explains why she was eating alone."

Giggling, they left, but Mary Pat sat in the stall and cried for ten minutes before she finally slipped out of the bathroom and edged out a side door of the restaurant to her car.

"Oh, God, help me just get back to the house," she muttered, crying as she drove down Glades Road. Rounding a curve and starting down a hill, she picked up too much speed and almost hit a car coming out of a side road.

The driver honked at her, offering a rude gesture, and Mary Pat pulled off into a parking lot for a minute, her heart beating and her hands shaking. Gracious, she didn't need a wrecked car right now on top of everything else.

Looking up after minute, she saw a row of shops, with a coffee shop, a large drug store, and a small business called Diet Options.

She laughed despite herself. "I can't believe it—a weight loss center in the Glades. Is this a sign from heaven or something?"

Mary Pat knew other businesses lay mixed among the shops through the Arts and Crafts Community, a clinic, a real estate store, a wedding chapel, the drug store and more. But the coincidence did seem providential.

"Okay, I'll check it out," she said to herself, moving her car closer to the front of the business and parking. Mary Pat looked in the mirror, wiped a few stray mascara smudges away, and added a little lipstick before she got out of the car.

At the door, she tried the knob but found it locked. Looking inside she saw lights on and knocked. A woman walked out from the back, slim with short, curly reddish brown hair and wearing a white lab coat over her shirt and slacks.

She opened the door and smiled. "We're closed now." She pointed at the sign in the window showing the hours. "But you can come back on Monday."

Mary Pat shook her head, backing away, tears starting again.

"Wait," the woman called as Mary Pat turned to start down the steps. "I think you need to come in. I was just catching up on paperwork before leaving. We can talk a minute before I lock up."

She held the door open and Mary Pat walked in. Shutting the door and locking it again, the woman turned and held out her hand. "I'm Charlotte Hillen the owner of Diet Options. And you are?"

To her horror, Mary Pat burst into noisy tears again. "I am so sorry." She apologized after a moment, struggling to get a grip on her emotions. "I shouldn't have stopped in right now."

"No. No, it's fine. It's only tears. But let's come back to my office." She glanced toward the window looking out front. "It will be more private."

Sniffling and trying to calm down, Mary Pat followed her. "This is so embarrassing," she said as she took a seat in a comfortable chair by a big desk.

The woman settled into the chair behind the desk and then

swiveled around so she faced Mary Pat more directly. She handed Mary Pat a few tissues from out of her desk drawer and smiled at her. "I think you've had a bad day. Your eyes look red, and I find people generally don't cry without a reason. Tell me what's wrong."

Mary Pat studied Charlotte Hillen's calm face and caring hazel eyes for a moment and then broke down and told her everything—about the restaurant and the girls, about Russell and the divorce, about losing her beautiful home and having to move to the mountain house, even about her kids being mad at her and her friends dumping her.

Charlotte listened, nodded occasionally, and made a comment or two now and then until the end.

"You must think I'm an idiot to come in here crying and then to dump all this on you—a total stranger," Mary Pat said, starting to settle down at last. "I am so sorry."

"Don't be. Like you said, you saw the sign at what seemed like an unusually coincidental time and you came in. You reached out." She smiled again, crossing her leg. "You do want to lose weight, don't you?"

Mary Pat glanced down at herself and rolled her eyes. "It's obvious I need to, isn't it?"

"But is it what *you* want?" Charlotte pushed a stray strand of hair behind her ear. "Life is full of people, events, hurts, calamities, losses, and situations we can't change. Like what happened to you with your husband. In many other areas though, life is full of choices about aspects of our life we can change."

She paused, looking thoughtful. "What is empowering is recognizing the areas in our lives that we can change if we want to and then having the courage and determination to do so." She smiled again. "Weight is actually one of the things we can always change in life. I find that comforting in an often upsetting and unpredictable world. It's one reason I got into this business."

Charlotte Hillen stood up. "Let me show you something." She led Mary Pat out into the hallway where framed pictures filled the wall. "We laughingly call this the Wall of Fame because these are all women and men who decided weight was one of those things they could change in their lives and they decided to make the choice to do so."

On the wall, Mary Pat saw row after row of "Before and After" photos of women and men, once heavy, who had become slimmer and more attractive.

"You make it sound easy but it's not." Mary Pat frowned at the photos.

"I never said it was easy. It *isn't* easy. It's hard, but most things worthwhile in attaining are hard and require work, determination, persistence, and effort to achieve." She swept a hand toward the pictures. "Many of these women also experienced hurtful painful situations in their lives before they came here—deaths of people they loved, job losses, divorces. One lost a home burned down by fire, another experienced abuse for years, and one woman lost her three children in a tragic accident. All gained weight for different reasons, but all realized one day that weight was one of those areas of choice in life they could change. And each decided they were ready to do that."

Her eyes met Mary Pat's, calm and sure. "The question is, are you?"

Mary Pat turned her eyes back to the pictures, uncomfortable now. "How do I know if this program will work for me? You haven't even told me about it."

"No, we haven't gotten to that stage yet." She gestured for Mary Pat to follow her back into her office. "I'm a registered dietitian and a registered dietitian nutritionist." She pointed to diplomas on the wall. "That may not mean much to you but it suggests I know what I'm doing." She grinned.

Mary Pat actually smiled then. "I personally majored in nutrition and dietetics in college, planned to work as a clinical dietician in the hospital." She looked down at herself and shook her head. "But I married before I got out of school, had four kids, and obviously forgot much of what I learned."

"I doubt that Mary Pat, and it's interesting we share background.

You may resonate with the principles of the program more than most."

Mary Pat glanced at Charlotte's diplomas. "Have you ever been heavy? Do you know how difficult losing weight is for some people?"

Charlotte opened a drawer and took out a laminated photo, handing it to Mary Pat. "This was me at one time."

Mary Pat's eyes widened at the obese women in the photo, much more overweight than herself.

"Unlike you," Charlotte said, "I struggled with weight from girlhood and through my teens. In college I finally got my weight down somewhat. That's when I met my husband. I was Charlotte Randolph then. My family owns Randolph Nutritional Products in Birmingham, Alabama, creating my interest in nutrition."

"Oh, that's a big international company."

She nodded. "I met Jason Burton at a big society event with my parents and didn't realize until after we married that Jason married me to get into the family business. I stuck it out longer than I should have, had two girls, and gained and gained weight while miserably unhappy, knowing my husband was seeing other women. Jason's indiscretions came out in a well-publicized lawsuit involving a married woman and I finally filed for divorce. Upset with my family because of their lack of support, I rented a house in the Smokies for the summer as a break from the scandal. I was thirty-one. My daughter Anne was seven, Trisha five."

"I'm so sorry, Charlotte."

"Like I said earlier, people go through hard times and hurtful things." She got up to get a bottle of water from a small refrigerator in the corner and handed one to Mary Pat, too, before sitting back down. "The girls and I loved the mountains and I experienced a sort-of-epiphany here, deciding to move here permanently and remake myself. Fortunately, I could financially make that decision more easily than some."

She paused, drinking some of her water. "I felt happier, free from Jason and away from my family, and the first thing I began to work on was my weight. I'd tried a lot of diets in past and failed at them or regained after, so I decided to find my own way back to good health. I used my knowledge and education to create my own diet program, and it began to work."

Charlotte smiled. "Looking better with time and having more energy, I found a part-time job in Rowan Cole Hillen's Art Gallery here in the Glades. He accepted my weight at the time and was kind to me. Not everyone is when you're heavy, as you've seen." She leaned back in her chair. "Over the next two years I lost ninety pounds. People and friends began to notice and ask how I did it. At their urging I opened a morning diet group in my home, teaching and helping others to lose as I had. It soon grew into a business."

Mary Pat drank her water, captivated with Charlotte's story.

"Over the years as the girls and my business grew, Rowan Hillen began to work his way into the fabric of our lives and Rowan and I married. With the girls and me moving in with Rowan, I began looking for a new place for my business. This spot next to the Smoky Mountain Pharmacy opened and it seemed ideal, not far from the highway or our home. I've been here fifteen years now, and I've been working to help people successfully lose weight and change their lives for twenty years."

"That's quite a story."

Charlotte shrugged. "I don't always tell it, but I saw parallels in your life and mine and thought it might help you realize others had gone through similar hurts."

"Your story is worse than mine."

Charlotte smiled. "Yet here I am and life is good. But the choices I made then, and continue to make now, are mine and only mine. Every day in life we choose, like the scriptures that advise each of us to choose life every day and to live our lives more abundantly so our joy will be full."

"You're a Christian."

"Yes. That was another wise decision I made along life's way and one that has helped and enabled me to rise to my best."

Mary Pat sighed. "You've given me a new ray of hope Charlotte, when I had little when I walked in here. Tell me what I need to do."

"I gather from what you shared earlier that you're not working right now?"

"No."

"Then you might like the Day Group at Diet Options best. I group my dieters into Day and Evening groups depending on work schedules. The Day Group comes to weigh and receive one-on-one counseling Tuesday, Thursday, and Saturday between 8:00 am and 12:00 noon. The Evening Group comes Monday, Wednesday, and Friday between 12:00 noon and 6:00 pm. As you saw on the hours on the door, I'm not open all day every day." She smiled. "I do like a life of my own, too, and sometimes I still fill in hours at Rowan's studio. He's an incredible painter. I hope you'll stop by sometime to see his work."

"I will, and I think I'd like the day group. Maybe I'll make some new friends there, too."

"I'm sure you will." Charlotte got up to get some materials off a shelf and from a file drawer across the room and then came back to sit down. "Let me tell you briefly about the program. I sell it only in six-week blocks. Six weeks is a commitment, and I want that from everyone I work with. I have a contract here for you to look over and some paperwork I need you to fill out." She laid it to the side to show Mary Pat a three ringed notebook. "This is our Diet Options notebook. Every dieter gets one of these, uses it, and brings it to every weigh-in and meeting."

She opened the notebook. "You will see the notebook has tabs just like a school notebook. Some information is already in the notebook, that you need to begin the program, and other information you'll add to it as you go along. The first section, the overview, tells all about the program with reminders about the center hours and class times. I do require weekly classes, Mary Pat. I don't believe in a diet that does it all for you, not teaching anything as you go along or preparing you to continue to keep up dietary changes you're learning."

She tapped a pencil on the table. "I'm strict about the classes and the weigh-in sessions. I will not renew contract with clients who do not come to class, who do not come to weigh-in sessions, and who do not seriously try to comply with all aspects of the program. Why waste their time and mine?" She shrugged.

"A new set of six-week day classes start on Tuesday. The Tuesday weigh in hours are from eight to noon, and the class starts right after. We have a nice classroom off the hallway, and my clients like the weekly classes, the things they learn, and getting together with other dieters. I think you will, too. Can you come to weigh in on Tuesday and stay for class?"

"I can do that," Mary Pat said.

"Good. Come around eleven and you can visit with some of my day clients, too, before class starts. It will help kick things off for you." She handed the open notebook to Mary Pat. "If you'll glance through the other notebook dividers, you'll see a tab for weigh-in records. I'll weigh you today and every time you come. Another tab is for food charts. To become aware of what foods are eaten, I ask clients to write down everything they eat and drink, and to count the calories in everything they eat and drink, too."

Mary Pat flipped to that section. "I don't think I've ever counted calories to this extent before."

Charlotte grinned. "You'll be amazed when you start learning calorie counts in foods. It really helps with awareness of what you eat and it helps you plan better eating patterns and a healthier lifestyle." She pointed at the notebook. "The other dividers are for class handouts, notes, and recipes from classes. I usually give out a few recipes at every class and dieters often bring recipes and ideas to share once they move along in the program. I expect clients to write down the exercising they do every day, too, and to decide on a type of exercise to fit into every day."

She passed the notebook to Mary Pat. "The concept of weight loss is actually simple in some ways. It basically involves eating less, eating more of the right things, and moving more."

"You haven't talked about what foods clients can eat and not eat."

"No, but you will find all of that in the overview section, clearly laid out. People only retain a small portion of what they hear so having materials to read and refer to later is helpful. It also makes the program and its food options very clear."

She reached across to open Mary Pat's notebook to details about Week #1. "The first week, that I call the Transition Stage, removes all carbohydrates and sweets from the diet to break their addictive hold and to flush the system out to begin a sensible eating plan. The week's food plan, however, allows a good variety of meats, eggs, vegetables, fruits and more. No starving going on, just good healthy eating."

Charlotte picked up her water bottle. "A lot more water is required daily than you might be used to. The body is predominantly water and water needs to be flushed and replenished every day. Keep in mind, excess fat is removed from the body mainly through water, so we don't want it to continue circulating around through the system." She laughed a little.

"As a dietician, you might be interested to know that most people in the United States are functioning in a chronic state of dehydration. It's also interesting to know the body often can't distinguish between the desire for food or water. Many times signals that seem like hunger are actually thirst. So drinking about six 8-ounce glasses of water a day is sensible anyway for good health and even more important for dieters." She pointed to Mary Pat's water bottle. "That's a 16-oz bottle, so four of those a day would do it as the minimum, but more is better."

Mary Pat glanced ahead at the food options for the first week. "This doesn't look too bad."

"It isn't bad, and you'll see for this week that I've given Lunch Options for the whole week and Dinner Options as well, just as a help, but the meals can be ones you design, as long as you select foods from the list provided."

Mary Pat studied the options. "I can do this."

"I believe you can, and I think you'll enjoy having a facet of your life you can control when so much of your life lately has been out of your control."

"That's the truth." Mary Pat laughed.

Charlotte stood. "While I clean up the rest of the materials from the class, I'll let you look through the diet instructions and food options for this week. If you would, also fill out the information sheet, and read over the contract and sign it if you still feel good about the program. Because my clients come in three days a week and participate in a one-hour class every week for the first twelve weeks of program, there is usually plenty of opportunity for clarifying any food and exercise options that come up."

She grinned. "If it's not on the list and you're not sure if you should eat it, don't until you come in to ask about it and discuss it. This week, in particular, adhering rigidly to the transition stage is vitally important. Sweets and carbohydrates are addictive in nature and we want all those flushed out of your system so they won't be calling your name every day."

Mary Pat giggled. "A lot of foods do that."

"We'll introduce a greater variety of food again, including carbohydrates and sweets, as we go along, Mary Pat, but in moderation so they don't take over an individual's life and thoughts."

Charlotte stopped at the door. "You'll need to go home and clean out your kitchen and your cabinets of all the foods you can't eat after you leave here. Since you're cooking only for yourself right now, that will make things easier for you. And you'll probably want to make a run to the grocery store to pick up foods on the program. Think of this experience kind of like going back to school. You'll be learning a lot of new things. Changing your lifestyle."

She straightened her lab coat and smiled. "I tell my clients, *today is the first day on the road to a New You* and that's the truth. You won't believe what a difference you'll see in yourself and feel as the weeks and months go by."

"How much weight do most people lose every week?"

"Usually two pounds a week and frequently more in the first two months." She hesitated. "You seem very purposed to do this now. If you'll weigh in for me, I can tell you more specifically what you can expect."

Mary Pat looked across the office at the big scale in the corner. "All right, but I hate for you to see how much I weigh."

Charlotte walked toward the scales. "Remember, I've been in this business a long time. I'm used to looking at weight. To me, it's simply a number getting ready to go down."

Mary Pat walked over to the scales to weigh and Charlotte made a note of the weight in Mary Pat's notebook chart and on another form she pulled from the file cabinet, putting Mary Pat's name at the top of it. She talked to her more specifically then about weight loss she could expect and desirable weights for her height, body frame and age, referring to the weight chart hanging behind the scale.

"I don't believe in those 'one-weight-only' charts by height alone. A good weight for each person is much more individual than that. All individuals should consider their body type, age, how active they are, and how much muscle they carry. For a woman five-foot-four, with a medium frame, at fifty-four years old this weight range would be good for you to shoot for." She pointed to the range on the weight chart. "I usually advise selecting the highest weight in the range as a goal weight. Then when you reach that weight, if you feel you'd like to weigh less you can continue to work to reduce, or you can start our Maintenance Program. We can talk about that more later and you can read about all aspects of the program in your notebook tonight."

Charlotte glanced over toward the shelf in her office again. "If you don't have a good calorie count book, I keep some paperbacks here to sell of the one I most recommend. I'd suggest you pick up several others later as you can find them from used or new book stores."

She picked up the paperback book. "I can add one of these books in with your program fee if desired and a bottle of good multi-vitamins. I get the vitamins wholesale, along with other minerals and nutrients I think are important to take, through my family's business, and I don't jack up the prices for my clients."

Mary Pat read all the materials, filled out the forms, paid her program fee, and headed out of the Diet Options Center a little later, armed with a copy of her contract, her new notebook, a calorie count book, and some bottles of vitamins and minerals. When she got home, she took Barker out for a walk, and then began to clean out the refrigerator and cabinets of temptations.

"I'm going to do this, Barker, and I'm going to do it well. You wait and see. I needed something to get my mind on right now, something new to get involved in, and what better than something that will help me look and feel better?" She grinned at the dog, sitting in the kitchen door watching her. "Charlotte seems to think there are several other women starting the program right now that I will really like, too."

She dropped a box of donuts, two sugar laden colas, a bag of potatoes, a box of cereal, assorted crackers, cookies, half a cake, a pecan pie, a bag of candy, a loaf of bread and more into the box she'd started to fill. Charlotte had given her the name of a minister in the valley that collected food for families in need who would run by and pick up any items that her new Diet Options clients wanted to get rid of. A thoughtful idea.

Finishing her clean out, she put the box out of sight in the laundry room for now and started making a grocery list for the store. She studied her notebook to know what to buy and soon headed out to drive down to the big Food City on the highway to shop.

Back at home later, she thought about her day again—the good and the bad. She also thought about Charlotte's story. "If Charlotte could do this, with all she suffered through, I can do this, too," she said out loud.

She wrote the motivational quote Charlotte said to her in bold on a piece of paper and put it on her refrigerator: *Today is the first day on the road to a New You.* "Lord, help me to make this be the truth for my life," she prayed out loud, running her fingers over the paper. "I really need a new me badly right now."

CHAPTER 6

On a Sunny Thursday in the next week, with the warm spell in the Smoky Mountains still holding, Owen took a hike up the Dawson Creek Trail behind his house. The old trail wandered in a gradual incline uphill behind Highland Drive to travel alongside Dawson Creek and across Providence Ridge before dropping downhill to its end near Birds Creek Road. The hike over and back was only a two-mile round-trip, a nice short walk for a sunny afternoon.

Coming back, Owen rounded a curve in the trail and started down a steep slope near Dawson Falls. Near the falls, sitting on one of the old railroad tie steps, built to stop erosion, he found Mary Pat crying.

She glanced behind her, hearing him approach. "Oh, great. You're going to think I don't do anything but cry."

He laughed and stopped to sit on the step beside her. "What are you doing up here?"

"I started a new diet program on Monday and we're supposed to get twenty minutes of exercise every day at least. The director recommended walking, so I thought I'd walk up the trail today. It's so nice out." She swiped at the tears on her face. "I was wheezing by the time I got halfway up these steps, and you know this waterfall isn't very far along the trail."

"The falls is a little over a quarter mile from the start of the trail."

She closed her eyes and moaned. "You're making me feel worse. I can remember easily hiking this trail's length to Birds Creek and back." She sighed. "Is that where you've been?"

"Yeah. It's only two miles over and back. Not a long hike but it might seem like a long distance if you're not used to walking or don't walk in the mountains often." He patted her on the back. "Remember, the first part of the trail winding up to the falls is the steepest. It levels out then to walk across the ridge top."

She glanced down at the old railroad tie under her feet. "I don't remember these stairs being here when I hiked this trail in high school and college."

"Clint Dawson, his dad and mine, built them later to stop erosion and make this steep trail section easier to navigate. This portion of the trail used to turn into a slippery mud mire in bad weather before."

"I remember." She glanced over at the falls, tumbling across a rocky drop in the creek, creating a pretty white curtain of water before splashing into the ongoing creek below. "The waterfall is still as beautiful as I remember though. It hasn't changed. I used to love coming up here when younger to sit on a rock by the falls to think and dream." She looked around her. "This is such a pretty spot."

"It is." He stood up. "You want to try walking on up the trail a little further or walk back home with me?"

"I think I need to walk on back." She pushed herself up from the step. "I'm in terrible shape. It's so discouraging."

"Every day you walk you'll get in better shape." Owen walked down the rest of the steps and onto the trail beyond, slowing his pace so Mary Pat could keep up with him.

"I walked down our street, Highland Drive, yesterday and back. That road is so steep. I hoped the trail might be easier."

"You might like walking over at Mills Park until you get in better shape. There's a walking trail there. I'm sure you remember the park behind the high school where we both went to school. You can cut across Proffitt Road from Glades Road to get to the park faster."

"I remember the way, and that's a good idea." She hesitated, slowing over a rocky section in the trail.

He grinned, glancing down at her canvas shoes. "You also might want to buy yourself a good pair of hiking boots before you hike any more Smoky Mountain trails again. They'll save your feet and ankles and they're better for the mountains."

"I'll do that." With the trail widening, she moved up to walk alongside him. "Charlotte Hillen recommended going to the Gatlinburg Community Center for swimming and aerobics classes, too. Do you ever go there?"

"Yeah. I like the gym, especially on cold or rainy days when I can't get outdoors. Clint and I play a little racquetball and shoot baskets there. You can get a membership for not much. The indoor pool is nice. Drive up and check out the center one day. It's not far from us and it offers all sorts of activities and classes. The new library is right beside it. Have you seen that yet?"

"No." She smiled. "I only remember the old one in Gatlinburg behind the Arrowmont School of Arts and Crafts. It's nice they built a library so close to the Glades now."

"It's beautiful, too, sits high on a hill with great views across the mountains. I remember you always loved to read. You'll like the library."

"I look forward to visiting it."

As the trail neared the end, she asked, "Do you want to come over to my place for a few minutes for tea or a cola? We can sit on the porch. It's nice out. I don't keep sugared colas in the house anymore, only diet ones, but I have unsweetened tea. You can sweeten it as you like."

He considered the invitation, glancing at his watch. "I'd like that. Thanks for the invitation. I don't need to head to the store to close until later."

The old Jennings house, or rather Mary Pat's house now, had a wide, open front porch with rocking chairs and a few side tables, while the back porch, to one side, was screened with a door opening to a rustic deck beside it. Owen hadn't seen much of the house interior since Mary Pat redecorated it after her parents moved.

"You've made the house nice with all the warm colors and an easy, casual feel. I think you have a flair for decorating."

"Thanks. I always feel good coming here."

She led him through the house to the kitchen and then outside with glasses of tea, Barker frisking around them, happy and excited to see Mary Pat back.

"He really wanted to go with me," Mary Pat said, leading the way into the screened porch room.

"You were wise not to take him on the trail. We've had bear problems around the area. A tourist's dog was killed not far from here, off Powdermill Road. The dog barked and ran at the bear, and the bear did what bears do when attacked."

Owen settled into a big wicker chair. "Tourism has its good and bad aspects. It brings rental homes, attractions, hotels, restaurants, and more visitors and income to the area. But it also brings new temptations and problems for the bears—overflowing garbage cans, pet food left out, grills not cleaned after use." His mouth tightened. "People get excited to see bears when visiting and they move too close to them to take pictures. Even worse, some people feed the bears, viewing them as cute pets. They welcome them around their rental cabins rather than scaring them away as they should. The bears then get too comfortable around people, lose their natural fear."

Mary Pat sat on a wicker sofa near his chair. "Wheeler fussed at me the other day and reminded me not to feed the birds. He said with winter ending, the bears would be coming out of hibernation soon. I'd hung up a hummingbird feeder, put a cute birdfeeder full of seed on one corner of the deck, and set out a bronze birdbath on a stand I brought with me from the Knoxville house. Wheeler made me take them all in. Said they'd attract bears as well as birds."

"He's right. Did you know that a bear's sense of smell is just as good as a bloodhound's? They can smell food from up to ten miles away and when they learn where a food source is—garbage, grills, birdfeeders, pet bowls—they'll come back again and again to the same spot."

She opened the door to call Barker to come in. "I've been letting Barker run around in the yard a little off leash where I can see him some days. Should I quit doing that?"

"As much as I hate to say it, you probably should walk him on a leash. The bear risk is great right now, plus snakes are coming out, and other critters will be moving around more with the spring. A dog sticking his head in a snake hole or digging into a yellow jacket nest can get hurt badly." He reached over to scratch Barker's head. "You can take Barker to walk with you over at Mills Park though. Let me know if you need to be away for a day or two and I'll come over and walk him or you can leave him with me."

Her face brightened. "Thanks. That's nice of you to offer, and Barker really likes you. Have you ever had a dog?"

"I had a part Husky Malamute named Cody for a time after I moved back here. We all loved him but he died two years ago. Larissa really misses Cody. She'd love walking Barker or keeping him if you need to take a trip, too."

"I really appreciate how kind you and your family have been to me since I came back. I feel undeserving of the kindness, too, when I think of how seldom I came up to the Glades to visit with anyone."

He waved a hand. "Growing up here, you're like family to us. We're all happy whenever family comes home. Everyone reached out to me like that, too, when I came back. Made me feel guilty, as well, when I thought about how long I'd been gone, how seldom I got to come home. How little I kept in touch."

"You always have a way of making me feel better about things."

He drained out the rest of his tea. "Are they letting you eat enough on that diet you're on?" he asked.

"Yes. It's a good program. I'm going to the Diet Options weight loss center on Glades Road near the Smoky Mountain Pharmacy. It's Charlotte Hillen's place. Do you know her? She's married to Rowan Cole Hillen who has that art gallery on Buckhorn."

"I know Rowan and I've met Charlotte. They seem like good people."

She smiled. "I signed up on Saturday, started the diet Sunday, and I went to my first class Tuesday at noon. Charlotte insists on all her clients coming to classes every week to learn more about nutrition and healthy eating and she requires weigh-ins three times a week. She insists the latter keeps you more accountable and on program. I weighed this morning and I've already lost three pounds."

"That's good."

She looked down at herself. "Well, as you can see I have a long way to go. It's hard, too. Charlotte explained in class that we're made in such a way that our bodies want to eat to maintain our current weight. So, in a sense, they cry out to eat enough food to keep that set weight—even if the weight is a wrong weight, which makes reducing more of a challenge."

"I didn't know that."

"Neither did I. I'm learning a lot, and I've had my moments already, I can tell you. I didn't realize how much precedence food took in my life or how many of the wrong kinds of foods I ate every day without thinking. Charlotte makes us count food calories. It's a wake-up experience."

"I'm not sure I know what a healthy calorie total should be per day for a man or a woman."

"There isn't a one right total for all, anymore than there is a one right weight for all. Just as a right weight varies by gender, height, body frame, and activity level, best calorie counts vary, too. An active man like you with your height and frame could probably eat up to 2000-2200 calories on average every day and still not gain, but you'd need to reduce that greatly to lose. For a short, basically sedentary woman like me, I could probably maintain with 1500-1700 calories a day, but to lose I'd need to keep that closer to 1000-1200. Most days I'm staying at around 1000, and I'm doing all right."

Barker jumped up on the sofa to lay his head on her lap, and she stopped to pet him. "I have to plan and think really carefully every day to meet that calorie count and to keep a three-meals a day healthy diet. Charlotte is sticky about that. She wants to build a healthy eating plan that will become a new life habit for everyone."

"That sounds sensible."

"It does." She giggled. "Our homework assignment from Tuesday's class was to look up calories for typical American meals, like most of us eat from day to day. My usual breakfast in Knoxville was to run over to Starbucks for one of their coffees. I'd usually get an Iced White Chocolate Mocha or a Cinnamon Dolce Latte, both about 300 calories each. While there, I'd usually pick up a cheese Danish with almost another 300 calories in it or a cinnamon bun with 400. I'd bring my coffee and sweet roll home and eat cereal with it, too, like Raisin Bran or Frosted Mini Wheats, two of my favorites. A bowl, or two cups, of either of those cereals and milk adds about 450 calories to my breakfast total. My usual breakfast totaled over 1000 calories a day, as much as I needed for the *entire* day."

Owen frowned. "Maybe I need to start adding up my calories."

"As long as you're fit and trim, like you are, and active, you're fine. A few days of over-eating here and there usually balance out with the bulk of days of healthy eating for most people. But I didn't eat healthy. I thought I did, but I didn't. That breakfast was heavily sugar laden and heavy in carbohydrates."

"What do you eat now for breakfast?" he asked, curious.

"This week I'm eating two eggs every morning with grapefruit or an orange, sometimes adding a cantaloupe slice if I want it. With that I drink a big glass of water and drink a cup or two of coffee with sweetener and a little skim milk. Next week for breakfast I change to one egg, fruit, and a piece of diet wheat toast or half an English muffin, with diet butter spray and a small spoon of diet jelly, if I want. Surprisingly, it's very satisfying. Both menus have only about 300 calories versus my usual 1000 plus." She shook her head. "It's been a revelation, I can tell you. It's no wonder I'd padded up like a giant walrus eating the way I did. But I thought I wasn't eating that much or that differently from most other people."

"You're really getting into this program. I think you're going to do great, Mary Pat."

"Thanks. I could tell you similar scenarios and comparisons about my other meals and snacks throughout the day." She shook her head. "Honestly, I had no idea of the amount of calories I wolfed down every day."

"I remember there was always good food at your house. Both your parents loved to cook and you knew your way around a kitchen, too."

"Cooking has always been one of my pleasures." She stroked the dog, asleep now and snoring softly. "I'm happy puttering in the kitchen, mixing up or making one thing or the other. My cakes and many of my special recipes became favorites with all my social groups—as well as my family. The kids were always in and out of the house with friends, wanting something to eat. I loved cooking big family meals, hosting dinner parties, planning luncheons, showers, taking lavish dishes to church dinners and other get-togethers. A lot of my life revolved around food, thinking about it, cooking it, and eating it." She laughed and patted her stomach. "And here I am."

"Change is the best result we get sometimes from new learning," Owen said. "I used to tell the men and women I trained in the military that."

"Were you a tough officer?"

He laughed. "All officers are tough officers. A weak, undisciplined soldier isn't prepared for combat and the other harsh situations military have to engage in. I think most of the time I was a fair leader and a trusted one, even when tough."

She reached over to pat his knee. "I can't imagine you being anything else. You were always strong, disciplined, and determined even as a boy." She grinned at him. "Stubborn and bossy, too. You seem more mellow and easy-going now."

He couldn't help laughing at her observation. "I had enough of power, leadership, and responsibility in the military, I guess. I'm glad to let down a little now, to live a more relaxed and easy life."

Mary Pat looked out the window. "Has it been hard for you,

coming back to the quieter, slower pace of the mountains after living all over the world in so many diverse, exciting places, staying in so many big cities?"

"At one time that's what I wanted and I liked that life, thrived on it most of the time. But I think we each have different sides to our nature. We can adapt and almost become different people when placed in different environments and situations." He turned to look at her. "Didn't you find yourself changing, becoming different with the environment you lived in while married and in Knoxville?"

She tapped her glass, considering his words. "I did. In many ways, I think I became what I needed to be."

He smiled. "That's my point. We adapt to life as it hits us, we acclimatize as we settle in to different lifestyles, cultures, adjust to different people. But down underneath, I think the essence of each of us—the depth of us—is still there, even if we suppress it for a season. At times in my life, I lost track of that deeper self and it felt good when I regained it, came back to myself more."

She watched a mockingbird on a tree limb nearby, considering his words. "So you think you've come back to yourself more here?"

"Yes, I do, and it surprised me at first to realize it. But I am more truly myself here. I have more control of my own life and my relationships are more true and real. That hasn't always been the case."

"I guess I'm in a searching stage right now. I'm like a little ship that's had all its moorings cut away and that has drifted out into rough seas. Before this I felt like I've had captains manning and directing my ship, but suddenly I'm out on my own. I need to find out how to be the captain of my own ship now."

"Remember to let the Big Captain help you. When He guides the ship all goes better."

Her eyes softened. "Charlotte and my mother reminded me of the same thing recently. You can be assured I'm trying to check in with Him often."

He stretched. "I need to go. I promised Dad I'd come down to close the store so he could leave early to go out to eat with Lamont. That's Clint's dad, in case you've forgotten. Lamont Dawson and dad, both widowed, are great friends and have been since they were kids. They like to go out to eat on Thursday nights and hang out. I do the same with Clint on Fridays."

Mary Pat stood and picked up both their empty tea glasses. "Well, thanks for being a good friend to me again today, Owen."

He headed out the back door of the porch with a little salute. "Hang tough with that diet Mary Pat. You can do it if you make up your mind to it."

CHAPTER 7

Near the end of March on a sunny Tuesday morning, Mary Pat smiled as Charlotte weighed her in, seeing a drop in weight from her last visit.

Charlotte smiled. "You have lost fifteen pounds since the first of the month, five pounds a week since you started the program. That's terrific. You've worked really hard this month following the program, getting out to exercise every day."

She sighed. "I know I should be thrilled, but I'm still fat in the mirror. A few people have noticed the change, but not many. I'm still big."

"You obviously need a pep talk." Charlotte pointed at a gallon of paint in the corner. "Go pick up one of those cans of paint. That's a ten pound gallon of paint. Rowan and I are repainting my office this afternoon. If you pick up that gallon and that smaller half gallon of paint, it will help you realize how much extra weight you were carrying on your body before today."

Mary Pat picked up the larger and smaller cans of paint. "They're heavier than I expected."

"Yes. Now walk around and imagine carrying both those cans everywhere you go today."

She walked around for a minute and then sat the cans back down in the corner, grinning. "You've made your point."

"Why are you so discouraged then? You've lost more than most of my clients in your first month. You're doing great Mary Pat."

"I know. It's just hard. I miss cooking. I miss eating out a lot. I miss pizza and spaghetti and pie and ice cream." She sat down in the chair beside Charlotte's desk. "I also don't really like aerobics classes or zumba or any of those group workout activities I've tried. But I do like walking. It's peaceful, but I hate always walking by myself. Although I've gotten to know some of the women in the class, I haven't made any real friends yet. I'm lonely more than anything, Charlotte. But it's okay."

"I thought you were walking with Viola?"

"I was for a time, but she kept making excuses for why she couldn't go. She also complained about the program, saying it wasn't healthy for her and that she thought it was too strict. When I defended it, she got miffed at me."

"Hmmm." Charlotte pulled a file from the cabinet by her desk and studied it. "Viola hasn't kept to program like you. She started strong, but then began to drift away. Her weight loss stalled and I remember she got mad about it, said the program was too hard."

Mary Pat wrinkled her nose. "She always wanted to go out to lunch after we walked every morning. The time or two we did, she didn't eat conscientiously and she pushed me to reward myself with a fattening treat every time for walking and dieting so hard."

"Did you order a treat?"

"No, and that seemed to make her mad."

Charlotte sighed. "One of the hard things with any diet program is that some people stay with it and some don't. Who Viola is really annoyed with is herself for falling off the band wagon while you seem purposed to stay on."

"I like her though. What can I do to help?"

"Nothing. Remember I told you that continuing on a weight loss program to goal is always a daily choice. I've talked to Viola and I will again, but I can't make her want this. She has to want it for herself." Charlotte leaned back in her chair and crossed her leg. "When I was heavy and first moved here, the friends I made seemed to be heavy, too. You know the old saying: Birds of a feather flock together. We were comfortable together, all liked the same things, all liked to eat, weren't active, and didn't like to exercise. None of those friends made me feel fat; they were all heavy, too."

"Are you still friends?"

"I am with some. Others began to avoid my company more as I slimmed down and especially when I started helping women lose weight at my home."

"You convicted them."

"Perhaps I did without meaning to, and perhaps you are convicting Viola without meaning to."

"Hmmm. Thanks for helping me see that." She looked out the back window, thinking for a minute. "What can I do to help her, Charlotte?"

"See, that's one of the things I love about you, Mary Pat. You really want to help others."

"I do. Maybe after I go back to school this fall, I can do that professionally. I think that would be so satisfying."

"Remember, though, that even when you offer the best counsel not everyone will follow it. People all have free will. It's easier, too, to take the course of least resistance, to keep following the herd, than to walk the narrow and harder path." She glanced at her watch as the door chime rang. "There's another of my dieters coming in to weigh."

Charlotte stood up. "I'll see you again at class later, Mary Pat. We're going to talk about eating out at restaurants and how to do that wisely and well in order to stay on program."

"That should be helpful."

Charlotte winked. "Remember to do your homework, too."

"I will. I'm going to take Barker and drive to Gatlinburg to walk around the streets of Mynatt Park. I discovered that cute neighborhood walking with Viola Bartlett. She lives there. Her husband's a vet." She hesitated before leaving Charlotte's office. "I think I saw Viola pulling away from my friendship as another rejection. Thanks for helping me think about that in a different way."

Charlotte smiled at her. "Mary Pat, you and I could be good friends if you weren't in the program with me right now. I want you to know that. I've learned over time to keep my work and private life separate, but I'd reach out to you in friendship if things were different."

"Thanks for telling me that. I appreciate it." The words warmed Mary Pat's heart as she gathered up her things to leave.

She drove back to the house, picked up Barker, and went to walk at Mynatt Park. At the house afterwards, she worked in the yard weeding part of the front bed before cleaning up, eating some lunch, and heading to class at the center.

The class, a good one, gave Mary Pat a lot to think about and helped to make her more determined to continue in the program. As she left class, she walked over to the drug store next door to pick up toothpaste and some nail polish remover.

"Mary Pat?" a voice called out, interrupting her thoughts.

She glanced up to see two women making their way across the drug store.

"It's Nancy Sue—or just Nancy now," the woman said, drawing closer. "My goodness, I thought that was you, but I wasn't sure. I haven't seen you in an age. Not since our twentieth class reunion, I think. Time has sure flown by since then."

She wrapped Mary Pat in a big hug and then turned to the woman with her. "Gloria, you remember Mary Pat don't you? She twirled with us in high school. We were the three cuties always strutting out in front of the band. Weren't those grand days?"

Gloria offered a smile. "I'm sorry Mary Pat. I didn't recognize you." Her eyes traveled over Mary Pat in an accessing way. "You've really changed a lot."

Embarrassed, Mary Pat said. "I have changed a lot, but you and Nancy sure look the same."

"Oh, now, aren't you sweet," Nancy said. "Girl, what are you doing here in the Glades? I think I heard you bought your folks old place. Are you here visiting for a time?"

"I am," she said, not adding more.

She noticed then that Nancy and Gloria were dressed in hiking boots, jeans, and flannel shirts.

"We've been hiking," Nancy said, noticing her glance. She ran a hand through her blond hair self-consciously. "I know we look a mess, but we had a great time on the trail."

Gloria straightened the blue visor over her short dark hair. "We hiked the Maddron Bald Trail and around the Albright Grove Loop today. The loop is a beautiful place with old growth forest. Things are starting to green up with spring arriving. We even saw a few early wildflowers. Nancy and I try to hike every Saturday when we're off work. We're so blessed to live here in the Smokies."

"Maybe you can go with us sometime if you'll be here a while," Nancy said.

Gloria's eyes moved over Mary Pat again. "We take some pretty long hikes, Nancy. We walked nearly eight miles roundtrip up and back today."

"Well, we can take one of our shorter hikes so Mary Pat can go," Nancy argued. "It will be fun. Just like old times, the three of us together again."

"You're sweet to think of me," Mary Pat said, looking at her watch. "I need to run though. I've left the dog alone a long time." She started toward the door. "It was good seeing both of you again."

She all but raced to the car to get away. Mad, she drove home frowning. At the house again, she changed into old clothes and attacked the weeds in the front bed again, simply for something to do to vent out her frustrations.

After about an hour she heard her dog barking and looked around to see a small car pulling into her driveway.

"Hey." Nancy Sue opened the door and got out. "I hope you don't mind if I stopped by a minute on my way home. I feel bad about the way Gloria acted." She shut the door and walked across the yard. "Gloria can just be so blunt. You remember she never was tactful even when we were girls. A fault of hers, but except for that she's as good as gold."

"It's all right." Mary Pat stood up.

"Are you here by yourself or visiting with your family?"

"I'm here by myself."

Nancy hesitated. "Well, maybe I didn't pick a good time to drop by but I was so thrilled to see you again. You were my very best friend all the way through school."

"Yes, and I'm being ungracious," Mary Pat said, brushing off her hands on the sides of her jeans. "Why don't you come in for a minute? I can make some peach tea. Do you still love it like you did?"

"Oh, honey, I do." Nancy wrapped her arm around Mary Pat's waist as they started up the stairs to the porch. "I remember your mama used to keep this peach syrup in the refrigerator all the time to add into the tea. It was marvelous."

Mary Pat laughed. Nancy had always been warm, loving, friendly and so fun to be with. "I have the syrup, but it's made with boiled peaches, water, and sweetener now rather than with real sugar. I'm watching my calories."

"Honey, we all have to watch our calories at our age." She laughed.

Inside the house, Nancy looked around and said, "Oh, look how cute you've made this place. I haven't seen it at all since I used to come over here all the time when we were in school. I just love how you've fixed it up."

Barker came into the room wagging his tail.

"Is this your dog you were talking about?" She squatted down, petting Barker and talking to him. "You're just the prettiest thing, aren't you?"

Mary Pat went in the kitchen to fix them a glass of tea and then brought their glasses back to the living room.

Nancy, settled in a chair now, was looking around the room. "You have some beautiful things in this room and all put together so nicely. You always did have the best taste. I need you to come over to my place and help me fix it up."

"Where do you live now?" Mary Pat asked, "still near Sevierville?"

Nancy laughed. "Honey, it has been a long time since we last caught up. I got married again and I moved up here about fifteen years ago when Dean opened the pharmacy in the Glades. That's our place where you ran into me today. I work in the store and help out a lot. That's how I met Dean originally, working in the drug store down in Sevierville where he was the pharmacist."

"I'm sorry I haven't keep in touch better. I guess the last time we caught up was at our twentieth reunion." She passed Nancy a glass of tea and sat on the sofa near her. "Where is your new home?"

"Oh, Dean and I went tourist and bought one of those rustic mountain houses with big decks looking out over a fine view. Not much yard to keep up and a great hot tub." She sipped her tea. "Um. Um. This is so good, Mary Pat. Just like your mama's."

"Thanks." Mary Pat made herself more comfortable, tucking a cushion behind her back. "How's your boy Brock?"

"I'm blessed that Dean took Brock in, too, just like he was his own son. He's such a good man. I got a daughter when I married Dean, too. Dean was widowed and had a girl Cali, a few years older than Brock." She flashed the big grin Mary Pat remembered so well. "Cali married the high school football coach at Gatlinburg Pittman. Can you believe it? It gives us the perfect excuse to go back to all the games now so I can remember when I used to go there."

She drank some more of her tea. "Brock decided to become a pharmacist like Dean. He works at the pharmacy now with us. Since he got his pharmaceutical degree, it gives us a chance to get away sometimes. Dean and I, along with Gloria and her husband Lewis, went on one of those Caribbean cruises this year. It was fun." Nancy propped her feet up on a footstool. "When we got married, Dean owned a farm and some property in Pigeon Forge. The farmland used to be nothing but country when Dean was a boy, before that crazy town started growing up all around. It got so hectic we decided to sell and move."

She laughed. "Honey, land in Pigeon Forge sure has gone up in value. We made out real good and Dean had enough to buy the business complex on Glades Road the pharmacy is in. He just wanted a small local pharmacy of his own this time, different from all the big chains that sell everything but the kitchen sink. Cali wanted to open a coffee shop in one end, so we helped her get that started as well. It's a cute place; you should stop in. Charlotte Hillen rents the other end space from us where she has her weight loss center."

"That's where I'd been before I ran into you. I'm working to lose weight in Charlotte's program."

Nancy put a hand to her chin thoughtfully. "That must mean you plan to stay around here a little while."

Mary Pat dropped her gaze to her lap, twisting her hands.

"Honey, something must be going on in your life." She leaned forward, reaching out a hand to pat her arm. "Remember, this is Nancy Sue you're talking to. It doesn't matter how long it's been since we bared our hearts and souls. We're still best friends. Remember our old motto: *No secrets among friends; no secrets shared outside friends.* You can tell me what's been happening with your life and it won't go any further. I won't even tell Gloria, but you know she'll ferret it out after a while. That smart thing. She and her husband Lewis own a title company out on the highway. I swear I think that woman can read faces and minds. But I'll let you tell her whenever you want. I promise."

Mary Pat smiled listening to all Nancy's chatter. Nancy had always been like this, talkative and as open as a book about everything.

"I hope life hasn't hurt you too much," she said. "I still remember how painful it was when Bobby died in that car crash before we'd been married six years, leaving me with a little baby to raise on my own, and me only a few years out of high school with no skills but baton twirling. Lord, those were hard times, but I got through. Whatever has happened with you, you'll get through, too."

"I'd forgotten that hard time you went through. It couldn't have been easy."

Nancy waved a hand. "All I can say is it's a good thing my daddy didn't let me drop out of that typing class I hated so much in high school. It helped me get my first job and led me to a better one so I could raise my boy."

Mary Pat took a breath. "Back in January right after the holidays, my husband Russell waltzed in and asked for a divorce. I thought we had a happy marriage." She felt tears gather in her eyes. "So I've been going through all that legal mess, selling our home, dealing with the fallout from our children, trying to figure out what I want to do with the rest of my life."

"Bless your heart. That's hard." Nancy reached over to take her hand. "I sure am sorry Mary Pat."

She poured out most everything to Nancy then, in the same way she and Nancy used to tell each other everything they felt and thought as girls.

"What a snake." Nancy commiserated when the story of the other woman came out. "I'll bet Russell regrets one day getting involved with a woman like that. Those slippery snake kind of women can be trouble."

"He doesn't seem to see that, and Cherise has spread it around they plan to marry as soon as the divorce is final."

"That will be hard for the children as well as you." She made a tsking sound. "But I'm glad you've come to the mountains to stay for a while. You've got friends here. You need that at a hard time."

"Yes, I'm beginning to see that." She reached across to take Nancy's hand. "I'm so glad you came by. I'll even tell Gloria all of this the next time I see her."

Nancy laughed. "She made me get into all this hiking, but it's been good for me. And great fun. You'd really love going with us."

"Well, let me get some more of this weight off and more walking stamina built up and I'll try it." She sighed. "Right now Gloria is right. I don't think I could keep up with you two on a long hike. I've been walking at Mills Park nearby and around Mynatt Park in Gatlinburg most every day."

"Have you walked the Gatlinburg Trail? You can take the dog there. It's an easy moderate trail, only two miles long. It starts off Ski Mountain Road, about where town ends, and winds its way back through park property to a point not far from the Park Headquarters Building. You know where that is."

"I do."

"Tell you what. My days are more flexible than Gloria's. She still works nine to five at the title company every day, but I only work part-time. You and I can go hike some short easy trails together if you want to some days. This time of year when the wildflowers start to bloom I know all the best places to go."

She grinned. "We'll soon turn you into a hiker so you, Gloria, and me can take on some longer trails together." She laughed. "Honey, that woman is strong and long-legged. Sometimes it's hard for me to keep up with her."

Mary Pat reached for a tissue to blow her nose. "I would really love that Nancy Sue—I mean Nancy."

Nancy reached down to scratch Barker's ears where he lay sleeping on the floor by her feet. "Back in school when the three of us twirled together, a lot of our friends used to call Gloria and me double names like yours just to tease us. I didn't care much, but Gloria did. It used to make her so mad when guys would cat call when we'd walk by. They'd holler: "Whoopie Do, it's sweet Mary Pat, Gloria Rae, and Nancy Sue.""

"I'd forgotten that. That used to make me mad, too." Mary Pat giggled. "We did have good times back then, didn't we?"

"Yes, and you'll have good times again, honey, and don't you think different," Nancy said in a softer voice.

She handed her empty glass to Mary Pat. "Now, before I have to head home to fix supper for Dean and Brock, who's living with us right now, I want you to make me another glass of that peach tea and take me on a tour around this house so I can see how you've fixed it all up." She grinned. "Then you've got to tell me about your diet. How much have you lost now?"

"Fifteen pounds so far."

Nancy put a hand to her heart. "Oh, honey, that's a lot. Good for you. I'd like to lose that much. Especially around my middle."

Smiling and feeling life was suddenly much better, Mary Pat led her old friend into the kitchen with her, Nancy still chattering away. Goodness, it was great to have a real, solid girlfriend again. Especially someone like Nancy Sue who knew all her past.

Nancy pointed at Mary Pat's note on the refrigerator. "Honey, I love that saying: *Today is the first day on the road to a New You.*" She held up her glass of peach tea. "Here's to us, too, and to this day of us getting back together again. I'm so glad you've come home."

CHAPTER 8

As April began, Owen couldn't help noticing that Mary Pat was losing weight. He admired her, taking charge of her life as she'd done, working on building a healthier lifestyle and a new beginning. He'd walked with her a few times at the park and on the trail behind their house. Living next door to her, he'd stopped over occasionally, too, when he saw her sitting outside reading on the front porch or working in the yard. He'd faced the fact he was still attracted to her and he tried to keep some distance because of it.

The woman was still going through the grief of betrayal and divorce, and Owen well remembered how painful that time could be. He knew her divorce had finalized. He'd caught her crying about it last week. One of her kids called, saying all the wrong things. It burned him. None of them had come to see her during this hard time. He knew Mary Pat had been a good mother. Where was their gratitude?

His house had a shop to one side, and he was working on some handmade kitchen cutting boards for the store this Monday afternoon when he heard Mary Pat scream. He dropped his tools and headed out the door toward her house, his heartbeat kicking up, as a second scream came again.

The front door stood open and Mary Pat held Barker in her arms, yapping and straining to get down, as she looked back at the house in terror.

"There's a bear in my house," she shrieked as she saw him coming.

He grabbed the dog from her, still wriggling and struggling. "Tell me what happened?"

"I went to the grocery, came in and put everything on the counter in the kitchen. Barker needed to go out, so I leashed him and walked him a ways down the street. When I came back and walked in the front door, I saw him. In the kitchen."

Her eyes, panicky, looked back toward the house. "There's a big black bear right in my kitchen, Owen. I promise. Thankfully, I still had Barker's leash on. I grabbed him up and headed out the front door with him barking and trying to get down. What am I going to do?"

"How did the bear get in? Did you leave a door open?"

She closed her eyes, her hand on her heart. "Oh, my gosh. I might have left the sliding door on the deck open. I brought the groceries in that way and then got distracted. How stupid."

"Listen. I'm going to make noise and see if I can scare him out of the house," Owen said. "Take this dog and put him in my house. I left the back door unlocked. Then call 911 and ask for the park emergency line. Tell them what's happened and they'll send a ranger or agent over. Go now." He started toward the house.

"Maybe you should wait til they get here."

"Don't worry. I'll keep a respectful distance but I plan to make some noise. Bears don't like people or noise. I'm hoping he'll take off when he hears some commotion. Go get that dog out of here before he gets loose and causes more trouble." He knew his voice sounded sharp, but the last thing he needed was for a dog and bear fight to start.

"Okay." Grappling to hold on to Barker she started toward his house.

Owen walked cautiously toward the house then, beginning to clap and sing loudly. He took his cell phone from his back pocket, too, tuned it to a loud radio talk show and turned the volume up as high as it would go. Usually bears disliked and feared people and when they heard a lot of people noise they'd flee.

On the porch, Owen shut the front door to leave only a back exit for the bear and then picked up a spade Mary Pat left leaning against the wall and started banging it against a metal milk can he found sitting by one of the rocking chairs. Starting cautiously around the side of the house next, he kept the noise up, carrying the spade and milk can with him.

As he neared the back of the house, he saw the bear head off the deck and through the back yard. "Get out of here, bear," he hollered as loud as he could, continuing his racket. "Get on back in the woods where you belong."

Seeing the bear disappear into the woods beyond the yard at last, he walked up on the deck and shut the sliding door. Then he started around to the front of the house to check on Mary Pat.

She met him as he came around the corner of the house and threw herself in his arms. "Oh, thank goodness you're okay. I was so scared, Owen." She pulled away to look at him for a moment. "Are you sure you're all right?"

"I'm fine, Mary Pat." He'd dropped the spade and milk can when she launched herself at him.

She wrapped her arms around him again and started crying. "I'm so sorry I left that door open. If anything had happened to you it would have been all my fault, too. I'm just so sorry."

Despite the situation Owen enjoyed the feel of her against his body. It had been a long time since he'd held Mary Pat like this and a sweep of old memories assaulted him, causing him to wrap his arms around her and pull her closer.

As if sensing a change in the moment, Mary Pat pulled away, her eyes meeting his with surprise for a minute before she looked away.

She glanced toward the house, collecting herself. "Is the bear gone or still there?"

"I saw him come off the deck, run through the yard and into the woods. I looked to see if there was another bear in the house, a cub or anything, but the coast is clear now." He shook his head back and forth. "Your kitchen is a wreck though."

"It's my fault if it is." She sighed. "I put the dog up and called the emergency number at your house. A ranger is on his way."

"Good." He wiped at the tears on her face. "We'll sit out here and watch for him. He'll need to file a report. He might know if this is the bear that's been causing problems the last month or so or a new one. I can give a pretty good description of this one. If others have reported problems nearby, it might help get a handle on the situation."

He took Mary Pat's arm and led her around to sit on the front porch steps.

She frowned. "Maybe I should go in and start cleaning up."

"No, let's wait. The ranger might want to see the damage."

She giggled nervously. "Like not disturbing a crime scene?"

He grinned at her. "Sort of like that." He brushed her hair back from her face. "Are you sure you're all right? You had a pretty good scare."

"I'll be okay."

A park ranger's car pulled up a few minutes later and they led him into the house and out back telling him what had happened.

The kitchen, strewn with groceries and torn up grocery bags, showed the bear's work well.

"Looks like he had himself a pretty good afternoon snack," the ranger said, shaking his head and looking around.

He turned to Mary Pat. "You'll need to keep a close watch on food, trash, grills, pet food." He glanced toward the dog's dishes in the corner. "Now that the bear's had a nice meal here, he might come back looking for more."

Mary Pat groaned. "Oh, great. What should I do?"

The ranger walked out to look at the deck and back yard. "Since you live here alone, you could add an electric fence out back. A little shock sometimes makes a bear decide to look elsewhere, but not always."

"I can help with that," Owen said. "Dad and I have done that with our properties. I might put a detector sprinkler near the deck, too, that would come on, make a little noise and spritz any bears or other critters that came too close to the deck."

"You could do that," the ranger said. "These things can help, but not always. We're worried this bear may be one that's gotten too acclimated to garbage and easy food. Your description of his size and that white blaze on his chest makes us know it's the same bear that's been causing other problems. I'm glad you called. We're hoping to catch him in a trap or tranquilize him so we can transport him to a more remote area. Sometimes that can work. If he gets too aggressive and people get in the way, we may have to euthanize him. I hope it won't come to that."

"Me, too," Owen said.

"How often do bears hurt or attack people?" Mary Pat said.

The ranger leaned against the deck rail. "People are more likely to be killed by a domestic dog, lightning, or bees before losing their life to a bear. Most bear nuisance complaints aren't serious or involve injury. There have only been a handful of fatal black bear attacks in the U.S. in the last twenty years and most happened in wilderness areas like Alaska. The ones in the states, mostly involving campers or tourists, were often initiated by tourist actions. For example, a woman in Colorado continually fed bears after being warned repeatedly not to and one day lost her life trying to feed a sick bear. Another death in New Jersey involved hikers who moved in too close to a bear trying to take pictures. Most black bear encounters between humans and bears were prompted by human behaviors."

Mary Pat rolled her eyes. "Like my stupid behavior leaving my back door open with groceries on the kitchen counter. I'm really sorry."

"Nobody's perfect," the ranger replied. "We all make mistakes. I'm just glad no one was hurt here." He glanced out toward the woods behind Mary Pat's yard. "I may come up with another ranger or two to check out this area more. So if you spot us, you'll know why we're here."

He turned to Owen. "You or Mrs. Latham, or any of your other neighbors around here, let us know if you see ole' Blaze again." He grinned. "That's what we've been calling this bear."

"We'll do that," Owen said reaching out to shake the ranger's hand. "Thanks for coming out today."

"You did good making noise, banging metal, hollering, making that bear feel unwelcome. It's important not to think of bears like pets, to talk sweet to them or throw out food for them. You can sign a bear's death warrant with kindness like that. I wish more people realized that fact."

He looked at Mary Pat. "If you see ole' Blaze again, back away slowly or sideways, talking calmly at first, then making noise like singing, waving your arms so he sees for sure you're human. Don't make any sudden movements that might trigger an attack. And don't run. A bear might chase you from instinct if you do, and bears can run faster than a racehorse, both uphill and down. You can't outrun a bear. Remember all the safety measures of living in the mountains like this. It's different from living down in the city."

"Thank you. I'll keep that in mind."

The ranger wrote his name down for them, Roger Humphreys, with a phone contact number, and then left.

Mary Pat glanced toward Owen's house. "I'd better go get Barker."

"Wait." He put a hand on her arm. "Let's go get the kitchen cleaned and sanitized first and try to get all the bear smell we can out. Then we'll go get the dog, if that's okay with you."

"That's probably a good idea," she said. "But you don't need to help me clean up. You've done enough."

He grinned at her. "If you think for a minute I'm going to let you go after all that mess by yourself you've got another think coming. Besides two sets of hands are better than one."

"Well...." She hesitated.

"You'd do it for me, wouldn't you?"

She threw up her hands. "Okay. You win."

It took nearly two hours to clean up the mess the bear had made of the kitchen. He seemed to have spread food scraps and pieces of grocery bags from one end of the room to another without being neat in the process.

Mary Pat surveyed the kitchen at last, nearly back to normal. "That bear was so destructive. I hate that he climbed over all my kitchen chairs and tore up the foam padding and fabric." She ran a hand over the wooden top of the kitchen table. "His big claws scratched up my table, too."

"I can fix the table and Noble can redo the chairs if you go to a fabric shop and pick out some material you like to recover them."

"I'll do that, and I'll want to pay for that work."

He lifted an eyebrow. "We'll see."

Owen glanced at the clock as Mary Pat tucked away the last of the cleaning supplies. "It's after six. Why don't you and I go out to dinner? I think we deserve that after all this cleaning."

She wrinkled her nose. "I'm not very fun to take out to eat on this strict diet program. There are so many things I can't eat right now."

"I have some place in mind that will do, and I'm hungry enough to eat anything you can't tonight."

She laughed. "All right. But I think I should pay."

He acted shocked. "How do you think that would make my manly pride feel?"

"Fine, but I need to change clothes and walk Barker before we go."

He started toward the door. "You get dressed. I'll go clean up, too, and walk the dog before I bring him back over to the house."

"Where are we going to eat?"

"Let me make a call to check and I'll tell you when I get back."

At the house, Owen walked Barker who was wagging his tail and happy to see him. He called to make a restaurant reservation, took a quick shower after handling all that garbage the bear left behind, and then dressed in a nice pin-striped shirt, clean slacks, and a corduroy sports coat.

He found Mary Pat dressed in a black skirt, a white overtop, and a long rose pink sweater that brought out the pink in her cheeks.

"You look good," he said.

She grinned at him. "This sounds silly, but I had to put a belt on with my skirt, the waist band was so loose. It made my day."

Mary Pat followed Barker into the kitchen to put down some dog kibble and fresh water for him. "He's sniffing every corner looking for that bear," she said, coming back with her purse.

"Well, gratefully he didn't find him."

She nodded. "Where are we going to eat?"

"I made a reservation at the Buckhorn Inn for seven o'clock."

Her eyes widened.

He held the front door open for her. "Don't get overly impressed. I did some work for the owners and they told me I could come over for two dinners sometime. It seemed like a place to take a date and I hadn't met any pretty girls I wanted to take until lately."

"You are making me feel good, Owen," she said, following him across to his car in his driveway. She sighed then. "I hope they'll have something on the menu I can eat."

"I asked," he said, as they started down Highland Drive. "I know from Francine's dieting a little about what women like to eat when they're being careful. Tonight's menu is a spinach salad with mushrooms and some sort of balsamic dressing, roasted tomato soup, grilled salmon, lemon garlic asparagus, rice pilaf, and some kind of fudge truffle tart for dessert. But they said they were familiar with Charlotte's diet program and that you could have a fruit cup of strawberries and blueberries for a dessert substitute. How will that work out?"

She smiled. "Actually very well. I'll probably have to pass on the rice pilaf and the crème soup, except for a taste or two, but everything else I can eat. It's nice they'll give a fruit cup as a dessert substitute."

Mary Pat straightened her seat belt. "Charlotte has visited restaurants in the area to get many to offer menu items that will work better for her clients. Isn't that thoughtful? She found most restaurants wanted to cooperate so Charlotte would recommend them on her preferred restaurant sheet she hands out."

The Buckhorn Inn sat on a hillside with commanding views out over the Smoky Mountain ranges. As Owen ushered Mary Pat to their pretty table by a window, he said, "You probably remember this inn opened in 1938. Founders Douglas and Aubrey Debb bought twenty-five acres where they could develop an inn in the new park region. The story of the development and history of the inn, and the woodlands and grounds around it, is great to read about. The inn stayed in the Debb family until the late 1970s, changed hands, and then the Mellors bought it in 1998. Lee and John made renovations to the Inn and grounds."

"It is a stunningly beautiful place rich in history. I haven't been here in years so this is a treat, Owen."

The waiter brought water and coffee, then salad and soup while they talked, and even laughed, over their eventful day.

Mary Pat told him about reuniting with Nancy again, going over to her house and on a short hike. "We walked on the Gatlinburg Trail and took Barker. I've been walking now for a month and did okay. I could tell Nancy wasn't even winded going up the few hills on the trail, but I kept up." She smiled. "She's promised to take me walking on the Porter's Creek Trail next week when she's off. She says the wildflowers on that trail are beautiful."

"They are and it isn't a hard trail either." He paused to finish his soup and salad. "Mary Pat, if you want to hike on Dawson Creek Trail behind our homes, plan a time to do that when I can go with you. I don't like the idea of you hiking there by yourself with ole Blaze possibly still sniffing around the area."

She bit her lip. "That's a good idea. What can Nancy and I do to be more safe on the trails when we hike?"

He laughed. "Talk a lot, and with Nancy Sue that shouldn't be a problem."

She giggled. "Gosh, I love her though. I'd forgotten how much. She's so happy, bubbly, warm-hearted and fun. And Nancy Sue's so entertaining."

"I remember that, too. I'm glad you two have gotten back together. You were always such good friends, and then in high school you, Nancy, and Gloria all three ran around together, spent the night and stuff. I guess because you all three twirled together."

She looked out the window, thoughtful for a minute. "I got out my old annual the other day and looked at pictures of us in those cute blue, gold, and white sequined costumes. I looked at pictures of you with the football team, too, and at all those fun photos throughout the annual. I loved those years in high school."

"You were head majorette. The school was really proud of you, and then you went on to become a majorette at the University of Tennessee."

She smiled at him. "And you were accepted to West Point. We didn't do too badly for two little mountain-raised kids."

"Yeah, we made out all right despite some upsets and sorrows."

Dinner arrived and they ate for a time, chatting lightly between enjoying the good food.

"Will you tell me about your wife?" Mary Pat asked, when they finished eating and were waiting for dessert. "I certainly bared my heart and told you all about Russell."

He sipped on the fresh cup of coffee the waitress had just poured. "After West Point, I was commissioned as a Second Lieutenant, working in the Engineering Branch I trained in. Two years later I advanced to Lieutenant and met Joanna Gillespi. She worked on base as a nurse. We began seeing each other and perhaps somewhat impulsively got married. The relationship seemed good at the time. Then I got deployed abroad and Joanna stayed behind."

Owen sighed, looking out the window. "We seemed to drift apart then. She didn't write or keep up much. When I came home, our relationship seemed a little strained. After one of my visits back she told me she was pregnant. We had a son." He paused. "This part of my life only a handful of people know about Mary Pat."

"I can keep a confidence when I need to. You should be able to look back and remember that." She put a hand over his on the table. "But you don't need to tell me anything more if you don't want to. Perhaps I shouldn't have asked."

"No. You shared with me." He drank some more of his coffee. "Our son's name was Garrett Dawson McCarter. Garrett's my middle name, and Dawson—as you know—is my mother's family name. Gosh he was a cute little boy and I was crazy about him. It made all the hard times overseas better, knowing he was there, looking forward to seeing him. My relationship with Joanna continued to be strained. I wasn't sure why, but coming home to Garrett was always a joy."

"You never know how special it is being a parent until that first child comes."

"That's the truth." The waitress brought their desserts and Owen stopped to take a few bites of his before continuing.

"My skills abroad were needed at that time and I ended up there a couple of years before coming back stateside; then I got deployed again for a shorter time, only about a year this time. I looked forward to coming home. I was being sent to Fort Carson in Colorado and thought the change might bring Joanna and me closer. Instead she asked me for a divorce, admitted she was involved with another man."

He looked out the window. "I was angry, did some checking and found the relationship had gone on far longer that she first intimated. I pushed aggressively for more time with Garrett, wanting joint custody rights. She dropped her bomb then that Garrett wasn't really my son. He was the son of the man she'd been seeing all those years. He was married, so she didn't want to seek a divorce from me. Now the man was in the process of getting a divorce. She said he wanted to legally adopt Garrett; he didn't have other children."

"Oh, Owen." She put a hand over her mouth. "That must have hurt so much."

"It was a rough time. For a season, I tried to stay in Garrett's life, too, but he was only six when we divorced. Having two fathers confused him and it was painful trying to stay a part of the new legitimate family mix. After a few years of occasional visits I stopped trying."

"You never met anyone else?"

"I didn't want to meet anyone else. I especially didn't want to take a chance on getting serious about anyone else again. Betrayal hurts, as you've learned."

"Yes, it does." She looked down, her voice growing softer.

He leaned forward. "I told you this because I wanted you to

know I haven't felt anything remotely like real feelings for a woman until you came back."

"Oh, Owen, this is too soon for me." She put a hand to her mouth.

"I know that Mary Pat. It's actually too soon for me, too." He ran a hand through his hair. "But I feel something has thawed out in me a little, that some crack has formed in my heart that had hardened over the years from all the hurts with Joanna and my life in the military. Even if it's only sweet friendship, it sure feels good."

He smiled at her. "I know how we looked at each other earlier today. Perhaps there are some old feelings waking up in both of us. I don't know. I wanted to say thank you though. I won't make any advances on you. I don't want anything of you. But I wanted to be real and tell you how I feel. That I'm grateful to know I can still feel."

"That's sweet, Owen. I'll be honest, too, and say I'm touched to know anyone could feel attracted to me right now with the way I look and with my emotional state. I've been deeply hurt, down to my soul, by all the critical and harsh things Russell said to me, how the children have acted, and how my so-called friends humiliated and rejected me when I needed them most. It's nice to know someone solidly male like you sees worth in me and is attracted to me."

He heaved a sigh. "It's another reason I told you. I wanted you to feel good and valuable about yourself, to realize how you can impact others."

She looked at him with a twitch of a smile then. "You're not going to try to kiss me goodnight or anything tonight, are you?"

"No. If the time is ever right for that, we'll both know it. But like a high school kid, I might think about it."

She reached over to take his hand. "You were always one of my best friends from the time we were two silly little kids. No matter what happens in the months to come as I heal from this mess in my life, promise we'll stay friends."

"You can count on it, Mary Pat."

The waitress stopped at their table. "This dinner is taken care of by the owners, Mr. McCarter. I hope you and your friend have enjoyed it."

Mary Pat smiled at her. "It will be a special night we'll both always remember. Thank you."

Heading out to the car, Mary Pat kissed him on the cheek, when Owen opened the door for her, and then grinned at him. "Charlotte says incentives are important for dieters. Maybe more than a kiss on the cheek might be a good incentive to think about for when I drop fifteen more pounds."

"We'll keep that goal in mind," he said, winking at her.

CHAPTER 9

On Sunday morning, Mary Pat got up early, dressed and went to church. The church she'd grown up in wasn't far down Glades Road. She'd been meaning to go as soon as she felt like she wouldn't break down and weep through the service, her emotions so ragged from the stress of the divorce and move.

The Glades Community Church, a pretty white country church with a tall steeple and bell tower, was built on a part of the old original Dawson farm. Up the winding road behind the church, the Dawson homeplace stood on a rise, an imposing two storied white farmhouse with high gables and wide welcoming porches. Clint Dawson's father Lamont still lived there as did Lamont's daughter Gaynelle and her husband, Dr. John Browder, now the pastor of the church and an instructor at nearby Walters State Community College.

Old friends immediately began to greet her with big smiles as Mary Pat came into church. Francine's little girl Larissa came to insist that she come to sit with her and her mother.

"Welcome," Gaynelle said, coming over with her husband, Pastor Browder, to greet her as she sat down. She reached over to give Mary Pat a hug. "Clint said you were back."

"And we've been hoping to see you one Sunday," John Browder added, giving her another hug himself. Leaning closer to her, he added, "Clint said you've been through a rough time, so let us know if there is anything we can do to help."

"We've already been praying," Gaynelle said. Then she grinned.

"I'd have brought you one of my famous Welcome-Pound-Cakes, but Francine told me not to—said you were dieting."

Mary Pat laughed. "Thanks for not tempting me."

The service proved to be a healing, blessed time, the music sweet, the sermon good, the people loving, all drawing Mary Pat back into fellowship with warmth and acceptance. Listening to the announcements, she learned the church would be hosting its traditional potluck dinner on Easter after the morning worship.

"I'm so pleased the church is still doing the Easter lunch," Mary Pat said to Francine after service.

"I am too." Francine said. "Everyone looks forward to that each year and the kids love the egg hunt we do after service while lunch is being set up." She stood, gathering up her purse and Bible to leave. "The church enlarged the outdoor pavilion a couple of years ago, added a side building with a small kitchen, refrigerator, a big ice chest, and nice restrooms. We don't have to run inside the building all the time when we host an event now. Dawson built us a pretty white gazebo, too—nice for weddings."

As she left, Mary Pat walked around to the back of the church to see the new pavilion and gazebo before heading home. She received invitations to eat Sunday lunch with several in the congregation, but declined graciously, deciding to avoid the temptation of a big Sunday meal.

Back at home, she fixed a small lunch and then decided to take Barker back down to the Gatlinburg Trail to walk. She wanted to keep building stamina so she wouldn't have such a hard time keeping up with Nancy on their planned hike in Greenbrier this week.

Returning home, she was glad to sit down to rest and picked up the phone eagerly when it rang, hoping it might be one of the children. Sometimes they called on Sunday afternoons.

"Where have you been?" Russell almost shouted when she picked up the phone.

"Hello, Russell." Mary Pat kept her voice calm. "It's Sunday. I went to church, grabbed a bite of lunch, and took Barker walking on the Gatlinburg Trail. It's such a nice day today. What can I do for you?"

"I'm not happy with you." He snapped out the words. "You've been poisoning the kids' minds so they don't want to come to my wedding."

"Actually, I didn't even know you'd set a date, and I haven't talked about it with any of the children."

"You expect me to believe that?"

She tried to bite back her annoyance. "Whether you do or not, I haven't talked to Todd, Craig, Patrick, or Victoria about this matter. Again, I did not even know you'd set a date."

He cleared his throat loudly, as he often did when upset. "Cherise set the date for Saturday, April thirtieth, at the Easter holidays so more of the family could come. Her parents and several others in her family are driving or flying in. My parents have passed away as you know. My brother Bill is overseas in Germany, so it's unreasonable to expect him to come. With the children refusing to come, I won't have any family represented."

Mary Pat couldn't help grinning. "I really don't have anything to do with their choices, Russell. As you've said, they're all adults now."

"I'm really upset about this," he said. "They've all talked ugly and disrespectfully to me. Todd called me an idiot. Can you believe it?" His voice rose. "After all I've done for him. He also had the nerve to tell me that when he and Allison get married, they don't want Cherise at their wedding. We had words over that, and I told him if my wife wasn't welcome then I wasn't welcome either. He said fine, that he didn't give a ripping flip if I came or not."

"It sounds like he was really upset." Mary Pat tried not to giggle.

"Craig acted almost as bad, said that despite his love and respect for me as his father that he didn't admire my actions right now. He had the nerve to suggest Cherise and I were marrying too soon after the divorce. What business is that of his, I ask you?" His voice grew angry and loud again. "When I called Patrick, he had the nerve to say I'd treated you like crap, trading you out for a younger woman, and all but pushing you out of the house. I can't believe my own son would talk to me like that. Said he was disgusted with me and didn't want to build a relationship with Cherise. Victoria acted nicer but she cried, said I'd ruined everybody's life. Honestly, that girl has always been too dramatic."

"Oh, my."

"Can't you talk to them? Help them see this is important to me?"

She couldn't believe he was asking her to do that. The nerve! "No, I don't think that is appropriate, Russell. As I said, they haven't even brought the matter up with me. I think this is between you and them."

He cleared his throat again. "Cherise won't be happy if they don't come. I want her to build good relationships with them, not negative ones. She's already mad over their attitudes and how they haven't reached out to her. If they slight her by not showing up, it won't help things."

She took a deep breath. "Listen, Russell, it is your place to re-contact the children and to express your feelings to them about this matter. I can't help you with this."

"You mean you won't."

Ticked now, she replied, "It is no longer my role to play intermediary between the children and you in disagreements." She started to add that she only infrequently talked with any of them anymore but she hated for him to know that.

"Well, great. I can see you're not going to help me at all with this. Thanks for nothing," he said and slammed down the phone.

She blew out a long breath after hanging up her own phone.

"Well, talking to my former husband for the first time since our divorce certainly didn't prove to be a congenial conversation," she said to Barker.

She walked into the kitchen to get a glass of water, fighting the old temptation to reward herself with something to eat when upset.

Glancing at the big calendar on the wall, she saw that April thirtieth was just over a week away. So soon. Cherise hadn't wasted any time after the divorce setting a new wedding date. She wanted to cry thinking about it but hated to waste any more tears on Russell. Especially after the way he talked to her.

She kept thinking, too, about the children's angry responses. Had they really said those things? Russell could exaggerate a situation sometimes to gain sympathy. They'd certainly never expressed any of those angry feelings about their father to her. In fact, she'd often felt they were madder at her than at Russell over the divorce, which she'd never understood.

"Oh, well, let them figure it out. There's nothing I can do about any of it."

To get her mind off things, she decided to head outdoors to weed more in the flowerbeds. In May she hoped to put out new flowers to cheer up the front of the house. She'd seen some old bulbs popping up already, ones her mother planted years ago, a few daffodils and tulips, but she wanted to plant vinca and other favorites, as well.

She brought Barker outside with her and hooked his collar on the long chain she'd attached to a stake by the porch. He could sniff around the yard there safely and enjoy the sunshine or climb up on the porch to nap.

About an hour later, her phone rang. The house phone again. Not many old friends knew that number; most used her cell number. She considered not answering it, thinking it might be Russell again, but then sprinted into the house to catch it. The children and her parents often still used this number.

"Hello?" She grabbed up the phone.

"Hi, Mom, this is Todd," her son said.

"Well, hi. It's nice to hear from you." She sat down on the sofa by the phone.

He sighed. "Look, I know Dad called you. He called Victoria back, trying to get her to work on us to go to this wedding of his. He let it slip he'd called you, too, and tried to get you to work on us. Victoria said Dad told her you didn't even know he was getting married again next weekend."

"Actually, no, I didn't know. I told your father, also, that whether you children attended his wedding or not was up to each of you."

Todd was quiet for a minute. "None of us want to go, Mom."

She hesitated. "It is your place to make your own decisions about that. All of you are adults now."

"Well, thanks for that." He paused. "Listen, I'd been planning to call. Craig, Patrick, Vee, and I want to come down to see you next week for Easter weekend. I was waiting to call to see if it would be okay to be sure we could all get off for a long weekend, but we've worked that out. Do you think we could come?"

She smiled. "I'd be delighted."

"I remember we all used to go to GiGi and Pop's church on Easter for service and to that big dinner after. When we were kids we loved the egg hunt, too. Are they still doing that?"

"They are. I planned to go and I'd be pleased for us all to go together."

"That's great." He paused for a moment. "We know we haven't been much of a support to you in all this. We were working, and to be frank, it was such a shock at first. I'll be honest and say we all got mad about it. I know that sounds stupid and childish, but we hated to see our family breaking up. For a while we really felt angry, angry at both you and Dad for messing up our home. We didn't want to talk with either of you about it. Then we started to see things more clearly. Especially when Dad started talking about this other woman and about getting married again. Geeze. We started to figure things out more then and we realized you'd probably been hit with as much a surprise as us. Probably worse."

"I experienced some of the same angry, shocked feelings, Todd. I naively thought your father and I had a happy marriage."

"I'm sorry, Mom."

"Well, life moves on, son. Like it or not. And despite anything that has happened with your father, my love for you children has not changed. I love all of you very much and I am simply thrilled you're planning to come to see me for Easter weekend."

"I think I remember the house has a couple of bedrooms upstairs besides yours downstairs. Will you have enough space for us?"

"Absolutely. There's the big room you boys used to share with three twins in it, Victoria's room with a double bed, and a guest room with a queen."

She hesitated and then added, "Your father mentioned that you and Allison might be planning a wedding."

"Yeah. We got engaged this week. I was going to tell you next weekend. We're planning to get married at the end of August." His voice grew warm and happy as he shared the news.

"Well, I am over the moon for you," she said. "And so excited. Would you like to bring Allison with you? We could put her in the guest room if all you boys don't mind sharing your old room together."

"Are you sure you wouldn't mind?" She heard the excitement in his voice.

"Surely you know I can't wait to meet her. She's joining our family."

Todd's voice choked a little. "Thanks for that, Mom. I'll ask her. I think she can get off work."

"When should I expect all of you?"

"Craig's flying from Massachusetts Thursday night to Charleston to drive over with Patrick early on Friday. Vee and I plan to leave Nashville early on Friday, hopefully with Allison, too. The three of us should get to your place before Craig and Patrick. What do you need us to bring?"

"Just yourselves."

"Will you bake a ham, make sweet potato casserole and deviled eggs like you always do at Easter?"

She smiled. "I'll do my best to make that happen."

"That's great. I'll call everybody else and tell them our plan is on. I'll go call Allison, too."

"All of you drive safe. I can't wait to see you."

"Mom." Todd's voice grew quiet. "We thought it might make this bad time not so hard for you if we all came."

Tears filled her eyes. "I appreciate that, Todd."

"Listen, none of us are telling Dad where we're going next

weekend, so if he calls you, please don't tell him we're coming. Vee worried he might come up and make a scene if he knew."

"He won't know from me, and I'd say he'll have a busy weekend of his own."

"He's really stupid to walk out on someone as great as you are, Mom. Marriages are supposed to be forever."

"Thank you, Todd. That's sweet." She tried to keep him from hearing her choked up voice.

"Well, we'll see you on Friday, Mom. Oh, and Patrick said to ask you to bake a carrot cake."

"I'll give some thought to that," she said, wondering when she hung up how she was going to manage baking sweets without sampling them.

"The children are coming for Easter," she said, going outside to pick up Barker and hug him. "Aren't we going to have a good weekend?"

CHAPTER 10

On Thursday after work, Owen drove over to the farmhouse next door to have dinner with his sister Francine and her daughter Larissa.

"Hi, Uncle Owen," Larissa said, flinging herself into his arms as he headed in the back door.

"Hi yourself." He swung her around. "I think you're growing more gorgeous every day. I may need to get my shotgun out soon to chase off the boys."

She giggled. "I'm only nine, Uncle Owen."

"Gorgeous is gorgeous, nine or nineteen or fifty-eight like your mother." He went over to give his sister a kiss on the cheek.

She made a face at him. "It's never wise to mention your sister's age but I guess I'll overlook it this time."

He dropped his jacket over a kitchen chair. "You're still a very beautiful woman, in case I don't mention it often enough—thick dark hair, pretty brown eyes, good figure, great smile."

"I'm beginning to be glad I invited you to dinner now." She grinned at him. "I knew I'd have extra spaghetti tonight with Dad eating dinner out with Lamont but I hadn't counted on the compliments."

Larissa looked up from the homework she sat working on at the kitchen table. "And we knew you liked spaghetti."

"I do."

"Come help me with my history," she invited. "We're reading about different regions around the United States and studying the

West right now. You lived out west in Colorado. Come look at my map and tell me more about the area. Hearing about it is more fun than only reading about it."

"Okay, that's pretty country out there." He got up and moved over to help her work with her homework while Francine finished up their spaghetti, salad, and bread for dinner.

After dinner they played cards and visited, and then when Larissa headed upstairs to take her bath and get ready for bed, Francine and Owen took their coffee out on the screened porch behind the farmhouse. They settled into two old rocking chairs where they could rock and relax as dark fell over the farm.

"You remember when Mama used to sit out here and sing songs with us at night?"

"Mostly old hymns, but I loved those times."

"Sometimes I feel like I can still hear her singing. I miss her and wish she hadn't died so young. Dad misses her, too. I catch him sitting out here late in the evening talking to her now and then. He always loved to tease her and call her Ida Belle. She had a pretty name Idaline; he only did that to get a rise out of her." She laughed softly.

"Do you think he'll ever marry again?" she asked after a few minutes. "He flirts with the young girls in fun but I notice he keeps a distance from the widows that sidle up to him."

"He told me that he and Lamont made a pact they're going to stay old bachelors together now that they're both widowed." He chuckled. "Clint and I made a pact like that once, too."

She raised an eyebrow. "Oh, really?"

He looked away, realizing what he'd said. "We were only joking around, Francine. Like guys do."

She rocked quietly for a few moments. "I've watched you around Mary Pat. There seems to be something there."

"Maybe there is, but it's too soon to know if it could go anywhere." He sipped on his coffee. "She's just divorced. Mary Pat may not even want to stay in this area. She's already talking about going back to college to upgrade her old credentials. Who knows where she may move after that."

She tilted her head. "You certainly are underestimating your appeal and charm. She may decide to stay around here because of you."

'That's a nice thought." He winked at her. "How is your relationship with Clint coming along?"

"It caught me off guard to learn Clint was attracted to me when Wheeler spilled the beans that morning at the store, but it stirred something in me." She smoothed a hand through her hair absently. "I could love Clint. I've always loved him in a way. I can visualize it as more, but he's shied away from me ever since."

"I've seen that," Owen said. "He's having a hard time letting his feelings out. As a young man, wildly in love and engaged to that cute little trick Lacey Harper, he got really hurt when he learned she'd been cheating on him. She got angry when he called her out about it, broke the engagement, said hateful things not needed. Clint's afraid to trust again."

She pushed the rocker back and forth with one foot. "You've been that way, too, Owen. You locked off your heart and feelings after learning Joanna was cheating on you."

"You're right. I think the worst for Clint and for me was that we didn't know. Others did but we didn't have a clue. That causes you to lose trust in yourself, in your ability to be wise in a love relationship."

"It makes you feel vulnerable."

"Yeah, I guess it does, and afraid to get in that place again, to risk that kind of hurt and pain another time. To risk the concept of being made a fool of."

"So you both closed yourself off to the idea of love, never let yourselves get close enough again to feel that much."

"I guess." He grinned across at her. "I never really though about it much until I felt Mary Pat starting to wake up the old ability to love in me again, that sweet desire to hope in even the idea of love again."

"What awakens the idea of loving again?"

He stopped to listen to a night frog croaking in the creek nearby. "You're trying to figure out how to get close to Clint now, right?"

She wrinkled her nose. "Yes, I think I am. He still seems to be holding back. Do you think it's because I've been married before, that I have Larissa?"

"No." He shook his head. "I think it's him. He won't care that you've been married before and he loves Larissa. She's crazy about him, too."

"What made you know you still carried feelings for Mary Pat again?"

Owen thought for a minute. "Being around her, having her need me, getting the protective instinct stirred up." He studied his sister. "You're so strong, Francine. You come across as not needing anyone."

"What?" Her eyes widened. "Do you think I'm never lonely? That I don't yearn for love, closeness, and intimacy again?"

He wasn't sure how to answer.

She grew thoughtful. "I guess I need to let Clint see that I want that."

"It might help." He tried not to laugh. "That day with the bear scare when Mary Pat threw herself in my arms stirred up some old passion in me. I'd forgotten I could get a rush like that. You know." He looked away, embarrassed. This was his sister. "Men are kind of physical sometimes."

She bit back a smile. "That's good to consider. With dad and Larissa usually around at the house and with others always at our business meetings at McCarter's or at the landscape office, there aren't many opportunities like that."

Owen scratched his neck. "True, but Clint lives alone. When I walk the Dawson Creek Trail, I often cut off after the old Dawson cabin down through the woods to the log house Clint renovated there."

"I remember his place." She laughed. "It's almost as primitive as the old Dawson cabin in some ways. You took me there on a hike one day; I do know how to get there." She smiled then. "It might not hurt to create an opportunity."

He looked out the window. "If such a thing should ever happen, it wasn't my idea."

She smirked. "Don't worry. What's said in the house stays in the house. This conversation we've had tonight stays totally between us."

She got up to take their coffee cups into the kitchen and brought back a tin of homemade cookies and two canned colas, balanced on the tin. "Here take one of these colas." She sat the tin on the table and popped the top on her own drink. "Are you okay to stay out here on the porch to talk? It's warm tonight, but we can go in if you prefer."

"No, this is great." He dug out a couple of chocolate chip cookies from the tin. "You make these?"

She laughed. "No, Maydeen did and Wheeler brought them over."

"That woman loves to bake and loves to feed people."

"Wheeler loves an excuse to visit, too." She nibbled on a cookie for a minute before picking up their conversation. "If anything ever happened between Clint and me, how would Dad manage if I moved out of the farmhouse?"

"He managed before on his own after Ma died. I didn't move in with him when I came back. I lived with Clint while I built my house."

She frowned. "Dad's strong-natured. I don't think it would suit Clint to move in here with us."

"You're got that right."

"But Dad's not getting any younger, Owen."

"Don't say that to him." He laughed. "You need to know, too, that Dad's been chuckling and making jokes about you and Clint getting together, plotting with Lamont to make it happen ever since Wheeler dropped that bomb. Obviously it's not worrying him. He's only seventy-eight. Our people generally live long rich lives, and it's not like you'd be moving to Maine. You'd still live around here."

"Don't say this to Clint, but I don't think I'd like living in that rough log house of his. It's small and hangs up on that steep hillside."

"No, it's not your sort of place nor Larissa's."

Her eyes brightened. "We could build a place on the farm property, like you did. Even on the next lot up from the farmhouse. Then we'd be close to Dad and close to you and the store."

He thought about it. "That could work—create a new place for a new life for the two of you." Owen glanced at his watch. "I need to head home."

She put a hand over his. "Thanks for coming for dinner and for the talk."

He gave her a kiss. "Always good to spend time with you, big Sis."

Owen followed Francine into the kitchen to get his jacket, helping to carry cola cans and the cookie tin.

As he drove up to the end of Highland Drive toward his own house a few minutes later he found his mind wandering along some of the same lines as Francine's thoughts. If Mary Pat and he ever got serious, would she like his place? Would she be content to even stay around in the mountains?

His mind far away, he almost didn't notice her out in the front yard in the dark, walking Barker. He slowed down to wave at her.

"Hi," she said, coming toward his 4Runner with a big smile.

"You look like you're in a good mood."

"I am. You want to come in and visit for a little while?"

He hesitated. "I tell you what. Why don't you walk over and visit with me this time? I know you dashed into my place to call the emergency park number that day, but I don't think I've had a chance to show you around my house before. You want to check out my place?"

"Oh, that would be nice." She looked toward the house. "I admit I've wondered about it, knowing you had the house built when you came back."

She put Barker up while he drove around to the back of the house to park his truck in the garage that sat at an angle to the house. A covered walkway led across to a side door into the kitchen area.

Mary Pat followed him inside, looking around with interest. "It's much bigger than it looks from outside, with the house sprawling up under the trees on the hill like it does."

He spread a hand, gesturing around. "I wanted a mountain home this time, after traveling for so long, with big open spaces, lots of windows looking out into the woods and up toward Providence Ridge." He gestured around at the rustic, but modern kitchen, opening into an expansive living area with a huge rock fireplace and beamed ceilings, looking out to a broad open deck.

"This dining area by the kitchen looks directly into the back yard through all the long windows there and out to the screened porch." He pointed. "In good weather I love eating on the porch and feel like I'm a part of the outdoors."

She peeked out at the porch with its beamed ceiling, paddle fan, and comfortable tan wicker furniture.

"It's beautiful. A lot of neutrals but with bits of color for warmth and variety."

"Definitely not as colorful as your place."

"No." She waved a hand. "But my place is a cozy old cape cod, with white clapboard siding. It needed a different look. But your furnishings are perfect for this place. So inviting with that wonderful mountain feel."

"Thanks." Pleased at her words, he added, "I wanted all my main living area, what you've seen here and the master bedroom, to be on the first floor. The upstairs rooms I mostly added for company—three bedrooms and a couple of baths—for times when friends or family come into town."

"Sounds like a good plan."

"I absorbed what could have been a garage to add a woodworking shop and office, and built the garage instead at an angle behind the house with a covered walkway straight into the kitchen. Another side entrance leads directly from the shop into the laundry and pantry area for times when I'm dirty from working in the shop or outdoors—sort of a mudroom."

She walked across the living area. "Does this hallway lead to the master bedroom?"

"It does." He led her down the short hallway to his bedroom.

Years in the military had taught him to make his bed every day and to keep things shipshape and clean, so he didn't worry about her looking around in his home, even unexpectedly like today.

"Oh, my," she said, putting a hand to her heart. "This is a wonderful spacious room, so unlike the small rooms in my mountain house, and I could die for big closets like these." She peeped into his huge closet and sighed. "You haven't even filled it up, Owen."

He shrugged. "I don't have that much."

Crossing the room, she asked, "Is this another screened porch off the master?"

"Yes, but this porch room is also glassed to use year round somewhat like a small den. I spend a lot of time out here."

"I can see why. What a marvelous room looking out into the trees." She sat on a small sofa and spread her hands out across the back of it. "I'd love a room like this. Even in winter you could sit out here with a roaring fire and watch the snow fall softly down, off in your own little world."

He liked her words. "Do you want to see the upstairs? I furnished all the downstairs first and then gradually finished the bedrooms upstairs, knowing I wouldn't use them as much. I've been surprised though at the old friends who like to drop in here in the mountains."

"Anyone would love this place and want to stay—and come back. The kitchen is a dream and it makes me itch to cook. You know how small that little kitchen is at my place." She sent him a teasing smile. "Next time we plan a dinner, I think we'll cook it here and eat in one of your wonderful porch rooms with the weather so glorious now."

She stood up. "Take me upstairs to see the rest and then to the shop, too. I want to see everything."

Mary Pat was equally enthusiastic over the upstairs rooms and she even enjoyed looking around his office and shop, asking questions about projects he was working on, looking at some of the pieces he had ongoing.

As they walked back into the main house, she said, "I had no idea looking up the hill to the front of your house, rustic barn red and blending into the woods like it does, that it was so nice inside. I really love your place." She spun around slowly. "It sort of reminds me of vacation homes we've stayed in while skiing out in Colorado."

He smiled, heading into the kitchen. "I lived in Colorado for a long time. Maybe some of the places out there inspired my design. I picked out a house plan from ones that the builder, Cooper Garrison, showed me. Delia Walker Cross, in Gatlinburg did the decorating. I give them more credit than myself. Both caught the vision of what I wanted and helped me bring it to life."

She perched on one of the tall chairs at the kitchen island.

"Could you drink hot cocoa?" he asked

Mary Pat frowned. "Only if it's diet. Do you have tea bags? I'd love some hot tea, and I tucked sweetener in my pocket before I left the house."

"You're really taking this diet seriously."

"Anything you do well has to be taken seriously. You know that."

"I do." He turned to put a teakettle filled with water on the stove to heat. "I think you said earlier you had some news."

He glanced back at her to see her eyes light up. "My children are all coming this Friday for the Easter weekend. I'm so excited. Todd is bringing his new fiancé Allison, too. I'll have a houseful, and I'm bringing them all to church and to the Easter potluck after. They remember coming to it as small children, in the years when Mother and Daddy still lived here and when you were off in the military. They loved the egg hunt."

The teakettle whistled and he poured hot water over their tea bags in two mugs. In a minute he handed her a big mug of hot tea. "After you sweeten that to your taste, let's sit over in the living area where it's more comfortable."

She tucked herself into a corner of the sofa, and then began to tell him about Russell's phone call and the subsequent one from her son Todd.

"It sounds like the kids are all coming around—and getting some good sense after their initial shock."

"Yes, especially the boys. They seem upset with their father the most. Victoria, always her daddy's princess, is having the most trouble with this."

"Has she said anything unkind?" he asked, noticing her frown.

"No, not exactly, but I feel her criticism. I think she still believes I'm partly responsible for the breakup." She sighed. "Maybe I am in a way. I didn't realize Russell had stopped admiring so many aspects of my life, my activities, my friends, my looks, and more. I look back now and wonder if I was living in a fog or something not to realize he was unhappy."

She rubbed her arms, thinking. "Mother said a lot of men go through a sort of midlife crisis at about Russell's age. They fear getting old, losing their youth, get restless, buy new cars, houses, or boats. Get new younger women." Her voice dropped on those last words.

"I didn't know Russell, but I've seen other men fall for a younger woman and lose all good sense."

"You're kind, and even the boys seem to agree the real problem instigating Russell's sudden desire for a divorce was probably Cherise. But as Patrick said, Russell didn't need to let her tie a string on his nose and lead him off."

"No, and that was his foolish choice." His eyes met hers for a long moment and he could feel the edge of their attraction surface.

She ran a hand through her hair nervously, and stood. "It's late. I need to head home, and you have work in the morning."

"I'll walk you home."

"You don't need to."

"I know, but with ole Blaze still out and about I'll feel better if I do."

She giggled. "I'd almost forgotten about him. I haven't seen him since that day but Maydeen and Wheeler have. They only live down the hill, not far."

"Maydeen didn't mention it." He frowned.

"I don't think Maydeen saw him, but Wheeler did. Said he was snooping around in the back yard, down near the edge of the woods."

He walked her home. "Be watchful out walking the dog or when working around the yard. And remember the ranger's advice."

"I will." She ran up the porch steps and then stopped at the door. "Thanks for the tour," she said and blew him a kiss.

And he walked back home imagining more.

CHAPTER 11

On Friday, the day the kids planned to arrive, Mary Pat left her cleaning and company preparations to zip over to Diet Options, when Charlotte opened for the day at noon, to weigh-in.

"Thanks for letting me weigh a day early before this busy weekend coming up," she said, following Charlotte back to her office after another client left.

Mary Pat weighed in and Charlotte grinned. "Well, this will make your day. You've now lost thirty pounds, Mary Pat."

As she walked over to sit down, Charlotte reached in her file cabinet, took out a balloon, and blew it up on the small helium tank she kept in the corner of her office. She tied it off, put a ribbon on it, and presented it to Mary Pat with a big flourish. "Ta-da! This is a big moment."

Mary Pat felt like crying as she looked at the bright yellow balloon with the large letters on it: "Congratulations. Thirty Pounds."

"Do you think the children will notice the change?" she asked.

"How can you ask that? Of course they will. People don't always notice a ten or fifteen pound loss, but they notice thirty." Charlotte sat down behind her desk. "Even more fun is that none of them even know you're in a weight loss program. That will double the surprise."

Mary Pat watched Charlotte write the new loss in her notebook and on the sheet she pulled from her file folder.

"I've dropped a whole clothing size now, and the new slacks I picked up are already getting loose." She pulled up her shirt to show Charlotte the loose pants. "My old dresses were baggy, too, so I actually bought a new dress for Easter and an Easter hat."

"Good for you. You're a pretty woman and your natural beauty is popping out more every day. So much of it was hidden under weight."

"I'm nervous about today." Mary Pat twisted her hands in her lap.

Charlotte smiled at her. "Don't be. Regardless of whether you're married to Russell or not, your children will continue to love you. My girls, when small, had a hard time understanding about their father when I needed to file for divorce, but they'd heard people talk and gossip. Like me, I think they felt relieved for a new beginning in a new place when we came here. Their father's photo had popped up in the newspapers and on television, embarrassing us all."

"Do they keep in touch with their father?"

She picked at a nail. "Somewhat. Jason has been married two more times and my parents said recently he has a fourth marriage planned. Constancy doesn't seem to be an attribute of his, although he is successful in business." She paused. "Adultery causes so many sorrows. The girls found it hard over the years to stay close to their father because of his lifestyle."

"Do you think people who cheat once will do so again?"

"It seems to be a pattern some fall into. In a recent fidelity study, researchers found partners who were unfaithful in one relationship were three times more likely to cheat again in another relationship. I saw that happen with Jason when married and after."

Mary Pat closed her eyes, shaking her head sadly. "Regardless, it's hard to think of Russell marrying again tomorrow—and so soon. Cheating aside, you'd think he could have waited a little longer to tie the knot again."

Charlotte tapped a finger on her desk. "I imagine others are wondering the same thing, and I'm glad your children decided to come this weekend to be a support to you while all this was going on." She glanced at the clock and changed the subject. "Let's talk about what you're doing with meal preparations for the weekend and how you're going to handle cooking more fattening foods with your family here. I asked you earlier to think out a plan for the weekend."

Mary Pat pulled a notepad out of her purse. "I drove down to Pigeon Forge this morning and picked up a honey-baked ham and a turkey breast for the weekend. I checked the calorie count and I can eat a little of either if I watch portions. I'm making the sweet potato casserole the boys asked for—which I can't eat any of; it's so fattening—but I'm baking a plain sweet potato on the side. I can eat half at one meal and half at another." She studied her list. "I'm using the green bean recipe you gave us at one of the classes, too, rather that making one of those fattening green bean casseroles I usually cook. I'm using low-cal mayonnaise for the deviled eggs; the kids will never notice the difference."

She paused. "I picked up brown-and-serve rolls, which I don't really like and can easily resist, instead of making my homemade yeast rolls, which I love. I'm making a big salad, too. For the Easter luncheon, I'm taking a broccoli apple salad to the church along with a plate of turkey and ham."

"It sounds like you've been thinking this out." She glanced at Mary Pat's notepad. "What about dessert?"

Mary Pat smiled. "Maydeen is making the carrot cake the boys requested, using my recipe. Knowing her, I'm sure she'll bake something else sweet as well, probably cookies. But I know those things are not on my list right now. I'm making a diet strawberry Jello salad with fresh berries that I can eat." She sighed. "This is only one weekend. I can manage."

"Good girl." Charlotte closed Mary Pat's file. "On Tuesday when you come back to weigh in, the goal should be to see no gain, even if there's no loss." She stood up, hearing the door chime and knowing another client was arriving. "This is your first big company challenge, but I'm proud you've thought out so well how to handle it."

Mary Pat spent the afternoon cleaning, changing bed sheets, and setting the dining room table. Then she moved to the kitchen to cook, answering the door once when Maydeen stopped by with the cake and a tin of cookies.

In the late afternoon the kids began to arrive, first Todd, Victoria, and Allison from Nashville and then Craig and Patrick from their longer drive from Charleston. With joy Mary Pat welcomed them all and helped them settle in to their rooms. After a little catching up, she moved back in the kitchen to let them visit and laugh in the living room while she finished dinner.

The kids popped in and out of the kitchen, helping her as she finished up, and they soon all gathered around the dining table to eat. Mary Pat noticed, with pleasure, that Todd, her oldest, took the end chair at the table where Russell would normally sit and offered to say grace.

As they passed dishes around, her eyes moved over them— Todd at the end of the table, dark-haired, brown eyed, tall and distinguished in appearance at thirty-three. On the right sat her other two boys—Craig, with wavy brown hair like his father's but with her gray-blue eyes, and beside him Patrick with his thick, dark unruly hair, brown eyes and casual ease. Across from Craig and Patrick sat the girls, Victoria, pretty and blond, looking a lot like a younger version of herself but taller, with her gray-blue eyes, and a sweet smile when she remembered to flash it. Beside her sat Allison, with short black curly hair, hazel eyes, and cute dimples when she smiled. A sweet and thoughtful girl. Mary Pat already liked her, and she loved the way she looked at Todd, his gaze back at her just as sweet. Every now and then, Mary Pat saw Allison twist her engagement ring on her finger, glancing down at it with pleasure.

"Mom, everything is great," Patrick said, reaching for another roll.

Todd looked across the table at her. "I still can't believe how much weight you've lost, Mom. You really look great."

Craig gave her a worried glance. "You haven't been losing because you're unhappy?" he asked.

She smiled. "No, I've been losing because I needed to."

"Daddy said nasty things to you about your weight, too," Victoria put in. "He told me some of the things he said to you."

Mary Pat dropped her eyes, not sure how to answer. She didn't want to talk negatively or critically about the children's father, despite all that had happened.

"Spoken with your usual tact, Vee," Todd chided her.

She made a face at him.

"Divorce is never pleasant," Craig said in his matter-of-fact voice. "I'm sure a lot of unpleasant words passed, and it's nice of Mom not to repeat them. We shouldn't push her to do so, either."

"All right, all right," Victoria replied crossly. "But don't expect me to tiptoe around all this like nothing ever happened. Our home is gone and our parents' marriage is over. In addition, our father is marrying someone else tomorrow, making it obvious to anyone that he was cheating on Mom long before he asked for a divorce. It's just sad, that's all."

Todd rolled his eyes. "Thanks so much for bringing all that up, Victoria. Now can we change the subject and talk about something else?"

Patrick caught the cue and jumped in. "What are we all going to do tomorrow? Do you have anything planned Mom?"

She smiled, glad for the change of subject. "Actually, I do. If it's all right, I'd like to take all of you hiking up the Porter's Creek Trail. A friend took me there not long ago, and it's a fun trail along the creek. It leads after a mile to an old cabin, a cantilever barn, and a springhouse, interesting to look at. We can sit on the porch and eat a bite of lunch, turn around to head back or walk on for another mile to Fern Falls if you'd like."

Victoria's mouth dropped open. "*You* want to take us hiking?"

Patrick leaned forward. "I'd love that."

"Me, too," said Craig. "Are you and Allison in?" he asked Todd.

Todd looked at Allison. "Are you game for a hike?"

Her eyes brightened. "I'd love it. You know I like to get outdoors and both of us stay cooped up in the hospital too much."

Todd glanced at Victoria with a smirk. "Do you think you can keep up? If not you can go shop while we all go."

Victoria lifted her chin. "If Mom can go, I certainly can." She frowned at her mother. "Since when have you started hiking anyway? I haven't gone on any kind of walk with you in years. Are you sure you can do this?"

Feeling a little annoyed, Mary Pat said, "I started walking in early March as a part of my weight loss program. Gradually, I built up stamina and as I lost weight walking grew easier. I ran into old school friends who like to hike and they soon had me out on some of the shorter, easier trails with them. I still can't take on the longer, more arduous trails yet, but I'm hoping to in time."

"Wow, I'd never have believed it," Victoria replied with that touch of sarcasm still in her voice.

Todd shifted the topic to start talking about the upcoming wedding he and Allison had started to plan. Again, Mary Pat was glad for the change of subject.

As they all talked, tossing out ideas, she studied her daughter, wondering again at the veiled hostility often underlying her words. When had that started? Back in middle school or high school? She couldn't recall exactly, but she knew the warm and close friendship she and her daughter once shared, when Victoria was a little girl, gradually disappeared over time.

She got up after a time to cut slices of cake for everyone for dessert. After she passed the dessert plates around, she sat back down with a wedge of diet Jello for herself.

"Aren't you eating cake?" Craig asked. "It's one of your favorites."

"It's probably not on her diet," Victoria put in.

Allison laughed. "It probably shouldn't be on mine. But it's wonderful." She smiled at Mary Pat, her dimples flashing. "Thank you so much for inviting me this weekend. I'm so glad to meet all of Todd's family."

"Tell me about your family," Mary Pat asked.

"My parents live just below Gallatin on the lake. My father and mother have a chiropractic practice. My older brother's in real estate, and I have two younger sisters still at home in high school. They are both so excited about being in the wedding." She smiled at Todd. "Of course I want Victoria to be one of our bridesmaids and my best friend to be the matron of honor. We plan to get married in my family church in Gallatin, nothing very fancy."

"Allison has a nice family, Mom. You'll like them," Todd added. "My brothers and Allison's brother will be my groomsmen, and Dickie, my best friend since high school and roommate in college, will drive in to be my best man."

"My parents go to an old family church in downtown Gallatin. It's pretty." Allison blushed. "We're not very party oriented, so we're just having the wedding reception in the church after. I hope that won't be disappointing."

"It sounds lovely. You let me know if there is anything I can do to help." Mary Pat got up from the table. "I'm going to clean up from dinner. You young people go out on the screened porch to visit if you'd like. It's a beautiful night."

The weekend sped by and before Mary Pat knew it, she was waving the children off on Monday morning after feeding them breakfast.

"How did it go?" Owen asked, walking across from his house when he saw her out with the dog.

"It went great." She glanced at her watch. "You're home early."

"Dad, Maydeen, and Noble are all at the store. Dad's closing so I wasn't needed. It's so pretty out, I thought I'd get outdoors for a while."

"It's gorgeous today. I hate to go back indoors."

"You want to hike up the Dawson Creek Trail with me?"

"I'd love that." She glanced down at her feet. "Let me go put on my boots and take Barker back in the house first though."

"I'll meet you back here in a minute," he said. "I need to put boots on, as well, and I'll throw a bottle of water and a couple of things in my waist pack. Since you've been walking and hiking more over the last two months, maybe we can walk all the way to the old Dawson cabin."

"That would be great."

A short time later they headed up the old trail that rose up Providence Ridge behind their houses. By the time they got to the falls, Mary Pat was a little winded but she walked on up the wood steps by the falls, stopping at the top to look down over the fall of water.

"You doing okay?" Owen asked.

"Yes." She smiled at him. "I'm fine."

"You're getting fit and sassy," he replied, moving on up the trail ahead of her. "You've kept up with my pace, too, and I didn't hear any whining."

His teasing made her laugh to herself, reminding her of the easy camaraderie they'd always shared while exploring these mountains.

With the trail leveling out and widening now, Owen slowed so she could walk along beside him. "I enjoyed meeting your children on Sunday at church. Nice looking, good kids. Dad especially enjoyed seeing them again, remembering them all when smaller."

"He used to hide Easter eggs for all the kids."

Owen laughed. "He still does. Gets out there with the little ones, too, and helps them find a few so they won't have an empty basket."

"It was a good weekend and I was so glad for the beautiful sunny weather. The kids really had a good time, I think."

"I think I heard one of them say you took them hiking."

"We hiked up the Porter's Creek Trail that Nancy introduced me to. I knew they could walk it even in tennis shoes, and I liked the idea of getting out and staying busy that day."

"Did Russell call like you worried he would?"

"He phoned a couple of the children, but they didn't answer or call back. I don't think it ever dawned on him they might come here."

"Well, I'm proud they did for your sake. I know it helped you get through what might have been a hard weekend otherwise."

She sighed. "I'm just glad to have relationships restored with them. I know they're adults now with their own lives, but I want to stay close."

"Any problems over the weekend?"

"Only a few small squabbles—like you'd expect with siblings. Victoria is still more upset over the divorce than the boys, I think. She and I haven't had a strong relationship for a long time. I'm not sure why, but the divorce hasn't helped, of course."

"She's a very pretty girl." He paused. "I made a point of meeting all your children and talking to them at church."

She put a hand on his arm. "I know I didn't invite you over while they were here, but I thought they might pick up on..." Her voice trailed off.

"The fact that your old boyfriend is still smitten with you?"

Mary Pat felt her face flush. "Kids are really sharp about picking up on things with their parents."

"You don't need to apologize, Mary Pat. It isn't the time for us to appear as a couple around your children, even as close friends—with me a man."

She giggled. "You are that."

They walked on, Owen reminiscing about the Easter service and gathering, catching her up on small happenings in his life. It surprised her how easily they'd fallen back into their old friendship.

After a mile, they came to the old Dawson cabin, sitting on a rise not far above the trail. They climbed up the short trail to the cabin, passing a small family cemetery to the right and the remnants of an old corncrib.

"The cabin looks good," Mary Pat said, surveying the weathered, hand-hewn log structure with its rusted tin roof.

"Dad and Lamont Dawson used to take care of it, now Clint and I do. He doesn't live far from here, up at the end of Reed Ridge Road." He brushed off the porch above the top step so they could sit down for a minute.

"I see daffodils over there around the rocks." She pointed.

"If you walk around the property you'll find more wildflowers—trillium, phlox, bloodroot, wood violets."

"When I sit on old porches like this one, I can't help wondering what it would have been like living in an old cabin like this so long ago."

"It was a hard life, not an easy one, but people had their joys."

Owen took his water bottle out of his wasit pack and offered her a sip.

"I should have brought my own waist pack," she said after drinking.

"We weren't hiking far today. It wasn't needed." He glanced toward the trail below them. "We can hike on another mile to the trail's end at Birds Creek if you want, but I thought after a big weekend, a short walk would be more in order."

"This distance was perfect for today, but I'd like to walk the length of the trail another day. I remember we used to cut over the creek and walk some trails at Camp Smoky, too. Is that old camp still there?"

"Yeah. It was bought out by a church denomination but it's still there, still used. The old trails are still there, too." His glance ran over her for a moment. "Now that you're slimming down so much, we can take some other hikes together if you wish. I remember you used to like the Dudley Creek Trail that starts at the Smoky Mountain Riding Stable."

"That would be fun. I would like that."

He grew quiet for a few moments. "How much weight have you lost now, Mary Pat—if you don't mind me asking? I'm real proud of the work you've done to get back in good physical shape."

She grinned at him. "I hit thirty pounds when I weighed last and I still have the helium balloon to prove it. Charlotte gives them out for big milestone points. It's bright yellow."

He studied her, his eyes moving over her in a new way, giving Mary Pat a chill. "Seems like I remember us discussing how you might like to celebrate the thirty-pound mark."

Mary Pat felt a rush of color wash up her neck. "You know I was teasing you that night, Owen."

"Don't spoil my fun, Mary Pat," he said leaning over to put a hand behind her neck and then moving his mouth to cover hers.

The kiss started light and playful but then moved into more,

Owen's arms moving to pull her closer, his kiss deepening. The sweetness of the moment quietly slipped into an explosion of unexpected passion. Mary Pat sighed, reveling in the rush of feelings, pressing closer to wrap her arms around Owen's back.

"Well," he said after a moment, breathing heavily and looking into her eyes. "That was better than I remembered."

Not sure what to say, she nodded and swallowed.

"I think we need to try that again," he said, moving in to kiss her once more, gathering her against him tightly.

As his hands began to rove, she pulled back. "Let's slow down, Owen. I'm sort of overwhelmed here. I don't know what I expected, but it wasn't this."

He traced a hand down her face. "We always did put off some sparks between us, but I don't think I expected it to still be the same, us being older and with all the years gone by. I certainly didn't expect it to be even better." He grinned at her. "It was good, wasn't it?"

"Yes." She looked down with embarrassment.

Owen leaned over and kissed her on the forehead then. "Don't be worrying that I'm going to be putting the make on you every time we get together now, you hear? But this was sure fun." He laughed. "I'm right glad to know I can still get all hot and bothered like this. It's been a while for me to feel this good."

She stood and then walked down the stairs. "We'd better start back. It's late and we both need to make dinner."

He caught her arm. "Don't decide you're betraying Russell to feel again so soon, Mary Pat. You and I, we're just picking up where we once left off."

CHAPTER 12

As April ended and May settled in, a beautiful time in the Smoky Mountains, Owen watched Mary Pat settle more easily into her life in the Glades. With her weight still dropping, she could enjoy more hikes and activities with Nancy Sue and Gloria, and she hiked with him occasionally on his days off. Sometimes they shared meals together. As he'd promised he didn't push on her emotionally. That kiss at the cabin proved a surprise to both of them—a good surprise to his way of thinking. It showed promise of a future. He could tell, too, he wasn't the only one often remembering it and wanting to repeat it either.

While thinking on this and putting new items on a row of shelves in the store one Friday morning, Mary Pat walked in the front door.

"Hi, Mary Pat," Maydeen called out as she spotted her. "I can't believe how this spring has flown by. Before we know it, the summer tourist traffic will be here and we'll all be as busy as beavers."

"That's good isn't it?" Mary Pat walked over closer to the register where Maydeen worked.

"It is and I always think busy days go by faster than slow ones, too." She finished sorting a pile of incoming mail. "You here to see Owen? I think he went upstairs to the office. You can check. If you're heading that way, would you carry this mail up? It would save me some steps if you take these bills and letters upstairs as you go."

"I can do that," she said. "While I go upstairs you be thinking about a nice gift I can get to ship to my dad in Florida for his birthday."

Owen walked to meet Mary Pat as she walked back through the store.

"Hi. I thought Maydeen said you were upstairs in the office."

"I'm heading that way now," he said. "We'll take the mail up and then get a cola. I'm ready for a break."

As they started upstairs, they heard a giggle. Owen paused and looked ahead to see Clint Dawson kissing his sister Francine on the stairs.

Clint glanced down to see them, winked, and then stepped away, whispering a few words to Francine, whose eyes widened as she saw them.

"Friends, I'll see you all later," Clint said with a roguish grin as he started down the stairs past them.

Francine straightened her hair. "Hi, Owen, Mary Pat. I guess you caught me in a moment." Her face flushed.

"Looked like a good moment to me." Owen grinned.

"I can't deny that." A little smirk crossed Francine's face. "Come on upstairs. I know you have some questions."

Mary Pat looked embarrassed. "Actually I came to get a birthday gift for my dad but Maydeen asked me to bring the mail upstairs for her. I don't need to stay. You and Owen can talk."

Francine took the mail from her. "No. I want you to stay. Come sit down and have a cola. We keep diet drinks, Mary Pat." She turned to Owen. "I also brought part of a coffee cake from the house. Do you want me to cut you a piece?"

"I'd like that *if* you'll give me the story of how you and Clint moved from embarrassed around each other and hardly speaking to kissing on the stairs."

She laughed, while she got cold drinks out of the refrigerator and cut a piece of cake. "If I don't tell you, I imagine Clint probably will." Francine flounced into a seat at the old conference table.

Mary Pat sat down, too, and pried the lid off her diet drink.

Francine sighed then. "When Owen and I shared dinner one night last month, he mentioned that I might need to instigate an encounter with Clint if I wanted to see anything happen with us." Her eyes turned to Mary Pat. "An old hurt in Clint's past has caused him to be real gun shy of any kind of serious relationship."

"I think Owen mentioned that to me once, said they even had a bachelor pact," Mary Pat said.

"Is that right?" Francine raised her eyebrows at Owen.

"Clint and I were only goofing around when we made that," Owen said. "It was a long time ago. Go on with your story."

"All right. First I want to admit that until Wheeler dropped his bomb, I was totally in the dark Clint had any interest in me beyond friendship." She drank a little of her cola thinking.

A little smile crossed her face. "Clint's a good looking man, as you both know," she said, continuing, "tall with that sun-streaked blond hair, that great dimple in his chin, blue eyes…" Her words trailed off. "It didn't take much for me to begin to see him in a romantic way."

Owen smiled as Francine talked. It seemed obvious Francine's interest in Clint had ratcheted up a notch since their last talk.

Francine turned to Mary Pat. "Owen mentioned that the log home Clint bought and renovated wasn't far off the Dawson Creek Trail. I remembered hiking to it, so I kept my ear to the ground to learn when Clint would be off work and at the house." She paused. "Wheeler let it slip one day that Clint planned to work on landscaping at his own place, so I decided it was a nice day for a hike." She grinned at both of them and Owen laughed.

"That sounds like my devious sister."

Francine shook her head. "I admit I acted really shameless. I ran down the trail near Clint's house carrying on like I'd seen the bear, threw myself in his arms, even worked up some tears."

Owen shook his head, trying not to laugh.

"What happened?" Mary Pat asked, leaning forward.

"Clint took me in the house to calm down, not seeing any bear pursuing. Then with a big ole twinkle in his eye—you know how Clint can be—he said, 'Let's try that hugging again, Francine. I think we can do better than that." She grinned. "He pulled me into his arms and kissed me silly then."

Mary Pat laughed out loud. "That's a great story."

Francine wrinkled her nose. "I felt like an idiot pulling off a juvenile stunt like that at my age."

"Do you think he figured it out?" Owen asked.

"No, and don't either of you tell him. Clint wouldn't even let me hike back home, insisted on driving me over to the house in his truck."

"Well, your secret is safe with me," Owen said. "After all, it was partly my idea that you go after him."

"Your secret is safe with me, too." Mary Pat smiled at Francine. "And thanks for sharing. I'm so glad we've become friends again. I always admired you growing up—older than me and so smart."

Francine smiled at her. "Life has a lot of sorrows along the way, but things do turn around for the good most of the time. Don't you think? I know you weren't happy coming here in the winter when you did, but you're feeling better now, aren't you?"

"I am." Mary Pat glanced down at her lap. "I have my moments, missing my life before, sometimes feeling sorry for myself. It still hurts how my old friends dropped me in that hard time like they did, but I've been grateful to renew old ties and friendships like with you and Owen. I wish I'd valued them more."

"Life is a great teacher if we're open to learn from it," Owen put in.

"That's true," she agreed.

Francine's voice softened. "I think I'm going to marry Clint Dawson. When my husband died I couldn't imagine I'd ever marry again or love again. But love seems to have found me even at mid life. It's a sweet and unexpected feeling. I'm glad I was open to explore the idea." Her eyes studied them both thoughtfully.

Owen well knew what she was thinking. "You'd be blind not to see some of the old feelings between Mary Pat and me revived a little," he said, deciding to be honest.

"I'm happy about that for you, Owen," Francine answered as if Mary Pat wasn't there. "You'd closed yourself off from feeling, from the possibility of ever loving again after Joanna's betrayal and losing Garrett."

Mary Pat panicked. "No one said anything about love, Francine, even if a little interest and friendship has revived. I've only been divorced for two months. It would be wrong to jump into another relationship so soon."

"You're worried about being on the rebound."

She fidgeted in her seat. "No. It's just too soon. I'm not ready for anything serious yet."

Owen could tell Mary Pat was getting upset and he started to intervene but then Francine continued.

"Don't get upset with me," she said in her matter-of-fact way. "Pointing out the obvious doesn't mean anyone expects you and Owen to make a mad dash to the church." She leaned toward Mary Pat. "But trying to deny feelings have revived between the two of you would be silly even if it's too soon. I still remember how hard it was for Owen to leave and go to West Point after high school because he was so in love with you. Maybe he never told you that."

Mary Pat looked at Owen then with a question. "He didn't."

"Well, it's something to think about." Francine stood up, looking at her watch. "Uh, oh. I need to be at a client's office in Cosby in twenty minutes. I almost forgot." She began to hustle around picking up papers from the table, searching for her purse.

"Thanks for sharing your story with us," Mary Pat said, getting up.

Francine waved a finger at her. "Well, remember to keep it to yourself."

"I will," she said, as Francine started down the steps.

"I'm sorry if Francine upset you," Owen put in, smiling. "You probably remember she can be pretty outspoken."

"Well, we grilled her and practically pushed her to tell us what happened with Clint. I guess we deserved for her to turn the tables on us."

He waited, watching her.

"Do you think it's that obvious to others that we're sort of interested in each other?" she asked, twisting her hands nervously.

"Maybe a few folks that know us well might be wondering. We spend some time together now. But I wouldn't worry about it, Mary Pat."

"Okay," she said after a minute. "Come downstairs and help me pick out a gift for dad."

In the store, they picked out a whimsical birdhouse for her dad and wrote down all the shipping information for Maydeen.

"I'm going to walk Mary Pat back up to the house, Maydeen," he said as Mary Pat started to leave. "It's nice out and I want to stretch my legs."

"You don't need to walk me home," she said.

He grinned at her. "It gives me an excuse to get outside for a few minutes and besides Noble's here and Dad should be back from lunch soon."

Shortly after passing the Lebanon Baptist Church, they ran into Wheeler coming down the road walking Sadie.

"Hey Mary Pat. Hey Owen." He waved at them.

Sadie, recognizing them both, barked a doggy greeting, too. A part corgi and Dalmatian mix, Sadie was a short stumpy, black and white dog with a big heart who thought of herself as more a lion than a small dog.

"Where you been?" Wheeler asked as Owen leaned down to pet Sadie.

"I've been down to McCarter's to buy a gift for my dad for his birthday," Mary Pat answered.

Wheeler frowned. "I miss my dad. Did you know him?"

"I did," she answered. "Remember that I grew up here, Wheeler. Your dad was a good man. I remember when he died; it was sad."

"He got injured on his work." Wheeler started to say more, but a loud scream interrupted them.

Two more terrified shrieks came again as they all looked around trying to figure out where the screams were coming from.

Sadie pulled on her leash, barking and straining forward.

"Them screams are coming from the parking lot behind the

church," Wheeler said, turning to sprint across the field behind the church. "We can cut through here to get there. Someone may need help."

Owen and Mary Pat followed, as they heard another scream or two.

As they all ran around the side of the church to the parking lot, they both stopped in shock at what they saw. A white van stood open near the back church door with a big bear inside it. Near the door, two women stood shrieking and hollering, obviously horrified.

Owen grabbed Wheeler's arm as he started to run closer. "Stay back, Wheeler. A bear in a situation like this is dangerous."

"I'm calling for help." Mary Pat dug in her purse for her cell phone and called the 911 emergency park number, telling them about the situation. "They'll be here soon," she said, hanging up.

"Good." Owen frowned. "I've never seen a bear situation like this before."

"That bear's tearing up jack in that car," Wheeler said, starting forward a little again in curiosity, Sadie barking and straining on the leash. "He's done tore the door off the car. What's he doing in there?"

"He must be after food." Mary Pat looked at Sadie, still barking furiously.

"Wheeler, maybe you should take Sadie back to the house."

He looked down at the dog. "I'll hold her. She don't like bears, and I think that's ole Blaze in there. I saw that streak on his side jest now." He picked up the dog to hold her, wrapping a hand in her collar.

"Don't let her go, Wheeler," Owen cautioned. "A bear will attack other animals or people when protecting their food."

He watched as one of the women walked toward the van, waving her apron and hollering. *Idiot.* Owen called out to her "Don't go closer, ma'am. If there's food in that van, the bear will try to protect the food. You could get hurt."

"He's tearing up all our cakes for the rummage sale," she

screamed, putting a hand to her face, crying.

"I called the ranger," Mary Pat hollered back. "They should be here in a few minutes."

The ranger's truck pulled up a few moments later and Owen recognized Roger Humphreys driving, the man who'd come to Mary Pat's house before. Another ranger with Roger leaped out of the van to start across the parking lot. As he moved toward the van, he called out to the women to go into the church.

Roger waved at them, too, urging them to step inside to stay safe.

"That's ole' Blaze in the van, isn't it?" Roger asked Owen.

"Yes, I think so. Wheeler and I both saw the markings on his side."

"What happened here?"

"Evidently, the bear tore into the van while the women were inside the church. They probably came out, saw the bear in the van and then started screaming. Mary, Pat, Wheeler and I were walking up the road." Owen gestured. "We came running when we heard the screams and when we saw the bear inside the vehicle, Mary Pat called your number."

Wheeler smiled at the ranger. "He sure has tore up stuff in there and I heared him growl at that lady when she ran toward the van swinging her apron."

"That was a foolish thing to do," the ranger muttered.

Mary Pat noticed then that the other ranger carried a gun. "Oh, my, you're not going to shoot that bear are you?" She put a hand to her heart.

"We're going to try sedating him. We've been trying to get close enough to this bear to put him to sleep so we can load and transport him. He's evaded all the traps we've set so far. This could be our chance."

As if sensing some innate danger, the bear began to edge out of the van. As he did so the ranger popped off a couple of shots.

"If we're lucky that might knock him out enough so we can cage and move him."

The bear, feeling threatened, growled loudly then, startling everyone. At the sound, Sadie jerked out of Wheeler's arms to head toward the bear barking furiously. Wheeler started to run after her but the ranger caught him. "No, son. It's too dangerous."

"He's right Wheeler," Owen said, realizing he'd almost done the same thing when the little dog took off.

Sadie ran toward the bear yapping away, as if heedless of her size. Annoyed, the bear reached out a claw and slapped at her, throwing her off to one side in the parking lot, before he stumbled from the van toward the woods behind the church. In another moment the bear staggered again and fell from the drug, just as another larger truck arrived with several more rangers and transport equipment.

As the rangers moved in cautiously to check the bear, now quiet on the ground, and to begin transport, Roger slipped over to check the dog.

"She's breathing," he called out. "I think she's okay. Just got a big claw lash on her side. You know a vet near here?"

Wheeler didn't answer, crying and upset.

"Call Maydeen at the store," Owen told Mary Pat. "She'll know their vet and can come help. Wheeler needs her, too."

He moved to try to comfort Wheeler who was rocking back and forth hugging himself. "I shouldn't have let her loose. I shouldn't have let her loose," he wailed. "She was just trying to save everyone. Sadie don't know about what bears can do."

He sent Owen an anguished look. "I'm sorry. I didn't mean to let her go."

"I know." He put a hand on Wheeler's shoulder. "The ranger thinks she'll be okay, and your mom's on her way."

Maydeen came running across the street, as another truck arrived with more help to transport the bear.

"Are all of you okay?" she asked, winded and out of breath.

Owen quickly filled her in on what happened, as one of the rangers brought over an empty box and lifted the little dog to put her carefully inside it.

Maydeen went over to squat down and croon to her. She turned to look back at Owen then. "Could you carry this box over to my car? I'll run Sadie straight to the vet's. They're just over on the highway. Not far."

He pulled out his phone. "Let me call and let the vet's office know you're coming with an emergency so they'll be ready." He started punching in the number. "You know I used the same vet for Cody; I still have the number."

After he finished his call, he said to Maydeen. "Do you want me to go with you or would you like Wheeler to stay with us?"

"No, I wanna go, Ma. I can help and Sadie might need me," Wheeler said. "Let me carry Sadie in her box, too. She knows me better and I can talk to her."

"Well, there's your answer." Maydeen offered Owen a small smile. "We'll be okay taking the dog. You need to get back to help at the store with me gone."

"I'll cover at the store. Don't worry," he assured her.

As Maydeen and Wheeler left to take Sadie to the vet, Owen turned back to find Mary Pat watching the rangers work with the bear. They seemed to be carefully trussing ole Blaze to safely load him into the big cage they'd brought.

As they watched, the women from the church edged out from the door and worked their way over to where they stood.

"Did that bear kill that little dog?" one of them asked. "We were watching through the window."

"I don't know," Mary Pat answered honestly. "They've taken her to the vet over on the highway."

"Poor little thing," the other lady said.

The first woman held out her hand then. "I'm Darlene Cutler and this is Wynelle Smith. We're members of the church here."

Owen took her hand. "I'm Owen McCarter. That's our family store across the road." He gestured to Mary Pat. "This is Mary Pat Jennings Latham. She lives at the end of Highland Drive."

Wynelle beamed. "I knew your Mama, Mary Pat; we both worked at the candy store together."

Roger walked over to join them. "How did that bear get in your van?" he asked the women.

"We're getting ready to hold a rummage sale tomorrow at the church," Darlene answered. "Wynelle and I made runs by a lot of members' homes, who can't get out easily, to pick up their baked goods and other items for the sale. When we pulled up out back, we took a load or two of things inside and then started setting up tables in the fellowship hall."

"We got to setting up tables and working, and I guess we stayed in the church a while," Wynelle added.

"When we came back out to get the next load, we walked toward the van, talking and laughing, and then we both about had heart attacks when we looked up to see that big black bear right inside our church van." Darlene waved a hand in front of her face.

"Did you lock the van?" Roger asked.

"Well, no." Darlene gave him a cross look. "We were going back and forth to it to unload, and it's not likely thieves would suddenly roar up behind our old country church to try to steal rummage sale items."

"The door was shut tight though," Wynelle defended. "How in the world did that bear get in?"

Roger shook his head. "Bears who have learned, mostly through the carelessness of tourists, to enjoy people food, grow bold to find more. They can tear off garbage containers to get into them, will walk right into people's garages and homes." He lifted an eyebrow at Mary Pat. "They can smell food from miles away and many bears have learned to open truck and car doors to get to any food they smell."

Wynelle put her hands on her hips. "Well, how were we to know a bear would open our van door, for goodness sakes!"

Darlene's gaze moved toward the van. "Looks like he tore the door open more than opened it politely, too. The pastor is going to have a conniption fit over that van being all torn up like this. That bear clawed up all the upholstery and slung food from one end of that poor van to the other."

Roger scowled. "I think we all need to be grateful neither of you were hurt. Bears can often become aggressive when trying to protect their food."

"It was hardly *his* food," Wynelle muttered.

Roger grinned. "Well, he saw it as finders keepers, I guess. Again, I'm glad no one was hurt."

"You're right to say that," Darlene agreed. "I watched with horror as that big bear tossed that little dog clear across the parking lot with only one swat of his paw. I hope that poor dog will be all right." She pointed toward the rangers now carrying the big cage to their truck. "What will happen to that bear?"

"We'll transport him to a remote area of the park, far away from here, and hope he doesn't find his way back or become a problem near the transport area," the ranger answered.

"Do you need us for anything else?" Darlene asked. "Wynelle and I have some calls to make, and we might see if there's anything in that van we can salvage for the sale."

"I'll need to get a phone number for each of you for my report." He took out a notepad from his pocket and made notes.

Owen and Mary Pat stepped away a few paces, walking toward the truck to watch the bear being loaded. Roger walked over to join them in a few minutes. "You two can go on home now." He paused. "Will one of you call and let me know if the dog makes it?"

"I will." Owen smiled. "Will you call and let me know if Blaze gets transferred safely?"

"Yes, please do," Mary Pat added. "I feel sorry for him despite all the trouble he's caused. Like you told me before, it isn't his fault he got tempted by people's carelessness out of his natural bear ways."

Roger watched the other rangers finish loading the bear. "Have you ever known anyone who smoked or drank and couldn't stop their habit? Getting started on garbage and people food becomes like that for bears sometimes. I wish I had an answer for the problem. We keep trying to educate people, but it's hard."

"You do a good job," Owen assured him.

Owen turned to Mary Pat as Rodger and the other rangers left. "I'll walk you home now."

"No," she said. "You go on back to the store. With Maydeen gone, you're needed." She smiled at him. "But call or drop by and let me know when you hear how Sadie is."

Later in the day, Owen knocked on her door.

"Hi," she said, letting him in. "How's Sadie?"

"She was lucky; she's going to make it." Owen walked over to sit down in his favorite chair. "The bear's claw tore into her skin, caused a lot of bleeding, nicked her spleen. The vet did a little surgery to fix that while he stitched up her wounds, but he found no further damage."

She sighed and sat down on the sofa near him. "I'm so glad to hear that. I worried so much how Wheeler would handle it if Sadie died."

"He was pretty torn up." He smiled at her. "He reminded me that you tried to get him to take Sadie home."

"Wheeler was holding her, but when the ranger darted that bear and he growled so loud, Sadie just went ballistic."

"I'm sure it was her protective instinct. In a lot of situations a black bear will run away when a dog chases them, even a little dog like Sadie."

"When will Sadie get to come home?"

"Probably in a day or two. I'm not sure."

"You let me know, okay?"

"I will." Owen stood up. "I'm going to head on home. I've had a long day, and I need to fix some dinner. I just wanted to stop by and check on you, let you know about the dog."

"Thanks," she said, getting up to see him out. Walking across the road, Owen couldn't help remembering the earlier conversations of the day with Francine and her candid comments about he and Mary Pat.

"Mary Pat sure is skittish," he muttered to himself. "I guess I'll just need to take it slow and easy and see what happens. If anything happens."

CHAPTER 13

On a warm Saturday in late July, Mary Pat stopped by Diet Options to weigh-in a few minutes before noon. She caught Charlotte getting ready to lock the front door.

"Opps, I'm running late," she apologized.

Charlotte smiled. "I'm glad you came near closing. I'd like to talk to you for a few minutes." She studied Mary Pat in shorts, a cute pink knit top, and sandals. "You look good."

Mary Pat grinned. "I had to buy more new clothes. Isn't that great?"

"It is," Charlotte said, locking the front door and leading Mary Pat back to her office.

Mary Pat weighed in and Charlotte's mouth spread in a wide smile. "You have lost fifty pounds now. You'll get another celebration balloon to take home."

"I can't believe it," Mary Pat said, staring at the scale. "When I first came in here weeping and crying on that first Saturday in March, I weighed over two hundred pounds."

"I remember that day." Charlotte recorded Mary Pat's weight, blew up a bright red helium balloon for her, and then settled into the chair at her desk.

She glanced over Mary Pat's calorie and food chart, asked a few questions, and then sat back, crossing her legs.

"Tell me your plans, Mary Pat," she asked." Do you expect to stay on here in the area?"

"I went into Knoxville to the university in the spring and

enrolled to go back to school this fall. I have less to update than I thought. I need to take a course or two and find a place to do some supervised internship work, but surprisingly that's all." She frowned. "I don't really want to pursue a Masters in the field. Financially, I'm somewhat comfortable, but I think I'd like to work in dietetics in some way to help others, if only part time."

Charlotte nodded. "Will you stay at your mountain house?"

"I hope to." Mary Pat studied the paperwork in her lap, avoiding Charlotte's eyes. "At least for a time."

"Until you can see how things develop with Owen?" Charlotte asked.

Mary Pat knew her eyes popped open.

"We've come to know each other rather well, Mary Pat. Also Rowan and I ran into the two of you at the Crystelle Creek Restaurant on the Parkway recently. We all shared dinner together. It seemed obvious to both of us the two of you care about each other." She grinned. "We like Owen a lot, and as Rowan said, 'the sparks practically lit up the room.' Am I wrong in thinking you care about him?"

She sighed. "Even if I do care, I won't act on it right away. My children experienced enough hurt watching their father marry quickly, pushing them to accept Cherise as a new mother figure. Their relationship is very strained with their father now; I don't want it to be strained with me, too."

Charlotte tapped her fingers on her desk. "I understand, Mary Pat. I'm sure you remember my own story. It took time for me to decide to enter into a committed relationship with Rowan, too."

Mary Pat bit her lip. "In a way, Owen and I are picking back up on an old friendship and an old love. I know that makes our situation different, but I still feel it's too soon to move forward into anything more serious. In my heart, I couldn't think about a serious commitment of any kind until the first of next year. Even though Tennessee doesn't require a waiting time to remarry after a divorce—Russell certainly proved that—I believe it is in good taste and wise to wait a respectful period."

"I tend to agree." She hesitated. "I don't usually probe into my clients' lives but I have a reason for my questions today. I'm wondering if you might consider working for me part-time."

Mary Pat put a hand to her heart in surprise.

"As you've seen, I run this center totally by myself, which isn't always easy. When I'm ill or need to be away, one of my long-time maintenance clients, Karen Abernathy or Stacy Myers, fills in for me. I know you've met both of them, but neither hold the credentials you do." She drummed her fingers on her desk again. "I couldn't pay like a hospital position would. My center is too small, but I think you might find working here rewarding, and as you said, you're looking more for an opportunity to help than a way to support yourself. It might give you a way to work and stay in the area, too."

"I'm so flattered you would think of me." Mary Pat tried not to cry.

Charlotte eyed her thoughtfully. "You've met your goal weight and would be an inspiration to our clients. I've watched you interact with warmth, interest, and encouragement with others in our classes, and I know you have the right educational credentials. Please know I didn't make the decision to talk to you about this lightly. I believe you could do a wonderful job here. I also believe we would work well together. Is it something you would consider?"

Mary Pat sniffed. "It's a wonderful opportunity. Do you think the university might see working here as an internship?"

"I don't see why not. I can write a proposal and submit it to the school. You would be counseling in dietetics, helping individuals form better nutritional habits, and teaching. I'd like to give some of the classes to you. I also believe you could begin to experiment to create recipes to discuss with our dieters. You've come up with so many recipe ideas on your own already and shared them with others in your classes." She paused. "If you enjoy working here, we might later expand the center's program and hours, too. What do you think?"

"I'm thrilled and so excited. Thank you."

Charlotte smiled then. "I hoped you'd be interested, but I wasn't sure. Do you want some time to think about this before we talk more?"

"I don't need any time." Mary Pat got up impulsively and hugged Charlotte. "I hope I can do a good job for you. I so admire everything you do for the women and men who come here." She sat down again, still grinning. "This has just made my day." Mary Pat glanced at the red balloon tied on the file cabinet drawer. "Along with my red balloon!"

Charlotte laughed as she pulled out some paperwork from her desk. "I've created a tentative twenty-hour a week work schedule that I think would work best for me and for the center right now. You know I'm open Tuesday, Thursday, and Saturday early hours from 8:00 am until 12:00 noon, and then on Monday, Wednesday, and Friday later hours from 12:00 noon to 6:00 pm. I have many more day clients than evening clients, and I'd like you to consider working Monday through Friday from 10:00 to 1:00 pm."

Mary Pat studied the schedule Charlotte passed to her. "I could do that."

"With day classes on Tuesdays and Thursdays at noon, I'm always swamped in the late mornings. Everyone comes right before class to weigh. With you here to help me weigh and counsel, it would lighten my load and give whichever of us teaches class more time to prepare."

"I've seen how you get piled up on those days."

"As you've noticed, too, a lot of my evening class clients pop in to weigh around their lunch hours. With you here every day 10:00 to 1:00, that offers everyone some broader hours for their weigh-in sessions."

Mary Pat studied the schedule sheet. "I don't see Saturday morning hours on my schedule."

"It's my slowest day. I can handle it alone or get you, Stacy, or Karen to cover any Saturday morning when I need to be away or can't get in. I want to use both those women occasionally to cover times that you or I can't work."

"They do a nice job and are always gracious and encouraging."

"They do." She paused. "So what do you think?"

Mary Pat grinned. "When do you want me to start?"

Charlotte laughed. "Are you sure you don't want to think about it over the weekend?"

Mary Pat wrinkled her nose in fun. "I don't need to think about it. For me this is a dream job. It will be wonderful to help others lose weight and feel better about themselves as you've helped me." She pointed to the old photo in her file that Charlotte took of her on her first day. "Look how much I've changed."

Charlotte stood up. "Yes and that reminds me we need to take a few photos today since you've hit your goal weight."

"I think I might like to lose a little more weight, move into the mid-range on my weight scale."

"You can do that if you want before starting maintenance." Charlotte got her camera off the shelf and walked with Mary Pat out into the hallway where they always took client photos.

"If you'd like to start work next week, I'd like you to come shadow me during four or five of my weekday hours, some day hours and some night ones. I think we should do that for a week or two until you get comfortable. Not all clients are as easy to work with as you have been and it will help you to see how I counsel a variety of personalities and different types of individuals."

"Oh, that's a great idea. I'd feel nervous otherwise. I need to learn how to do the paperwork and everything, too."

Charlotte took Mary Pat around the center then, showing her the second counseling office where she would work, taking her into the work room and kitchen area, walking her around in the classroom to show her switches for lights and technology used in the classes.

Mary Pat left on a high, carrying her red balloon—not even minding some of the stares she got from people milling around in the parking area.

Back at the house she called her mother to share her good news, fixed lunch, walked Barker, and then headed to her favorite outlet mall in Pigeon Forge to shop. As her mother had said, "Go buy some new clothes for your new job and celebrate, darling." Truthfully, she would need some nicer outfits to wear for work at the center. Like Charlotte, she'd wear nice slacks, a top, and a white lab coat with her name and the Diet Options logo on it for work. Charlotte believed the lab coat added a touch of professionalism and Mary Pat agreed.

As Mary Pat was unloading shopping bags from her car later in the day, Owen slowed as he drove up the road from work to say hello. "Looks like you've been shopping," he said.

"I'm so excited," she exclaimed, skipping over to his 4Runner. "I hit goal weight today and Charlotte Hillen offered me a part-time job at the center. Isn't that fantastic?"

He winked at her and smiled. "That is fabulous news." He glanced at his watch. "Why don't I take you out to dinner to celebrate?"

She put a hand to her heart. "I would be honored. Where are you planning to take me?"

He considered her question. "How about Howard's Steak House down on the Parkway in Gatlinburg? I'd love a steak tonight and you can have a small one or grilled shrimp or chicken there. They serve great salads, too. I can give you a little of my baked potato and you can order zucchini or broccoli or something that works for you."

"You've certainly learned the things I can eat and not eat through this spring and summer of dieting." She laughed. "And Howard's sounds wonderful to me. Maybe we can sit out on the patio by the stream tonight?"

"I'll call and see if I can make a reservation." He glanced at his watch. "It's only 4:30; I got off work early. If you don't mind going right away, we'll have a better chance to find a place to park and get into Howard's ahead of the crowd. It's Saturday night and summer in the mountains. Gatlinburg can be crowded."

"I'm already dressed from being out shopping. I only need a little time to freshen up and walk Barker."

"I'll need a few minutes, too. How about if I pick you up in about fifteen minutes?" he asked. "Will that work?"

"Perfect," she said, heading into the house.

Thirty minutes later they'd driven the short distance to Gatlinburg, parked, and were now seated at one of Howard's outdoor tables with a big green umbrella sheltering it.

They'd both ordered steak tonight, Owen the Ribeye and Mary Pat a small Filet Mignon. Mary Pat liked Howard's because they offered a grilled zucchini mix she really liked and lovely salads. It bothered her less now to watch Owen eat bread and a large baked potato. She'd learned to enjoy so many other foods and her appetite and cravings for more fattening foods was down.

While they ate their salads, Mary Pat told Owen all about her job offer. "It's just perfect for me," she said. "I never dreamed Charlotte might offer me this opportunity or offer anyone an opportunity to work with her. She's run her center by herself since it started."

He smiled at her. "I doubt she's had anyone go through her program with your credentials before. She probably doesn't get many dietitians as clients."

"Do you think she might have been thinking about asking me for some time? I gathered she'd talked to her husband Rowan about it. Maybe she'd been watching me for some time, considering it."

"Charlotte doesn't strike me as an impulsive person. I'm sure she thought her offer out carefully." Owen lifted his glass of tea. "But here's to her making an excellent decision."

Mary Pat lifted her glass to his, grinning, and then frowned. "I hope I'll do all right working at the Center. I haven't worked in forever, Owen."

"You've worked in all sorts of volunteer ways. I've listened to you talk about them. It sounds to me like you did more work in some of those philanthropic and social clubs than most people do on a nine-to-five job."

"That's nice of you to say."

His eyes met hers. "Russell was unkind to you in the things he said about your social activities. Don't take those things to heart.

Charity work is important, and few people give time to it."

She stirred her salad thinking about his words. "Some things I did were important, made a difference. Others were pretty frivolous. I see that more now. I could have sought out more worthwhile activities after the kids grew older. I did, as Russell said, sort of stagnate in my life." She looked out over the creek. "I don't need to work to make money now but I want to work to make a difference. To do and be something in my own right."

"I understand that." He finished off his salad and pushed his plate to the side. "As retired military at my level, I don't need to work. But I like it. I've found pleasure again working with wood as my dad and granddad taught me, and I like working in the family business. Skills I developed in the military come in handy. Like Francine, I brought in my own set of skills to McCarter Woodcrafts. I find I'm proud now that our family continues to run this business started so long ago."

Their steaks came and they ate quietly for a time, enjoying the warm July evening, the sound of the stream, and the murmur of conversation of other couples and families around them enjoying a happy evening.

"Wonder if ole Blaze settled in okay to his new life after the park service relocated him?" Mary Pat asked.

"I ran into Roger Humphreys the other day and he said he hadn't heard any problem reports about Blaze. Maybe he'll stay out in the wild this time where he belongs."

"I hope so."

He chuckled. "A couple of years ago, a waitress dropped off an order of food to one of the tables out here on the deck and a small bear climbed right up from the creek and started helping himself to the meal. When he finished, he just politely moved right along. Didn't cause any trouble except upsetting staff and scaring a lot of tourists."

Mary Pat laughed. "That's funny. Bears are as much a part of the mountain life here as tourists. I imagine people eating here at the restaurant that night told that bear story to their family and friends for a long time after."

"Generally, bears and other wildlife in the Smokies stay about their own business." Owen cut another wedge out of his steak as he talked. "Most bears don't want to run into people any more than people want to run into them."

"Nancy and Gloria say people see few bears when hiking if they stay on the maintained trails." She giggled. "I'll tell you something funny if you won't tease me about it."

"What?"

"We tie jingle bells on our waist packs so we'll make a little more noise when hiking. Gloria is convinced making noise alerts wildlife that you're in the woods so they'll scatter."

Owen's lips twitched. "My grandmother sang on the trail and when she walked through overgrown fields and wooded areas. She had a little rhyming song she sang warning snakes and critters away. Francine probably remembers it."

"I'll ask her about it." She pushed her plate back. "I used to clean my plate and eat every bite when I went out to eat—and order a rich dessert as well. Now, unless I order light, I can't finish what I get. I usually take home half of every dinner meal anymore and then eat it for lunch or supper the next day."

"Do you still gain when you go out to eat?"

"Sometimes I'll be up a pound the next day. It's hard to control what restaurants season their food with, and they use a lot of butter, more oils, and salt. If I cut back the next day though, drink a lot of water, and eat carefully I lose that pound again." She squeezed a lemon wedge into the refill of water the waitress had brought. "People eat out so much more today than they once did. It's one reason so many more people are overweight. It's easy to overeat when you eat out and the temptation to eat more of the wrong things is hard to resist."

"Francine and Clint would like us to go out to eat sometime with them. Would that be all right with you? They're a bit older than us but not much. Clint's a lot of fun to do things with. I love how he makes my serious sister laugh so much more than she used to. She needs that."

"I'll be glad to go out with Clint and Francine one night."

He nodded. "Good. Clint and I will set something up."

"How is Larissa handling her mother having a man in her life again?"

"She's crazy about Clint. That won't be a problem." Owen bit back a smile. "We've had some interesting conversations trying to help her understand that she won't get a couple of new brothers and sisters later on with the deal, though."

Mary Pat giggled. "Nine is a little young to figure that out, I guess."

Finishing their meal, Owen paid their bill and then they made their way back to his car to start home.

They drove in the quiet, enjoying the evening, talking about this and that.

When Owen pulled up in Mary Pat's driveway, he turned off the car and turned to look at her. "I'm real happy about your job offer, Mary Pat, and sometimes I still can't believe the change in you from all the weight you've lost, looking so different than before. You stirred me up even before you lost, but I have to admit, this weight loss of yours has kicked my attraction up another level. I hope it doesn't make you mad for me to say that."

She shook her head and smiled. "No, it doesn't make me mad. Sometimes I look in the mirror with surprise myself."

"I used to have trouble keeping my mind on my homework when we studied together while in high school. Oh, I'd pretend I was reading my book, but I admit now I was studying your legs when you weren't looking or imagining kissing you or more. I have to tell you it's been a surprise to me as a middle-aged man to find those same feelings and ideas rolling through my mind."

Mary Pat looked down at her lap, not sure what to say. She didn't want to encourage Owen more than she should.

"My first thought when you told me you were taking the job with Charlotte was a happy one for me as well as for you." He reached a hand across to touch her cheek. "It meant you were staying and not leaving right away."

She turned her face to kiss his hand. "I need time, Owen, for myself and for my children. You know how shocked and hurt they've been over their father leaping into a relationship and marriage with Cherise so soon. I won't do that to them. They need time."

"I understand that, Mary Pat. I just feared you'd move away before we had the time to see what might happen between us."

She smiled at him, studying his warm eyes, his kind face. "You're a handsome man with a good heart. I'd be a fool not to let time show us what we might be together."

"You'd better watch those sweet words. A boy in a dark car with a pretty girl gets ideas."

She leaned toward him. "I don't see why we can't make this special day and special evening end in a special way."

Not needing another hint, Owen pulled Mary Pat into his arms and kissed her with a fiery passion that made her toes curl. Oh, my, he'd always been good at this even when they were teenagers, she thought, reeling in the rich feelings sweeping between them, heating her blood, and warming her heart.

She kissed him back eagerly, loving the feel of him close to her, his earthy sandalwood scent weaving around her senses.

"Oh, Owen," she said after a time, pulling back. "I am so glad life brought us back together again." She touched his face. "Did you really love me and hate to leave me when you went to West Point like Francine said?"

He kissed her again. "I almost didn't go because it nearly killed me to leave you. I did love you. Didn't I tell you so?"

"We were so young," she whispered. "We said a lot of things."

He cupped her face in his hands. "I meant those words of love I said. I hoped when I finished West Point and got settled to come look for you."

"But I met Russell."

"You did. And I met Joanna not long after." He stroked his hands through her hair. "But look how good God is. He's given us a second chance to get it right."

She laughed softly. "That's a sweet way of looking at it."

"It's how I look at it, Mary Pat."

He kissed her again and then said. "You'd better go in while I'm still acting gentlemanly."

She opened the door to get out and then paused. "Thanks for a sweet night tonight, Owen."

"It was that," he said, blowing her another kiss.

Mary Pat drifted into her old family home then, smiling like a teenager coming home from a happy date.

CHAPTER 14

A little over three months after Owen and Mary Pat ran into Clint Dawson and his sister kissing on the stairs, Clint and Francine married on a warm Sunday afternoon in late August at the Glades Community Church.

After the church service, Owen and Mary Pat mingled with the wedding guests around the new pavilion on the grounds behind the white country church.

"Everything was simply beautiful," Mary Pat said to Owen. "I'm glad it wasn't raining today, too, so the reception could be outside."

"I imagine this small event a little colloquial compared to city weddings you've probably attended." Owen gestured to his neat slacks, gray tie, and charcoal suspenders over a pinstriped shirt with a grin. He'd been Clint's best man and he, Clint's brothers, and the groom were all dressed the same. "Clint didn't want anything to do with what he termed 'monkey suits' for the men, and Francine was happy to go casual, too."

"You all look very handsome," she said, straightening his tie. "And I loved Francine's simple, white dress with that sweet lacy top and those soft gray bridesmaids dresses. What a lovely color choice. A gray and white color scheme set off the richly colored floral bouquets beautifully." She smiled. "Larissa looked cute, too, in her little white dress. I'm glad Francine let her be the flower girl for the wedding. She felt so special leading the way down the aisle as the wedding music started."

"Larissa was crazy excited for weeks about this wedding. I'm glad, too, the day was fine and fair." He led Mary Pat over to the long food table in the pavilion to get something to eat.

Maydeen Ellis, in front of them, turned to send a sunny smile their way as she filled her plate. "I just love tasting all these pretty finger foods, don't you? And don't the church tables around the lawn under the trees look pretty draped in those old white lace tablecloths loaned out by the women in the church?"

She heaped mini quiches, ham, hors d'ourvres, cheeses, chocolate drizzled bon bons, and petit fours onto her plate while she talked. "Did you know Clint's sister Glaydeen sewed every one of those floral runners you see on the tables? They look so nice with those big vases of colorful flowers. I swear, I think every woman in the church donated flowers from their garden to make everything beautiful—roses, crepe myrtle, snowballs, and anything else they could find."

"It's all gorgeous," Mary Pat assured her.

Owen noticed how carefully Mary Pat selected foods from the table, choosing meats, salads, fruits, and skipping the richer items.

"Will you sample the wedding cake?" he whispered, leaning closer to her.

She smiled at him. "I probably won't need it after all this." She skipped the rich punch, too, and pulled a chilled bottle of spring water from the tin wash tub full of ice at the end of the reception table.

As they looked for a seat, Duggan waved at them from across the yard. "I've saved you two a seat," he called.

Mary Pat walked ahead of him, giving Owen a chance to admire her from the back, noticing how her sky blue dress flirted around her legs below her knees.

Duggan got up to pull out her chair. "Lordy, woman, you get prettier every time I see you. We sure are glad you came on back to your family's place—and that you've stayed." He winked at Owen. "Maybe we can figure out a way in time to make sure you don't run off again."

Owen rolled his eyes. "Dad, watch your speculating."

He grinned at Mary Pat. "You forgive that meddlin, girl. It's just this day that's got me in a matchmaking mood with my girl and Clint getting married." He glanced across the table at Lamont Dawson, Clint's father. "Who would have thought our family would get hitched together in marriage?"

"I don't see it as odd," Lamont said, pushing back the weathered brown cowboy hat he almost always wore. "You married Idaline. She was a Dawson cousin of ours." He laughed. "Why shouldn't two good families like ours link up when they can? Makes for good breeding."

More fun-loving chitchat passed back and forth among the family members at their table. He, Mary Pat, and his father sat at the big table with an assortment of Dawsons—Clint's dad Lamont, Clint's two brothers, Wade and Tommy, their wives Evalyn and Jean, and Clint's sister Glaydeen and her husband John, also the church minister. Larissa and the other children attending the wedding were off playing and eating separate from the adults, with the service finished.

"This day really has been perfect," Glaydeen said, looking around with pleasure. "Sunny and warm. Clint and Francine look so happy, too." She smiled at Mary Pat. "I'm pleased you could be here with us."

"I wouldn't have missed it for the world," Mary Pat replied, "and you and the other church women did a beautiful job decorating. I'm so impressed."

"Thank you," Glaydeen said, pleased. She began to chat then to Mary Pat about planning and decorating for the wedding.

Owen sat enjoying time with all the family, liking the laughter and shrieks of the children playing, the warm lull of conversation around him. Across the yard he could see Francine and Clint eating at a little table in the gazebo, friends going over to visit and talk with them. Francine's face glowed in a happy way, making Owen's heart glad. She'd grieved a long time after Davis died so young.

"Where are Clint and Francine going to live now that they're married?" Evalynne asked.

Duggan answered with a big grin. "They're building themselves a fine new log home on the lot next door to me. Not too close, mind you—they need their own lives—but close enough that I can mooch some meals off Francine now and then." He laughed. "Larissa is staying with me while they take a little honeymoon trip to Florida; then they'll live at Clint's place until the new house is done. That new architect Cooper Garrison designed a nice floor plan for them and he's supervising the building of the house, I hear. They ought to get settled into their new place about March, if bad weather don't hold things up this winter."

Glaydeen grinned. "You'll be an old bachelor on your own again."

"I doubt I'll have a chance to get lonely with Francine back and forth all the time, Clint and Mary Pat up the street, Maydeen and Wheeler across the road, and Lamont dropping over."

"I heard Maydeen is going to clean for you and help a little with the cooking," John said.

"Aw, she's been doing that even while Francine lived with me. I'd say she'll be fussing over me more than I'd like." He laughed again.

After everyone finished eating, a little local band set up in the pavilion to play. The Backwoods Boys soon began to entertain everyone with a lively selection of bluegrass and dance tunes. Clint led his new wife out in a waltz when the band started playing "The Tennessee Waltz," with others soon joining in.

"Wanna dance with your old boyfriend?" Owen asked Mary Pat.

She put her hand in his in answer, and he led her into the pavilion to sweep her around, enjoying being close to her, catching the scent of gardenia in her perfume as he tucked his face nearer her neck.

"Be watchful about how cozy you get," she whispered. "We're at church, remember?"

"It's hard to keep good etiquette in mind when I get this close to you." He chuckled, but stepped back a little.

"We don't seem to have forgotten how to dance well together." She smiled up at him. "This brings back a lot of memories."

"Good ones, too." He grinned at her.

They enjoyed more dancing and visiting over the next hour or so until it was time at last to see Clint and Francine off.

He held Larissa's hand as Francine and Clint ran out of the church amid the crowd of well-wishers tossing rice on the laughing couple.

"Why does everyone throw rice?" Larissa asked.

"To wish the couple good fortune, prosperity, and a happy life." As they watched the couple climb into their car, Owen asked, "You okay about your mama marrying Clint?"

She smiled up at him. "Yes. I like Clint, and I like how he makes Mama and me laugh more. He's fun."

"Well, if you get lonesome while they're gone, you can come up and spend the night with me, you hear?"

"I'll be fine." She giggled. "Grampa has promised to do some special things with me while they're gone."

He leaned over to kiss her cheek. "You mean some spoiling that your Mama won't usually let him get away with?"

She wagged a finger at him. "Don't tell her and spoil it Uncle Owen."

"I won't. You and Grampa deserve to make a few special memories."

After Clint and Francine drove away and the crowd began to break up, Owen went to find Mary Pat. "Are you ready to head home?" he asked.

"I am. It's six now already. The afternoon has flown by."

He walked toward his truck with her. "Why don't we drive down to the Food City and pick up a big flat iron steak for me to grill at my place, some mushrooms and vegetables—like peppers, onions, new potatoes, and squash—to stick on skewers and toss on the grill, and salad makings? I'll grill the steak and the kebobs if you'll make the salad. I think that would make a perfect ending to our day, don't you?"

"That does sound nice." She smiled. "You can get one of those mini apple pies in the bakery for yourself, and I'll warm sliced apples with cinnamon, diet butter, and sweetener for my dessert. I already have whipped topping."

"Diet whipped topping, I figure."

She wrinkled her nose at him. "You know you can't tell the difference."

"Not with pie underneath." He chuckled.

At the store, they bought the groceries they needed and then headed back up the highway to the Glades.

As they pulled up in Mary Pat's driveway, Owen saw an unfamiliar car in the driveway. "Anyone you know?" he asked.

She frowned. "It looks like Victoria's car but I can't imagine what she'd be doing here on a Sunday evening."

As Mary Pat opened the truck door, a girl streaked down from the porch. "Mom, where have you been? I've been sitting out here on the porch forever."

Owen couldn't help noticing her eyes red and swollen, her face blotched, from crying.

"Honey, I've been to a wedding. I had no idea you were coming." Mary Pat hugged her daughter and then pulled back to look at her. "Whatever has happened, Victoria?"

The girl burst into tears and threw herself on her mother again.

"My life is totally over, Mother. Kevin's been cheating on me. We were talking about getting engaged and everything. We even looked at rings. Now I've found he's a horrible, awful person I could never trust." She wept some more.

Owen leaned against the car watching. Victoria was taller than Mary Pat but a beautiful girl who made him think so much of Mary Pat when younger. She had long honey-blond hair, tied back in a loose ponytail, blue-gray eyes like Mary Pat's with pretty long lashes, and a peaches and cream complexion. He noted her figure slim and curvy, too, her clothes casual but obviously expensive. Owen knew Victoria was the youngest of Mary Pat's children, twenty-five now, not long out of pharmacy school, into her first apartment and her first job. Pampered in her early life, he also knew she was still living in those youthful years of idealism before life taught you its disillusions.

"I don't know what I'm going to do, Mom," Victoria babbled

on, while crying. "I really don't. How could Kevin do that to me? How could he cheat like that? I thought he was a nice person. I trusted him."

"How do you know he cheated?" Mary Pat asked, smoothing her daughter's hair with one hand, her voice gentle.

Victoria put a hand to her throat. "I caught him. I caught both of them—Kevin with Carol, my roommate. As if it wasn't bad enough he cheated, it was with my best friend. How could she do that to me? I thought I'd die." She closed her eyes, shaking her head. "I saw them, too, and it was simply awful."

"When did this happen?"

Victoria hugged herself as if in pain. "Around lunch, I guess. I came home early from the conference. It was so boring, and I found only one session today even relevant to me. It was at eight so I went to that and then left. I changed my flight and flew on into Nashville early. I drove to our place—my apartment with Carol—and let myself in. I was trying to be quiet so I wouldn't wake Carol. She loves to sleep in on Sundays. But as I walked by her door, I heard some noise. I looked in to see if she was up, and I saw them."

She started to sob again. "Do you know how awful it is to see your best friend and your soon-to-be fiancé naked in bed together in the act? I thought I'd simply perish on the spot. I don't sleep around, Mother. You know that. I didn't think Carol did, either. We go to church together. Kevin goes with us, too. I couldn't believe what I saw. I guess I gasped or something because then they looked up and saw me."

"I'm so sorry, honey."

"They just stared at me, then they looked at each, lifted their eyebrows, said 'whoops' and started giggling. Can you believe it? They actually started giggling. Then they started scrambling for their clothes and Kevin said, 'This isn't what it looks like, Victoria. We were just having fun. It's not serious.'" Victoria's voice grew shrill. "Like that was supposed to make me feel better or something?"

"What did you do then?" Mary Pat asked softly.

"I grabbed up my bag, got in my car and drove away. Then I

came here. I couldn't stay there in Nashville. I don't ever want to see either of them again. Ever! Carol will just have to get another roommate and if she wants to nail me for rent because my name is on the lease, she can sue me." Victoria began to sob again. "They've just ruined my life, Mother. I can't even go back to work at the pharmacy tomorrow. Kevin works there with me. You know that. I can't work with him every day like nothing has happened. I simply can't!"

Mary Pat looked toward Owen, still leaning against the side of his truck. "As you can see Victoria is upset."

Victoria, as if noticing him for the first time, looked toward him, eyes widening. "Who is that? Oh, my gosh, I didn't realize you were with someone."

"This is Owen McCarter, my neighbor. I drove to the wedding with him." She patted Victoria's arm. "You met Owen when you came at Easter. It was his sister who got married today."

Her eyes moved over him.

"Owen and I stopped by the store and picked up food to make dinner." Mary Pat smoothed a hand down her daughter's arm. "Have you eaten at all today?"

"This morning before the first session I grabbed something and I ate a snack bar and a drink I picked up at a gas station along the way." She shrugged.

Mary Pat looked at Owen and smiled. "When Victoria is upset she forgets to eat; when I'm upset I want to eat to make myself feel better."

He chuckled, and then looked toward the house as they all heard the dog barking inside.

Mary Pat put an arm around Victoria. "Let's go in and let Barker out. Bless his heart. He's been alone all day. Then we'll go help Owen fix dinner and talk some more."

Owen could tell this didn't go over well with Victoria. "Look. Maybe we should take a pass on dinner for tonight," he said. "You and your daughter will want some time alone."

Her eyes met his with a plea in them. "No, we've bought dinner.

And we all need to eat. Victoria and I can talk after."

"All right," he agreed. "I'll go over to the house, take in the groceries, and start the grill. I want to get out of my dress clothes and put on some jeans."

Mary Pat glanced down at her dress. "Yes, I want to change, too, and I need to walk Barker. We'll be over in about twenty minutes. Is that okay?"

"That sounds good," he said, climbing back in the truck.

"Do I have to go?" Owen heard Victoria whisper as she and Mary Pat started up the stairs to the porch.

"Yes," Mary Pat said, and Owen liked the sound of her firm voice. As she'd mentioned, they all needed to eat.

A little later, Victoria followed her mother over to the house. They brought Barker with them, as comfortable now in Owen's house as in his own.

The girl acted subdued, and perhaps a little sullen, but she'd washed her face and cleaned up.

As Mary Pat headed into the kitchen to start making a big salad, she trailed behind her, perching at first on a stool at the island to watch them. When her mother turned to lift her eyebrows at her, Victoria faked a smile and asked, "What can I do to help?"

"There's a pretty table out on the screened porch." He gestured toward the door leading to it. "You could set the table out there. I've already put out some plates, silver, and napkins you can use."

"What are we drinking?" she asked, going to pick up the tray Owen had loaded the plates and silver on.

"Your Mom picked up some of those sparkling waters she likes and I keep sweet tea in the refrigerator. Take your pick but give me time to grill before you put the drinks out."

After she let herself out to the screened porch, Owen turned to Mary Pat. "She didn't want to come, did she?"

"No, but I *wanted* her to come. Victoria has always been the sort to get highly emotional over situations to the point of making herself sick. She'll go on and on about anything that happens, even something awful like this, not realizing she fuels the emotions to a greater degree by continuing to spew out her upset and anger, like fueling a fire. Of course, then she only gets more and more upset. When she was little I had to put her in her room to calm down when upset or angry." She smiled at him. "I know Victoria isn't pleasant company tonight but she needed a diversion to arrest that train of emotions she had going."

He glanced toward the screened porch. "I knew a lot of guys in the army who had trouble getting their emotions in check. A lot of people don't know that venting anger and troubles excessively just throws fuel on them to explode more."

Mary Pat sighed. "God bless her, though. I hate to see her hurt like this. I always liked Kevin. I could see he was a little spoiled and self-centered but so is Victoria sometimes. They're so young yet." She wrinkled her nose. "But I hadn't expected Carol to turn out to be such a snake. Those girls have been friends a long time. I'm really shocked Carol would go after Victoria's boyfriend even if he flirted with her. Girls generally share an unspoken law that they never go after each other's boyfriends."

"That law exists with men, too." Owen finished putting the last of the vegetables on the kebobs and placed them, along with the marinated flat iron steak, on a big metal tray to carry out to the grill.

After he'd grilled outdoors for a short time, Victoria came out to join him.

"You have a nice place," she said. She sat on a bench on the patio and looked out at the woods.

"Where's your mom?"

"In the house making some kind of diet dessert." She made a face.

Owen grinned as he turned the steak. "I've eaten that apple dessert she makes. It's surprisingly good."

"Maybe, but I noticed you bought deli apple pie for yourself."

"The store bakery has good pie." He walked over to sit down beside her on the bench. "I'll share mine with you."

A smile twitched her lips. "Thanks."

She sat silently for a few minutes and then said, "Why would Kevin do something like he did? You're a man like him. Why would he cheat like that and with my best friend in my own apartment? It's just so gross."

He considered her words. "First, I'd like to think I'm *not* a man like Kevin. I hope I would never act as he did, and I'm sorry for the way he treated you. It must hurt like a knife to the heart."

She winced. "It does."

He got up to turn the skewers on the grill.

"What am I going to do Mr. McCarter? I'm supposed to go back to work at the pharmacy tomorrow. I signed a lease with Carol on the apartment." Tears dribbled down her cheeks again.

"It's Owen," he said. "And do you really want my advice?"

She nodded. "I could use an outside view."

"All right. I'd call the head pharmacist you work for, tell him a difficult family situation came up, making you need to come home unexpectedly. Tell him you're sorry but that you need a week off." He turned to look at her. "You wouldn't be lying to say that."

She thought about his words. "Mr. Remmick is an older man and really sweet. I think he would be understanding."

"It's a chance you might need to take." He smiled at her. "I imagine he knows you and Kevin have been seeing each other. Tell him Kevin will probably cover some of your shifts."

She actually laughed. "That's a great idea. I'm sure Kevin doesn't want Mr. Remmick to know why I'm really taking a week off."

"During your week off, you can look for another job if you want. I imagine there are other pharmacy jobs out there if you decide you really don't want to go back."

She shook her head. "I just can't imagine myself working side by side with Kevin Walsh now. Seeing him every day, working behind the counter with him. It makes my skin crawl to think about it."

"Most people want to avoid a person once they realize they're a snake."

"Boy, that's the truth." She sighed. "What about Carol?"

"I'd say Carol has shown you what she is, too. She isn't someone you want to continue sharing your life with either."

"What about the lease?"

"Text her and tell her she'd better find someone to sublease with her. Suggest she and Kevin split your part of the rent until she finds somebody."

She giggled. "That's a great idea, too."

"I don't imagine Carol will push too hard on you to fulfill the lease after what she's done. She'll know she forced you out. I think she'll find a way to deal with it. If she threatens you, talk to an attorney. Most apartment leases can be terminated early if both parties agree. Landlords are used to these situations." He turned the meat and skewers a final time. "I doubt Carol will push on you to come back. She probably realizes it would be awkward."

She groaned. "It would be the worst."

He looked at her. "Do you want to stay in Nashville?"

"Not after this." She rolled her eyes.

"Look for jobs near your dad, your brothers, or around here. You'd have someone to live with for a time while you resettle and find a new place to live."

"That's smart, but yuk—I could never live with Dad and that awful Cherise." She pushed a strand of her hair back. "I could live with Mom for awhile while I look, though."

"If you'll be nice to her." He leveled a stern glance at her.

"What?" Her eyes widened.

"You heard me. You too often talk disrespectfully to your mother and don't treat her with the kindness she deserves."

She put her hands on her hips. "You have no right to say that to me."

"Don't get on your high horse. I mean no offense, but if you're honest, you know I'm telling the truth. All I'm saying is that you're a grown woman now and it's time you started acting like one." He began taking the meat and skewers of cooked vegetables off the grill now. "My dad can be crotchety, interfering, and irritating at times, but I treat him with respect none the less. He's my father; he birthed and raised me and there is much to admire in him. At an earlier time in my life, I acted less wisely."

Owen turned toward her. "You've just experienced an ugly hit in life. I'm real sorry for it. People can hurt and disappoint you worse than anything else in life, and I know of what I speak. But then you look around and see the people that love you, that are in your camp, on your team. You treasure them more then. You'll find your mother is one of those on your team. Good, honest, loving, kind. I've known her since we were kids. Loved her when we grew a little older, too. She's someone you can count on all through your life, Victoria."

She studied him, a considering look in her eyes. "Do you still love my mother?"

"If I do it's my thought to keep because it isn't your mother's time to love again yet. Like you, she's been through a hurt and a betrayal. She's trying to heal, deciding if it's safe to trust anyone with her heart again. I'm sure you know the feeling." He scraped off the grill a little, put the tools on his tray, and placed the lid back on the grill. "A lot of time has passed in your mother's and my life since we were young like you. But now that she's on her own, I watch out for her."

She moved a little closer to him. "Will you watch out for me a little, too?" she asked in a soft voice. "I think my father's forgotten how."

"I will do that," he said, leaning over to kiss her on the forehead. "Now let's go and eat this nice dinner."

As they ate on the porch, Victoria told her mother her plans to call Mr. Remmick to ask for a week off and to text Carol to start looking for another roommate. She explained that she thought she'd start looking for another pharmacy job to avoid returning to work with Kevin again, too.

"Well, it sounds like you've thought things out well." Mary Pat smiled at her. "Those are good ideas."

"Owen helped me think things through," she acknowledged, pushing a few more vegetables off her skewer to eat. She looked up and smiled. "This dinner is so good. I didn't realize how hungry

I was."

Owen watched Mary Pat try to hold back a small smile.

"Victoria has talked me into sharing my apple pie with her, too," Owen said. "It's a sacrifice, but I think I can manage it."

The atmosphere lightened a little then.

Before they started dessert, Victoria slipped out of the room for a few minutes. When she came back, she said, "I called Mr. Remmick at home. He was nice and said they'd manage without me this week. He only works part-time, so he said he can fill in my hours with Kevin's help."

Victoria sat down at the table again. "I texted Carol, too. I didn't want to talk with her. She texted back a bunch of apologies and stuff, trying to make excuses, but she did say she thought she knew another friend who'd like to move in with her." She gave her mother a hopeful look. "Would you mind if I stay with you this week, Mom?"

Mary Pat smiled. "Surely you don't even need to ask," she said.

"To be frank I'm going to start looking for another job this week. I simply can't go back and work that closely around Kevin at the pharmacy." She frowned. "It would be worse than awful."

"You'll find your way," Mary Pat said, reaching a hand across the table to pat her daughter's hand.

"I hope so; right now I feel like I'd just like to die."

As Victoria and Mary Pat started out the door a little later to head home, Victoria held back a moment while Mary Pat walked down the steps with Barker.

"Thanks for talking to me, Owen," she said softly, so Mary Pat couldn't hear. "Can I come see you if I need to talk about anything else?"

"Sure," he said, and then watched her move on down the steps to start across the lawn. As he went back in the house, he thought about Garrett and all he'd missed not having children of his own. Not having more moments like this to impact young lives for the good.

CHAPTER 15

The next day, Nancy Sue knocked on the door at Diet Options a few minutes after closing at noon. Charlotte had left and Mary Pat was finishing cleaning up and getting ready to leave herself.

"Hi, sweetie." She smiled at Mary Pat when she unlocked the door. "I hoped to catch you before you left. I'm off today and thought you might like to go hiking. If you haven't had lunch, we can pack a light lunch to take with us on the trail."

Mary Pat gestured her friend inside for a moment and relocked the front door. "I'd love that, but my daughter Victoria came home last night. I probably need to spend the afternoon with her."

Nancy's eyes lit up. "Honey, she can go with us. It would be fun. Or maybe we can all go out to lunch together. I'd love to see her. I don't think I've seen her since she was a little thing."

"Come sit down a minute." Mary Pat sat on one of the sofas in the waiting area. "Victoria just had a boyfriend cheat on her and a girlfriend betray her. This is kind of a rough time for her."

"Oh, my goodness. What happened?" Nancy settled beside her.

Mary Pat related the story to her briefly.

"Well, bless her heart." Nancy shook her head in sympathy. "That's a hard thing for a young girl to experience." She hesitated. "Maybe Dean will know someone at one of the pharmacies around the area who's looking for an employee. I'll go talk to him and let you know."

"I know Victoria would appreciate that. So would I."

After locking up again, Mary Pat drove home. At the house, she found Victoria sitting at the dining room table working on her laptop.

"Hi, Mom." She looked up and smiled. "I still can't get used to the idea of you working. You've always been home."

"That's true." Mary Pat dropped her purse on a side table and sat down at the table with her daughter.

"I know you told me last night how much you liked your job. As I told you, I'm so impressed you took charge of your life after Dad asked for a divorce." She glanced down at her laptop. "I realize more now how you must have felt, what a hard time that was. Kevin and I had only been serious since I graduated and started working at the pharmacy with him. But you and Dad had been married and together forever."

"Time heals somehow. Like you, I wanted to just hole up and die after it happened. But every morning I woke up again, still alive, and gradually found a way to go on."

"And now you're happy again. Aren't you?"

"Surprisingly, I am." She glanced toward Victoria's laptop. "What are you working on?"

"I updated my resume this morning and started searching for pharmaceutical jobs."

"Found anything interesting?"

"A few possibilities. None close to you but one near Patrick in Charleston that looks interesting. I'm sure, like Owen said, something will open up."

"We also need to think about going to Nashville to get your things."

Victoria smiled. "Actually, I thought about that earlier, too. You remember Carol's grandmother gave us furniture for the living and dining room area in our apartment, so regardless of how I feel about Carol, that furniture is hers. You remember Carol's grandmother was moving to a smaller home because her granddad died, so she gave us kitchen things, too—even bathroom towels. All I bought was a bedroom set."

"That's right. I remember when I came over to help you girls move from the dorm at school that you didn't have to buy much."

"No, and I called Todd today and asked if he and Allison wanted my bedroom furniture. They're buying a house, since they're getting married at the end of this month." She drummed her fingers on the table. "It would cost more for me to move that one room of furniture here than it's worth, but I will need to go get my clothes and other things."

"I'll drive over with you. We can take some boxes and pack everything easily—your television, personal items, pictures, and such. Todd can come up to help us load the car."

"Thanks, Mom. I admit I dread facing the memories there, facing Carol and possibly Kevin. Does that sound cowardly?"

Mary Pat shook her head. "No. When your father asked me for a divorce, I was so shocked and hurt. I cried and sobbed all afternoon, and then looked around and panicked at the idea of spending the night alone in that house by myself with all the memories. I got in my car and drove here."

She nodded. "I remember. Gigi came up to stay with you a couple of weeks then. She was so mad at Dad."

"I'm grateful for her support at that time. I really needed it."

Victoria reached across the table to put a hand on hers. "I'm grateful for your help right now, Mom."

The doorbell rang and Nancy Richardson opened the screened door to lean in. "Can I come in?'

"Sure," Mary Pat said. "Did I leave something behind?"

"No, but I'm so excited. I just had to come right over." She bounced across the room and leaned over to give Victoria a hug. "Look at you, darling. You're just as beautiful as your mother. I'm so tickled to meet you. I'm Nancy Sue, Mary Pat's best friend since we were girls.""

Nancy gave Mary Pat a hug, too, and then sat down at the table with them. "I have the best news, so I had to come over to bring it myself. Remember I told you I'd asked Dean if he knew anyone looking for a pharmacist? Well, he does."

"Oh, wonderful," Victoria said. "You're so kind to help me."

Nancy put her hands together with excitement. "Well, I hope you'll still say that when I tell you the job is at our drug store, Smoky Mountain Pharmacy. Dean and Brock have been handling everything, where most pharmacies, even smaller ones like ours, have three or four pharmacists to fill prescriptions and work behind the counter. Dean's tickled you're already living in the area. He and Brock just contacted East Tennessee State, where Brock got his pharmaceutical degree, for possible employee names and they were even working on an ad, too."

Mary Pat watched Victoria's face, deciding to leave the decision of whether to pursue a job with the Richardson's pharmacy totally to her.

"I'd love to talk to them about the position," Victoria said. "The pharmacy I worked with in Nashville was a small independent one versus one of those big grocery store or chain store pharmacies. I really liked the community feeling of it. Should I call to make an appointment to come in to talk with your husband? To see if he thinks I have the credentials and experience he's looking for? I know the way everyone gets along together in a pharmaceutical business, especially a small one, is important. You know he'll want to talk to me, check my resume and credentials, and contact my references before making a decision."

Nancy pointed to Victoria's laptop. "Do you have your resume and information on your computer?"

She smiled. "I do. I spent the morning updating my resume and references."

"Can you email it over to Dean?" Nancy pulled a card out of her pocket. "Here's his card with the email address. I told him I'd try to get you to send it right on over."

Victoria studied the card. "I'll be pleased to do that."

"Honey, if you could send it on right now, we can run over to the store and you can meet Dean and Brock and look around the pharmacy to see if it would be a work place you'd like. I know you've been living in downtown Nashville. A pharmacy, no matter how nice, in a small place like Gatlinburg might not be your cup of tea. It won't hurt our feelings one bit if that's so."

"It might be good if you did go over and check out the pharmacy," Mary Pat put in. "If it isn't what you have in mind, Dean won't need to contact your references and everything."

Victoria glanced down at herself. "I'll need to change from these shorts into something a little more suitable."

"You can hook up your laptop to my printer and print your resume and reference list to take with you if you'd like," Mary Pat suggested. "While you're doing that and getting dressed, I can fix us some lunch. Nancy, do you want to eat with us?"

"Well, shoot. I was hoping to take you both out to lunch after we go by the pharmacy, Mary Pat." She leaned toward them, grinning. "Maybe we'll have something to celebrate at lunch."

Victoria smiled at her. "I'm sure your husband will want some time to consider whether he wants to hire me or not, Nancy. But I'd love to go to lunch and I'd like for it to be my treat since you've been so nice to help me."

Nancy put a hand to her heart. "See? I knew it. She's just as sweet as you are, Mary Pat." She went over to give Victoria another hug. "Honey, I have the feeling this is going to be the beginning of a good new time for you. You know your mama went through a hard time this year, and I lost my husband when only about your age. I had Brock then, too, just a little thing. We've both known hard times, but we got through them."

"I'm still kind of in the train wreck stage now, working my way past the shock." Victoria made a face and shrugged. "You know."

"Yes, and a new job and keeping busy is exactly what you need, darling. Trust me. Sittin' around and stewing and feeling sorry for yourself never helped anyone. I didn't have any choice but to go right to work after Bobby died. Looking back, though, I know that was the best thing I could have done." She patted Victoria on the cheek. "And if you have a bad day or cry or anything at work, we'll just give you a tissue."

Victoria giggled.

Mary Pat laughed, too. "Nancy, come in the kitchen and we'll get a glass of tea to drink while Victoria prints out her paperwork and changes clothes."

At the Smoky Mountain Pharmacy a short time later, Mary Pat watched with pleasure how the warm-hearted and fatherly Dean Richardson took her daughter in hand, making her feel welcome and wanted.

He looked down at her paperwork he'd been studying. "Honey, I was hoping to get someone with your credentials and experience for the store, but I sure didn't count on getting a pretty girl to look at every day as a bonus. Mercy, I'll have to remind myself I'm a well-married man and I'm sure Brock will be tickled to enjoy your fine looks along with all these high grades, skills, awards, and experience you bring. My, my, I feel blessed we learned you were visiting here and job searching."

Dean was white-haired now and partially bald, but tall and still fit, with a warm smile and an easy manner. Brock, Dean's stepson and Nancy's boy, must favor his father—so much taller than Nancy, with sun-browned hair, dark blue eyes, and broad shoulders. Mary Pat noticed his good looks wasn't lost on Victoria, either, and when Dean led her around the pharmacy on a tour, she saw Brock's eyes follow her with admiration.

Nancy leaned over to whisper to her. "They'd make a cute couple, don't you think? I was so excited about getting Dean some help here at the drug store, so we can take a little trip now and then, that I didn't even stop to consider those two are about the same age and both single."

Mary Pat pushed at her friend's shoulder. "Victoria is just getting over hurt and betrayal. She's not ready to think about getting involved with anyone again."

"Honey, your girl's young. They move past these upsets of the heart a lot faster than we did from losing husbands. Don't you remember how we'd weep and carry on over the loss of a boyfriend in high school and then be dating someone new by the next week?"

"You're so crazy. But I will agree your son is a fine-looking man." She watched Victoria laugh with Dean across the store.

"Your husband is a sweetheart, too. I love how nice he's being to Victoria."

"I'll tell you this, if Dean's being nice and welcoming it's because he's checked out her resume and likes what he saw. And because he likes your girl. He looks for employees for the store who are comfortable and easy with themselves and with others. I know that man, and he likes Victoria."

"She seems to like him."

"Nancy," he called out. "Why don't you and Mary Pat go over to the coffee shop and get a cup of coffee from Cali? I want to spend some more time with Victoria if it's all right, talk shop."

A little later Victoria came over to find them, beaming. "Dean and Brock think I'd be a great fit for the pharmacy. And I really love it here." She slid onto a stool beside them at the counter. "I've been offered a job, Mom, if everything checks out well. Do you think I could live with you for a time?"

"Of course," Mary Pat said, leaning over to give her a hug. "I'd love that. And I'm so pleased if you like the pharmacy here."

"I just knew it." Nancy clapped her hands. "Girls, I just couldn't be more excited."

"Cali," she called to the tall young woman working behind the counter. "Come meet Mary Pat's daughter, Victoria Latham. It looks like she's going to be working with Brock and your daddy at the pharmacy." She turned to Victoria. "Cali is Dean's daughter and became my girl, too, when Dean and I, two widowers, married when she and Brock were only kids."

The young woman flashed a wide smile at them as she walked over. "I'll be tickled to have some more female company around here." She held out her hand to Victoria. "I'm Cali Richardson Branam. Welcome to the Glades, if you're just moving here."

"Oh, I hadn't looked at the coffee shop yet." Victoria's eyes moved around the cute café and then to the billboard of coffee selections available. "I can already tell I'll be a regular here every day."

Nancy stood up. "Listen, you girls can get acquainted later. Right now, I want to take Mary Pat and Victoria to lunch. We're all about to starve, and I have the perfect place in mind for us to go to for a little celebration time."

Mary Pat started to get her keys out as they walked toward the door.

"I'm driving, Mary Pat," Nancy insisted. "It's a pretty sunny day, and I'm putting the top down on my little yellow convertible and we're going to sing our way down to Bubba Gump Shrimp Co. on the Parkway in Gatlinburg. I am craving some of their coconut shrimp." She waved a finger at Mary Pat. "And don't you be reading the calorie count to me, do you hear? I know I'm splurging a little. You can get boiled shrimp and a nice salad, and Miss Victoria can order any little thing her heart desires."

She led them over to her bright yellow Mustang. "You girls climb on in and we'll be off. Life sends some bad things our way sometimes but just look at this day today. Warm and sunny, and here we are fit and healthy when so many others aren't so blessed and lucky." She smiled at Mary Pat. "I've got my best friend back in the mountains with me again." She kissed Victoria as she climbed into the back seat. "And now I've got her pretty girl to love on as well. It don't get no better, girls."

Nancy backed out of the parking lot, laughing. Then she turned on the radio, popped a CD in the tape player and soon started singing along with "Footloose" by Kenny Loggins.

Later that evening, Victoria looked up from scrolling through Facebook. "I had a great day today. I still can't believe it."

Mary Pat lifted her eyes from the book she was reading to smile at her daughter. "I'm so happy a job opportunity opened up so quickly."

"Almost as good today was spending time with your friend Nancy. Gosh, she's fun. Why haven't I ever met her before?"

"We sort of lost touch through the years. I went off to college, met Russell, and Nancy stayed. She got married right out of high school, had Brock. Our lives seemed to go in different directions."

A little smile twitched over Victoria's face. "Brock is really good looking, don't you think?"

Mary Pat grinned. "He is that. Even a girl my age would need to be blind not to notice."

Victoria laughed. "See, Mom? Even you've become more fun since you came here." She made a face. "You'd gotten a little stuffy back in Knoxville and your friends were all so ..." Her words trailed off.

"Plastic? Snobby?"

"I didn't say that." Victoria's eyes widened. "Don't get mad, Mom."

"I'm not mad. I thought many of those women were my best friends, but when my social status changed, they dropped me—seemingly without any remorse."

"Ouch. Even your Monday Group friends? You'd known them forever."

"It was a neighborhood group. Once I moved out of the neighborhood, they lost interest in keeping up with me." She put a bookmark in her novel and shut it. "I got ousted rather curtly from the doctors' wives group I'd belonged to for nearly thirty years as well. One of the members let me know Cherise applied for membership even before the ink was dry on the divorce papers."

Victoria made a face. "Gosh, I'm sorry, Mom."

"I know it hurt when Carol treated you the way she did. You and Carol had been friends a long time, too."

Victoria sighed. "In some ways it hurt more finding out Carol was a creep than it did learning Kevin was a scumbag. Somehow you expect your women friends to stay true."

"That's the truth." Mary Pat picked up her glass of tea from the table beside her to take a sip. "When I ran into Nancy and Gloria, I didn't feel happy to see them. They were both a little shocked at the change in me. But Nancy came over here to the house before the day was over, got me to laughing and reminiscing, and let me know she was tickled to have me back. She was always my best friend, Victoria. I was foolish not to hold on to that tie. She's reminded me what a real friend is supposed to be like. She and Gloria both."

"I'll look forward to meeting Gloria. The three of you used to twirl together, didn't you?"

"Yes. Those were good times."

Victoria looked thoughtful. "My best friends all the way through Webb School were Dana Riley, Isabel Everbach, me, and Anna Burnette. We called ourselves the DIVAs for the letters in our first names. We all danced in ballet and tap together. Gosh, we had good times."

Mary Pat smiled. "I remember sewing a lot of sequins on some of those tap dance costumes and hosting many spend the night parties at our house."

"We had matching T-shirts made that said The DIVAs on them. I think I still have mine."

"Have you kept up with those girls?"

"Sort of." She shrugged. "We all went off to different colleges, but I think they all still live around the East Tennessee area."

"Maybe you should reach out and try to get together again."

"I'd like that. It would be fun to spend a long weekend together in a mountain cabin up here in the Smokies."

A little later Mary Pat took Barker for a walk before heading to bed. Across the street she could still see a light on at Owen's. It wouldn't be easy for them to share impromptu times together any more with Victoria here. In addition, Mary Pat knew her daughter would be quick to pick up on any feelings between her and Owen if Victoria spent enough time around them.

"I wanted to wait before getting more involved with Owen," she told Barker. "Now, I'll not only have to wait, I'll need to be careful, too." Although she was the one who told Owen she'd need a long wait, she admitted she'd miss those sweet moments that sometimes flared to life between them.

CHAPTER 16

Owen felt glad to see his home again after being away for a few days at a woodworking trade show in Atlanta. He'd driven home this Monday morning after four days at the show. After putting his gear away and grabbing a bite of lunch he headed out to his 4Runner to head down to the store. As he did, he glanced over to see Mary Pat working in the flowerbed in front of her house, Barker tied on his lead by the porch.

He walked over to say hello before heading to work. "It's a nice afternoon to be outside."

She looked up from where she sat on the grass. "Yes, it is, and not as hot now that September is here. I thought I'd put out some pansies to enjoy through the fall." She dropped another plant into the hole she'd dug, patting soil around it.

Owen petted Barker and then sat on the porch steps beside her. "I haven't seen you for a while."

"I needed to make a quick trip with Victoria to Nashville to get her things and then we drove back again for Todd's wedding in Hendersonville the next week." She lifted another pansy plant out of its container to settle into a hole she'd dug with her trowel. "Of course, Victoria had to go shopping for new clothes for her job at the pharmacy, too, when we got back. You know how girls that age are—they never seem to have enough clothes or shoes."

He laughed. "Larissa is starting to lean in that direction already and she's only turned ten. She was showing me new clothes and school items about a week ago when I had dinner at Clint and

Francine's place."

"How are Clint and Francine doing? I haven't seen either of them since they married."

"Both are still in those lovey-dovey stages." He grinned. "It seems funny to see my old bachelor friend Clint so smitten—and with my own sister."

"Well, that's a happy situation. Did they enjoy their honeymoon?"

"They did." He scratched Barker behind the ears. "They brought back a stack of photos I'm sure they'd be delighted to show you."

"I've heard about those pictures." She giggled. "Wheeler was so excited to see them. He's trying to talk his mother into a trip to the beach now."

"Actually, I'd like to see Maydeen get a little break like that; Wheeler, too. They live a pretty simple life."

"Hmmm. You know Mom and Dad own a rental in Florida near their house. I'm sure they'd let Maydeen and Wheeler come down to stay for a week." She wiped some dirt off her hands. "They could cook most of their meals in and would only need gas money and a little spending money with a free place to stay."

He smiled at her. "If you could work that out with your folks, Dad and I will see to it that Maydeen gets a week off and some spending cash if we can talk her into taking it."

She laughed. "Wheeler will be so excited. He told me he's never seen the ocean. So often we have so many more blessings than we realize in life."

"We do." He studied her tan legs, remembering last winter when she'd never have dreamed of being seen out in public anywhere in shorts. "You're keeping your weight off well."

"I'm in maintenance now." She put another plant into the ground. "Working with the dieters every day keeps me conscientious about my eating habits. They watch your life as an example. When they see you succeeding, know you've lost weight, are keeping it off and building a new healthier lifestyle, it inspires them to do the same. I'll never forget what an impact it had on me when Charlotte showed me her "before" photo taken when she was heavily overweight. I couldn't help thinking that if she could do it, so could I."

"You're liking your job."

"I admit I love it and Charlotte is letting me teach some of the introductory classes, too." She paused. "I started my first college course to update my credentials. The class meets one afternoon a week, and Charlotte got approval through the nutrition department at the university for my work at the center to count as my internship."

"That's good."

She paused to look up at him before digging another hole with her trowel. "Maydeen said you went to a woodworking fair in Atlanta."

"Yeah, it's a major woodworking trade show. I mostly go to look for wood products and tools we might need for business." He shifted on the step to get more comfortable. "I enjoy even more going to the Wood Pro Expos where professional woodcarvers congregate. Those fairs offer classes and workshops along with an opportunity to get new ideas for the business."

"While you were gone, I bought one of those beautiful walking sticks you made at the store. I wanted a lightweight one I could use on rougher trails with a lot of creek crossings, and I love the colorful paracord grips you put on each stick. Gloria and Nancy bought one of your walking sticks, too. Gloria's stick has a brown grip, Nancy's red, and mine blue. That way we never get them mixed up."

"I feel flattered that you all like them." He smiled. "The paracord I use is actually parachute cord, a lightweight nylon rope used as a general purpose utility cord in the military. It's strong and holds up well. I like having something under my hand on a walking stick to grip when I hike."

"So do I." She sat back and looked up at him, her voice softening. "I miss coming over to the shop to watch you work, and I miss our dinners out and little times together."

"I figured out you were keeping your distance knowing Victoria would be scrutinizing your activities now that she's here." He chuckled. "I think I've seen more of her than of you the last month."

Her eyes widened.

"She likes to come over to visit and talk—mostly when you're gone."

"I didn't know that."

"Well, don't tell her, and don't think more of her interest than what it is. She seems to be substituting me for a father figure right now. Basically told me that."

Mary Pat looked wistful. "That's sweet. Victoria was always sort of a Daddy's girl; I know she misses her father. He reaches out to her so little now."

"She told me he ended up coming to Todd's wedding."

"Yes." She made a face. "Todd refused to allow Cherise to come to the wedding at all. It caused some nasty scenes between Todd and his father, but Todd stood his ground. Russell kept saying he wouldn't come without Cherise, but in the end, he drove over for the day. He wore a tux, even helped to greet and usher. He also stayed for the family photos and he hung around for the reception before starting home."

"Victoria said he had a good time. She also said he looked sad."

"Well, I'm sure he endured an ugly scene with Cherise over coming. He said as much to several."

"Victoria also said his eyes about fell out when he saw you at the wedding."

A smile twitched across her face. "He did seem to do a double take. The last time he saw me I weighed over two hundred and ten pounds. I have changed a bit."

Owen laughed out loud. "I'd love to have seen his face."

She finished putting the last pansy plant in the bed and began to gather up her tools and the empty plant pots. "I guess I'd better clean up here." She brushed off her shorts and stood up. "Thanks for stopping by to talk with me."

"It's been hard to stay away." He walked closer and put a hand on her face.

She turned her mouth to kiss his palm and he leaned in to kiss her then, softly and sweetly. "You're so precious to me. I hope you know how much," he whispered as he pulled away from her.

Mary Pat put her hands on his shoulders and leaned forward to kiss him back. "Maybe now that you and Victoria are getting closer, we can share some dinners and times together—the three of us."

"When she sees the way I look at you sometimes, Mary Pat, she'll figure out how I feel. She's a smart girl. Will you mind?"

She threaded her hand through his hair. "I imagine she'll notice how I look at you sometimes, too. But I think I'm ready for her to notice now." She smiled. "Mostly because I've missed you more than I imagined I would."

"Oh, those are sweet words." He gathered her closer and kissed her again, letting his hands roam a little familiarly through her hair and down her back.

She pushed him away after a moment. "Owen, we're right out here in the front yard," she whispered, straightening her hair. "Anyone could see us."

"We do live at the end of a dead end street, Mary Pat." He glanced at the dog. "I doubt Barker would tell anyone, but I admit we'd be in trouble if Wheeler wandered up this way and caught us."

She laughed. "You'd better get back to work, and I need to go do some laundry before Victoria comes home."

"Think about coming over to share dinner on Friday night—you and Victoria," he said. "I'd like to grill ribs and corn on the cob."

"Ummm, that sounds good, but you know I can't eat all that sweet barbeque sauce you'll probably put on the ribs."

"I know. I can put a little dry rub and some of that diet dressing on yours."

"Good." She smiled at him. "I'll make slaw and green beans."

"I'm heating garlic bread, too, and Maydeen's promised me a homemade pecan pie, so you'd better bring something in that area to suit yourself."

"I will." She unhooked Barker's leash and turned to start up the porch steps.

Owen watched her from the behind, and as if sensing it, she turned to wave at him. "See you on Friday if not sooner."

Owen walked to his 4Runner with a lighter step and whistled all the way down Highland Drive to the shop.

"You're in a good mood," Maydeen said.

"I am, and I'm looking forward to that pecan pie you said you'd make me this week."

She laughed. "I get off early on Thursday. I'll make it then and send Wheeler to bring it to you."

As he started back through the store, Maydeen called after him, "Your dad is looking for you. He said to tell you when you came back to walk over to the construction site where they're working on Clint and Francine's house."

He scowled. "I have work to do in the store, some products to unbox and get out on the shelves."

She shook her head. "I imagine it will wait. You know how your father is when he gets something on his mind. Noble is in the back caning chairs today for a customer. We'll mind things all right until you get back."

Resigned, he said, "Okay. I'll run up to the office and check for messages and then head over to the site."

A short time later, Owen headed out the back door, crossed the log bridge over the small creek, and started across the back of the McCarter farm property. An old trail wound from behind the family farmhouse up into the woods and to the site on the ridge where Clint and Francine were having their new house built.

Owen had watched the building crew clear the land earlier, and now he could see, as he drew closer, that the home's foundation was complete and the basic house framed. He saw his dad sitting on a rough bench under a big maple that the crew had obviously erected as a spot to rest on.

"You took your time getting here," his father said, frowning at him.

"I had to drive home from Atlanta if you remember and then went home to unpack, get some lunch, and take care of a few things before heading to the store." He walked over to sit down by his dad. "Is anything wrong? If so you should probably talk about it with Clint and Francine and not with me."

His dad waved at a young man by the construction site, who waved back and started toward them.

"I got somebody I want you to meet."

The young man, dressed in jeans, a tan golf shirt, and a Garrison Homes ball cap, came over with a smile.

As the boy drew closer, Owen saw his father watching him carefully instead of the boy. "You don't recognize him, do you? I'm not surprised. It's been a long time."

The young man stopped in front of them, his look expectant.

"Owen, this is Garrett McCarter, Joanna's son. His mom never did change his last name, which I was pleased to learn."

Owen instinctively put a hand to his heart, totally shocked to see his boy again, now a man and grown so tall.

Duggan, Owen's dad, chuckled. "Garrett, you've rendered him speechless. He'll come around here in a minute or two and find his tongue."

Owen studied the boy a moment longer, then stood, reaching out to shake his hand. "You've turned out to be a fine looking man, Garrett."

A look of yearning in the boy's eyes made Owen forget the formalities and move forward to hug him. "You were once the brightest spot in my life, son," he told him honestly. "I can't tell you what a joy it is to see you again."

He saw the boy make an effort not to get tears in his eyes. "I'm sorry we didn't stay in touch more, that my mother didn't encourage it."

"Well, life is what it is." Owen stepped back. "What brings you here all the way from out west?"

"The boy's taken a job as architect for Cooper Garrison's log home business. He'll be living here in Tennessee now," Duggan answered.

Owen could hardly think what to say. It was such an odd twist of fate.

Duggan stood up. "You two need to talk. Catch up. I suggest you take Garrett up to your house where you can talk in private. I'll go back to the store to cover things there."

Owen started to make an excuse, that he had a lot to catch up with after his trip, but his father gave him a steely look before he could say anything. "Trust me, son, that you need to do what I suggest this time. Garrett has already cleared it with Cooper Garrison to take some time off this afternoon, as well. You two go have a catch up. It's important."

Garrett cleared his throat. "If you could see a little time clear, sir, I agree it would be a good idea."

Yielding to the inevitable, Owen conceded. "We can walk up to my place if you'd like. It's only a block or so further. Or we can walk back down to the store and get my 4Runner."

"I wouldn't mind the walk," the boy said.

Owen turned to his dad as Duggan began to walk down the trail toward the store. "Dad, I'll come down later and help you close, catch you up on contacts I made on the trip, and things I ordered for us."

"Take your time," he said, heading into the woods.

Garrett spoke to the men on the site to let them know he was leaving, and then led the way around the construction site to the driveway.

He hesitated there. "We can take my little Jeep Wrangler if you'd like." He glanced over to an Army green jeep parked in the grass."

Owen couldn't help grinning. "Yeah, I'd like that. I'll feel like I'm back in the military riding in that jeep, except the Navy jeeps were usually gray." He walked over to study the vehicle. "Nice jeep."

"It's a Rubicon. It's good for getting around in the mountains."

Owen pulled himself into the passenger seat. "Just follow the road to its end and swing left into the driveway at the end of the street. That's my place, the rustic red-barn looking home."

"I've noticed it," Garrett said, gunning the jeep to start out of the gravel driveway.

They rode in silence for a time and then Garrett said, "Your dad said all this land from the main road to your place and beyond it to Providence Ridge is McCarter land. He told me you built your house on the burned out ruins of your great grandparents' original home-site."

"That's true. The old log home, that burned to the ground, was built by my great grandparents, Wiley Garrett McCarter and Sally Ownby McCarter. Their son Owen married Francis Anne Weber and built the big white farmhouse by the store on the lower farm property. They birthed one son, Duggan, my father, before dying of influenza one winter. Wiley and Sally had moved down to live with Owen and Francis at the farmhouse after their home burned, and after my grandparents died, Wiley and Sally raised my Dad."

"My name Garrett came from Wiley Garrett's name, didn't it? And my middle name Dawson came from your mom's family. Right?"

"That's right," Owen answered, wondering why it mattered to the boy.

They pulled into Owen's driveway and both climbed out of the car.

He led Garrett into the house, watching his easy stride with interest.

"I've wanted to see this place," Garrett said. "Cooper told me Garrison Homes built this house for you."

"They did."

"It looks great," he said, looking around with the eye of an architect.

"Would you like a cola?" Owen asked.

"Yes. Thanks."

Owen grabbed a couple of icy drinks from the refrigerator and handed one to Garrett. "Come over and make yourself comfortable," he said, walking over to the grouping of sofas and chairs around the big rock fireplace.

Sitting down, Owen knew he'd need to ask about Joanna, but he hated doing it. "How's your mother?" he asked at last.

"She died this summer," he said.

"I'm sorry." He hesitated. "And how's your father?"

"I haven't seen him in almost twenty years."

Owen knew his eyes popped open in surprise.

"He divorced my mom when I was nine or ten. We moved from out west back to Blacksburg, Virginia, where my mother's parents live. You may remember them."

Owen thought for a minute. "Frank and Polly Gillespi, I think. They came out west a few times, once for the wedding, another time when you were born, probably other times when I was gone. I think Frank was in engineering and Polly…." He tried to remember.

"My grandmother stayed at home, and when we moved back, she kept me while my mother worked at the hospital as a nurse."

"Are they both still living?"

"They are; they're good people. My granddad, like you and your dad, enjoys working with his hands. He owns some rural property—a small farm—and a shop. He taught me to work with tools. He was an architectural engineer before he retired recently, so that's where my interest in architecture developed. I used to love looking at the rolls of blueprints and all the magazines full of floor plans my granddad kept around the house."

"I'm sorry. I guess I lost touch gradually with your mother after she remarried and no one told me you'd moved." He frowned. "I thought I remember your father Ryan Clements wanted to adopt you, give you his name. That he didn't have other children. I was surprised to hear you still carry the McCarter name."

"This is the awkward part." Garrett shifted in his seat in obvious discomfort. "I met Cooper Garrison when he came to a Log and Timber Home Show in Asheville, North Carolina. I was out of college and working for Barna Log Homes in Blacksburg then. I'd graduated with a Bachelor's of Architecture Design from Virginia Tech in Blacksburg, did an internship with Barna, and then got hired with them full time. I was always interested in log homes. I loved the log homes I saw around the mountains in Virginia and the company often sent me to the log home shows for new ideas."

Garrett ran a hand through the stubble of beard on his chin, uncomfortable. "I knew Mom was dying when Cooper offered me a job with his company in May. In fact, I told him I couldn't accept because of that. He said he understood, his own mother a single mom much of her life, too. He said he'd hold the job open for me and he did. Mom died in July and I moved down here to Gatlinburg in early August. I've been living with one of the other single guys who works with Garrison Homes since."

Garrett got up to walk over to look out the window.

Owen tried to think what to say. "Listen, Garrett, if your mother told you some unpleasant things about our relationship, there's no need for us to talk about it. Your mother and I fell for each other and married in a little haste. I don't think your mother realized how hard it would be, married to a man in the military. I was deployed not long after we married. I came home and then got deployed again. It's hard for a couple to be split up so soon after marrying."

Owen studied the boy, now tall and good-looking with wavy brown hair and dark eyes. "Garrett, I'm sorry things didn't work out with your mother," he said, "but I never regretted my time with you."

"I remember those times, too," Garrett said, coming to sit back down. "I also remember when Ryan Clements started coming around a lot. He wasn't fun like you. I don't think he ever really liked me much. He never took me fishing, to the park, or to the movies like you did. He never read to me or tucked me in bed, wrestled with me in fun or rode me piggyback the way you did. I know I was only a little kid in early elementary school when you and my mom divorced, but I really loved you as my dad. It was tough on me when Mom and Ryan told me he was really my dad and not you. I know it had to be a hard time for you, too."

Owen searched for words. "I tried keeping in touch, coming to visit you, writing letters, and all, but Joanna and Ryan didn't welcome my contacts and efforts to continue our relationship. They said it confused you, having two fathers, that it made other kids talk about you. I didn't want to make problems for you, so I gradually backed away."

Garrett smiled at Owen then. "My mother told me you sent money to put away for my education. It really helped. Thank you."

"I finally lost touch with your mother when the holiday gifts I sent to you got returned. I think you were about nine then."

"That's when we moved back to Blacksburg," Garrett said. "Ryan got involved with another woman that year and basically dumped my mother." He looked away. "Sort of like she dumped you. I remember my grandmother telling mother once, when she was feeling sorry for herself, that she'd been foolish not to realize what a good man you were. They didn't know I was listening."

"Well, I never wished your mother ill, even though I did get hurt by her actions." Owen put his legs up on an ottoman. "It hurt to lose her. I'll admit that, but it hurt almost as bad or worse to lose you. I'm glad I got a chance to tell you that after all this time."

Garret got up to walk over to the big rock fireplace, tracing his hands over the stones. Then he turned back to Owen with an anguished look in his eyes. "Ryan Clements is not my dad. I think that's one reason he never wanted to adopt me."

Owen tried to conceal his shock. He knew, from what the detective he hired in those past years uncovered, that Joanna had fooled around on him while he was deployed even before she hooked up with Ryan. He studied Garrett. Did Joanna even know who the boy's real father was? Had she never told him?

"Mom told me all this when she was dying," Garrett added, coming to sit back down. "She also told me you were really my father."

Owen dropped the bottle of cola in his hand, spilling the last of it across the wood floor. "What?"

Garrett got up to go to the kitchen to get some paper towels. He came back and dropped down to wipe up the cola, sitting the empty bottle on the coffee table.

"I guess this is a big shock, huh?"

Owen tried to find his voice. "Your mother told me clearly Ryan Clements was your real father. She said she hadn't wanted to tell me before because Ryan was married to someone else when she found herself pregnant. She also told me often that Ryan wanted to adopt you because he didn't have any children in his first marriage. Why would Joanna tell me that if it wasn't true?"

Garrett sat down across from him again and leaned forward. "She told me she was afraid you'd gain custody if you knew. She admitted, crying, that she hadn't been faithful to you while you were deployed, that she'd been young and stupid. She said she fell in love big time with Ryan and wanted a divorce but she also wanted to keep me. So she lied to you. And she lied to me."

"Good heavens." Owen sat there totally in shock. "Are you sure about this?"

Garrett nodded. "My grandparents told me it was true, too. She told them the same story in those last weeks of her life. She said she was always afraid you'd fight for me if you knew. And she said she felt too ashamed about what she'd done to ever tell me or her parents before." Garrett twisted his hands in his lap. "Mother was a nurse, you know. She said you could look at the blood types to know for sure. Back when I was a kid people didn't push DNA paternity tests much."

"That's true. I didn't even consider pursuing that avenue. I simply assumed Joanna was telling the truth. I didn't doubt her word. It never dawned on me she'd lie about something like that." He leaned over and put his head in his hands.

Owen heard Garrett sigh. "If it helps any, Mom said to tell you she was sorry. She said she hoped you could forgive her for lying, for being scared of losing me. Scared, too, to encourage you to stay in touch more because Ryan was jealous of you."

"Did you know all this when you accepted the job with Cooper Garrison here in Gatlinburg?"

"No, like I said, it was just a great opportunity. And I told Cooper no at first because I knew Mom was dying." He winced. "Mom said she hoped I would try to find a way to know you better when she learned I planned to move here. She said you were a good person and a good father. She cried a lot telling me all this."

Owen felt tears smart at the back of his eyes. "Do you want us to build a relationship?" he asked.

Garrett chewed on his lip. "I'd really like that if you'd be willing. I wouldn't blame you if you didn't want to."

Owen got up then, pulled the boy to his feet and wrapped his arms around him. "Of course I want to. In my heart you were always my son. Always. I've dreamed of you, thought of you, prayed for you all these years. Hoped you were happy and well. My heart is overflowing to know, even if suddenly like this, that you really are my son."

He put his hands on his boy's shoulders and looked at him with love. "Even if you'd come here tonight, saying you remembered me with fondness from your boyhood years, and only asked for my friendship, I'd have said yes without reservation. But now, I feel like the Lord has simply laid an unbelievable gift in my hands." He smoothed his son's hair. "What an unforgettable day. I've found my son again. How blessed I am."

They sat and talked for a long time catching up on all the years. Laughing together. Sharing together. Owen kept wanting to pinch himself with the knowledge that Garrett actually was his son.

Garrett grew serious at one point. "I want us to do a paternity test. It's not that I doubt Mom but I want it certain for our sakes because both of us were lied to." He hesitated. "Would that be all right with you?"

"Sure. We can go to the hospital and get a legal test done. I want it done right if we do it—none of this sending away for some kind of results that wouldn't stand up in a court of law."

Owen got up and walked to the kitchen, turning to smile at the boy who so resembled him the more he studied him. "All this stress has made me hungry and it's getting late. You want to stay for dinner? I can rustle up something. I make good chili."

"That sounds great but….." He stalled on finishing the rest of his sentence.

"Listen, if you need to be somewhere else, that's fine," Owen said, smiling at him. "We'll have other chances to spend time together in the future."

"It's only that I thought we might call Duggan and invite him to come up to eat with us, too."

"Whew." Owen shook his head. "I don't think I can go through all this again in one day, Garrett. Although the thought is nice. And we'll need to get Dad in on this soon, as well as my sister and others in the family."

"Well, about that…" Garrett rubbed his neck. "Your dad already knows."

"What?"

"When he first met me at the construction site and I told him my name, he said, 'Son, are you sure Owen McCarter isn't your real dad? The resemblance between you two is striking." Garrett shrugged. "So I ended up telling him everything,"

Owen laughed. "Well, yeah, I guess we should call Dad to come up and have chili with us. Why didn't you tell me this before?"

"I was afraid to tell you because I didn't talk to you first before him." He blew out a breath of relief. "I was afraid you'd be mad."

"Well, I'm not." Owen clapped him on the back. "If you have Dad's phone number you can call him now and invite him up while I start the chili."

Garrett hesitated. "There's something else I need to tell you."

Owen grinned at him. "You're married? You have a couple of kids?" He teased. "You have a weird tattoo?"

Garrett laughed. "No, I'm living with your dad."

"You're what?"

"You see when he talked to me on Friday, you'd left to go to the trade show in Atlanta. When your dad learned I was hanging out staying with a coworker and looking for a place to live, he talked me in to moving in with him at the farmhouse." Garrett shrugged. "He said he felt lonely there by himself, needed company, and that living with him would put me right by the worksite I'm supervising now."

Garrett sat on a stool at the kitchen island. "Your dad can be a pretty persuasive guy. He sort of insisted and he said if I didn't like it there I could move out anytime." He grinned. "But I really like Duggan. He wants me to call him that instead of Grandad. He's teaching me some new woodworking skills and to play poker. He's a mean poker player, even playing for dimes."

"Well, if he starts driving you crazy, you can move up here."

Garrett looked down at his hands. "He said you kind of had a relationship started with someone, working toward getting serious, and that you might need your privacy and space for canoodling around a little."

"Is that what he said?" Owen laughed out loud.

Garrett nodded.

"Well, that woman I'm interested in has a daughter living with her right now. Come up on Friday and you can meet both of them. I'm grilling ribs and corn on the cob."

Owen began to chop up onion to toss in his chili pot. "Call your grandfather to head this way and I'll fill you in on Mary Pat and Victoria's stories before he gets here. I'd rather you'd hear my version on that than Dad's."

Garrett pulled out his cell phone to call Duggan, but stopped suddenly to grin at Owen. "I just realized I have a whole new family now. Isn't that cool?"

"Yeah, it is," Owen said, and he meant the words more than he could say.

CHAPTER 17

On Thursdays after work, Mary Pat drove into Knoxville for her class at the University. With the old Hoskins library building practically next door to the building where her class met from six to nine, Mary Pat usually drove to campus early, studied at the library, and then grabbed a bite to eat before class. Today, she dropped by the University of Tennessee hospital ahead of class to see Dorothy Warren, her former neighbor in Knoxville.

"I'm so glad you're going to see Dorothy," her mother said when they talked on the phone earlier. "She was such a nice woman, always so sweet to the kids, treating them like a grandmother. I really liked her and her husband Harold. I can't believe she had a heart attack, but I'm glad she's going to be all right."

"So am I, Mom. I'll tell her you sent your best."

Dorothy and Harold Warren, an older couple who'd lived next door to Mary Pat in Knoxville, had always been good neighbors. They'd been thoughtful and kind to Mary Pat after Russell asked for a divorce, coming over several times to visit with her, too.

With time tight, Mary Pat decided to eat dinner before class at the hospital. After hugging Harold and Dorothy goodbye, she took the elevator downstairs and made her way to the cafeteria. She chose fish almondine and green beans and then fixed a quick salad at the salad bar before finding a quiet corner in the cafeteria.

As she checked the messages on her phone, a shadow fell across her table.

"I hope it's okay if I join you," Russell said, sitting his own cafeteria tray down on the table and dropping into the empty chair across from her. He smiled at her then, that charming smile she so well remembered. "I thought I saw you across the room as I went through the line."

Immediately suspicious, Mary Pat asked, "And you just happened to be in the cafeteria right now?"

He shrugged. "All right, I admit I saw you on the cardiac floor visiting Dorothy. She's my patient. Harold mentioned you'd invited him to come eat a bite with you at the cafeteria, but that he wanted to eat with Dorothy."

"I see."

"Dorothy is doing well," Russell continued. "I think she'll be able to go home tomorrow or the next day barring complications. Her heart has settled down, but she'll have a long recovery time and need to make big changes in her life. I'm concerned about her diabetes but we've talked about that."

Mary Pat looked around. "Russell, I don't think it's appropriate for you to be chatting and having dinner with me here in the hospital cafeteria. You work here. I've already seen several of your colleagues glancing over in this direction, wondering about us eating together."

"We shared a life together for thirty-four years, Marian. I don't see any reason why we can't be friends, even if divorced." He offered her another wide smile again, before eating a few bites of his meat loaf.

She tucked her cell phone into her purse, trying to decide how to answer. "I hope to always be civil for our children's sakes, Russell, but I don't care to be friends. I doubt Cherise would like the idea of us spending time together, either."

He made a face. "It would be just one more thing for her to get on her bandwagon about then." Russell scowled. "She's a very difficult woman, much more controlling and domineering than I expected. She practically polices my life, wants to know everywhere I go and with whom, everything I do, and when and where I do it."

"This isn't appropriate for you to share with me, either."

He leaned forward. "You look so beautiful, Mary Pat. I could hardly believe it when I saw you at Todd's wedding. My heart kicked up like in the old days and I kept watching you throughout the wedding and reception."

Mary Pat started to gather up her purse and tray to leave, but Russell put a hand over hers. "I wanted to tell you that. I'm proud of what you've been doing with your life—losing weight, going back to school, working now in your field. It's what I always wanted for you."

She pulled her hand away from his. "I don't recall you ever telling me that or ever encouraging me to pursue goals in any of those areas. You always said you wanted me to stay at home, to keep the house in order, to cook and supervise everything in our lives because of your intense work schedule, to be there to entertain your friends, to keep up with the children, to be in all the right clubs and groups. The first time I ever learned you wanted something different from me was when you asked for a divorce."

A small frown crossed his face. "I did try to talk to you a few times, Marian."

"Well, obviously so obscurely that I can't remember the occasions." She stood up then, draping her purse across her shoulder.

He started to reach out again to catch her arm.

"Don't make a scene here, Russell." She forced a small smile for anyone watching them. "I'm glad to know you're taking good care of Dorothy and being a kind support to Harold. I hope Dorothy continues to improve. She was always a good neighbor to us and sweet to our children."

Russell gave her a pained expression. "You hate me now, don't you?"

"No. You are a good doctor, and although I don't want to pretend a friendship I don't feel, I don't wish you anything but continued best in your life." She glanced at her tray still on the table. "If you'll take my tray when you take yours, I'd be grateful." Then she turned and walked away.

The episode with Russell was upsetting, and Mary Pat found it difficult to focus fully during her class. In fact, she slipped out before the end of the class to head back to Gatlinburg.

"You're home early," Victoria said, glancing up from the couch where she sat watching television. Her eyes narrowed. "You're upset, too. You've been crying. What happened, Mom? Did you fail an exam or something?" Victoria's mouth dropped open as a new thought hit her mind. "Oh, my gosh, did Ms. Dorothy die?"

"No, Dorothy is improving." Mary Pat dropped her purse, laptop, and books on the table and walked into the kitchen to get a bottle of her favorite flavored water from the refrigerator. "I didn't fail an exam, either," she added, walking back into the room to settle into her favorite chair by Victoria.

"So what happened?" Victoria turned off the television.

Mary Pat put her feet up on the ottoman and sighed. "I stopped at the hospital cafeteria to get supper and your father came and sat down with me."

Victoria sat up, eyes alert. "Uh, oh. Did you have a fight?"

"No, but I made it clear I didn't want to spend time with him." She leaned her head back, closing her eyes. "We were in the hospital cafeteria—a highly visible place. He works there, Vee. I saw several of his colleagues walk by and send speculative looks our way."

"What did he want?"

Mary Pat decided to be honest. "He wanted to flirt and to complain about his wife. He came looking for me specifically. Dorothy is his patient and he learned from her husband Harold that I planned to eat at the cafeteria."

"Well, that's flattering, I guess, isn't it?"

"No. I don't want more problems in that area. Cherise acted nasty enough to me through all the divorce and home sale proceedings. I noticed her always being very possessive around Russell, too, looping her arm through his, leaning against him, giving him suggestive looks—always making sure I noticed." She hesitated. "I shouldn't say this to you, but one time I dropped my pen at one of those conference table meetings with our lawyers, leaned over to get it, and saw her hand where it didn't need to be."

Victoria laughed. "That woman is a piece of work. Do you think Dad's finally figuring that out?"

"I don't know, but all is not well in paradise."

Victoria snickered. "I shouldn't laugh but you'd think Dad would have been more discerning about Cherise or listened to the talk about her. Everyone said she was shopping for another rich husband. I don't think she's a very nice person."

"I heard similar commentary among my friends, but your father seemed to greatly admire Cherise at one point. He certainly sang her praises to me."

Victoria got up to get herself a cold drink and came back to sit down again. "I haven't told you this, Mom, but Todd said that Cherise called him up and talked awful to him about not inviting her to the wedding. Cherise threatened him that she'd alienate Dad from all of us and see to it we were written out of Dad's will if Todd didn't accept her presence in his father's life."

Mary Pat sighed and rubbed her neck. "That is extreme."

Victoria wrinkled her nose. "I'll bet she does get Dad to change his will, too, especially after he went against her and came to Todd's wedding without her." She flounced in her seat. "Besides, everyone says she married him mainly for his money anyway."

"Let's look on the good," Mary Pat said. "Your father provided well for you children and was wealthy enough, as a surgeon, to see all four of you through private school and college. That is rare today with college costs so high and the income levels of average Americans not keeping pace with the rising cost of living. I'm learning more about the financial struggles most people face from counseling with many of my dieters. So many young people today are forced to take loans for higher education because it's the only way they can go to college."

She smiled at her daughter. "Even my brother Brandon and I took some student loans to help us through school. Mom and Dad were struggling with the restaurant business here in Gatlinburg when our time to enter college came. Mom worked in a candy store to help out. You can see from our home here, that we lived comfortably but certainly not lavishly. I never wanted for food or clothing but I didn't get many of the extras I wished for."

Victoria looked around. "It's comfortable here and you decorated the house to be warm and inviting after Gigi and Pops moved to Florida." She smiled. "I remember happy times coming here with my brothers to see my grandparents as kids, but once we got into high school we all got busy with other things."

Mary Pat sipped on her drink, curling her legs up in the chair. "Children change in their teens. It's a time for breaking away from parents, trying to establish their own identity and independence. That's when peers become more the center of one's world than parents many times." She smiled at her daughter. "I'm glad we've become closer again now."

She saw Victoria squirm and make the face that showed something was on her mind. "Mom, I need to apologize for something."

"What, sweetie?"

"When I started moving into middle school you started gaining weight and by the time I started high school you'd really gotten big." She looked down at her hands. "I pulled away a lot because of that. My friends said stuff and when we went places together, people stared at us and said things they didn't think I could hear. It was sort of embarrassing."

Mary Pat smiled. "I'm glad you shared that with me. I should have realized it. Anytime someone we're close to seriously crosses the norms in appearance or behavior, it can be hard to deal with— excess weight, overly weird clothes, too many obvious tattoos or piercings, or other extreme aspects of appearance or behavior that draw too much attention." She paused remembering. "You were young, fashion conscious and peer driven, and I had a problem appearance I wasn't dealing with. You didn't know how to say anything so you just pulled away."

"I didn't want to hurt your feelings but I felt mad at you sometimes for it. I didn't understand why you didn't want to try to change, why you wouldn't work at it for your health and your appearance. Even for us." She spread her hands. "It's not like you were in a wheelchair like Myrna Loy's mother. She couldn't help her condition. As an overseas reporter, she stepped on a bomb or something trying to rescue some kids. I mean, everyone's heart went out to her."

Mary Pat winced at some of the memories Victoria's words evoked. She, too, remembered those stares, those words—like in the bathroom at the restaurant this March. The words she heard that time though started her down a new road to improvement.

She turned to see Victoria biting her lip, watching her. "Are you mad at me? You already had a bad night and I shouldn't have dumped on you."

"You only told the truth." Mary Pat smiled at her. "I'm glad you're not avoiding me anymore."

Her daughter's eyes twinkled. "The last time we went shopping that clerk in the gift shop thought you were my sister. Hearing her say that made me feel so good for you and for me."

"It made me feel good, too."

"I'm glad we're having this talk. It's kind of like a truth session."

Mary Pat managed a teasing smile. "It seems to me like you and Brock Richardson are developing more than a friendship. Can we talk about that with some candor? You've been out on quite a few dates now since summer. I know you keep telling me you're only friends and work colleagues, but your actions and eyes tell me more—especially when Brock and you are together."

Victoria leaned back on the couch dramatically. "Gosh, I admit I really like him, Mom, but I'm so scared it might be like with Kevin. How do you know when you can trust someone enough to let your heart out a little?"

"I'm not sure you ever know fully when the moment is right. But gradually over time trust grows, you learn someone's character, you realize you can count on them. You watch their lives, how they interact with others, with their family members, friends, the people they work with. Somehow, down in your heart, you begin to know. The old fears thaw out and give place to trust and love again." She smiled. "But loving is always a little scary."

Victoria hugged a sofa cushion to her. "Brock is talking of love already. He's so sweet but strong and smart, too. Surprisingly, we even work well together. Kevin and I quarreled and snipped at each other at work all the time. He always wanted me to try to dumb down, let him take the credit for anything we learned, back away and let him offer advice to any of the customers. Mr. Remmick didn't do that but Kevin certainly did." Victoria looked thoughtful. "Brock doesn't mind me being smart. We share ideas and insights. I really like that."

She sent Mary Pat a sweet smile then. "You always told me it's important to like a man's family. I'm crazy about Brock's parents Nancy and Dean and about Brock's sister Cali and her husband John." She leaned forward, her voice conspiratorial. "Cali told me she and John are going to have a baby. She's so excited. Don't tell anyone else yet. They're waiting to tell people until the pregnancy is further along. But oh, mom." She rolled her eyes. "Cali and I went shopping the other day and looked at the sweetest baby things. Brock wants children, especially because his dad died young. He said he wants to be a great dad to his children like Dean was to him. I don't think Kevin wanted kids at all but Brock is so good with all the little kids that come in the store."

Mary Pat smiled, realizing her daughter and Brock's relationship had progressed further than she thought in the last months. Nancy had certainly been right about the young recovering more quickly from hurt and betrayal.

Victoria glanced over at Mary Pat's hiking stick leaning against the fireplace and changed the subject. "Owen is really happy about Garrett living here now, don't you think?" She frowned. "I can't believe Garrett's mother lied to him about his father though. That's such a sad story."

"Yes, it is."

"It's wonderful, though, that they got back together," Victoria continued. "It's changed Owen and Duggan, having Garrett around—three generations, so much alike in many ways." Her lips twitched. "Owen told me Garrett and Duggan get along like two peas in a pod. Duggan is teaching him all sorts of new woodworking skills, too. They already put some of Garrett's items in the store. Owen says Garrett really likes to make utilitarian things—coat racks, book ends, chairs, trunks, quilt racks."

"I've seen some of his work. It's very good."

"I enjoyed meeting Garret that Friday night when we went to Owen's for ribs and corn on the cob. He's a nice guy. We all played cards, that rummy game. I had fun." She wiggled her eyebrows. "Garrett is good looking, but I don't get any of those vibes around him like I do with Brock. We're just easy friends." She giggled. "When Brock is around though my mind drifts to kissing and what Owen's dad calls canoodling."

Mary Pat laughed.

Victoria grew quiet for a moment. "Mom, what do you do when you're thinking out hard decisions, trying to decide about important things?"

"I pray about them, pray for direction, more now than I used to. I've learned a lot from John Browder, the pastor at our Glades Community Church. He's so wise. He makes God feel so much more real than most ministers I listen to."

Victoria nodded. "He's helped me in my faith, too. So have you. I'm glad we've been sharing about faith. I mean, you always did when we were growing up and everything and we all went to church, but I've been moving into a deeper personal relationship here in the mountains. It seems like people talk about God and their beliefs more freely, don't act like it's not cool. It feels more real. Do you think it's partly the mountains, being close to nature?"

"Maybe a little, but when you're around people of strong faith, it builds your own faith up. I read a quote once that said you can only be lifted up to higher ground by people who walk there."

"That's a good thought. But you can grow your own faith, too, by studying and wanting to know more."

"I agree, but when I get around people who are excited about their faith it gets me more excited, makes me want to study more and know more." She smiled. "You asked me about what I do when I want some answers. I walk up Dawson Creek Trail to the waterfall or the old cabin to pray. Even when I was a little girl it seemed like I always felt God there more keenly, got the answers I needed. I still do. I sit on the steps of the old cabin or on one of those big rocks in the stream, get quiet, and pray, and usually I get the peace and the answers I need."

Victoria gave her a teasing look. "Have you prayed there about Owen, whether you can love him?"

Mary Pat knew her mouth dropped open.

Victoria giggled. "Oh, come on, Mom. There are as many looks and fireworks going off around you and Owen as around me and Brock."

Mary Pat looked away, not sure what to say.

Victoria leaned over and put a hand over hers. "It's okay, Mom. I've known since August Owen has feelings for you. He said they resurfaced from the time when you fell in love when younger, but he also told me you weren't ready to love again, that it was too soon after dad."

Uncomfortable, Mary Pat felt a flush rise up her neck.

"I didn't mean to embarrass you. I just wanted you to know it would be okay with me if you and Owen got together. After what happened to you with Dad you deserve a little happiness. So does Owen, I think."

Anxious now, Mary Pat said, "You haven't talked to your brothers about this, have you?"

"No, but I will if they say anything catty, and you know they'll see how you and Owen feel when they come for Thanksgiving." She waved a hand. "So maybe we should drop a few hints."

"Let me think about that, Victoria." She twisted her hands in her lap.

Victoria watched her. "You don't want them to think you're like Dad, running from one relationship into another. That's it, isn't it?"

"I admit I'd thought of that, and I needed time, too. I still need time."

"Owen's a really good man, Mom."

"I know, but let me move from A to Z in my own timeframe."

"I will." Victoria glanced over at her Bible lying on a side table. "There sure is a lot in the Bible about adultery and how it tears up lives. It hurts not only the people involved but the kids and family around—like hurtful ripples spreading out in waves. Look how it messed up Joanna and Garrett's lives. It messed up our family, too. Sometimes I admit that I miss our family all together. I look at old photos in our family scrapbooks of you, Dad, me, and the boys, all laughing and happy. I thought we'd always have our big white two-storied house in Sequoyah, that I'd come back there with my family one day, that the boys would, too. I never imagined it would all fold up one day and be over. That dad would betray you and betray us. It seems so wrong somehow for people not to stay faithful to their vows."

"Yes, it does." She smiled across at her daughter. "But God is also a God of second chances. That's a good thought, too."

"It is." Victoria yawned. "We'd better go to bed, Mom. We both have to work in the morning."

In her bed later, Mary Pat had a lot to think about. Some of her daughter's candor hurt. But sharing so honestly was bringing them back closer together, too. She felt happy for that. Leaning down to nuzzle Barker, curled up at the end of the bed, Mary Pat smiled thinking of Owen. Maybe her kids could understand her reaching for a second chance at love more than she'd thought. Like the little girl she'd once been, she wrote the word "love" on her palm with her finger, liking the feel of the word, happier to imagine it possibly entering her life now.

CHAPTER 18

On a late September Monday morning, close to noon, Owen worked in his shop at the house. The fall tourist traffic had started to pick up again around the Smoky Mountains, with the foliage beginning to show early color, especially in the higher elevations. The weekend at the store had been a busy one, and Owen's hiking sticks had almost sold out in many sizes. He needed time in the shop today to work on replacements.

Wheeler helped Owen in the shop this morning, chatting more than Owen liked, but his help was still appreciated.

"These are all looking good," Wheeler said, running his hands over the sticks Owen had finished removing the bark from with a power sander. "How come you work on them with your knife, too? The sander is faster."

"I use the knife for more of a layering effect and for more color variation in the wood. Personal handwork makes each stick more distinctive." He smiled at Wheeler. "My granddad used to make his walking sticks on an old shaving horse. It's still sitting in the corner over there. He used only hand tools for all his work, too. Power tools like this sander hadn't been invented."

Wheeler got up from his worktable to study the old shaving horse. "I wondered what this bench thing was. Will you show me how it works one day?"

"I will but not today. We need to get a lot of new sticks made fast for the store." He pointed at Wheeler's worktable. "You need to get back to staining those sticks on your table, too."

"Okay." Wheeler ambled back to his work. "When you finish that last oak stick you're working on, start on the maple sticks I just finished and use the redwood stain on those."

"We use different colors because it makes them prettier."

"That's true. Some people like more natural tans or light brown sticks, like you're staining now, while others favor a deep brown or redwood stick. Variety in the staining, in the kind of wood used with each stick, and whether we wrap them with colored paracord, or add a leather cord through the top, makes them all more individual."

Wheeler went back to work brushing on stain and them rubbing the stain into the wood with an oilcloth. Setting his finished stick aside to dry, he picked up a stick from the new pile, the wood twisted instead of straight and smooth.

"Duggan told me that vines wrapped around little trees or branches give them this twisty shape." He ran his hand over the stick's twists and turns. "It's pretty, don't you think?"

"Yes, some people really like those more than a smoother stick."

"These are harder to sand and to get the bark off of, though, and they're harder to stain."

"They are. They're harder to find in the woods and fields, too. Sometimes I order them from a dealer I know in Kentucky."

They worked in silence for a few minutes.

Wheeler stirred the new can of redwood stain well, dipped his brush into it, and began to add a light layer to the walking stick on his worktable. "After we finish the staining and let the sticks dry overnight, how come we paint on the polyurethane layers outside instead of in here?"

Owen paused from sanding a small protruding knob, trying to reduce and smooth it without losing its character. "The resins and solvents used in polyurethane varnish are harsh. Breathing in the fumes in a closed up shop like this can make you feel sick or dizzy."

"It stinks, too."

"You're right. It does. The fumes are strong."

A knock came on the side door. Wheeler went over to open the door and let Brock Richardson in.

"Hey, Owen and Wheeler. Sorry to bother you all but I'm looking for Victoria and thought you might have seen her. She was off today and told me to drop by the house for lunch." He glanced at his watch. "It's past noon and she's not there."

"Maybe she went shopping or to the store and forgot the time," Owen said.

He shook his head. "No, her car is here."

"Did you knock hard on her door?" Wheeler asked.

"I knocked hard on the front door and the back," Brock answered. "I could hear Barker whining inside the house, too."

"She could be in the shower or something," Wheeler added.

"No." Brock shook his head. "I've been here for about twenty minutes now, looking around."

Owen laid down his sandpaper. "You're worried."

"I admit I am. Victoria is sort of anal about being on time for everything. It's not like her to forget I planned to drive over on my lunch hour. I just talked to her this morning, and yesterday we planned the lunch date when we drove over to Cosby to Carver's Orchard. We bought apples and she said this morning she was making some kind of apple salad with chicken, celery, and stuff in it."

"Did you text her?"

"I did. She hasn't answered. I texted her to confirm it before I left the pharmacy and then after I got here. I also phoned. She isn't answering." He rubbed his neck. "This doesn't feel right Owen."

"Did you call Mary Pat?"

"No. She's really busy before lunch on Mondays and teaches a class from noon to one, too. I hated to bother her." Brock glanced around. "I saw your car and thought Victoria might have walked over here or that you might have seen her."

Owen brushed off his hands. "Tell you what. I have a key to Mary Pat's house so I can get in to walk Barker when she and Victoria are working or away on a trip. We'll go check the house."

Brock sighed. "Thanks. I hope nothing has happened to her."

At Mary Pat's they checked through the house without finding any sign of Victoria.

Brock looked around with a frown. "It's odd she hasn't even started lunch or anything. Usually she sets the table, gets out glasses and stuff."

Owen walked into Victoria's room and looked around one more time. Clothes were strewn on the bed, shoes under a chair, but nothing unusual to suggest a problem.

"Let's go outside and walk around the yard, too," Owen suggested. "If we still don't find her, I think we'd better call Mary Pat. Victoria might have told her mother where she was going and forgot to call you for some reason."

"Man, I'm really worried about her," Brock said. "It's private and isolated up this street, and she was here alone."

They went out the front door to find Wheeler sitting in one of the porch rocking chairs.

"We're going to look around the yard and property for Victoria," Owen told him. "If she comes back or if you see her, holler at us."

"You might want to walk up the Dawson Creek Trail behind the house. I saw her walking that way earlier."

Owen frowned, provoked. "Why didn't you tell us that, Wheeler?"

He shrugged. "Cause she went hiking up the trail a long time ago, about the time I came up to your house to work. She waved at me." He grinned. "I figured she'd have been back from a walk by now. Besides I forgot it."

Brock rolled his eyes. "I'll head up the trail to look for her, Owen. You and Wheeler don't need to go."

"No, I'll go with you in case we run into a problem or something." Owen glanced at his watch. "Wheeler, can you walk Barker and stay here until Mary Pat comes home? She should be here soon."

Wheeler grinned. "I can do that. Barker likes me."

"I know he does, and when Mary Pat comes home ask her to call me. I have my cell phone with me."

"Okay." Wheeler looked at his own watch. "It's my lunch time,

Owen. You were going to fix me a sandwich."

Owen heard Brock snort.

"Wheeler, you can make a peanut butter and jelly sandwich in Mary Pat's kitchen and eat an apple," Owen told him. "Look around in the kitchen and you'll find what you need."

"Will Mary Pat get mad?"

"No. Tell her I told you it was all right because you're helping. That's important."

He nodded. "I like to help."

"I know you do." Owen smiled at him. "When Mary Pat gets back, you can go on home. We'll work some more in the shop another day."

Contented, Wheeler went into the house whistling for Barker.

As Owen and Brock started toward the trail in the woods behind the house, Brock glanced back. "Will he be all right?"

"Yes, and I'll call Mary Pat as a back-up in a few minutes. She should be finishing class soon and she can cut out early to stay at the house."

"I sure hope nothing has happened to Victoria," Brock said with a ragged edge to his voice.

"She might have lost track of time out on a pretty day like this," Owen said to reassure the boy, but he was worried, too.

As they headed up the trail into the woods, Owen phoned Mary Pat. She was anxious, of course, and promised to stop class early and head straight home.

"Mary Pat will stay at the house in case Victoria comes back or calls," he told Brock, hanging up and tucking his cell phone in his back pocket. "She's concerned, too."

At different points along the trail, they stopped to look around more, calling out to Victoria in case she'd walked off the trail. At Dawson Falls, they explored around the rocks near the falls in case she'd stopped there to think and forgotten the time. At about a mile up the trail they came to the turning to the old Dawson cabin. A small side trail wound up the ridge past an old family cemetery and to the cabin.

Brock called out again as they started up the side trail to check the cabin, "Victoria! Victoria! Are you around here somewhere?"

A voice came back on the air. "Brock! I'm here. In the cabin!"

They quickened their pace, but Owen put out a hand to slow Brock's progress as they drew closer. "Look," he said, pointing.

A black bear and her cubs milled around the grounds of the cabin. The mother bear hung in an old crab apple tree stuffing herself with crabapples and her cubs milled around below, eating the apples that had fallen on the ground.

"Mama bear will catch our scent in a minute, if she hasn't already," Owen told Brock. "Bears are normally wary of people and her natural instinct will be to climb down from the tree and take her cubs off to safety. So we don't want to crowd her or she'll get defensive."

"Can't we holler to encourage her to leave?"

"Yes. Without moving forward start talking loud when I do and spread out your arms. This will alert Mama we're in the area. Keep talking and let her start climbing down the tree. Then we'll do a little hollering, too, to encourage her more as she starts moving out. Noise generally makes a bear want to leave. If she grows aggressive, we'll back off slowly facing forward. But don't turn and run, Brock." He kept his eye on the bear as he talked, and noticed when she looked down the trail spotting them.

"Hey bear!" Owen called out, spreading his arms out and waving them a little. "Time to take your kids and head on home. There are people in the area. It's not safe."

"Victoria," Brock called out, waving his arms, too. "We're hollering to scare off some bears. When they leave, we'll move in to help you."

Owen saw the mother bear shinny down the tree now. As she reached the ground she began to herd the cubs away from the area. "Climb up on that rock beside you to look bigger," Owen said, pointing to a large mountain rock by the trail.

Brock did and waved his arms from on top of the rock, continuing to holler to the bear to head off into the woods.

With gratitude, Owen watched mama bear hustle her cubs out of the area and into the woods behind the cabin. "She's leaving but we need to wait a little while before moving in. Keep making noise until she gets out of range of the cabin. We don't want one of the cubs cutting back, encountering us, and getting Mama upset and defensive."

To pass the time and keep the noise up, Owen began to sing the lyrics to "Anchors Aweigh" the old Naval fight song.

Laughing, Brock joined in on the chorus, changing the words "my boys" to "my bears" making Owen laugh with him.

"I forgot you were in the Navy," Brock said, when Owen paused.

Owen grinned. "It's the first song that came to mind when I got tired of just hollering to make noise."

"Are you all out there singing?" Victoria called out, sounding annoyed.

"Yes, just making noise to be sure the mama bear and her cubs moved on off," Owen called out. "We couldn't afford to move in with her in the area."

"Is she gone now?" Victoria called in answer.

"Yes, I think so," Owen hollered back. He nodded to Brock to start slowly up the trail again.

"Are you okay Victoria?" Brock called.

"No, I'm hurt." Her voice held an edge of tears.

With caution, they worked their way up to the cabin. They pushed the old door open to find Victoria huddled on the floor against the wall by one of the cabin's front windows. Tears washed down her face as Brock raced over to squat down beside her.

"What happened?" Owen asked, walking closer, too.

"I decided to take a walk this morning to the falls and the cabin. When I got up near the cabin, I heard something." She sniffed. "I turned around and saw this little cub. Like an idiot I walked toward him, and then heard a growl and saw his mother and another cub coming out of the woods."

She shook her head. "I was so scared and acted stupid then. I turned and ran toward the cabin. Mom has told me you shouldn't run, but I just wanted to get somewhere safe. I knew mother bears can get really aggressive to defend their cubs. As I ran in the cabin door I tripped over a loose board or something, turned my ankle in, and went down. I managed to crawl over and push the door shut, but I can't walk. I tried standing up and the pain was awful."

Brock began to remove Victoria's boot to examine her ankle. "It's swollen and red," he said as he got her boot and sock off.

"Ouch." She winced with pain as he moved the foot a little, examining it.

"There's black and blue discoloration, too," Owen said, squatting beside Victoria, too. "How long ago did this happen?"

"Over two hours ago, I guess. I've been here forever." She made a face. "Every once in a while I pushed up to look out the window. The bears were still there, which kept freaking me out, worrying they might try to come in the cabin or something but they only seemed interested in eating." She shrugged. "Even if they'd have been gone, I couldn't have made my way back."

"Why didn't you call?" Brock asked.

She rolled her eyes. "When I saw the mother bear and freaked, I dropped my cell phone. It's out there somewhere I guess unless the bears ate it, too."

Owen tried not to laugh. "You've sure had a rough time."

"Why have those bears stayed out there so long?"

"They're eating to get ready for the winter. They eat voraciously this time of year to add weight. This farm property has several fruit trees, planted back in the days when members of the Dawson family lived here, including crabapples, an old Winesap tree, and even an old Limbertwig apple tree."

"That mother bear was up in one of the crabapple trees, gulping down apples and branches, with her cubs below chowing down on what fell to the ground," Brock added.

"Wild bears like an area like this where settlers planted fruit trees and other trees dropping nuts this time of year," Owen explained. "There are a lot of big oak trees behind the cabin, a few hickory and pecan trees. Even a big walnut tree."

Brock made a face. "Can bears eat those huge walnuts? They're bigger than golf balls."

"Yeah, they chomp them right up. They have strong teeth," Owen replied.

Victoria cleared her throat. "Excuse me. I hate to interrupt, but I'd like to figure out a way to get out of here. I need to go to the bathroom. Bad."

Owen chuckled. "Sorry." He turned to Brock. "If you'll call Mary Pat at the house and your dad at the drug store to let everyone know we've found Victoria, I'll carry her around back of the cabin and help her find a way to relieve herself. Then you and I will make a chair of our arms and carry her down the trail back to the house. From what I'm seeing of her ankle, I don't think she can bear weight on it to walk back, even with help."

"I can carry her outside," Brock said.

Victoria gave him a panicked look.

"No, you're a boyfriend and I'm more like a daddy. It will embarrass her less with me. You make the calls." He lifted her and then took her outside, keeping an eye peeled for the bears.

"Do you think they'll come back?" she asked.

"When we're gone, I feel sure they'll come back." He glanced around. "It's a virtual smorgasbord here at the cabin. Look at all the acorns, buckeyes, and hickory nuts on the ground, and there's still fruit dropping from some of the old apple trees. We come to pick late Winesaps and Royal Limbertwigs to eat when they ripen, but most folks don't want the work of making crabapple jelly anymore. We're happy for the bears and other critters to enjoy them."

"How did you end up coming with Brock to look for me?"

"I was at home working in the shop today with Wheeler. When Brock couldn't find you, he came to see if you'd come to my place." Owen looked for a spot behind the cabin where Victoria could prop herself against the house while squatting down. "After we checked your house, Wheeler remembered seeing you heading toward the trail this morning, so Brock and I came hiking up the trail looking for you."

"Thank goodness."

After they managed an awkward bathroom stop, Owen carried Victoria back around to the cabin, sitting her on the porch steps.

"I called Mary Pat and my dad," Brock told them. "Everyone is so glad you're okay Victoria."

She looked down at her foot and frowned. "Well, hardly okay. Do you think my foot is broken?"

"No, I think you have a sprained ankle. I've seen a lot of them in the military," Owen said. "It's a common injury, occurring with an unnatural twisting motion when you trip as you did or place your foot awkwardly." He paused. "Did you hear a popping noise when you turned your ankle?"

Victoria shook her head. "No, I don't remember hearing anything."

"Good. It means you may only have overstretched or partially torn a ligament, but I want to drive you over to the ER at the hospital in Sevierville to be sure."

"Do we have to do that?" She wrinkled her nose.

"Yes," Brock said, leaning over to give her a quick kiss. "We need to be sure it is a sprain and not broken and you need to learn exactly what to do to be sure it heals well."

Somehow, with occasional stops to rest and changing sides in carrying Victoria's weight, Owen and Brock made it down the trail from the cabin back to the house.

Rejoicing and hugs went on after they arrived with Mary Pat and Victoria both hugging and weeping. After a little time for this, Owen suggested they drive on over to the ER.

"I'd like to take Victoria to the hospital now," he said. "She does need to get checked and I can lift her in and out of the car if needed."

Victoria turned to Brock. "You go on back to work now. The pharmacy will get busy toward the afternoon and evening and Dean will need you. You can run over later tonight after you get off work if you want to.'

"I'm sure Dad would cover for me," he started to argue.

She smiled at him. "I know he would, but both of you will probably have to help out enough for a time until I can recover enough to stand on my feet all day." She rolled her eyes. "I hate this has happened, causing everyone so much trouble."

Mary Pat hugged her. "This wasn't your fault, dear. Accidents just happen sometimes."

After some more arguing with Brock, they managed to send him back to work and then Owen loaded Victoria into Mary Pat's car for the trip to the hospital. An x-ray and visit with the doctors thankfully confirmed Victoria only had a sprained ankle.

"Sprains are painful but heal on their own," the doctor said, before releasing them. "Yours is a moderate sprain with a very minor partial tear in the ligament at the most—border line between a grade one and grade two sprain—so with rest it should heal up in two to four weeks. You'll need rest to give the tissues time to heal. Use ice and cold packs to reduce swelling and take some anti-inflammatory medications to ease the pain as needed. Keep your foot well elevated in these early healing stages. As a pharmacist, you know the importance of that." The doctor paused. "I want gentle compression on this ankle, too—an elastic wrap, like on your foot now, or an ankle support—and crutches for a time or a scooter to keep weight off the foot."

"I imagine Dean Richardson at the pharmacy has some contacts to find a scooter for you to use, Victoria," Owen put in. "That would be easiest to free your hands for work."

"I think so, too," she agreed.

"We can set up a little physical therapy, also, to help you regain full range ankle motion," the doctor added. "It helps with balance, as well, and they'll teach you home exercises to use. You're young and strong. You'll come along quickly."

He added a few more instructions, answered questions, scheduled a follow-up appointment, and then released them to leave.

Back at the house, Owen carried Victoria inside and helped her get settled on the sofa.

Mary Pat smiled at him. "Thank you so much for your help. I'm going to fix dinner now. Will you stay and eat with us?"

He shook his head. "Not this time. I have work to finish at the shop, but I appreciate the offer."

Mary Pat walked out with him as he left. "I'm so grateful to you for going with Brock to look for Victoria. Brock said he might not have known how to handle those bears if you hadn't been there. You always keep such a cool head. I so admire that." She reached out to put a soft hand on his chest.

"You're welcome and I don't *always* keep a cool head," he answered, grinning at her, and leaning down to kiss her.

"Me neither," she whispered, leaning into him and kissing him back. "I think you're becoming a very essential part of my life, Owen."

"Good, because I think I'd like to make you a *permanent* essential part of mine." He traced a hand through her hair.

"Oh." Her eyes widened as she searched for an answer.

Letting her off the hook, he started for home. "You'd better go take care of your patient," he said, winking. "And if you need any help, give me a call."

He whistled as he made his way across the yard. Mary Pat might not be fully ready for a commitment, for she was sure getting close.

CHAPTER 19

Two days later, on Wednesday, Mary Pat sat in the cozy living room of her mountain house with Victoria and Brock. Brock had stopped by on his lunch hour from work to check on Victoria's progress.

"I'm really glad you're doing better," Brock said.

Victoria stuffed another cushion under her foot on the ottoman to raise it a little higher. "Me, too, and tell your dad I plan to come back into the drug store for some part-time hours this weekend. Hopefully, on Monday, with my scooter, I should be able to work full time again."

"Don't push it," Brock cautioned. "You know proper rest after an injury impacts healing. Dad and I can manage."

"I'm being good." She pointed at her elevated foot wrapped neatly in compression bandages. "I'm going to the physical therapist on Friday, too. He can advise me about the activity level I can safely manage."

"Victoria is doing exceptionally well," Mary Pat added. "The pain and swelling are improving and movement is less painful. The scooter your dad found is helping her to get around more easily, too."

Brock sat back on the couch, relaxing. "I still can't believe we ran into those bears on the trail. I grew up around the mountains here but I seldom saw bears when hiking, exploring, or at summer camps, only the occasional bear raiding a trash can in a picnic area."

"I looked up some information about bears and watched some

incredible YouTubes since this happened," Victoria said. "I want to smarten up for the next time I ever run into a bear again. Owen knew so wisely what to do and I panicked and acted really dumb."

Brock nodded. "Owen said that usually if you run into bears, like we did, that backing away quietly and leaving the area is the wisest action. With you hurt in the cabin though we needed to try to chase the mother bear and her cubs away from the area. Owen told me later there is always risk in doing that, especially with a mother and cubs."

"Bears can be aggressive when they are eating, too," Mary Pat said. "I've been learning more about bears, as well." She told them about her encounters with ole Blaze and how he had to be transported.

Victoria put a hand to her heart. "Oh, my gosh, Mom. I would have totally freaked if I'd walked in the house and found a bear here."

She grinned. "It's a funny story to tell now, but it wasn't funny then."

"No kidding." Brock laughed. "Well, I'm glad the bears we ran into at the cabin were still wild bears. The mother vamoosed and herded those little cubs off in a hurry when she picked up our scent and heard our noise."

A knock at the door interrupted their talk and Brock jumped up to open the door. Russell walked in with a smile, Barker greeting him with excited barks and a lot of tail wagging.

"I learned from one of the boy's Facebook posts about Victoria's injury," he explained, smiling. "I decided to come check on the patient." He leaned over to kiss his daughter on the cheek and than sat down beside her on the sofa. "How are you doing?"

Despite a little tension in the room, Mary Pat noticed tears at the edge of her daughter's eyes over her father's unexpected visit.

"How did you get away from the office and your patients?" Victoria asked.

"I'd scheduled some golf time for this afternoon, but decided checking on you was more important. I figured with a sprain, I'd find you at home, too."

"That was nice of you," Victoria replied. She turned to Brock to make introductions. "Daddy this is Brock Richardson who works with me at the pharmacy. Brock, this is my father, Russell Latham."

"Pleased to meet you," Brock said, rising to shake Russell's hand.

"You, as well," Russell replied as Brock took his seat again.

"Would you like some iced tea, Russell?" Mary Pat asked, remembering her manners.

"I would. Thank you."

As she got up to head to the kitchen, Russell asked Victoria to tell him what happened to her ankle, and she and Brock began to relay their story.

Mary Pat came back with a glass of tea to find them laughing, Russell acting like the warm and charming man she remembered from the past. She could see Victoria was touched and excited he'd come to visit.

Making an excuse that she needed to walk Barker, Mary Pat left them to talk and visit. She walked Barker down Highland Drive and back, taking her time, and then came in the back door to settle down on a rattan sofa on the screened porch. Mary Pat knew Brock had left to return to work. She'd waved at him as he drove down the road, and she wanted to give Victoria private time with her father.

The October day was unexpectedly warm, and Mary Pat enjoyed the color beginning to show in the foliage of the trees in the yard and woods behind the house. The big screened porch had always been one of her favorite rooms at the mountain house and she'd painted and bought new cushions for the old rattan pieces that had been her mother's, adding new items to supplement, and creating a colorful cozy space.

She was soon lost in a paperback book she'd found among a pile of magazines on a side table, Barker settled contentedly at her feet.

"I thought I might find you out here," a voice said.

She looked up to see Russell coming through the door.

"You always did love this porch." He smiled at her and sat down in the chair beside her. "It's a pretty day, isn't it?"

"It is."

A small silence fell, then Russell said, "I had a good visit with our daughter and then helped her upstairs to her bedroom before coming to look for you. The dark circles under her eyes told me she hadn't been sleeping well. I admit I pushed a nap on her."

"She hasn't slept too well the last two nights. Turning her foot awkwardly while she sleeps kicks up the pain and wakes her."

"She's lucky she wasn't hurt worse. Her sprain, even with a minor tear in the ligament, should heal easily."

"Does an x-ray show the extent of the tear?"

"No." He shook his head. "But examining the foot does. A good orthopedic doctor can tell in the exam, by looking at and moving the foot, the extent of ligament damage. From what Victoria said, the tear was very slight, which as she was told, makes healing quicker." He smiled. "I gave her some medical advisement myself, of course."

"Yes, and I'm sure that helped. Victoria doesn't like confinement and she gets impatient with illness."

"I remember." He sighed. "I had a heart-to-heart with Victoria, too, after Brock left, let her know how sorry I am that I broke up our family, told her how much I missed her and the boys being more a part of my life. Cherise isn't good with them. In fact, she's catty and rude to them, obviously jealous of my affection even for my own children."

Mary Pat stayed silent, not sure what to say.

"Barker is glad to see me." Russell reached down to pet the dog, who'd moved near his leg when he came out to the porch.

"I'm glad you got to meet Brock," Mary Pat decided to say.

"Me, too. I gathered from time with the two of them that they are dating. Brock let me know, too, in front of Victoria I might add, that he was serious about her and wanted them to get engaged."

She grinned. "That was bold. How did Victoria take that?"

"Blushed and looked pleased, so I guess we'll have another wedding to go to in the next year."

She looked off into the yard. "I still can't believe Todd is married, that our children are growing up, getting married, and starting lives of their own. It seems like only yesterday they were little, running around in the yard, whooping and hollering, playing some sort of imaginative game."

Russell sighed. "I miss those times." He turned to Mary Pat. "I've been a monumental fool, Marian, to break up our family and our marriage. I know I handled my midlife itch poorly, became discontent and ungrateful for the good in my life, started wanting more. I don't know what got into me."

She lifted an eyebrow at him.

"Yes, Cherise was a major part of that. I admit." He had the grace to laugh. "Cherise, like a cat watching a mouse, seemed to know exactly when to pounce on me, fanning my discontent, promising new excitement. As she worked her way into my life, running with me in the mornings, she began to make me feel I deserved more from life. She tempted me in a lot of ways and I fell right into her machinations hook, line, and sinker."

"As I've been learning, so many things in life are a choice, Russell."

"Yes, and I made dang poor choices." He rubbed a hand through his hair. "Cherise has made my life a misery. She's difficult, controlling, has emotional tirades that are often over the top. I never saw that side of her before we married. I don't think she's stable. When we go out to public events, she hangs on me, follows me around and polices me. After we leave she suggests I've shown interest in other women. Throws angry, jealous rages."

"Has she any reason to be jealous?"

"It's a pleasure to be in the company of any woman who is emotionally sane and normal these days." He blew out a long breath. "I don't know if I can stay married to Cherise. She's making my life a living hell."

"I'm sorry, Russell," she said, and she did mean it.

He leaned toward her. "If I get free, do you think there is a chance we might get together again, Marian? We had a good marriage. I'm sorry I didn't see that."

Stunned, Mary Pat didn't answer.

Russell shifted from the chair to move onto the sofa beside her. He leaned forward and kissed her before she could think or react, then started to wrap her up in his arms, moving closer.

She pushed him back, standing to her feet in shock.

As she stood, Russell did, too, trying to move closer to her again. "You see, Marian, it's still good between us? We can begin again."

"No." She stepped back away from him. "No, it's not good between us anymore, Russell, and we cannot begin again. I don't wish unhappiness for you, but there is no future for us together any more. I want to make that very clear."

She moved across the porch further away from him. "I'm happy for you to be reestablishing better relations with our children. That's important. I want to remain civil with you whenever our paths cross, too. But as I told you at the hospital, I don't want more than that. Not even a cozy friendship."

"That's harsh."

"No, it's realistic. We're divorced. You ended our relationship with hostile, critical, angry words. I learned all in one morning that you didn't want a life with me anymore, that you all but disliked me, that you had someone else in your life you liked better, and that you had a buyer lined up for our home. A heart doesn't easily forget that sort of hurt and betrayal, even when you forgive."

He lifted his hands. "I know other couples who got back together, healed their relationships after a break up."

"That will not be me, Russell."

He sighed. "I had to try once I realized the mistakes I've made."

She watched him, feeling a little sorry for him. "I'm grateful for your apologies and your honesty today. It will make it easier for us in future to interact with events with the children." She hesitated. "But don't move in on me again. I won't have that, Russell."

He shrugged and grinned. "I had to try. You always did stir my blood, and now ...." His eyes roved over her. "You're as beautiful as when you were a girl."

Hmmmph. So much for loving me through good and bad, thick and thin, Mary Pat thought, but didn't say the words out loud.

"I guess I should go," Russell said, glancing at his watch. "Would you let me know when significant things happen with the children, in case they don't call me? I'd rather learn they're hurt, getting ready to marry, changing jobs, moving, or whatever in some way other than from Facebook."

"You should call or visit and let each of the children know that yourself, Russell. I can't be the go-between anymore unless there is an emergency. You'll need to find your own way to build back a close relationship with each of your children. Coming to see Victoria today in person was a start in the right direction."

He nodded and pulled his car keys from his pocket. "You're right. I'll work on that. It is my responsibility."

"I wish you well." Mary Pat held out a hand.

Russell took it. "I wish you well, too, and much happiness to make up for all the unhappiness I brought to you. I do mean that."

"Thank you," she said, as he opened the screened door to walk out the back of the house.

"Tell Victoria I'll call and check on her next week." He paused. "Victoria said all the kids were coming here for Thanksgiving. Do you think I could come by sometime while they're here? I can't invite them to my place with all the problems with Cherise."

"Ask them to see what they think," she said. "They'll be here through the weekend. You might plan a time to take them all out to eat at one of the restaurants in the area."

He considered her words. "That's a good idea. A friend of mine has a condo in Chalet Village above Gatlinburg. I might even come up and stay a night. I don't want to lose my relationship with my children."

She saw him out the door, glad to hear those last words. Even if divorced from her, Todd, Craig, Patrick, and Victoria would always be Russell's children, and they needed him in their lives.

Mary Pat let Barker back in the house with her and then slipped upstairs to check on Victoria.

As she opened the door a crack and then started to shut it again, Victoria called out. "Mom? I'm not asleep. Come on in."

She came in to her daughter's room, cluttered a little as Victoria always kept it, and perched on the end of the bed. "Do you need anything?"

Victoria pushed herself up to prop on some pillows at the head of the bed. "No. I took an ibuprofen pill and slept a little after Daddy helped me upstairs. I feel better now. Is he still here?"

"No. He had to get back to work."

Victoria sniffed. "It was sweet of him to come by, wasn't it?"

"It was."

"I'm glad he got to meet Brock." Her eyes widened. "Brock said right in front of him that he wanted to get engaged."

"Your father mentioned that." She smiled. "And what did you say?"

"Nothing." She rolled her eyes. "I admit Brock has asked me about getting engaged and married, but I stalled. The whole Kevin thing makes me wary."

Mary Pat chuckled. "Doesn't sound like Brock is wary."

"No." She giggled. "I sort of respect that. No one likes a wussy sort of man."

"I agree."

Victoria fiddled with her pillows. "Daddy told me how sorry he was for breaking up our family. I think he really meant it. He's super unhappy with Cherise, really confided to me how awful she acts. Did he talk to you, too?"

"He did." She hesitated before saying more.

"What? You're not telling me something."

Mary Pat sighed. "He let me know he was sorry he ended our relationship, too. He pushed some to reconcile ..." She let her words drift off.

Victoria's mouth dropped open. "Did he put some moves on you?"

"Yes," she said with embarrassment. "Uninvited ones, too, I might add. I quickly stopped him. He caught me totally off guard."

"I don't suppose it would work for you to try to get back together," Victoria said with a slightly hopeful tone.

"No, it wouldn't. Would you want to get back together with Kevin now?"

"Gosh, no!" She looked shocked.

"Well, despite the length of your father's and my marriage, I feel exactly the same way." She smiled at her daughter. "I did encourage your father in continuing to work to rebuild good ties with you and your brothers. He really wants that, Victoria, and I'm glad about that."

"Me, too, but I'm sorry he's unhappy." She bit her lip. "Even if he got himself into this fix all by himself, I still feel bad for him. Cherise sounds kind of scary if what he tells me about her is true."

"It's hard to know for sure as little as we spend time with them." She stood up. "I'm going to go downstairs to do some household tasks and to start some dinner for us. Do you want me to help you back downstairs?"

She grinned. "I think I might nap a little more and maybe watch television, just be lazy." She picked up the remote to the television that sat on her chest of drawers across the room. "Daddy is right that I need to rest this ankle while I can these first days. He read me the riot act on caring for even a stretched ligament, or minor ligament tear, and he directed me to fully follow the directions of my doctor and therapist. I probably needed that reminder lecture."

"He is a good doctor. You should heed whatever advice he gave you."

Mary Pat got up to leave.

"Mom?" Victoria asked with question. "Will you mind if Brock and I get engaged? I sort of think I'm ready for that."

"I'd be delighted, and I know Nancy and Dean will be thrilled; Cali and John, too."

Victoria grinned. "Nancy Sue Richardson will probably throw a party!"

"I don't doubt it." Mary Pat laughed. "Tell her to plan it Thanksgiving weekend when your brothers come in."

"Oh, that's a great idea!" She leaned back with a dreamy look on her face. "Brock's father Dean has a beautiful old vintage engagement ring that was his grandmother's. It has a gorgeous diamond and pretty scrollwork in the white gold setting around it. Brock showed it to me to see what I thought about it."

"You like it, I can tell."

"I do, and it's sort of romantic that it's an old family piece. Do you think it's okay not to get a new ring?"

"I think it's the love and thought that counts and what you would like and be happy with. I'm sure Brock's first thought is to please you.'

"It is. He said we could go shopping for rings, but I fell in love with that ring the moment I saw it." She sighed. "It fits perfectly, too. That's like a sign, don't you think?"

"Yes, and you be sure and hint to Brock you want a memorable moment in which to receive that ring. We women remember that sort of thing."

"We do." Her voice softened. "I love you, Mom."

"I love you, too, sweetheart," she said, and went down the stairs smiling.

CHAPTER 20

On the last Saturday in the month in October Owen took Mary Pat on a hike in the Smokies. The day was a glorious, warm one, expected to rise into the seventies and both wanted to get out of doors to enjoy the fall colors before colder temperatures settled in for the winter.

In an effort to avoid the "leaf looker" tourist crowds in popular areas of the Smoky Mountains, they decided to hike on nearby Dudley Creek Trail off Highway 321. The old trail was little known to most hikers since the horses from the Smoky Mountain Stable also used the crisscross of quiet pathways winding up and down the mountainside between Twin Creek and Dudley Creek.

"This is a glorious day to be out," Mary Pat said as they started up the trail walking by the corral fence beyond the stable.

"Yes, I'm glad Victoria is better and that we could both get away today." He adjusted his waist pack, containing a light lunch, water, a small first aid kit, and other needed items for the trail.

"She's really doing well, back at work full time and only using the scooter as needed to keep swelling from setting up when she's on her feet all day." Mary Pat stretched out her pace to keep up with him as they started into the woods.

"Instead of hiking the six mile loop, I thought we might hike on past the turning to the Grapeyard Ridge Trail. On that higher trail, we might catch some fine views of the fall colors on the higher mountains."

"That sounds like a great idea." She pointed ahead. "Look at that glorious golden orange tree. Is that a beech?"

"Yes. There are a lot of them on this trail, along with oaks, maples, and other hardwoods. We should see some pretty color all along the way."

With the old roadbed trail wide on this lower end, they could walk along side by side.

"Look at that brilliant red maple and that stunning yellow tulip poplar? Isn't it amazing to see all the different colors the trees turn in the fall?"

"It is," he said, kicking his way through the colored leaves across the path.

At about a half-mile they rock-hopped across the first creek crossing. A few more would follow, but the last week had been dry so the water in the creeks would be low and easy to ford.

"Gloria, Nancy, and I got our feet soaked crossing some of these creeks one day when we hiked this trail after a week of rain." She straightened her own waist pack after getting across the creek.

They admired the colors along the trail as they hiked on, pointed out rushing cascades in the creek, birds they spotted twittering in the trees overhead, a deer they saw deep in the woods. The trail, although gradually ascending, wasn't a difficult one.

Further up the trail, Owen spotted a huge, familiar beech tree near the trail. He slowed to move closer to it. "Many settlers lived in this area before the park took the land," he told Mary Pat. "Most of the land around here belonged to the Coy Ogle family. They hated leaving their land and all the children signed their names on this old tree before they left."

"I love the old stories about the early families here." She traced her finger over the word Ogle etched into the trunk.

"Not all the children's names are still legible after all this time, but you can still find some."

They took time to look for a few of the names and then walked on.

"Nancy, Gloria and I explored the Ashley Ogle Cemetery one day on the cross trail and there are several places where you can find clearings where old settlers' homes stood off the trails, too."

"McCarters owned a lot of the land along Little Dudley Creek on the other side of the loop and if you look off the trail nearer Grapeyard Ridge, in the right spot, you can find remnants of the Richard Clabo place and remains of an old mill."

"You'll have to show me that spot one day."

"Mike Maples knew the backwoods and trails around this area like few others. If you ever got the chance to hike with him, he could lead you off the main trails to all sorts of interesting places. He also wrote several books about the families and history of this area. All are packed with little known stories and vintage photos."

"I'll have to look for those books."

"I own a few you can borrow; Dad has others. He likes to collect books about the history of the area."

"He should probably write one, too. Your dad knows so many old stories."

"That he does."

The trail wound uphill, moving under trees ablaze with fall color. They often stopped to take a few photos and Mary Pat picked up special leaves to carry along with her to admire.

At about three miles, they climbed to the intersection with the Grapeyard Ridge Trail. They turned left, walking east, soon finding spots where they could look north toward Mount Winnesoka, Lookout Rock, Brushy Mountain and on to Mount Le Conte high above. The trees at these higher elevations sang with rich gold, russet red, and vibrant orange autumn colors, creating a beautiful panorama across the overlapping mountain ranges.

"I see where the Grapeyard Ridge name came from." Mary Pat pointed to the tangled vines along the trail and the Gordian knots in the hemlocks, cucumbers, and red oaks along the way.

Owen walked over to test a grapevine swing looped between two trees. "Clint and I used to love to play on these as kids and pretend to be Tarzan of the jungle."

Mary Pat laughed and snapped his photo.

With the day so beautiful, they hiked on toward James Gap. At

Injun Creek, they stopped to look for the remains of the old steam engine in the creek.

"There's a wheel." Mary Pat gestured toward the rusted metal wheel in the creek. "How in the world did a steam engine end up down in this creek?"

Owen walked over beside Mary Pat to study the old wheel and turbine. "In the 1920s an old railroad bed ran along where the Grapeyard Ridge Trail is today. As the driver of an old steam engine started over James Gap and downhill one of the engine's wheels got too close to the edge, toppling the engine into the creek. The driver jumped off, luckily, but the engine was toast, of course. They salvaged most of the parts but a few pieces got left behind to tell the story."

"The mountains are full of wondeerful stories." She gave him a sunny smile. "I'm hungry. Can we eat lunch here?"

"Let's walk back up trail and eat at Campsite #32. It's a pretty spot with cascades and some nice rocks and logs to sit on."

They hiked about a quarter mile back up trail and down a side path to the campsite. They ate their lunch there and talked.

Mary Pat told him about Russell's visit.

"I don't think you mentioned that visit from Russell before."

"No." She looked down at her lap, not meeting his eyes.

"You going to tell me the rest or make me guess?" He grinned at her.

"He's unhappy in his marriage to Cherise. He says he may not stay married to her…"

"Let me guess. He wants to get back with you, realizes he made a mistake in ever leaving you."

She looked up in surprise. "Did Victoria tell you that?"

"No, but most fools come to their senses after a while." He studied her. "Are you interested in that idea?"

"No!" She practically hollered the word.

"Well, I'm relieved to hear that. You spent a long time married to Russell. I often wondered what you'd do if he came sparking again."

She blushed.

"How much sparking did he do?"

She rubbed her arm, obviously embarrassed. "He kissed me before I realized what he intended. Caught me off guard."

"Was it good?"

She threw a pinecone at him. "No, and I pushed him away right after. I don't want to go there again with Russell."

"I worried I might have a rival for my affections."

She reached out a hand to put it on his knee, her voice softening. "You shouldn't worry. It rather helped me realize more fully the new direction of my heart now."

"Oh, sweet words." He turned on the log they shared as a seat to kiss her, pulling her close as she kissed him back with warmth and pleasure.

Owen pulled back after a minute to trace a hand down her cheek. "Do you think you might want to think about another name change sometime in the new year?"

"Is that a proposal?" Her lips twitched.

"It could be if I thought the answer might be yes." He let his hands play through her hair, enjoying being here in this quiet, beautiful place alone with her.

"You know I love you, Mary Pat, want to spend my life with you. I love the idea of waking up every morning to find you lying beside me, and I dream far too often of the rich pleasure of knowing you in a closer way."

They sat looking into each other's eyes for a moment.

"I love you, too, Owen McCarter," she said at last. "I did as a girl, and that old love has flamed back up again and only grown stronger."

She put her hands on his chest. "I'd like to say yes now to that sweet proposal, but I'm asking you to be patient a little longer. Victoria and Brock have just gotten engaged. Nancy and Dean are planning an engagement party for them at Thanksgiving when my boys come home." She sighed. "I think it would be a little much to spring two engagements on them at once. But I think Christmas would be a lovely time to get engaged, don't you?"

He smiled and leaned in to kiss her again. "I've always heard the best things are worth waiting for."

She swatted at him. "You may change your mind by then."

"No, I won't, but it might be a little cold to propose outdoors again."

She giggled. "I think the Buckeye Inn would be a lovely indoor spot for a proposal, maybe with candlelight and a nice dinner."

"I'll work on making that happen."

They packed up the remains of their lunch and started back toward home on the trail. At the intersection to the Dudley Creek Trail 1.7 miles later, Mary Pat stopped to rest a minute on a rock.

"Owen, I've been thinking about something."

"What?" he asked, after drinking water from the bottle in his waist pack.

"Well, I'd assume if we got married that I would move in with you."

He grinned at her. "Most married people don't live in two houses."

She wrinkled her nose. "Be serious. I was just wondering what you'd think about me offering my mountain house to Victoria and Brock. He's still living with Nancy and Dean right now in their basement and I'll soon have an empty house. Do you think they might like it? Would Brock be offended for me to offer? Would it bother his pride or anything?"

Owen propped a foot on the rock she sat on, considering the idea. "I can't imagine it a problem. You could call it a first year wedding gift. If they wanted to stay on, they could pay rent. Would you want to sell the house to them in time if they wanted to buy it?"

"I'm not sure." She frowned. "It's my parents' place, my home, too. I want it to stay in the family. I'd like it to be a place in time where the kids could always come to stay, like a vacation home."

"Brock and Victoria would understand that." He smiled. "I own a lot of land around my place if they wanted to build nearby, but they might have other ideas. Offering the house for the first year or so is a sweet idea though."

"Thanks." She sighed. "I really needed an outside view."

He leaned over to kiss her. "The best idea in this is that we'd need to get married before them so you can move in with me. Those two seem eager to tie the knot. Would you be willing to become Mrs. McCarter a little sooner than planned if needed?"

Her eyes widened. "I hadn't thought of that. I just envisioned they'd wait until spring or early summer."

He laughed. "I wouldn't count on it."

"I imagine you're right," she said blushing. "They do give each other rather smoldering looks these days."

Owen gave her a hand up and they hiked on, continuing down the Dudley Creek Trail. They chatted along the way.

"Can you share some part of Thanksgiving with us?" she said at one point. "I'd like you to get to know the boys better."

"I'll find times to come around." He wanted to talk to the boys alone at some time, too. "You know, Francine wants to host a big Thanksgiving at Dad's at the farmhouse with her, Clint, Larissa, Dad, Garrett and myself. Would you consider joining in with that? The farmhouse is big. The dining room table seats at least twelve with the leaves in. With six of you and six of us that would make an even dozen to enjoy a good day together."

"I'll see what Victoria thinks about that idea," she said. "This Thanksgiving is her special time, getting engaged. She might want something smaller with only the family." She paused. "With the children marrying and maybe starting families, it could be one of the last times we all get together at Thanksgiving."

He turned to see her frowning at that idea.

"They'll always find ways to come home, even if not always together for every holiday," he said, slowing for a moment. "They'll soon have other families to think about as well."

She looked thoughtful. "Yes, I'm sure you're right. And I don't want to be one of those difficult parents who doesn't understand that."

"You'll find your way with those changes just like you have in other things with grace and love."

"What a nice thing to say." She offered him a sweet smile before they walked on.

As the horse corral and the end of the trail came into view, she slowed her steps again, stopping to lean against the fence. "I hate for this day to end," she said. "It's been such a really nice day." She looked around at all the fall color with a smile.

He let his eyes move over her, a fine looking woman for her age, her blond highlighted hair glowing in the sunshine like her face, her slacks fitting well over her legs, strong from walking so much, a lightweight rosy sweater highlighting the color in her cheeks.

"This has been a good day." He winked at her. "I'm all but secretly engaged and the woman I love has let me know she loves me, too. She's even making plans to move in with me. The day couldn't get much better."

She laughed. "Well, it might. I could go home, get dressed and cleaned up, and you could take me out to dinner."

He went over to link his arm in hers. "Well, honey, that is a fine offer, and you can pick the place. That will make a perfect ending to our day and we can whisper sweet nothings to each other over dinner and before we say goodnight."

Her warm giggles rang out after his words.

"We are going to have a happy life, aren't we Owen?"

"The best," he said. "The very best."

CHAPTER 21

Mary Pat seemed to float through her next days after her hike with Owen, remembering so often their words shared on the trail and later over dinner. At work at Diet Options on Thursday, she hummed as she locked the door at noon and began to tidy up to close.

"You certainly have been in a good mood all week," Charlotte commented.

Mary Pat looked up to see her leaning in the doorway. "I always love the fall when the colors turn in the Smokies," she said.

Charlotte chuckled. "Somehow I doubt it's the fall colors causing you to hum while you work and walk around with a big smile on your face."

She blushed.

"There's nothing wrong with falling in love, even at mid life," Charlotte added.

"Is it that obvious?" Mary Pat bit her lip. "I feel a little silly."

"I'd say only those who know you well see the change this week. You tend to be an upbeat, positive person."

She straightened a stack of magazines on the coffee table. "Owen and I shared some feelings this weekend."

"I see. Did he propose? Can I do a happy dance?"

Mary Pat laughed. "Yes, but keep the information confidential for now. We're waiting to share the news or make any plans until after Thanksgiving. It's such an important time for Victoria and Brock right now, and I want to give the boys an opportunity to get to know Owen."

"I understand you taking your time." She smiled. "But please know I'm so happy for you. I like Owen and I'm glad for your news."

"Thanks."

Charlotte changed the subject. "You have a college class tonight. How's that going?"

"Good. It's mostly a refresher course to catch up on all the legal changes related to nutritional practice—that sort of thing."

"I have a form for you to take in about your internship here, all positive of course. You can read it." She passed it to Mary Pat. "One of the best decisions I ever made was hiring you to work here with me. For a long time, when getting started, I wanted to do it all myself, didn't trust the idea of hiring anyone else. Probably smugly thought no one else could do it as well as I could, but over time, with the workload heavy, I began to think I might hire someone if I could find the right person."

"I've really been happy working here."

"That is obvious in the love and care you give to all our clients. You also are an excellent teacher." She twisted her necklace. "Next spring when all your personal issues are resolved, Rowan and I would like to take a trip abroad. As a painter Rowan would like to see some of the well-known galleries in Europe like the British Museum and the National Gallery in London, the Louvre in Paris, the Vatican in Rome and the Uffizi Gallery in Florence, and others we've been reading about—and, of course, see all the sights. Do you think you could run things for a while with some of the girls to help you?" She grinned. "I could return the favor when you need time away."

"What a wonderful idea! I'm so excited for you." Mary Pat went over to hug Charlotte. "I will definitely cover for you and Rowan, especially if you promise to show me all your pictures when you get back."

"You can count on it. I'll probably bore everyone senseless showing them over and over."

They talked about a few of their dieters they had concerns about then, how to counsel and encourage them, and Mary Pat left to go home. With Victoria working today at the pharmacy, she planned to make a big salad for lunch and toss some shrimp into it. Later at campus after studying for a time in the library, she'd get a bite to eat before her class at 6:00.

At the house, after walking Barker, she fixed her salad and ate it while studying the text readings for her class. The sound of the doorbell interrupted her focus, and she got up to walk over to open the door.

To her surprise, Cherise stood there, a businesslike look on her face.

"Hello, Cherise. This is a surprise. What can I do for you?"

"I need to talk with you. Can I come in?" She moved past Mary Pat into the living room, not waiting for an answer.

Mary Pat gestured to the sofa, deciding to be gracious.

"You did downsize to move up here." Cherise glanced around, obviously unimpressed, as she sat on the sofa. "But several women in the Auxiliary said they heard you'd dropped a lot of weight. You do look well." Her eyes moved over Mary Pat in assessment.

What was this woman doing here? Trying to hide her annoyance, Mary Pat studied Cherise for a moment as she sat down across from her in a chair. In professional business dress, she wore a trim grey houndstooth suit, a neat black shell, and a simple strand of pearls. Her dark shoulder length hair lay neatly in place, the cut obviously professional, and her makeup perfect. Admittedly, she was still a stunningly beautiful woman. Her physical appeal to any man could hardly be questioned, but her eyes were not kind.

"What brings you to Gatlinburg to see me?" Mary Pat asked at last.

"I'm here for a two-day real estate conference at the Edgewater Conference Center in Gatlinburg. I had a break between meetings and followed my GPS directions to your place. The address was in Russell's file."

She glanced around again. "I argued with Russell about handing you this place on a silver platter. It should have been a part of the estate, but with a sale offer on the house in Sequoyah, it was convenient for you to have a place to relocate to quickly." Her eyes settled on the dog, eyeing him without welcome. "It does surprise me, however, that you haven't sold the place, found something nicer. It's hardly the sort of home you're used to. I know a realtor in this area if you're interested in selling."

Gritting her teeth, Mary Pat chose her words carefully. "I have no interest in selling my home. I grew up here. With that issue aside, what did you want to see me about?"

Cherise leaned forward. "I want you to quit seeing Russell. Don't try to tell me you haven't been seeing him. I know you met him at the hospital one day. I know one day he came up here." Her glance grew steely. "You had your chance with him and that time is finished. Do you hear me?"

Mary Pat knew her mouth dropped open in surprise, but then she smiled. "Cherise, be assured I am not seeing Russell again, nor do I want to. I ran into him at the hospital cafeteria one day while visiting an old neighbor and friend. He came by the house to see Victoria after learning she got injured. She is his daughter."

She sneered. "I knew you'd offer some sort of excuse and try to deny it, but I know it's more than that. Don't tell me different." Her voice rose, her eyes angry and challenging now. "I can tell by the way Russell acts when we talk about you. It's different than the way he talked about you before the divorce. So don't tell me it's nothing. I can tell he's attracted to you again and I expect you to quit encouraging his interest. I will not let him go without a fight."

Mary Pat tried to think what to say. "No matter what you may discern in Russell's actions, I can only assure you again I have no interest in resuming a relationship with him. My life has moved on. I do not want to revisit the past."

Cherise all but snarled. "I'm sure you wouldn't tell *him* that."

Provoked, Mary Pat said, "Actually I did."

"See?" Cherise waved a finger toward her. "I knew you'd been encouraging him."

"No. I have not," Mary Pat said emphatically, standing up. "Listen, I'm sorry if you and Russell are experiencing marital problems but I can assure you I am *no* party to them. If you are seeking someone to blame, it is *not* me, and I don't appreciate you coming here throwing out unfounded accusations and suggesting I am trying to break up your marriage. You are welcome to Russell Latham. I only see him at all to help him and our children keep ties. If you ask him, he will make those facts clear to you."

"I don't believe you." Cherise stood up. "I know he's seeing someone else. I can sense it."

"Then you will have to look elsewhere if you think that is so. Or discuss this issue with Russell. I'd advise that course over coming here and making ridiculous accusations to me. This helps in no way."

She moved toward Mary Pat with an angry look. "I'll find out if you're seeing him. Be sure you know that."

Barker growled low in his throat.

"You'd better go, Cherise. I have nothing more to say to you, and your continued accusations are becoming offensive."

Mary Pat watched the anger snap across Cherise's face, her eyes narrowing again. "If it's not you, I will find out who it is, and if it is you, I will find that out, too. I won't have anyone cheating on me, do you hear?"

She'd raised her voice again and Barker growled once more.

Mary Pat walked to the door and opened it. "You need to go now. I wish you no ill, Cherise, and again, I am not interested in your husband. You are welcome to him and I suggest the two of you get some counseling. It looks like you need it."

Cherise spit out a few final accusations, needing the last word, and then swept out of the door.

Her legs shaky then, Mary Pat sat down on the couch. Barker came to put his nose in her hand.

She petted the dog to calm him—and to calm herself. "That woman is not a healthy person," she told Barker. "I have to admit I almost feel sorry for Russell today."

Mary Pat sat on the sofa for a little while to calm down, and then cleaned up her lunch and packed her books, papers, and laptop to head to class. She kept thinking about Cherise's visit over the next hours while she studied at the old library. At four, she finally decided to call Russell. He needed to know Cherise had visited and threatened her, and she wanted him to encourage Cherise not to come to her home in Gatlinburg again or to call or bother her in any way.

She punched in his cell number on her phone.

"Russell here," he answered in an abstract tone.

"I'm sorry to call if you're with a patient, Russell, but I'd like to stop by your office for a minute to speak to you if it's all right."

"Actually I'm on my way home, Marian, turning into my street. Are you at the campus today?"

"I am."

"Well, why don't you run down to my place? It's just down Kingston Pike, a condo in La Rue, the gated condo community right before you get to Sequoyah. I'm on the main street in, fourth condo on the left." He gave her a street number. "It's near the campus for you and as close as driving to UT hospital and my offices in the medical building."

"I rather wanted to avoid Cherise for this meeting, Russell."

He hesitated a moment. "No worry there. Cherise is in Gatlinburg at a real estate conference. I have a meeting later or I'd come out to meet you somewhere, but I don't mind if you drop by for a minute. Or maybe we could simply talk on the phone. I'm pulling in my drive now."

Mary Pat thought about it. "I'll drive over to your place, but I can't stay long. I need to talk to you for a minute, but I have a class at 6:00."

"Well, see you in a bit," he said. "Here's the code for the gate." He recited off some numbers and Mary Pat wrote them down.

A short time later, after retrieving her car from the parking lot and driving down Kingston Pike to the entrance to La Rue, Mary Pat turned into the beautifully manicured and gated development to drive past a row of stately brick condos to find Russell's house number. Parking her car in the drive, she walked to the front door and rang the bell.

"Hey," Russell said, opening the door. He still wore a crisp dress shirt from work but without his usual lab coat now. "Come on in."

She watched his eyes slide over her, accessing her with interest, and wondered if she'd made a mistake stopping by.

"Cherise came to see me today," she said following him into the house, deciding to move to the subject of her visit quickly.

He groaned. "I'm sure that wasn't a cozy visit." He gestured to a white sofa in a beige and white room, modern, stark, but tastefully decorated.

She sat on the sofa, while he dropped into a chair beside it.

"This is a beautiful place." Mary Pat glanced around.

"It was Cherise's before we married and bigger than my condo by the hospital. So I moved over here. It's still close for me when I need to flash back for emergencies."

"Yes." She remembered those times when an emergency with a heart patient sent him off to the hospital at three or four in the morning many times.

"Why did Cherise come to see you?" he asked.

"To warn me off. She thinks we're seeing each other again."

He laughed. "Not for my not trying."

She leaned forward. "This is serious, Russell. She was angry, all but threatened me. I don't like that. I want you to talk to her. If necessary, get some counseling."

He rubbed his neck. "I'm tired of her emotional tirades, her threats and accusations. I swear the woman practically stalks me now. Shows up when I've told her I have a meeting. Checking up on me."

Annoyed, he got up and paced over to the fireplace with a large flat screen television mounted over it. "I signed some papers today to take my old condominium back near the hospital. She'll probably throw a fit but I don't care. I've had it with her instability. And when you really get to know her, she's cold inside. She may be beautiful, but her soul is dark."

"I don't want to get in the middle of this. She seems certain you're seeing someone else."

He rolled his eyes and looked away from her.

"Are you?" She recognized that shift in posture that suggested Russell wasn't telling her everything. "I have no right to interfere in your life, but I'd like to suggest you close out one life entirely before starting another. It's a better course of action usually."

He turned to grin at her. "You have a point. If I'd taken things slower, gotten to know Cherise better, I'd never have left you."

"I hate to sound pious, Russell, but adultery is wrong. When you are married, even if there are problems, you should attempt to work them out before embarking on another relationship."

"You have a point there, too, but Cherise is the sort of woman that soon has a man wanting to run into any kind and loving arms he can find."

She pursed her lips, not saying anything.

He smiled then. "Look at you, sitting there sweet and prim and proper, worrying about me like you always have. I was an idiot to start fooling around on you and I'm still sorry you won't think about taking me back."

She shook her head and stood. "That isn't an option, but Russell, take care how you handle this situation with Cherise. Seek counseling and help, try to work things out. You admired so much about her before you married. Maybe you can begin to see those attributes again."

"It's easy to see why you make a good counselor." He glanced at his watch and then flashed a grin at her again. "I do have a dinner meeting to get ready for, but if you'd like to stay on, I could cancel it."

She shook her head.

"I figured that would be your answer but you can't blame a guy for trying." He followed her to the door.

Mary Pat turned at the door and put a hand on Russell's arm. "Talk to Cherise and convince her there is nothing happening between us. Promise me that. I don't want more problems with her or any more angry visits."

He shrugged. "I'll speak to her. We need to talk out quite a few things." He kissed her on the forehead. "You take care and find some happiness. You deserve it. I'm sorry again I wasn't a better husband."

She smiled at him. "I have no complaints until the last year or so of our marriage."

He touched her cheek. "Then those are the sweet years we'll both remember."

Driving back to school, Mary Pat felt happy in a way that she'd gone to talk to Russell. Maybe he would get help and work things out with Cherise. It seemed obvious Cherise still cared for him and was panicking that Russell might be growing discontent.

Back at home later, she told Victoria about Cherise's visit and going to see Russell.

Victoria shook her head. "I told you that woman was a hard, mean number. I can't believe she came up here, uninvited, to accuse you of trying to steal Dad back. I hope they work something civil out."

"I do, too."

Victoria propped her foot up on a pillow on the ottoman.

"Is your foot bothering you?"

"No, it's good. It just swells a bit after a long day on my feet at the pharmacy sometimes. The therapist and doctor said I could expect that for a time. They said to elevate it after a long day. It helps."

Mary Pat stood up. "I think I'll make a cup of diet cocoa. Would you like one, too?"

"Ummm. Sounds good. I would."

When she came back with both mugs and sat down, Victoria asked. "What is Dad's new place like? I've never been there."

She smiled. "I doubt I'd have stopped by if Cherise hadn't been away." She sipped her cocoa. "It's a posh, modern condo—nine foot ceilings, beautiful hardwood floors, elegant crown molding, very modern and elegantly decorated. The color scheme I saw was all predominantly white and beige with a lot of sleek black and gold accents. It's in La Rue, right by the turn into Sequoyah Hills. You've seen the development, I'm sure. Gated, immaculate grounds."

"I know where it is, right next door to Boxwood Square before the Boulevard starts."

"Yes." She hesitated. "Is that the sort of place you and Brock want? Modern and new?"

Vicotria made a face. "No, we want a homier place, more like this or like Nancy and Dean's log house." She grinned. "We'll need to find something before we get married, though. I don't want to live with Brock in Nancy Sue and Dean's basement."

Mary Pat sipped her cocoa trying to decide whether to tell Victoria about the house. "You like Owen, don't you?"

"I'm crazy about Owen." She eyed her mother with suspicion. "Why are you even asking me that? Are you still worrying I might disapprove if you decide to get married?"

Mary Pat blushed. "I did wonder what you'd think about it. And the boys."

"Like I told you before, you and Owen both deserve some happiness." She paused. "I've been telling the boys a lot about Owen lately when we talk, how much I admire him, that I think he's still in love with you from your school days."

"What did they say?"

"They remember him a little from last Easter. They think he's nice. Since you've known each other forever, and since you grew up together, they all feel better about him. He's not like a stranger would be." She grinned. "I gather Gigi has been working on them about Owen, too."

Mary Pat sat up straight, surprised.

Victoria giggled. "Gigi and Pops have come to visit a couple of times since you moved here. They know Owen and they know you. They'd need to be stupid blind not to see there is something going on with the two of you."

"Mom has dropped some hints a few times."

"She likes him, just like I do." Victoria sipped her cocoa. "If

Owen was someone new in your life, the family might be more concerned. But it's sweet you found each other again the way you did. You're not strangers that don't know each other." She wrinkled her nose. "Besides, when you find the right person, you simply know sometimes. I worried about falling for Brock so soon, but it happened anyway. It's hard to stop love. It sort of sneaks up on you."

"Would you and Brock like to live here for a time after you marry?"

"With you?" Victoria's eyes popped wide.

"No. I mean if I lived somewhere else."

Victoria sent her a questioning look. "What do you mean? Do you want to leave Gatlinburg? Leave your job and everyone?"

"No." She knew she answered crossly. "It's just that ..."

Suddenly Victoria threw a hand over her mouth. "Are you and Owen wanting to get married?" She all but squealed out the words.

Mary Pat twisted her hands. "We have talked about it."

Victoria dropped her foot from the ottoman and jumped up to hug her. "That is such fantastic news! I'm so excited for you."

She tried to temper her daughter's enthusiasm. "I didn't say we'd made definite plans, only that we talked about it. And if we do marry, the house here would be empty."

Victoria sat back down, propping her foot up again. "I'll talk to Brock about it. It's a great idea, and it would give us time to save money for our own place, look around, think about what we want to buy."

Mary Pat sighed. "I hoped you might like the idea. I'd be pleased for it to be my wedding gift to you, to stay a year or two here."

"It's a fun thought." She scratched her chin. "We've talked about getting married on Valentine's Day weekend in the New Year. If we do that, you and Owen will need to plan something *ahead* of us." She grinned. "I'm sure Owen would like that."

Mary Pat blushed. "Well, we'll all talk about this when you two set an actual date. Right now, it's time to be happy about your and Brock's engagement."

Victoria looked thoughtful. "I'm sorry about Dad. It seems like people cheating doesn't bring anything but sorrows and unhappiness, like bad karma. But look how nice things have turned out for you and me, Mom? I think it's true that things work for good in time for nice people. I'm glad we're getting a second chance to be happy."

"Me, too, sweetie." She got up and picked up their empty mugs to take to the kitchen. "I think I'm going to head to bed with a good book. I've had a long day."

"I hope you have a better day tomorrow."

"Me, too." She blew her daughter a kiss and headed to her bedroom, but despite her good talk with Victoria, she tossed and turned through the night, worrying about Russell. He seemed to float constantly through her dreams.

CHAPTER 22

Owen dropped by for lunch the next day with Mary Pat, Victoria and Brock. Victoria didn't work at the pharmacy until later in the evening, so she'd fixed lunch for them all, timing it to coincide with Brock's lunch hour.

"This casserole is really good," Owen said, reaching for a second helping.

"It's called Turkey Mexican Lasagna, one of mom's recipes and with a surprisingly low calorie count per serving, especially with salad as a side."

Brock grinned. "Well, I'm not counting calories so I'm eating a second helping, too. I'm glad you're a good cook."

"Mom taught me. She's always been a great cook. She's working on a recipe book for the Diet Options center right now, compiling all the recipes she, Charlotte, and other dieters have created or adapted over the years."

Mary Pat finished off a bite of salad. "I suggested it might be a good idea to compile a book for our dieters and Charlotte loved the idea. We can spiral bind and print it locally for very little, like churches and civic organizations do."

They ate and talked about work and ongoing activities. Owen listened happily to the conversation, pleased to learn earlier that Mary Pat had shared their plans to get married in future. It seemed Brock and Victoria were excited about the idea of living in Mary Pat's house for a year or two, as well.

When Brock went back to work, Owen, Mary Pat, and Victoria

sat visiting in the living room after cleaning up from lunch.

"I still can't believe Cherise came by here yesterday with all those crazy accusations," Victoria said, putting her foot on the ottoman to rest it.

"Well, hopefully, when Cherise gets home from her meetings in Gatlinburg today, Russell will talk to her." Mary Pat curled a foot up under her on the sofa.

"Did she say she stayed over last night in Gatlinburg?" Victoria asked.

"She mentioned it when she stopped by and I don't think Russell expected her home last night. It was a two-day conference."

Victoria tucked a pillow under her foot. "Well, I hope she doesn't stop by here again before she heads home today!"

Owen leaned over to pet Barker, who had curled up by his feet. "I also hope in future, Mary Pat, you won't go to see Russell alone as you did with so much turmoil going on between that couple."

"Looking back, I admit that probably wasn't the smartest thing to do. I'd expected to simply drop by Russell's office." Mary Pat wrinkled her nose. "But Cherise acted so crazy yesterday, I thought Russell should know."

The doorbell rang, and Owen got up to answer it.

Two police officers stood at the door. "I'm Officer John Roland and this is Officer Innis Salter," said the older of the two, flashing badges to Owen. "Is this the home of Mary Pat and Victoria Latham?"

Alarmed, Mary Pat stood up, walking over to join him at the door. "I'm Mary Pat Latham." She gestured to Victoria, still sitting on the sofa. "And this is my daughter, Victoria. What can we do to help you?"

"Can we come in?" the officer asked.

Mary Pat gestured them in, encouraging them to sit down. "Is anything wrong? Has someone in the neighborhood or in our family been hurt?"

The two men took seats, and the older officer with short-cropped hair, a neat mustache and a touch of grey beard, leaned forward to speak again. "We're with the Knoxville police department. We contacted Bill Magee, the police chief in Gatlinburg, before stopping by to see you." He hesitated, his eyes settling on Victoria and then Mary Pat. "I regret to bring you the news that Russell Latham was found dead in his home this morning. We had this address for his daughter and ex-wife. We wanted to bring the news to a family member personally."

Mary Pat gasped and Victoria began to cry.

"What happened?" Owen asked.

The officer lifted his eyes at Owen, uncertain of his identity.

"I'm Owen McCarter. I live next door and I am a close friend of the family," he explained.

The officer nodded.

"How did Russell die?" Mary Pat asked, upset. "He was a doctor, in good health. I saw him only yesterday. He wasn't even sick."

Owen watched the two officers exchange a significant glance.

Officer Roland took a breath before adding, "Unfortunately, Russell Latham was murdered."

Mary Pat began to cry then, too, obviously shocked. "Oh, how terrible. How could that have happened? Who could want to kill Russell?"

"We're investigating that now," Officer Roland answered.

With Mary Pat and Victoria still crying, Owen asked, "Can you tell us what happened?"

"When Dr. Latham didn't show for surgery this morning and couldn't be reached, we were contacted to check his home. Staff at his office told us his wife was out of town at a real estate meeting. With no continuing answers to calls or messaging to her or the house, we entered the home and found Dr. Latham dead from a gunshot wound, the body discovered in what we assume the family room."

"Have you reached his wife?" Owen asked.

"We did finally make contact with her. She had been swimming morning laps in the hotel pool when Dr. Latham's office first tried to reach her. Naturally, she's driven back to Knoxville now and is equally distraught."

Officer Salter, the younger of the two officers, leaned forward, "Ms. Latham, you mentioned that you had seen the victim yesterday. Can you tell us about that visit?"

Victoria's eyes widened. "Oh my gosh, you can't think my mom had anything to do with this? If anybody had wanted to hurt Daddy, it would have been his crazy wife Cherise. She came here yesterday, threatening my mom."

Owen groaned. "Victoria, this might not be the best time to air out family problems."

She clapped a hand over her mouth. "Should I not have said that?"

Mary Pat sighed.

Officer Roland turned to speak to Mary Pat. "We would like to ask questions about those visits and especially about your visit to see Dr. Latham yesterday."

Her face blanched white and she glanced at Owen. "Do I need an attorney?"

Officer Roland shook his head. "We were sent to bring the death notification to the family and to ask for information that might help us in the investigation. We have no suspects at this point but we would appreciate your cooperation in helping with any facts and information you could provide."

"You don't need an attorney now, Mary Pat," Owen answered. He glanced at Victoria. "And I think you've watched too many TV crime shows."

He saw both officers try not to grin.

"As Officer Roland said," Owen explained, "Mary Pat is not a suspect, nor could she be. If Russell was killed late last night, Mary Pat was here in Gatlinburg at home with her daughter."

Owen turned to the officer. "What time did Dr. Latham die?"

"The approximate time of death was estimated at shortly after midnight," he answered.

Mary Pat turned to both officers. "If you tell me what you know about Russell's death, I will tell you about my visit with him yesterday, if you think it could help your investigation. Naturally, we want to do all we can to help."

Officer Roland nodded. "We know he left his office earlier than usual yesterday at about 4:00 pm. A neighbor, raking leaves, waved at him as he pulled in his driveway about twenty minutes after that." He glanced at Mary Pat. "The neighbor also said a woman in a red car pulled into the driveway shortly after and went into the home."

"That was me," Mary Pat said. "I called, hoping to drop by Russell's office to speak with him briefly. He let me know he was nearly home at that time and suggested, since I was nearby at the university for a class, that I drop by the house instead. I did so. We talked for about fifteen or twenty minutes and I left. I went back to campus, ate dinner at the cafeteria, and went to class in the human ecology building, the Jessie Harris building, from 6:00 to 8:00. Then I drove back home to Gatlinburg. I got home about an hour later. Victoria and I visited and then we went to bed at about 10:00."

"She got home a few minutes after 9:00," Victoria put in. "I was finishing a favorite TV show that ends at 9:00 when she came in the door. Neither of us went anywhere after Mom came home and we were both here all night. I got up to go to the bathroom about midnight. Mom's door was open and she was asleep. I remember shushing Barker so he wouldn't woof and wake her up."

Owen smiled. Victoria wanted to be certain the officers didn't suspect her mother of leaving and returning to Knoxville. Quite frankly, with this situation, it was good she had a solid alibi. A recent ex-wife is often one of the first suspects of interest in a homicide investigation.

Tears welled in Mary Pat's eyes again. "Is there anything else I can tell you that might help?"

Officer Roland pulled out a notepad to check it. "Dr. Latham's nurse at the office said he mentioned a meeting scheduled that night. Do you know where he went for that?"

She frowned. "No, I don't. I assumed it a medical or business meeting. He did mention that he left work early for a meeting but he didn't offer any details about it and I didn't ask."

"Will you tell us why you went to see your husband yesterday?"

Mary Pat's eyes went to Owen. "Do I need to share personal information?"

"Since Victoria already offered information about that earlier, I think you should," he answered.

He saw Victoria roll her eyes. "I'm sorry. I was upset."

Mary Pat smiled at her. "We have nothing to hide, Victoria." She turned to the officers. "Yesterday proved an upsetting day. Russell's wife Cherise came to our home, uninvited, pushed her way in and accused me of seeing her husband."

"Have you been seeing him?" Officer Salter asked.

"Only on needed occasions as related to our children. We share four children together. I've tried to keep a civil relationship because of that. I saw Russell at our son's wedding in Hendersonville this August, inadvertently at the University hospital when visiting a sick friend this fall, and when Russell came here to see Victoria after she fell and suffered an injury recently." She hesitated. "Cherise saw these simple interactions as something more. I clearly told her I had no interest in resuming a relationship with Russell but she left still angry, throwing out unfounded accusations."

"She said she thought Dad was seeing someone else," Victoria added. "Maybe he was. Maybe that's where he went last night, knowing Cherise was out of town. He cheated on Mom for a long time when they were married. Maybe he was cheating again."

Mary Pat frowned at her. "Victoria, we don't know that. Let's not speak negatively about your father. This situation is tragic enough."

Victoria started crying again. "I'm just trying to help, you know. They need to know everything so they can find who did this."

"All information is appreciated," Officer Roland replied. "We'll ask questions among Dr. Latham's friends and at work, also, to see if we can learn where he went last night, how long he stayed out, when he returned, and if alone."

Owen's mind churned while the officers asked other questions to help in the initial investigation. Who could have wanted Russell dead? Was the murder premeditated or impulsive?

Mary Pat and Victoria both cried often throughout the remaining questions asked. But they answered every one with honesty—perhaps with more candor than needed, but without any guile.

"We will keep you informed with what we learn," Officer Roland said as they left. "I'm sorry again to bring you such sad news today, but thank you for helping us with the investigation by answering our questions with such honesty."

Mary Pat put out a hand to shake his in parting. "You have been kind. Thank you." She paused. "Has Cherise made funeral arrangements yet?"

"I believe she was working on that today," Officer Roland answered.

"She mentioned Highland Memorial," Officer Salter added. "I think she planned to go there today."

Mary Pat nodded. "Our family owns gravesites at Highland Memorial Cemetery. Thank you. I can call them later to learn arrangements and then notify my other children and our close family."

The afternoon proved a sad and upsetting one. Owen stayed with Mary Pat and Victoria for a time to talk and comfort both of them. Mary Pat contacted Highland Memorial and learned Russell's body had been taken there and that Cherise had set a funeral time.

She hung up from her call and shook her head. "That woman set the funeral for Sunday afternoon at 2:00 pm, only two days from now. I'll need to contact the boys, my parents, and any friends of Russell's that Cherise may not know right away for them to have time to make arrangements to get here."

"I'll help, Mother. I know Dean and Brock will cover my hours for me this afternoon and evening. I'm too upset to work anyway." She wiped tears away again. "Dad and I were just starting to get close again, too. I'm so glad, at least, we had that special time recently. This is so awful. I can't believe it's happened."

"Yes, things like this are shocking," Mary Pat agreed. "Even though Russell and I were divorced, we shared a long married life together. I simply can't take this in at all. Whoever would want to kill Russell?" She looked at Owen. "Do you think Russell might have come home and interrupted a burglary?"

"It's possible. I'm sure the police will find the answers."

"I hope so. We all need resolution, even Cherise. I'm sure she feels awful, knowing she questioned Russell's faithfulness. Surely she realizes now how foolish that was."

Mary Pat went to get her address book in order to find the needed addresses and phone numbers not in her cell phone. When she sat down at the table to begin a list of family and friends to call, Owen decided to leave.

"I'm going to head home and make a few calls of my own," he told her. "I'll call Dad, Clint and Francine, our pastor, Maydeen and Wheeler, and Charlotte, if you'd like."

She smiled at him in gratitude. "Oh, that would be nice. Thank you."

Victoria settled down beside her mother at the table to look over the list she'd started. "Brock said his mom Nancy would make calls, too, to Dean's and her daughter Cali and John, to Gloria and Lewis Oliver, and some other friends you know around here."

Mary Pat smiled. "That's good. That will help." She took a deep breath. "I'll need to call the boys first. I hate to call them at work, but they need to know as soon as possible to talk to their employers to make arrangements to come for the funeral." She gave Owen a panicked look. "I'll need to get to the grocery to get food, with the boys and my parents coming in."

Owen leaned over and gave her a kiss on the forehead. "I'll go to the store in the morning for you, get anything you might need. As for food, the Glades Community Church women will bring food over, as will Maydeen and others. You'll soon have more than you need."

She sighed. "There's so much to think about."

"You'll be fine," he said, leaving to start home.

After making a ream of calls from his house, Owen sat by the big fire he'd started in the fireplace thinking about the day. He imagined that no matter how much Russell had hurt Mary Pat that she deeply grieved his loss. She'd loved him for so many years, cared for him, birthed and raised his children. The days ahead would be difficult for her and it was likely the police would be back for more questions as they tried to learn who murdered Russell Latham.

A thought came to Owen as he sat looking into the fire in the fireplace. He pulled out his cell phone, punched in a number and made a call to his old high school friend Arnold Tipton.

"Arnold," he said when he heard his voice. "This is Owen."

"Hey, what's up with you?"

"I'm good. Are you at work?"

"Yeah, pulling late shift tonight. It's the weekend and I'm a manager in the hospitality industry, you know." He laughed. "The Edgewater is packed tonight with another conference. Folks like to schedule them here when the fall colors are still pretty in the Smoky Mountains. What can I do for you?"

Owen told him briefly about the murder. "The victim's wife, Cherise Latham, was staying at the Edgewater Thursday night for that two-day real estate conference." He hesitated. "I'll be candid and tell you she had a lot of hostility going for her husband Russell Latham. I wondered if you might ask around, check with your staff, ask any garage attendants, maybe check security camera footage, and see if this woman might have left the hotel for any length of time on Thursday night, acted suspicious or anything."

"You think she might have had anything to do with this?"

"I don't know. Just a hunch. I didn't really know the man. He could have had enemies. It might have been a burglary gone wrong. Like I told you before, the police are looking into it." He paused. "I guess I ought to keep my oar out of it."

"Nah. When you have a hunch, you need to follow it. I'll be here with all of the night staff tonight. I'll ask some questions. If someone saw her in her nightgown going to the ice machine around midnight it will ease your conscience. I'll give you a call after I check around." He laughed. "Maybe after this busy time we can do a little fishing on one of the streams."

"I'd like that Arnold. Give me a buzz when you're free."

Owen hung up. He imagined the police would check out everyone's alibi for the time when Russell Latham had been killed. Perhaps it was only his own annoyance over Cherise coming to threaten Mary Pat that made him wonder what she might be capable of in a rage, but there it was. He wondered.

He decided, too, to keep it to himself that he'd made any inquiries at all.

He laughed. "Heck, I don't even have a good alibi for where I was last night, and I certainly didn't like Russell Latham much or how he treated Mary Pat."

CHAPTER 23

Mary Pat slept little Friday night, her mind a whirl with the events of the day. How did people deal with the concept of murder? With such a sudden, shocking, grievous event tossed into your life? Even though she and Russell had divorced over nine months ago, it hadn't been that long since she'd cared for him, cooked for him, watched over his life with love and concern. She felt brutalized with the knowledge of his death and the horror of the idea someone had shot and murdered him. Coming to terms with the death of someone you care for is hard enough but to know they were murdered? It hurt down to the bone in a way hard to describe. Who would do such a thing anyway? She'd never understood murder except perhaps as a last resort in self-defense or to save another.

"Did you sleep any last night?" Victoria asked the next morning as they sat down at the breakfast table to try to eat.

"Very little," Mary Pat admitted. "I tossed and turned, trying to come to terms with the idea your father is gone, especially in such a horrible, tragic way."

Tears leaked out of Victoria's eyes. "I kept waking up thinking I'd dreamed all this, that it couldn't really have happened."

Mary Pat sipped at her coffee, needing the caffeine to help her face all she needed to do today.

"When will everyone be here?" Victoria asked.

"The boys are all on their way. Craig is flying to Charleston to drive over with Patrick like he did before. After Todd finishes several early surgeries that couldn't be cancelled, he and Allison will come. Mom and Dad are leaving this morning, but it's a nine to ten hour drive from the coast. They won't arrive until late. Of course, relatives and friends who live nearby will come to pay their respects." She shook her head. "I hate that Cherise planned the service so quickly. It makes it so difficult."

"What about Daddy's family?"

"You know his parents died when he was young, that his grandparents raised him. They're gone now, but he has a few aunts, uncles, and close cousins. You contacted them yesterday. I know you said some would try to come."

Victoria made a face. "They said Cherise hadn't contacted them at all. I think that's awful. I hope she let Daddy's friends know about the service."

"Perhaps she's too distraught," Mary Pat said.

Victoria snorted. "No more so than we are and we've all done our part." She closed her eyes. "I so dread tomorrow. It will be such a hard day."

Mary Pat reached across to take her daughter's hand. "We'll all get through it. We have each other."

They both ate eggs and English muffins quietly for a moment.

"Do you think that black dress I have will be all right for the funeral?" Victoria asked.

"It's lovely and very tasteful," Mary Pat replied. "I'm truly grateful now, too, I bought that black suit last month to wear to a funeral at church."

"What else can I do to help this morning?"

"Change the sheets on all the guest beds, if you would. I'm going to sleep in the other twin bed in your bedroom, so Mom and Dad can have my room downstairs. Craig and Patrick will share their old room as before and Todd and Allison can have the guest room. We'll have to manage somehow with only two and a half baths, but it will be okay."

The doorbell rang and Barker woofed, running to the door.

Mary Pat smiled. "It must be Owen."

Victoria went to let him in, and he came into the kitchen carrying an armful of dishes. "Food is already showing up," he said, putting the containers and dishes on the counter in the kitchen. "Maydeen made a cake and a pie last night, Francine sent over a casserole, and Glaydeen said to tell you she and other women in the church would be bringing everything you'd need for dinner tonight."

He came to hug them both. "How are you two doing?"

She smiled at him. "Better now that you're here."

"If you'll make me a grocery list, I'll go to the store to get whatever you need so you don't have to deal with shopping."

"Thank you." She glanced at a sheet of notes on the table beside her. "Russell's office called this morning. They are catering the reception after the service. They already contacted the funeral home to make arrangements. I'm glad they called to tell me. I've heard nothing from Cherise."

Victoria flounced back into her chair. "What do the boys and I need to do at the funeral Mother? Usually the family stands in the receiving line to greet everyone who comes in. Do we have to stand up there with Cherise?"

"Yes, you do." Mary Pat sent her a stern look. "This is your father. No matter what you feel about your stepmother, you will show respect and honor tomorrow for your father."

"What will you do?"

"I will sit to one side of the funeral home, near the back with my parents, where those who want to find me can."

"And with me." Owen leaned over to kiss her on the cheek after pouring himself a cup of coffee in the kitchen. "Dad, Garrett, Francine and Clint, Charlotte and Rowan, Brock, Nancy and Dean, Gloria and Lewis, and others from the Glades will be there for you, too."

"They didn't even know Russell," she said. "They don't all need to drive down to Knoxville."

"But they know and love you." He sat down at the dining room table, bringing a loaf of Maydeen's homemade banana bread with him.

"What's that?" Victoria asked, eyeing the bread.

"Maydeen also sent several loaves of her homemade breads. I decided one would be nice to try now." He grinned at them.

"Ummm. Cut me a piece, too," Victoria said, pushing her plate toward him.

They talked then about groceries Owen needed to buy and about plans related to the service on Sunday.

The doorbell interrupted them, with no familiar doggy woof this time from Barker.

"Do you think that's more food already?" Mary Pat asked.

"I don't know." Owen got up to go to the door, and Mary Pat followed.

Another policeman stood at the door, this one older with short-clipped grey hair and glasses.

"Is this the home of Mary Pat Latham and Victoria Latham?" he asked.

"Yes," Mary Pat answered, tensing to see another officer at the door. "Can we help you?"

"May I come in?" he asked.

She nodded, opening the door to direct him in and gesturing to the grouping of sofas and chairs for him to sit down.

"You're not one of the police officers who came last time," Victoria said, getting up from the table to come over and join them.

"No, I'm Bill Magee, the Chief of Police in Gatlinburg." He sat his hat on his knees as he settled into a chair. "Officer John Roland from the Knoxville Police Department, who visited you earlier, contacted me this morning relating to the ongoing investigation of your husband's murder."

Mary Pat winced at the words.

"A suspect has been arrested and charged. Officer Roland called to advise me of the arrest and known facts in the case and I decided to come speak with you personally to tell you about that rather than calling. Officer Roland said you were helpful when he came to let you know about Dr. Latham's death. My wife and I also knew your father and mother well, Mary Pat, and remember you as a young girl. I thought you'd appreciate getting this sort of news in person. A murder is always so hard on any family."

"Yes, it is." Mary Pat tried not to cry again.

"Who's been arrested?" Victoria asked.

"Cherise Laverne Latham was arrested and taken into custody early this morning at her home."

Victoria gasped, and Mary Pat put a hand to her mouth and began to cry.

"After questioning and with evidence found, she admitted to the murder," Bill Magee continued. "She is claiming self-defense, but has admitted to firing the shots that killed Dr. Latham. The weapon was found on the premises, locked in a safe, and revealed in a search. It is a firearm Dr. Latham kept in the home for security purposes, registered in his name."

"How can this have happened?" Mary Pat asked, shocked. "She is his wife."

"As with many murders, like this one, the situation developed from an escalated domestic quarrel." He twisted the cap in his hands. "According to the accused, she believed her husband was cheating on her. The Knoxville police found a GPS tracker on the victim's car while conducting the house search. The accused admitted to having it installed, telling the installation technician it was to help locate the vehicle if stolen."

"Is that legal?" Victoria asked.

Bill Magee nodded. "It is legal to put a tracking device on a vehicle with proof of ownership. The accused provided a signature to the installation technician from her husband requesting the device for his vehicle. The police doubt it was his signature now."

"Do the police know where Russell went Thursday night?" Mary Pat asked. "I know the officers were trying to learn that when they came here."

Uncomfortable, Bill looked at both women and then down at his lap. "He evidently spent the evening with a hospital nurse he'd recently become involved with, Gweneth Pearsons. She has been questioned and has affirmed they were together Thursday night until about 10:00 pm. Dr. Latham returned home then to be met by his wife."

"I thought Cherise was in Gatlinburg Thursday night?" Victoria asked, confused.

"She said when the tracker showed Dr. Latham at an address that she now knew belonged to Ms. Pearsons, she decided to return home to confront him about his unfaithfulness. She claimed she hoped that talking with him would cause him to stop the relationship."

Mary Pat shook her head. "I can't believe she was tracking him. I'm sure that's how she knew your father came here to see you, Victoria, and probably how she knew how to get here."

"What clues led you to go to the Latham home with a search warrant?" Owen asked.

"Officer Roland said a neighbor they interviewed last afternoon claimed he thought he saw Cherise Latham's car return home last night when they were out walking their dog. It is a yellow sports car and somewhat distinctive." He paused. "In checking with the manager of the Edgewater Hotel in Gatlinburg, they learned a staff member had seen Cherise Latham leave the parking lot late in the evening. Another front desk employee saw her come through the front lobby at around two a.m. It's very quiet in a hotel at that time of night and hard to miss anyone coming or going. Evidently someone already contacted the hotel manager earlier to ask him to question staff as to whether Mrs. Latham might have left that night and returned later. With the neighbor's evidence of seeing Mrs. Latham's car, the hotel's evidence of her leaving and returning, and with extensive evidence from Gweneth Pearsons, the police had due cause to search the Latham home and arrest Mrs. Latham as a suspect."

"What evidence did Gweneth Pearsons give?" Victoria asked.

"She told the police that Dr. Latham was leaving his wife and had signed papers on a condo near the hospital. He told her Thursday night that he planned to confront his wife with his desire for a divorce when she returned from Gatlinburg." Bill Magee hesitated.

"Several sources confirmed the couple had marital problems and frequent fights, and that the accused had a somewhat short fuse."

"We sure saw that on her visit here," Victoria said. "But I still hate to think she killed my dad, no matter how mad."

"She claimed she arrived home hurt and angry, waited for Dr. Latham's return, and that they then began to argue. She wanted him to stop seeing Ms. Pearsons but said he laughed at her and began to say cruel things to her."

Victoria snorted. "Knowing Cherise, I imagine she was in there slinging cruel words at Daddy, too."

"I guess we'll never know exactly what happened," Bill Magee said. "Ms. Latham claims he got angry and hit her. She claimed she got scared and got the handgun they kept in the home for security from the desk drawer in the family room. She then threatened him with it, telling him he'd better not hit her again. The argument escalated. The accused claims that Dr. Latham then informed her in anger he was filing for divorce and had signed a lease on another apartment. He also admitted to an ongoing affair with seemingly no regret. A lot of threats and harsh words passed between them, according to the accused. She said he lunged toward her at one point to get the gun away from her and that in her panic, the gun discharged, killing him."

"Oh, my. How simply terrible." Mary Pat started to weep.

Victoria sobbed, too. "That awful, awful woman. Didn't she have enough sense to know waving a gun around can only lead to trouble?"

Mary Pat looked thoughtful. "I remember Russell always kept any gun in the home locked in his safe. I'm surprised to learn it was out in an unlocked desk drawer in their home."

"Officer Magee said they found the gun locked in the safe when they searched the house," Owen added.

Victoria sniffed. "With Daddy dead, we'll never really know what happened. Cherise might have gotten the gun out of the safe, fuming and waiting to kill him when he got home."

"It's hard when only one party in a crime can tell the story, but you can be sure the police department in Knoxville will thoroughly investigate the crime." Bill Magee stood to leave. "Mrs. Latham has not been released on bond. She showed so much rage at her arrest and threw out threats in relation to Ms. Pearsons that she may be detained at some length. Officer Roland said she acted cool and collected when they first arrived at the home but then grew very angry."

Mary Pat's mouth dropped open then. "Oh, my goodness. I just remembered the funeral is scheduled for tomorrow. The expectation is that Cherise will be there to meet all those who come to offer their respects."

Bill Magee scratched his head. "You could cancel it. I imagine the media will pick up this story and get it in the news before the day is out with a prominent Knoxville surgeon murdered and his wife arrested."

"Oh, this is awful." Mary Pat turned to Owen. "What do you think we should do?"

Owen thought for a moment. "The man deserves for his death to be grieved by his loved ones and friends and to be respectfully buried. At this point everyone has been notified of the funeral. Many are traveling in for it. I would have it unless you and Victoria don't think you can make it through the funeral. Postponing won't change the sorrow of the situation."

Mary Pat lifted her chin. "You're right. Russell deserves a service and for his friends and family to grieve his death. Even if he and Cherise argued, she was wrong to kill him. No one will doubt that fact and all will feel deeply sad he had to lose his life so young."

Bill Magee started toward the door. "Contact the funeral home to put on a little extra security to keep media out. They will do that. You should let the minister conducting the service know so he can modify his message, too."

Owen looked at Victoria. "You and your brothers, with your mother's help, and any of Russell's family will need to act as the primary family members now and see to it that the funeral is conducted with dignity and respect and without undue emotion."

"That's wise counsel." Bill Magee stopped before leaving. "I'm sorry again for your loss."

Mary Pat reached for his hand. "You were so kind to come in person to talk to us. It would have been awful to learn of this from the news media first or only by a phone call from the police department. I'm truly grateful to you for coming to share with us as you did."

He put on his hat, starting down the porch steps. "Tell your folks hello for us when they get in. We used to love eating at your dad's restaurant."

Mary Pat closed the door and stood there a moment in shock.

Victoria pulled out her cell phone, starting to cry again. "I'm going to call Brock," she said.

Mary Pat looked at Owen. "Should I call the boys, my parents, and others about this before they get here?"

He gathered her into a big hug, letting her lean her head against his chest. "As hard as this is, you probably should. You'd hate for them to hear something about it first on the news or get a text from one of their friends about it."

"That would be awful." She leaned against him, trying to draw strength from him. "I dread the calls though."

Owen kissed her forehead. "People already know Russell was murdered. They'll be happy, in some way, to know the police arrested the person who did it, that justice is being served."

"I'm sure you're right. I wanted the murderer to be caught, but it's so hard to learn it was his wife. That she would do such a thing." Mary Pat tried to hold back another sweep of tears.

Owen started toward the table where they'd been sitting before. "If you'd like, I can help you with some of the calls. Victoria can, too, after talking with Brock." She'd stepped out of the room to call him privately.

"I shouldn't ask you to do that," Mary Pat said.

"It needs to be done and there are a lot of calls to be made. I saw that big list you created." He pointed at it on the table. "We can split the names up. I can call all the people around here and people you're less close to. You need as many people as possible to know about this before they show up tomorrow."

They sat down at the table, and she reached a hand across to take Owen's. "I'm so grateful you were here with Victoria and me today and with us yesterday when the police came to tell us Russell had been killed."

He kissed her hand. "I am going to be in your life from now on Mary Pat, through good and bad, sickness and health. No matter what has happened today and no matter what happens tomorrow, we'll see everything through together."

The next two hours were filled with phone calls. In an odd way, Mary Pat found herself in charge of the funeral and arrangements for her ex-husband. Victoria leaned to her. Her boys were in transit. Russell had no parents to handle the funeral, no siblings to take charge of things, with his only brother overseas in Germany.

After all their calls were completed, Owen drove to the store to get needed groceries for the company coming in and Victoria went to the pharmacy for a short time to help with the busy Saturday traffic at the store. Mary Pat sat down on the sofa to rest, glad to enjoy the quiet for a little while.

"What an eventful year we've had," she said to Barker, who'd climbed up on the sofa to put his head on her lap, seeming to realize she needed a little comfort. She stroked his shaggy fur, glad for his company.

She had only a short time to rest before the phone rang again. Recognizing the caller, she answered.

"I'm sorry for all this sorrow," Scott Litchfield, the family's longtime attorney said. "My secretary said you'd called while I was at lunch."

Scott Litchfield was the family's estate administrator. He'd also been one of Russell's fraternity brothers and a long time friend. In his legal capacity, he hadn't represented either Russell or Mary Pat in their divorce, but Russell had retained Scott to handle his estate planning. He'd mentioned it to her on several occasions.

"I hope you know how torn up I am about this. I loved Russell like a brother. You know that."

"I do. Thanks for your call."

"My wife Darla and I will be at the funeral tomorrow, of course. I agree it's best to go ahead and have it." He hesitated. "I know Victoria is living with you right now. Will all three of the boys be coming in for the funeral?"

"They're on their way."

"This is awkward, but I'd like to suggest that the family get together after the funeral and reception to meet with me. The funeral home has a conference room we can use. I'd like to read the will and go over assets, such as life insurance and joint property while the boys are in town." He paused. "I often do this with a family when they're scattered."

"Is that really needed? I assume Russell changed his will after he and Cherise married."

Scott cleared his throat. "Actually, I will admit Russell talked about that last spring but by the time I got some paperwork together, he and Cherise were already having problems and he stalled on going further with any changes. The will in place before you and Russell divorced still stands. You and the children are the primary beneficiaries. You may recall he set up some trusts for them, but the insurance and most other assets come to you."

Stunned, she asked, "What about Cherise?"

"Even if Russell had changed his will, legal rulings prohibit inheritance from a victim by the murderer. Neither Cherise or any members of her family are in any position to contest the will Russell made." He hesitated. "Russell didn't write any changes to leave her monies or property. He candidly told me on several occasions he'd made a mistake to marry her. Russell also deeply regretted divorcing you and hurting the family. I wanted you to know that."

"Thank you." Mary Pat felt the tears start again.

"I won't keep you. I know this is a hard day, but if you wouldn't mind a brief meeting after the service and reception, I will set it up with the funeral home. I do that often there and they are always very accommodating."

"Of course. The boys, Victoria, and I will be pleased to meet with you."

She put her phone down on the table and leaned her head back against the couch then. "Lord, while I have this quiet moment, I ask for your help and grace to get through this time. I admit my heart hurts and my mind is swamped with sweet, old memories of my life with Russell. I so loved him. We shared so many years, so much love, the births and raising of our children together. You know, no matter how much he hurt me, that those good years will remain in my heart."

She paused in her prayer a minute. "Isn't that what Russell said the last time we were together, that we should remember all the good times and the good years? Help me to do that. Help me to forgive Cherise, too. What sorrow and tragedy she's brought to her own life. I hurt for her and the awful mistakes she's made. I hope you will find a way to help her as she struggles to live with the consequences of her impulsive actions, the ruin of her life."

Mary Pat shook her head thinking over everything. "Help me to help the children in this hard time. To not fan their anger. To encourage them to forgive and not hold bitterness to their harm. To move on and live their lives in a way their father would have been proud of. To, like me, remember the good and all the happy times and memories. To forgive their father, too, for his decisions that may not have been wise. I ask for your peace and strength and help to get through tomorrow and the next days. To grieve, as I should, but then to move on. To not let these sorrows color my future. Charlotte taught me that so many things in life are choices. I choose life and not staying bitter and angry over this death. I choose to move on, to serve and love, to find meaning and fulfillment in the rest of my life, and to give my love again, without fear, to Owen, who has been so good to me."

The door opened, and Owen pushed his way in with one foot, his arms loaded with bags of groceries. He smiled at her. "It's quiet here. Are you all right?"

"I am." She grinned at him. "I was just praying about you."

"You were? I'm happy to get any prayers I can anytime. I hope they were good ones." He walked into the kitchen to set the groceries on the table.

"They were lovely ones." She looked across the room at him. "But I'd be happy if you'd come over here and kiss me before all my family starts to come in. I might be pretty tied up the next days. We might not have much time for canoodling."

She giggled as Owen strode across the room with a laugh to swoop her into his arms and oblige her.

CHAPTER 24

Owen stood in the small lounge and dressing area in the men's bathroom at the church, two month's later, adjusting his bow tie at the mirror.

Clint, beside him, grinned at him in the mirror. "I guess the bachelors' club officially ended this year."

Owen laughed. "Last Christmas, I'd never have imagined in a million years either of us old, settled bachelors would decide to offer 'I Dos' this year, especially me. Yet here I am and eager to say the words, as well."

"Well, I can vouch for the married state as a happy one, if it helps."

Owen studied the black bow tie and tuxedo he wore. "Thanks for being willing to suit up in a tux to be my best man. Mary Pat wanted something pretty for a wedding at Christmas time. To match the church, she said."

Clint smirked. "How'd you get Mary Pat to decide to get married sooner than planned?"

"Actually her kids pushed her to do it," he said. "I got close to the boys through all that mess following Russell's murder, the funeral after, helping Mary Pat through everything. The boys saw how I took care of their mother and their sister. It built respect and trust."

He moved to sit on the couch inside the bathroom with Clint. When the church added its big fellowship hall, they wisely planned a lounge area in the front of both the men and women's bathrooms for the frequent weddings and events the church hosted both inside and on the grounds.

"I can see Mary Pat's boys are easy and comfortable with you."

Owen nodded. "At Thanksgiving the boys came back home again, along with Todd's wife Allison. They shared a big family dinner with us down at Dad's place, got to know my Dad, my son Garrett, you and Francine, and Larissa. It built ties. Sometimes hard times build friendships, you know. You learn who matters when times grow tough. You see who will pull with you and who will pull away."

"That's true."

"With Victoria egging them on, the boys starting pushing with her for us to get married at the Christmas holiday when they'd all be back. It made sense, really. With Victoria and Brock's wedding scheduled for Valentine's weekend in February, we needed to see about getting married ahead of them." He chuckled. "I surely didn't discourage it. After a little arm twisting, Mary Pat started to warm to the idea of a Christmas wedding, too, so we set the date for Saturday the twenty-eighth, while the kids were still here visiting and while the church would still be decorated pretty for a holiday wedding."

Clint pulled at his bow tie, uncomfortable with fancy dress. "Glaydeen and all the women of the church always decorate up everything real fine for the holidays—garlands, holly, poinsettias, candles, and all. They've worked like beavers with the caterers to make the fellowship hall real nice for the reception after." He paused. "You don't think Mary Pat, living in the city with wealth for so long, is disappointed in marrying in a country church?"

"Nah. Life taught her this year a lot of things are more important than big houses, cars, money, and fancy society groups. Not that there's anything wrong with having some money or things. God wants good for us."

Clint laughed. "You don't need to preach that to me. I'm on the same page with you there." He glanced at his watch. "It's nearly 11:00 am now. I guess it's about time."

The two men walked down the hall to join the minister John Browder at the back door to the sanctuary, moving inside with him to stand at the front of the church. Martha Goodby, a fine pianist and member of the church, was already playing for the full house in the sanctuary.

Owen felt a little nervous looking out at the sea of faces.

As the back doors to the narthex opened, Martha began to play a processional and Todd walked Mary Pat's mother Charlotte Jennings down the aisle. He couldn't help wishing his own mother Ida still living for Garrett to walk her down to sit by his father. He missed her especially at times like this but imagined her watching from above and enjoying the day, seeing her family growing and expanding again.

A smiling Larissa led the wedding processional next, scattering rosebuds with obvious pleasure. She wore a sweet claret red dress with a satin cummerbund, her long dress the same color Owen knew he'd see on the matron of honor and bridesmaids soon to come.

Victoria followed next, Mary Pat's Matron of Honor. She'd had a joyous time helping to plan this wedding for her mother, and she winked at Owen as she arrived at the front of the church.

The church, with the lights dimmed this morning, and candles lit all around, looked really beautiful as the ushers and groomsmen— Garrett, Todd, Craig, and Patrick—led Mary Pat's bridesmaids down the aisle. His sister Francine, Charlotte Hillen, and Mary Pat's friends Nancy and Gloria, looked glorious in deep burgundy red, their satiny dresses V-necked with loose sleeves and slightly full skirts, each skirt dropping below satiny cummerbunds like Larissa's long dress.

As Martha began to play Wagner's "Bridal Chorus," which Owen had always called "Here Comes the Bride," he caught his breath as Mary Pat appeared in the doorway. She looked like an angel on her father's arm, in an ivory satin dress, shimmering in the candlelight, her hair pulled back with flowers tucked in the back, a lush bouquet of red and white roses in her hands. She didn't want to wear a veil—insisted it symbolized virginity and the uncovering of a bride. He almost grinned remembering her argument with Victoria about it. She wouldn't wear white, either, but chose a deep cream ivory gown she thought more appropriate for a second marriage. She looked unbelievably beautiful. He was surely a blessed man.

The service, like most wedding services, moved quickly then, their vows soon said. Owen's nerves began to quiet as he kissed his bride and exited the sanctuary. With the congregation standing and smiling, they walked down the aisle, while Martha pounded away on the piano with verve and vigor playing Mendelssohn's "Wedding March."

He and Mary Pat, along with family and the wedding party, had posed for pictures earlier that morning before the guests arrived, so they moved now to a receiving line to greet friends, family, and church members as they filed from the sanctuary into the fellowship hall. Afterward, they cut the cake, toasted each other and their guests with sparkling water in pretty, little engraved flutes, and then settled at a small bride and groom table in a corner of the fellowship hall. Someone brought them plates filled with a selection of foods from the lavish brunch buffet spread over beautifully decorated tables as their guests lined up to fill their own plates. But Owen didn't have much appetite.

"You're staring at me," Mary Pat said, her mouth twitching in a grin.

"I'd be a dumb man not to. You're the most beautiful woman in the room."

Pink color flushed her cheeks. "It's nice to hear that."

"It's nice to realize you're finally Mary Pat McCarter. I'm awfully happy to be saying that Mrs. McCarter."

"You're certainly acting very romantic." She touched the rose bouquet she'd laid on the table beside them. "The wedding was beautiful, wasn't it?"

"It was gorgeous and perfect," he replied.

He studied her hand with her wedding ring now in place behind her engagement ring. Victoria showed him the wedding set Russell bought her, and Owen purposely chose an engagement and a wedding ring different and distinctive from her first set. The engagement ring had little diamonds down the band to match the small diamonds across the top of the wedding ring. His wedding ring, too, had some diamonds across the top of the band, a little fussy for him but a nice match with Mary Pat's.

"I love my rings," she said, following his gaze. "And you remembered to propose at the Buckhorn Inn, like I hoped you might."

He lifted her hand and kissed it. "We had our first real date there since coming together again, I proposed there, and we held our rehearsal dinner there last night. Maybe I'll take you there for our first anniversary."

"That sounds nice. I like the idea of it being our 'special place.' It's nice for couples to remember special places, special songs, and such."

"We have a special song."

She looked surprised. "We do?"

"Yeah. It came out in 1981 when we were in high school. We danced to it together at two proms and a couple of different dances, always called it our song. Have you forgotten?"

She smiled then. "Lionel Ritchie's "Endless Love." I do remember. You used to sing it to me."

He laughed. "Considering my voice, that probably isn't the best memory."

"Oh, but it is." She gave a deep sigh. "It's sweet that we got together again after all this time, after all our hurts and sorrows."

"A dream come true for me," he replied. "You were my first love, just like the words of that song, and I expect you to be my last."

She swatted at him. "I'd better be your last."

They heard a tap on the microphone and looked to see Nancy Sue Richardson standing at the mike. "I hate to interrupt all this fun," she said. "But I wanted to say a little word here. Not all of you may know it, but Owen and Mary Pat were good friends growing up as children, lived on the same street, played together, and then in high school fell in love and were sweethearts. Gloria and I were Mary Pat's best friends in high school. The three of us twirled together at all the high school games, at pep rallies, and sometimes at talent shows. Mary Pat was the best, but we were all good twirlers. The kids called us double names like Mary Pat's to tease us—Mary Pat, Gloria Rae, and Nancy Sue. We had some fine times, I'll tell you."

Everyone laughed. "Now you know both Owen and Mary Pat went off and did other things for a time, married other people, had children, but we think it's so sweet that they've gotten back together after all these years. So for fun Gloria, Francine, Mary Pat's daughter Victoria, and I hunted up some photos to create a little slide show for you—complete with music Garrett helped us tuck in. We hope you'll all get a kick out of watching the bride and groom back when."

Mary Pat groaned as the lights dimmed and the video began on the big television screen on the wall.

Owen soon laughed out loud as photos popped up, with songs from that day, showing Mary Pat, cute and blond as a little girl, her hair in pigtails playing with him outside in the sprinkler and posing in her first sequined twirling costume. Photos of him showed a slightly freckle-faced little boy, laughing and smiling, often teasing or chasing Mary Pat. Photos of their friends and family were mixed into the batch and soon photos of the two of them in high school, him playing football, Mary Pat strutting out on the field, twirling with Gloria and Nancy.

"Where did they find all those pictures?" she whispered to him.

"I'd say it took some looking."

Early pictures of the two of them dating popped up then, taken at school dances, plus a candid shot someone must have snapped of them kissing after a football practice.

"I don't remember that photo." Owen grinned. "But I do remember that moment."

"So do I." Her eyes danced. "I think we simply forgot anyone else was around."

Another cute shot followed in the video of them as queen and king at some school dance, wearing crowns and grinning in front of a backdrop of balloons and silver. The song "Endless Love" played with that photo and several to follow, making them both smile again.

Some through-the-years photos jumped onto the screen next— Owen in West Point military dress, Mary Pat on the field as a majorette at the University of Tennessee, then a few photos of Owen with Garrett when younger, Mary Pat with her kids when they were small—tastefully omitting photos of their former spouses. Finally a few photos from their rehearsal dinner last night ended the video with the words: Together Again.

Nancy ran over to their table when the lights came up. "You're not mad at me for this, are you honey?" she asked Mary Pat. "They don't do dancing at the church after the weddings here so we needed something fun."

"I loved it," Owen assured her. "Everyone else did, too. Thanks, Nancy for putting together those memories for us."

Mary Pat grinned. "I hope you're giving me that video."

"Well, sure, honey. But let me add a few wedding photos at the end for you and maybe some honeymoon shots." She wiggled her eyes. "But some tasteful ones, of course."

Owen laughed.

"Remind me where you're going again. Somewhere in Bermuda."

"It's called Grotto Bay, a lovely resort that Owen found on the Internet and read about," Mary Pat said.

"Charlotte went there with Rowan one time. They loved it," he added. "We've neither one been to Bermuda, so we thought some place warm near the beach would be nice for a change in the winter from the mountains."

"Well, you two have a wonderful time," Nancy said. "And as Victoria said you'd better throw that bouquet her way when you leave in a little while. She and Brock are next and we get to have this fun all over again in February."

She headed off, leaving Owen and Mary Pat to smile and laugh after her.

"While Victoria helped to plan our wedding she constantly found ideas for hers." Mary Pat nibbled a piece of wedding cake.

"Is she doing a red and white wedding, too, for Valentine's Day?"

"No." Mary Pat shook her head. "Her colors are rich rose and sweet pink, with the groomsmen wearing grey tuxes and pink ties. She's already found a lovely, white chiffon wedding dress, too, with a train and a veil to sweep behind her. You know whatever Victoria plans will be dramatic, and they want a party with dancing after for a reception. I think she has half the details worked out already."

"Well, I'm believing for this wedding to be her first and last," Owen said.

"Me, too." Mary Pat looked wistful for a moment. "Every couple enters marriage with that hope. I hope and pray they'll both know only a long life and marriage filled with joy. We both know some of the heartaches that can come with broken vows and broken dreams."

He reached over to squeeze her hand. "Yet God graciously arranged for us to have a second chance at love and happiness."

"That he did." She smiled. Glancing around, she said, "Let's go mingle and talk to everyone. Then we'll probably need to go change to leave. What time is our flight?"

"At about three out of the Knoxville airport. It will take us about five to five and a half hours to get there, changing planes in Atlanta but we only have a short wait before boarding again." He straightened his bow tie. "We probably won't get to Bermuda until about nine I guess."

Her eyes twinkled. "We'll have days to explore though."

He sneaked a quick kiss as they stood to start their walk around the room, leaning to whisper in her ear. "We can sleep in tomorrow, too."

"That we can," she said primly, but her eyes held a fun promise.

"I love that it's *only* going to be you in my life, like the Lionel Ritchie song, together for a whole week, off on some beautiful island."

She touched his cheek, straightening his jacket after. "It's going to be me in your life forever more, Owen. And we're going to purpose to have a happy, long life together. Being happy, like many other things is a choice."

"Well, being happy with you every day will be an easy choice." He winked at her and then led her over to visit with their friends.

———

Dear Readers...

I hope you enjoyed this book and that you will hold fast to the belief that life can always offer us new choices and new chances for happiness if we are open to seek and pursue them.

If you are interested in learning more about Mary Pat's Diet, you will find excerpts from her Diet Options Notebook, inspirational quotes, and the Diet Options complete diet—if you would like to downsize a little—free on my author's website. You'll find week-by-week diet instructions, food lists, dieting counsel, and even some of Mary Pat's diet recipes. The diet is available at: www.linstepp.com. Click BOOKS under the menu bar; select Mountain Home Books and choose Downsizing - Book 2; scroll to bottom of the book synopsis and click the link shown next to the Diet Options Notebook. This is a nearly forty page booklet FREE for my readers.

Today could be the first day of a New You.

A Reading Group Guide

DOWNSIZING

Lin Stepp

About This Guide

The questions on the following pages are included
to enhance your group's reading of
Lin Stepp's *Downsizing*

DISCUSSION QUESTIONS

1. This book begins on a normal, ordinary day when Mary Pat's husband Russell drops by their home unexpectedly at mid-day. She's surprised to see him and can tell he's uncomfortable about something. What things does she imagine might be troubling him? What does she learn is really the problem? What reasons does Russell cite for wanting a divorce? What other shocks does this meeting bring? Do you think Russell was kind? How did Mary Pat react and what did she do after Russell left?

2. Mary Pat also learns she is losing her home as well as her marriage. How would this make you feel? What other disappointments does she experience in relation to her friends and social groups, and in her relationships with her children as word of the divorce gets out? If you experienced a hardship or divorce in your life, do you think your friends and family would be a support? Have you ever experienced a difficult time in your life and been disappointed in how others changed toward you because of it?

3. With emotions overwhelming her, Mary Pat runs to her family's old home outside Gatlinburg in the Glades. What is this home like in comparison to her house in Knoxville? Why did she and Russell own this home and why does he offer it to her? What reasons caused Mary Pat to decide to stay at this house for a time? Have you ever driven through the Glades Arts and Crafts Community and stopped to visit at the craft stores, shops, galleries, and restaurants there? What do you remember about it?

4. An old saying says: Old friends are the best friends. Owen McCarter, a neighbor and old friend of Mary Pat's and her family, came back to the Glades after retiring from the military. How was Owen a friend to Mary Pat the first night she came? What did you learn about their childhood, former relationship, and about

Owen's life since he left?   Do you think Owen's past marital sorrows helped him better understand Mary Pat's problems? Do you think people have more empathy and understanding to others problems when they've experienced similar problems?

5. Owen works in the family business McCarter Woodcrafts. As the story moves along, you meet others in his family who work in the business, too—his father Duggan, his sister Francine, a cousin Noble McCarter, Wheeler and his mother Maydeen Ellis. What losses have each of these characters known? What special problems does Wheeler have? How does Wheeler inadvertently "spill the beans" about an interest forming between Francine and Owen's long-time friend Clint Dawson? What are some of the things you liked about Wheeler and these other characters in the story?

6. As Mary Pat and her mother talk about disappointments Mary Pat has faced with friends, neighbors, and groups, her mother asks, "What about your church friends?" How does Mary Pat answer? How has she found the response of her church friends and minister disappointing? Do you think people hold a greater expectation that church friends will be more of a support in hard times than others? Why? What did you think of Mary Pat's mother's counsel: "Well, don't blame God for it … He is always faithful, and He still loves you. Reach out to Him and He will be right there?" Have you found that to be true for yourself in times of trouble?

7. Russell claims a divorce won't impact his and Mary Pat's children very negatively because they are grown now. Do you think he's right that divorce is easier to accept for older children? What does Mary Pat tell him? How did the children, Todd, Craig, Patrick, and Victoria act after learning the news? How did their feelings change over time and why? In what ways did they later show their support for their mother more than they did earlier?

What did you learn about these children as the book progressed? How do you think your children would handle a divorce or hardship you might endure?

8. Trying to cheer herself after some time has passed, Mary Pat decides to go shopping in the Arts and Crafts community and out to lunch. What happens at the restaurant where she eats that upsets her? When she almost has a wreck trying to drive home after, and pulls off the road, what business does she see? Even though the Diet Options business is closed, what does the owner Charlotte Hillen do when she sees Mary Pat is upset? Charlotte tells Mary Pat that even though we can't change some situations in our lives there are others we can change. She adds: "What is empowering is recognizing the areas in our lives that we can change if we want to and then having the courage and determination to do so." Do you agree? What sorrows does Charlotte confide that she's known?

9. In writing this book, I needed to create both a "fictitious business" and a "fictitious diet" for Mary Pat. I drew on research and personal experiences in creating the business and used a diet plan I'd developed and used successfully to lose weight. Most successful diets involve three things: eating less, eating more of the right things, and moving more. How did you see all three of these factors playing out in Mary Pat's weight loss efforts? Have you ever participated in a weight loss program to help you lose weight?

10. Mary Pat and Owen were sweethearts in high school, and their old relationship begins to resurface in this book. What broke them up and caused them to meet and marry other people? How does their relationship gradually develop over time, despite their reluctance to acknowledge and pursue it? At the Buckhorn Inn, much later, what does Owen confide to Mary Pat about his feelings, even knowing the time isn't right for their relationship

to develop further? Many months later, when they share a first kiss, how does it surprise them? As more time moves on, Owen lets Mary Pat know on a hike they take together that he'd like to marry her. How does she respond? How are the roadblocks between Owen and Mary Pat finally resolved?

11. Along with reuniting with Owen, Mary Pat reunites with two former school friends, Nancy Sue Richardson and Gloria Oliver. What is their shared past? While Gloria is somewhat outspoken, Nancy Sue is more warm and nurturing, yet both women have their strengths. What did you enjoy most about Nancy Sue? Do you have friends that are very different from each like this? Do you still have friends from your school days among your many friendships today? What lessons about friendship did this book suggest to you?

12. What brings Mary Pat's daughter Victoria unexpectedly to the mountains? What upsetting thing has happened in her life? Victoria and Mary Pat's relationship has grown somewhat problematic over the years. Why? How did this time bring them closer together again? How do both Owen and Nancy Sue play a part in helping Victoria? Where does Victoria meet Brock and how does that begin to change her future?

13. Bears play a big role in this story—as they do around the Great Smoky Mountains. What "bear-scare" happens to Mary Pat early in the book? What reasons does the ranger give for the bear, ole Blaze, becoming a problem? When Victoria goes missing later in the story, what part did bears play in this incident? What happens in a third bear encounter at the church when a group of women are unloading baked goods for an upcoming church sale? What problems did the bear cause in this situation? How was the ongoing issue with ole Blaze resolved by the rangers in this scene? Did you learn a lot about bears in this story, like what to do if you encounter a bear, the reasons bears become a

problem in the park, or how people can avoid creating difficulties for bears?

14. Russell Latham gets involved with Cherise Levene long before he asks Mary Pat for a divorce, and the two plan a wedding for almost immediately after the divorce is finalized. Just before the wedding date, Russell calls Mary Pat, angry at her and his children. Why? What does she tell him when he expects her to jump in and resolve ongoing difficulties with his children? How does a later call from her son Todd let Mary Pat know that the children are not happy with their father's behavior? What do they want to do on Easter weekend when their father is being married? As the book progresses, Russell Latham realizes he has made a mistake in marrying Cherise. When he says he regrets his divorce and tells Mary Pat he'd like for them to get back together, how does she respond?

15. The romance of Owen's sister Francine with his friend Clint Dawson encounters some difficulties getting off the ground. Why? What does Owen tells Francine about some issues he thinks might be slowing the relationship from developing? What does Francine do to turn things around? When Francine worries about leaving her father alone in his home, but doesn't want to live permanently in Clint's rustic cabin, what resolution does Owen help her come up with? Did you enjoy getting to know Francine, Clint, and Larissa in this story?

16. The young architect, Garrett, working for Cooper Garrison's company building Francine and Clint's new home, ends up having a surprising link to Owen's family. What is that link? What does Garrett tell Owen that shocks him about their relationship? What did you think about Garrett's mother Joanna for her part in this past? Ongoing events throughout this story show that family relationships are often complicated and filled with problems but that family is still important and meaningful. Do you agree?

17. A theme in this book, and a quote Mary Pat puts on her refrigerator is: Today is the first day on the road to a New You. Despite the hurts and betrayals she's faced, how does Mary Pat begin to build a new life? Reaching back to old goals, she decides to go back to school to update her educational and work credentials. What does she want to do? At a later point in the book, what part-time job offer does Charlotte Hillen make to Mary Pat? Is she excited about it? Does she take the job? How is this a benefit to both Mary Pat and Charlotte? When people go through difficult times, they can let those times make them bitter and cause them to stagnate in life or they can push to make a new life. In what ways did you admire how Mary Pat handled all the hardship that came her way?

18. Just as Mary Pat's story seems to be moving toward a happy ending, Russell Latham is murdered, and at first Mary Pat is a suspect. Why? How was Russell killed? How does Owen help Mary Pat and Victoria in this difficult time? As the police begin to investigate, who is arrested for the murder? What was the motive behind the murder? Later, after Christmas, when Mary Pat's family is home again for the holiday, she and Owen are married in a small service at the Glades Community Church. What was their wedding like? Did you enjoy this happy ending for Owen and Mary Pat who had both known so many life sorrows?

About the Author

Lin Stepp

Dr. Lin Stepp is a *New York Times*, *USA Today*, and *Publishers Weekly* Best-Selling international author. A native Tenessean, she has also worked as a businesswoman and educator. A previous faculty member at Tusculum College, Stepp taught research and a variety of psychology and counseling courses for almost twenty years. Her business background includes over twenty-five years in marketing, sales, production art, and regional publishing.

CKatie Riley

Stepp writes engaging, heart-warming contemporary Southern fiction with a strong sense of place and has sixteen published novels set in different locations around the Smoky Mountains and the South Carolina coast. Her coastal novels in the Edisto Trilogy are *Edisto Song* (2021), *Return to Edisto* (2020) and *Claire at Edisto* (2019). The latest Tennessee and North Carolina mountain novels are *Happy Valley* (2020), *The Interlude* (2019), *Lost Inheritance* (2018) and *Daddy's Girl* (2017), with previous novels including *Welcome Back* (2016), *Saving Laurel Springs* (2015), *Makin' Miracles* (2015), *Down by the River* (2014) and a novella *A Smoky Mountain Gift* in the Christmas anthology *When The Snow Falls* (2014) published by Kensington of New York. Other earlier titles include: *Second Hand Rose* (2013), *Delia's Place* (2012), *For Six Good Reasons* (2011), *Tell Me About Orchard Hollow* (2010), and *The Foster Girls* (2009). In addition Stepp and her husband J.L. Stepp have co-authored a Smoky Mountains hiking guidebook titled *The Afternoon Hiker* (2014) and two state parks guidebooks, *Discovering Tennessee State Parks* (2018) and *Exploring South Carolina State Parks* (2021).

For more about Stepp's work and to keep up with her monthly blog, newsletter, and ongoing appearances and signing events, see: *www.linstepp.com*.